The Doomed Oasis

A Novel of Arabia

Alfred · A · Knopf NEW YORK

THE
DOOMED
OASIS

Hammond Innes

Cold voices whisper and say—

"He is crazed with the spell of far Arabia,

They have stolen his wits away."

WALTER DE LA MARE

THIS IS A BORZOI BOOK,
PUBLISHED BY ALFRED A. KNOPF, INC.

I would like to express my appreciation of the help I have received from Neil Innes during the actual writing of *The Doomed Oasis*. He was Minister of External Affairs to the Sultan of Muscat at the time I was journeying in Arabia; not only did he check the final typescript for me, but at the various stages of the writing I benefited greatly from his knowledge. I should perhaps make it clear, however, that I have ignored his advice on the spelling of two Arab names, in particular believing that my own spelling of Makhmud would be more helpful in conveying the sound of that name than the correct Mahmud. Both the sheikhdom of Saraifa and the emirate of Hadd are, of course, entirely imaginary Arab states.

Contents

Part One

THE COURT OF FIRST INSTANCE

1

Part Two

THE WHOLE TRUTH

I:	*Escape to Saraifa*	9
II:	*Enquiries of an Executor*	57
III:	*The Empty Quarter*	103
IV:	*The Doomed Oasis*	140
V:	*The Quicksands of the Umm al Samim*	185
VI:	*Fort Jebel al-Akhbar*	237

Part Three

THE COURT STANDS ADJOURNED

291

The Court
of First Instance

I

Call Aubrey George Grant!

Aubrey George Grant!

The moment had come. My mouth felt suddenly dry. The Court was waiting and I knew the ordeal ahead of me was a long one. And at the back of my mind was the knowledge that in telling the truth, the whole truth, I might convict an innocent man. I felt the touch of her hand on mine, the quick pressure of her fingers, and I rose to my feet, the sweat sticking the shirt to my back as I followed the attendant. The doors of the courtroom stood open. I checked, a moment's hesitation in the entrance; the place was packed, the atmosphere tense with expectancy.

Quickly I walked down through the Court, the setting familiar to me, a part of my working life; only my role had changed. It was the first time I had entered Court as a witness. I kept my eyes on the Judge, on the pale London face above the tropical suit. He had been specially appointed to try this unusual case, and he looked tired after the long flight, shrunken almost, the suit too large; without the scarlet robes he seemed less awe-inspiring and the Law robbed of some of its majesty. Counsel, too, looked ordinary without wig and gown, and the courtroom itself—all open shirts or pale, loose-fitting jackets, a scattering of Bahrainis in flowing Arab robes. The Code of Criminal Procedure in this Court was based on the Indian Penal Code, yet in essence it was the same Law, and as I moved towards the witness box, the Judge leaned slightly forward, peering at me short-sightedly, his hands clasped together.

Once in the box, I faced the crowded courtroom, no longer a mass of unidentifiable humanity, but a sea of faces all lifted to stare in silent expectation, waiting for the full story which they now knew I alone could give.

I had been called as a witness, not for the Defence, but for the Prosecution. Every word I uttered would be taken down and rushed out of Bahrain by telephone and radio, and thousands of miles away the metal drums of the presses would pour the story out to waiting millions. Representatives of almost every London newspaper were here and half the world's press, packed so tight in this improvised courtroom that they could hardly breathe. And outside in the broiling, humid heat were the photographers and the newsreel men and the television recording units, and at the airfield across the water on the island of Muharraq, special planes waited to fly the pictures that would be flashed on the screens of television sets in the homes of countless people.

Here and there in that sea of faces below me were people I recognized, people who had taken part in the events I was going to have to describe. There was Sir Philip Gorde, director of Gulfoman Oilfields Development, looking old and battered, his heavy-lidded eyes half closed; and beside him, Erkhard, very neat and cool. Colonel George was there and Captain Berry, easily distinguishable, smart in their uniforms of short-sleeved khaki shirts and well-creased khaki longs. Sue had followed me in, and it came as something of a shock to me to see that she had seated herself next to that strange, half-Arab, half-French girl who called herself Tessa. Captain Griffiths, too, his beard neat and pointed—a reminder of Cardiff and the visit that had started it all.

Raise your right hand.

I did so and my gaze shifted involuntarily to the prisoner in the dock. He was watching me, and for a moment our eyes met. I thought he smiled, but I couldn't be sure. I had a sense of surprise, almost of shock. Perhaps it was the tropical suit, the neatly brushed hair; he looked a different man. There was only the arm still in a sling to remind me that this was the man whose singleness of purpose had captured the world's imagination. The Book thrust into my hand disrupted my thoughts.

Repeat after me. My lips were dry. I had turned away from him, but I knew he was still watching me. *I swear by Almighty God.*

"I swear by Almighty God . . ."

That the evidence I shall give the Court.

"That the evidence I shall give the Court . . ." And as I said it I was wondering how the public at home would react to what I was going to have to tell the Court. Until today they would have had quite a different picture of the prisoner—a mental picture culled from garbled versions of his exploits heard over radio and seen on television, read in newspapers and periodicals, a colourful, larger-than-life picture entirely at odds with the neat figure standing alone there in the dock accused of murder.

Shall be the truth,

"Shall be the truth . . ." They should never have brought the case. He was a national hero and, whatever the verdict of the Court, the public's reaction would be a violent one. But would they be for him or against him?

The whole truth,

"The whole truth . . ."

And nothing but the truth.

"And nothing but the truth."

Your full name, please?

"Aubrey George Grant."

And then Counsel for the Crown, on his feet and facing me: "You are a solicitor by profession, I believe?"

"Yes."

"Were you called upon to act for the prisoner on his arrest?"

"Yes."

"When did you cease to act for him?"

"As soon as I realized I was being regarded as a material witness for the Prosecution."

"You have acted for the prisoner before, I think?"

"Yes."

"When was that?"

"Just over four years ago."

The Judge's voice suddenly interjected: "How long ago?" His hand was cupped to his ear.

"Four years, my Lord."

The Prosecution moved a step nearer, hands hung in the lapels of his jacket, the skin of the face cool as parchment in the humid heat. "I will ask the witness to take his mind back now to the afternoon of March twenty-first four years ago. On that afternoon you received a telephone call from a Mrs. Thomas of Seventeen, Everdale Road, Cardiff. And as a result of that telephone call you went to that address."

"Yes."

"Perhaps you will now tell the Court in your own words what happened. . . ."

Part Two

The Whole Truth

I

Escape to Saraifa

Everdale Road was in the Grangetown district of Cardiff. It was one of those terrace streets of grim Victorian brick, roofs hunched against the wet west wind, windowed eyes peering blindly for the view of river and sea that was blocked by other similar houses. Two streets away and you could look across the Taff to the litter of cranes, the glimpse of funnels that marked the Bute Docks. It always depressed me, this area of Cardiff; it lacked the squalid colour of Tiger Bay, the bridge across the Taff seeming to cut it off from the toughness and sense of purpose that gave a lift to the real dock area. The street was deserted except for one car, a small black sedan. It stood outside Number Seventeen, and as I drew in to the curb behind it, I glanced quickly at the house. There was nothing to distinguish it from the others, except the number. A light was on in one of the downstairs rooms. Neat lace curtains were looped back from the windows.

I got out and rang the bell, wondering what I was going to find inside. Trouble of some sort; nobody ever called me to this district unless he was in trouble. And the voice over the phone —it had been a woman's voice, low and urgent, near to panic. I glanced at my watch. Four thirty. The light was already going out of the cloud-filled sky. A slight drizzle gave a black shine to the surface of the street.

Across the road a curtain moved; hidden eyes watching, something to gossip about. I knew the black sedan parked at the curb. It was Dr. Harvey's. But if there had been death in the house, the curtains would have been drawn. My hand was reaching out to the bell-push again when the latch of the door clicked and voices sounded: ". . . nothing else I could have done, Mrs. Thomas. A case for the police . . . you understand, I hope. And the ambulance will be here any minute now." The door was flung open and Dr. Harvey bustled out, almost cannoning into me. "Oh, it's you, Grant." He checked in mid-flight, black bag gripped in his hand, no overcoat as usual, a young, fair-haired, very serious man in a perpetual hurry. "Well, I suppose you'll be able to make some sort of a case out of it in Court. The boy's certainly going to need legal advice." There was no love lost between us. We'd tangled over medical evidence before. "Got to deliver a baby now. Can't do anything more for that chap." And he almost ran out to his car.

"Mr. Grant?" The woman was staring at me uncertainly.

I nodded. "Of Evans, Jones and Evans, solicitors. You telephoned me a little while back."

"Yes, of course." She held the door open for me, a small, neat-looking person of between forty and fifty with deep-set, shadowed eyes. Her hair was greying, swept straight back from the forehead, the face dead white against the dark background of the passage. "Will you come in, please?" She shut the door behind me. "Dafydd didn't want me to call you. But I thought you wouldn't mind, as your firm it is that handled that little allowance for me."

It was the first I knew we acted for her in any way. I thought she'd phoned me because I'm willing in certain circumstances to take a case without a fee. "What's the trouble, Mrs. Thomas?" I asked her, for she was standing motionless as though unwilling to let me go further into the house.

She hesitated, and then almost in a whisper: "Well, it's Dafydd really, you see. He came back—and then . . . Oh dear, it's all so difficult to explain." Now that she had shut the street door, I could see no more than the outline of her face, but her voice, trembling to a stop, told me she was having to fight to keep control of herself. She was frightened, too. "I don't know what he'll do," she whispered. "And Sue not here. Sue could always manage him when I couldn't."

"Sue is your daughter, is she?" I knew it would steady her if I asked questions.

"Yes, that's right. She works at the Infirmary, but I didn't phone her because she'd never get back here in time."

"And David—that's your husband?"

"No, Dafydd's my son. He and Sue are twins. She understands him, somehow."

"I see, and he's in some sort of trouble?"

"Yes." And then she added hastily: "He's not a bad boy, not really." She drew in her breath quickly as though gathering herself together. "If I hadn't written to him like I did, it wouldn't have happened. But I'd had about all I could stand, you see, and then he came home and there was a bit of a row and Mr. Thomas, he said things, you see, that he shouldn't have done, and suddenly they were hitting out at each other. It wasn't Dafydd's fault. He'd had a terrible shock, poor boy. And Mr. Thomas, he'd had a few beers, and then—" She sucked in her breath again as though gulping for air. "Well, then he had this stroke, you see, and I called Dr. Harvey right away and then I telephoned you because I knew it meant trouble for Dafydd." It had all come out in a rush as though she couldn't contain it any longer. "My husband looked so bad, you see," she added lamely, "and I didn't know what would happen. I just didn't know what to do, Mr. Grant—not for the best, as you might say. And then Dr. Harvey came and he said there wasn't much hope for him and he phoned the police, so it's glad I am that I called you now. You'll know what to do and what Dafydd should say to them. He's not a bad boy," she repeated in a voice that was suddenly on the defensive. "Just a bit wild, you know." And she added quickly: "Mr. Thomas hit me, you see."

"There was a family row, in other words?"

"Yes. Yes, you could call it that. But I wouldn't like you to think that because Mr. Thomas was a bit of a drinker there was anything wrong between us. He's good at heart, you know."

"And he's had a stroke, you say?"

"Yes, that's right. That's what Dr. Harvey called it." She seemed to have got a grip on herself. "Come in now, won't you, Mr. Grant? He's lying on the couch in the parlour. And Dafydd's there, too. I expect you'd like a word with him. But don't try and rush him, please," she added in a whisper, and I got the impression she was afraid of her son. "He needs a bit of handling, you see. And he's had a shock, as I say—a dreadful shock." She pushed open the door and stood back for me to enter. "This is Mr. Grant, Dafydd—Mr. Grant the lawyer."

The room was lit from the ceiling, a stark, glaring light without compromise. It showed me a couch with the body of a man lying on it. He was in his shirt-sleeves, the brass gleam of a stud showing where his shirtband had been loosened. His eyes were closed and he was breathing with difficulty, his rather heavy, florid features fallen away so that the bone showed through the flesh. The nose had the veined look of a heavy drinker's. Close against the gas fire, one elbow on the mantelpiece, leaned a youth of about twenty. He was rather over-dressed in a jacket with a lot of elaborate pockets and tucks and a pair of tight-fitting trousers. His face was as white as his mother's; the same features, too, except that the nose was more beaky, the jaw stronger. He didn't shift his position as I entered the room, didn't even look up. He was staring down at the gas fire and his immobility was oddly disconcerting.

Close by his feet was a litter of broken glass from the smashed front of one of those over-pretentious china cupboards. The mahogany beading as well as the glass had been broken in the struggle, and the bric-à-brac with which the cabinet had been filled, mostly white china souvenirs from seaside towns, lay in confusion on the worn carpet. A vase, too, lay where it had fallen from the table by the window. It was unbroken, and beside it lay a much-thumbed photograph album spilling press-cuttings. There was something a little macabre about the whole room—nothing cleared up after the struggle, and the father lying there half dead on the couch with a blanket tucked round him, and the mother and son standing, facing each other, absolutely still.

I could feel the tension between them. It wasn't hate, but it was something just as strong, an emotion so violent that the man on the couch, myself, the state of the room didn't exist for them.

"Well, now." I addressed the boy, my tone as matter-of-fact as I could make it in that sort of atmosphere. "Suppose you tell me what happened." But it was like talking to a brick wall. He had a sullen, withdrawn look.

"I've told you what happened," his mother said in a whisper.

"Quite so, Mrs. Thomas, but I'd like to hear it from your son." She looked deathly tired. I turned to the boy again. "You've had a shock," I said gently. "It's natural you should be a bit dazed by what's happened. . . ." But even as I said it I knew the boy wasn't dazed. The knuckles of the hand that gripped the mantelpiece were white with pressure and there was a muscle working at the back of the jaw. He was holding himself in like a boiler under pressure and I wasn't sure how best to handle him. His gaze had shifted now and he was staring at his mother. I felt sorry for the woman. "Listen to me, young man," I said. "I understand Dr. Harvey has called the police. They'll be here any minute now. If you want me to act for you, then you'd better start talking now, before they arrive."

A slight movement of the shoulder, that was all the answer he made. It wasn't a shrug, more a muscular twitch as though he was impatient for me to go.

"Mr. Grant is only trying to help, Dafydd."

"*Dammo di!* What the hell good is a lawyer man now? It's done, and arguing about it won't alter anything." His voice trembled. And then he turned on me, a flash of pale amber eyes, and told me to get out, the words violent, laced with obscenities.

"Dafydd!" But she was frightened; she had no control over him.

"All right," I said, and I moved towards the desk, where I'd left my hat. "I hope for your sake," I added, "that your father's condition isn't serious."

"He's not my father." The words flashed out from between clenched teeth. "I'd have killed him if he'd been my father." I turned to find his pale eyes fixed on his mother. "I mean that, Ma. I swear I'll kill the swine—if I can ever find him." The words had a violence and a bitterness that appalled me.

"He's not himself," his mother murmured. "He doesn't know what he's saying." Her hands were plucking at the apron round her middle, and her brown, doe-like eyes were wide with fear. She knew he'd meant it.

"You'd better get control of yourself," I said. "You've done enough damage for one day without threatening more and frightening your mother."

But now the pressure inside him couldn't contain itself any more. "You get out of here." He said it quietly, and because of that his words had force. "What's happened here is nothing to do with you or any one else. It's between my mother and me." He spoke through clenched teeth as though he were still trying to keep some control over what he was saying. And then suddenly he lashed out wildly, all control gone: "When you're suddenly told you're illegitimate, and your sister's illegitimate, too, you want to know a little more about it, don't you? You want to talk it over with your mother—ask her a few questions, find out who and what the hell you really are."

He flung out an arm, pointing dramatically at the album on the floor. "See that? Uncle Charles's scrap-book. She subscribed to a press-cutting agency. Every story the newspapers published about him—it's all there, pasted in with loving care. My own mother clinging to the worn-out bed of an old love. Jesus Christ! It makes you want to weep. And me and Sue coming up the wrong side of the bloody blanket, and being fooled into calling that poor drunken sot Dada." He stared at me balefully. "Eight years old I was when I first stole a peek at the contents of that book. A relation, that's what she said, an uncle of mine. Started me getting interested in Arabia, it did. I thought he was a bloody hero. Instead, he's just a low-down, dirty heel who left my mother flat. Well, what do you say to that, eh? You're a lawyer. Maybe you can tell me what I ought to do about it?" And he glared at me as though I were in some way responsible.

And then he suddenly moved, a quick step forward that brought him face to face with me. "Now you just get the hell out of here and let me talk to my mother alone, see?" His eyes had a wild look, the sort of look I'd only seen once before on a boy's face, but that had been in the midst of battle.

I'd known how to deal with it then. But this kid was different. It wasn't only that he looked tough; I had a feeling he *was* tough. Well, I'm not exactly soft, but I don't walk into things with my eyes open. But then I glanced at Mrs. Thomas, saw how scared she was of him, and after that there was nothing for it but to stand my ground, not knowing what exactly he'd do, for I could feel the tension building up inside of him again. He was like a spring coiled too tight.

And then the ring of the ambulance bell sounded down the street and the violence suddenly died out of him. The ambulance drew up outside the house and a moment later two hospital attendants came in with a stretcher.

The attention of the three of us was focused then on the man on the couch. He murmured as they shifted him, an inarticulate sound, and Mrs. Thomas, fussing over him now, spoke his name. The tone of her voice had a quality that is only possible between people who have shared their lives together, and it seemed to reach him, for his eyes flicked briefly open and he murmured her name: "Sarah." It came quickly from his twisted lips, obscured by the effort of moving half-paralysed muscles. "Sarah—I'm sorry." That was all. The eyes closed, the face became clay again, and they took him out.

Mrs. Thomas followed them, sobbing uncontrollably. The door swung to of its own accord and the room was still. "I shouldn't have hit him. It wasn't his fault." The boy had turned away and his shoulders were moving. I realized suddenly that he was crying. "Oh, God!" he sobbed. "I should have known. If I'd any sense, I should have known."

"You couldn't have known he'd have a stroke," I told him.

He turned on me then. "You don't understand." The tears were standing in his eyes. "He and I—we hated each other's guts. I can see why now. But at least he stood by us, poor sod." And he added viciously: "He was a dam' sight better than my real father. If I can ever lay my hands on that bastard . . ." He checked there and gave an odd little laugh. "Bastard! That's funny, isn't it, me calling him a bastard." He turned away then, brushing the back of his hand across his eyes. "I wish I hadn't hit him," he said quietly.

"He'll be all right."

"You think so?" But then he shook his head. "No, he's going

to die. That's what the doctor said. He was the only father Sue and I ever knew," he added, "and now I've killed him."

"Don't talk nonsense. It's not as dramatic as that. He's had a stroke and anyway you're entitled to defend your mother when a man hits her."

He looked at me. "Did she say that?" And then he laughed, a little wildly. And after a moment he said: "Yes, that's right— he hit her." And he added: "Christ! What a bloody mess!" The door of the ambulance banged in the street outside and he turned to stare out of the window. The engine started and it drove off. As though its departure had started an entirely new train of thought, he swung round on me. "You're Whitaker's lawyer, aren't you?"

The name meant nothing to me, but then no doubt Mrs. Thomas's allowance had been arranged by Evans years ago and it would be handled by my clerk as a matter of routine. "Whitaker is the name of your father, is it—your natural father?"

"That's right. My *natural* father." He spoke the word slowly, savouring it for the first time. And then he said: "I want his address."

"Why?"

"Why the hell do you think?" He was back at the window again. "A bloke's got a right to know where his father lives, hasn't he?"

"Maybe," I said. "But I'm afraid I don't know his address."

"That's a lie." He came back to me, his eyes searching my face. "Well, you've got it on your files, haven't you? You could look it up."

"If he's a client of mine, then I'm not at liberty to disclose—"

"Not even to his son?"

"No, not even to his son." I hesitated. The boy's temper would cool and, after all, he'd a right to know where his father was. "If I've got his address," I said, "then I'll write to him if you like and get his permission—"

"Oh, don't give me that crap. You know bloody well where he is." He caught hold of my arm. "Come on. Arabia, it is— somewhere in Arabia. Tell me, for Christ's sake." He saw it was no good then and began to plead: "Please, I haven't much time and I got to know. Do you hear? I got to know." There was a desperate urgency in his voice. And then the grip on my arm tightened. "Let's have it." I thought he was going to hit out at me and my muscles tensed, ready for him.

"Dafydd!"

Mrs. Thomas was standing in the doorway, her hands plucking again at the apron. "I can't stand any more." There was an edge to her voice that seemed to get through to him, and he relaxed slowly and stepped back from me. "I'll come for that address," he muttered. "Sooner or later I'll come to your office and get it out of you." He was back at the window again, looking out. "I'd like to talk to my mother now." He stared at me, waiting for me to go.

I hesitated, glancing at Mrs. Thomas. She was still as stone, and her eyes, as they stared at her son, were wide and scared-looking. I heard the slow intake of her breath. "I'll go and make some tea," she said slowly, and I knew she wanted to escape into her kitchen. "You'd like a cup of tea, wouldn't you now, Mr. Grant?"

But before I could reply and give her the excuse she needed, her son had crossed over to her. "Please, Ma." His voice was urgent. "There isn't much time, you see, and I got to talk to you." He was pleading with her—a small boy now, pleading with his mother, and I saw her weaken at once. I got my hat from the roll-top desk. "It's all right, Mrs. Thomas," I said. "I'll leave you now." There was a phone on the desk, an old-fashioned hook-up instrument standing amongst a litter of books on greyhounds and racing form. "You can always phone my office if you want me."

She nodded dumbly. She was trembling slightly and I could see she was dreading the moment when she'd be left alone with him. But there was no point in my staying. This was something that lay between the two of them alone. "Take my advice," I told him. "When the police arrive, be a little more co-operative with them than you have been with me if you want to avoid trouble. And stick to your mother's story."

He didn't say anything. The sullen look was back in his face.

Mrs. Thomas showed me to the door. "I'm sorry," she said. "He's upset."

"It's not unnatural." I was remembering how I'd felt when I learned that my parents were divorced. I'd heard it first from a boy at school and I'd called him a liar and half murdered the little swine. And then when I discovered it was true, I'd wanted to kill my father and had had to content myself with a letter, which for sheer brutality had been inexcusable. "It's a pity you didn't tell him before."

"I always meant to," she said. "But somehow . . ." She shrugged, a gesture of hopelessness, and as I went out to my car I was wishing I could have done more to help her.

As I turned out of Everdale Road a squad car passed me. There were four of them in it, including Sergeant Mathieson of the Cardiff CID. It seemed an unnecessarily large force to an-swer Dr. Harvey's call, but I didn't go back. It was past five already and Andrews would be waiting to clear the day's business.

Andrews was my clerk. He was also secretary, switchboard operator, office boy. Poor devil, he had come to me with the furniture and the two-roomed dingy office, all that remained of the once prosperous business my uncle had left to me in a fit of misplaced optimism, for, though I'd passed my law exams, I'd never practised. There'd been the war and then I had drifted to Tanganyika and tea-planting, a venture which had turned out badly, leaving me virtually broke at the time of his death, so that the legacy of that miserable place seemed like the smile of fortune.

"Know anything about a Mrs. Thomas?" I asked Andrews as he helped me off with my coat. He had drawn the curtains, and with the coal fire burning brightly in the grate, the place looked almost snug, despite the dust and the piles of documents and the black deed-boxes littering the floor by the open strong-room door. "It's a matter of a small allowance she claims we handle for her."

"Mrs. Thomas is it?" I had seated myself at the desk and he stood over me, tall and slightly stooped, the skin stretched taut as vellum across the bones of his long face. "You know, Mr.

Grant, almost half our clients are named Thomas." It was part of the game that he must always make the simplest thing appear difficult.

"It's one of your old clients," I said. "Something I have apparently quite unwittingly inherited from the old man."

"From Mr. Evans, you mean."

That, too, was part of the game, and because his position was privileged I had to humour him. "All right, Andrews. From old Mr. Evans." The firelight flickered on the lined, hang-dog face bent obsequiously over me. He'd been with my uncle since before he was articled and had stayed with him right through his long illness until he had died two years ago. God knows how old he was; his scrawny neck, covered by a hard stubble, stuck up out of the soiled stiff collar like the flesh of a plucked fowl. "Well, what about it?" I said impatiently. "I inherited so little in the way of business that it rather narrows the field. Does the name Whitaker ring a bell?"

"Whitaker?" His Adam's apple moved convulsively. "Ah, yes, of course. Colonel Whitaker. A little matter of a settlement. It used to come to us quarterly from Bahrain in the form of a banker's draft, which we cashed and forwarded to an address in Grangetown."

I asked him to get the file. But of course there wasn't any file. However, whilst I was signing the letters, he managed to dig up some record of the arrangement. It was written on the firm's notepaper in my uncle's sloped writing and went back to before the war. In it Charles Stanley Whitaker undertook to pay *to Sarah Davies the sum of twenty-five pounds quarterly for a period of fifteen years* or, in the event of his death, *a lump sum from the estate equivalent to the balance ALWAYS providing that such sum* . . . The clue to what it was all about was contained in the final paragraph, which read: *THIS settlement to be binding on my heirs and assigns and to be accepted by the said Sarah Davies in full settlement of any claims real or imagined.* The signature at the bottom was a barely decipherable scrawl, and below it Sarah Davies had signed her name in a clear, schoolgirl hand.

"If you ask me, Mr. Grant, the Colonel got this young lady into trouble."

The dry snigger with which Andrews accompanied this appraisal of the situation annoyed me. "The young lady, as you call her, is now an unhappy and rather frightened woman of middle age," I told him sharply. "The son, according to this, is nineteen and he's only just discovered that he's illegitimate. There's a twin sister, too. Not a very amusing situation." And Whitaker—was he still in Arabia? I wondered. "Do you think the man has any idea he has a son and daughter here in Cardiff?"

"I couldn't say, sir."

"Have we got his address?"

"The bank in Bahrain. That was the only address we ever had."

And Bahrain was in the Persian Gulf. But it was over three years since the last payment had come through. He might be anywhere now—back in England, retired, probably. "A pity we haven't got his address," I said. I was thinking that the son must take after his father: the beaky nose and strong jaw were both physical characteristics that didn't suit his circumstances. "This is all we've got on Whitaker, is it?"

Andrews nodded.

"Then how the devil do you know he's a colonel? There's no mention of colonel in this settlement."

Apparently Andrews had seen his rank given in some newspaper story. "Something to do with oil concessions, I think. There was a picture, too, with some sheikhs in flowing robes and Colonel Whitaker in the centre dressed in khaki shorts and a military cap."

"How did you know it was the same man?"

"Well, I couldn't be sure. But I don't think there could be two of them out in that area."

He was probably right there. "I'll ask Captain Griffiths about him." A man who spent his life taking his ship in and out of Arabian ports should know, and he was due in the office at five thirty. "Is the conveyance on that property of his ready now?"

Andrews produced it from the bottom of the pile, a bulky

package that looked as though it contained enough deeds to cover a twenty-thousand-acre estate instead of a little cottage on the Gower Peninsula. "There's still a map to be inserted in the conveyance. Otherwise it's all there, title deeds, searches, everything."

I told him to get on to the man who was doing the map right away. "Griffiths wants all the documents before he sails tonight." The phone rang. It was Mrs. Thomas and I knew by the tone of her voice that something had happened. "They came just after you left, and I'm so worried, Mr. Grant, I don't know what to do. And now Sue has got back and she said to ring you. I'm very sorry to trouble you when you were so kind and came out here all for nothing, but you did say to telephone you if I needed any help and so I thought perhaps . . ."

"Just tell me what's happened, Mrs. Thomas," I said.

"Well, you see, they've taken Dafydd away and . . ." Her voice broke down then. "I'm so terribly worried about him, Mr. Grant. I don't know what's going to happen. So determined he is, you see. Once he's got an idea into his head . . . Always been like that, he has, ever since he was little, you know. Nothing would ever make him change his mind once he had made it up."

"Never mind about what's in your son's mind. What happened when the police arrived?"

"They just said he was to go with them."

"To the police station?"

"I don't know."

"For questioning, was it?"

"They didn't say. I asked them why they were arresting him, but they wouldn't tell me. Been in trouble he has, you know, and them behaving as though—"

"Did Sergeant Mathieson say he was arresting him?"

"No, he didn't say that exactly. He just said he was to come along with them. But it's the same thing, Mr. Grant, isn't it?"

"Did he charge him?"

"No. No, I don't think so. He just said he was to come along, and he went. He didn't try to resist or anything. They just took him, and now I don't know what is going to happen to him."

"Mrs. Thomas," I said, "there's something I want to ask you. Can you tell me where Colonel Whitaker is now?"

The quick gasp of her breath and then a long pause. "No. No, I don't know. But somewhere in Arabia it will be."

"He's still alive, then?"

"Oh, yes."

"You've heard from him?"

Again the pause. "No. No, I never heard from him. Never." And she added quickly: "Only the allowance. Very good he was about the allowance." She sighed. "Never a penny I took for myself, but spent it on Dafydd. Clever he is, you know—a quick brain and good with his hands. I thought perhaps he would become an engineer." Her quick tongue ran on, about the books she'd bought him and how she'd sent him to night school, and I let her talk because it seemed to help her. "He couldn't understand it when the money ceased. It was then he began to run wild, you see; down in the docks all the time and his heart set on getting to Arabia. Speaks Arabic, you know." She said it with pride, and in the same breath added: "I tried to discourage him, but it was no good. He had books, you see, and all those Arabs down in the Tiger Bay district. In the blood it is, I suppose—in the blood and in their stars. And that book of cuttings. I should never have let him see it." And then she added: "A pity you weren't here when they came for him. I know it would never have happened if you'd been here."

"Well, don't worry about it any more," I said. "I'll phone them and find out what it's all about. Have you heard how your husband is?" But she'd received no word from the hospital. "Well, that's good," I said. "They'd have been in touch with you if they were worried about his condition. I'll phone you if I've any news about your son." I put the phone down. "First thing tomorrow, Andrews," I said, "get on to the newspapers and see if they've anything in their files about Whitaker. What that boy needs right now is a father, the sort of father he can look up to."

I hurried through the rest of the business, and as soon as Andrews had gone I phoned Dr. Harvey's surgery. "George Grant here," I said when he came on the line. "Any news of Thomas?"

"Yes," he said, "and it's bad, I'm afraid. I've just had a call from the matron. He died in the ambulance on the way to hospital."

"I see."

"Did the police pick that boy up?"

"Yes." It could well mean a charge of manslaughter. "Has anybody thought of notifying Mrs. Thomas that her husband is dead?"

"The matron is telephoning her right away."

"About time, too," I said. Incredible how soulless an institution can be. But, in fact, it was the boy I was worrying about more than the mother. "They've taken David Thomas into custody," I said.

"Good."

His comment angered me. "Why did you consider it your duty to notify the police? Did you know the man was going to die?"

"I thought it likely." And then, after a pause, he added: "He was a bookie, you know. Greyhounds, mostly. Heavy drinker, heavy smoker, immoderate in everything, if you get me. That type goes quick. But I couldn't be certain, of course." And he added: "Frankly, I wouldn't have expected the boy to stay there till the police arrived. I'd have thought he'd clear out. Probably would have done if you hadn't been there."

"I wasn't there," I told him. "I'd left before they arrived."

"Oh, well, doesn't make any odds. He's no good, that boy."

"What makes you think that?"

"Oddly enough," he said on a note of asperity, "I don't hold with boys hitting their fathers. Far too much licence allowed this new generation. He's a street arab, that boy—dock arab, rather." He gave a quick, awkward laugh. "It's the war, of course, but that doesn't excuse them entirely."

I asked him then to tell me what he knew about the boy. But he couldn't tell me much. The Thomases had only been going to him since the start of the National Health Service, and he hadn't set eyes on the boy more than once or twice. He'd grown up with the dock gangs, he said, mixing too much with the Arabs, had been in and out of a number of jobs, and had finally been sentenced for his part in the beating up of a rival gang leader. "I imagine he's only just been released from Borstal," he said. "Dockside toughs like that are the devil in my parish."

"And that's why you called the police?"

"Well, he killed his father, didn't he?" His voice sounded on the defensive.

"You don't make much allowance for human nature," I said.

"No. Not with boys like that. You try stitching a few flick-knife wounds and bicycle-chain gashes; you'd soon see it my way."

"All right," I said, and left it at that. He didn't know Thomas wasn't the boy's father or what had caused the row between them. "Life's not all as straightforward as you chaps see it in your clinics," I said and put the phone down.

By then it was five thirty and Captain Griffiths had arrived. He was a small man with a pointed beard and a high, cackling laugh, and he wore a tweed suit which was a little too large for him. This and his scrawny, wrinkled skin gave him a shrivelled look. But though he was not an impressive figure, long years of command had given him the knack of making his displeasure felt. "You promised me the documents before I sailed, man." He thrust his beard at me accusingly.

"Don't worry," I said. "You'll get them. When are you sailing?"

"Nine thirty on the tide."

"I'll bring them down myself."

That seemed to satisfy him, and since he showed an inclination to chat, I asked him about Whitaker. "Colonel Charles Stanley Whitaker," I said. "Do you know him, by any chance?"

"Yes, indeed. The Bedouin, that's what they call him out there. Or the Bloody Bedouin in the case of those that hate his guts and all his Arab affectations. That's the whites, you know. The Arabs call him *Al Arif*—the Wise One—or *Haji*. Yes, I know Colonel Whitaker. You can't trade in and out of the Gulf ports without meeting him periodically."

"He's still out there, then?"

"Oh, Lord, yes. A man like that would never be happy retiring to a cottage in the Gower." His small blue eyes creased with silent laughter. "He's a Moslem, you know. He's been on the

Haj to Mecca, and they say he keeps a harem, and when it isn't a harem, there's talk of boys. . . . But there—" He shook his head. "It's just gossip. If I took account of all the gossip I heard on my ship, there wouldn't be any one with a shred of reputation left. Too much time, you see. Everybody's got too much time, and the damned humidity . . ." He gave that high-pitched, cackling laugh. "But, dear me," he went on, "there's a real character for you. You don't find men like Whitaker back here in Britain—not any more. One-eyed and a patch, and a great beak of a nose that makes him look like a bloody bird of prey."

"And you've met him?"

"Yes, indeed. I've had him on board my ship, too—often and often. I've had him on board in all his flowing Bedouin robes, with the silver of his great curved *khanjar* knife gleaming at his girdle and the black *agal* of Arabia around the *kaffyah* that covered his head; yes, and holding court on my own boat deck with the prayer mats out and his bodyguard all round him, armed to the teeth."

"A sort of Lawrence?" I suggested.

"Well . . ." He sounded doubtful. "He hasn't quite that standing with the political crowd. Too much of an Arab. Changing his religion like that, it made a difference, you see. But the oil boys all treat him like God, of course—or used to. But for him, the Gulfoman Oilfields Development Company wouldn't have had a single concession out there. And then there was his theory—the Whitaker Theory, they called it. He believed that the proved oil-bearing country that runs down from Iraq through Kuwait, Dahran, Bahrain and Qattar would be found to continue, swinging southeast along the line of the Jebel Mountains, through Buraimi and into the independent sheikhdom of Saraifa. Well, there's no knowing whether a man's right about a thing like that except by prospecting and drilling. And there was Holmes, you see—he'd had the same sort of bee in his bonnet about Bahrain and he'd been proved right."

"And Whitaker wasn't?" I prompted, for he had paused, his mind engrossed in the past.

"No. It cost the Company a lot of money and nothing but dry wells for their trouble. And now things are changing out there."

He shook his head sadly. "There's a new type of man coming to the top of these Middle East oil companies, technical men who understand oil, but not the Arab. Whitaker and the world he represents—it's doomed, you know; finished. You can't lord it in the deserts of Arabia, not now, with the oil flowing and half the world trying to grab a stake in it. And he's the manner of a ruling prince, you know. He might have been descended from the Prophet himself, the way he behaved at times."

It was an extraordinary picture that Griffiths had drawn for me, and when he left to go back to his ship I felt that my drab office was the brighter for the colour his musical tongue had brought into it. I put some more coal on the fire and settled down to finish the day's work.

It was about half an hour later that I was interrupted by the sound of the street-door bell. It startled me, for I very seldom have a caller after office hours except by appointment, and a glance at my diary confirmed that I'd no appointment for that evening.

My visitor proved to be a girl, and as she stood there in the driving sleet, clutching her bicycle, she seemed vaguely familiar. She had the sort of face that comes together around the nose and mouth, a face that was attractive, rather than pretty, its composition based on the essential of bone formation. She smiled, a little nervously, a flash of white teeth, the bright gleam of pale eyes. I remember that it was her eyes that attracted me at the time. She was just a kid and she was brimming over with health and vitality.

"Mr. Grant? I'm Susan Thomas. Can I speak to you a moment, please?" The words came in a quick rush, breathless with hurrying.

"Of course." I held the door open for her. "Come in."

"May I put my b-bike inside?" There was a natural hesitancy in her voice that was oddly attractive. "I had one stolen a few weeks back." She wheeled it in, and as I took her through to my office, she said: "I was so afraid you'd have left, and I didn't know where you lived."

In the hard glare of my office lighting I was able to see her clearly. The beaky nose, the strong jaw—they were both there, recognizable now. But in her these facial characteristics were softened to femininity. Unlike her brother, she had no resemblance to the mother that I could see. "It's about your brother, I suppose?"

She nodded, shaking the sleet from her blond hair whilst her long, quick fingers loosened the old fawn coat she wore. "I only just got back from the Infirmary. Mother's beside herself. I had great difficulty . . ." She hesitated, a moment of uncertainty as her clear wide eyes stared and she made up her mind about me. "She—she's reached an odd age, if you know what I mean. This is just too much for her."

Nineteen years old, and she knew everything about life, all the hard, unpleasant facts. "Are you a nurse?" I asked her.

"Training to be." She said it with a touch of pride. And then: "You've got to do something about him, Mr. Grant . . . find him, stop him from trying to kill his—from killing somebody else."

I stared at her, appalled. "What are you talking about?" I said. She was over-dramatizing, of course. "You've heard about your—" I stopped there, uncertain what to call him. "About Mr. Thomas?"

"Yes." She nodded, her face as withdrawn as her brother's had been, set and white. "Mother told me."

"The hospital phoned her, then?"

"About half an hour ago. He died in the ambulance, they said." There was no emotion in her voice, but then her lip trembled slightly. "It's David I'm worried about."

"I was just going down to the police station," I said. "It was an accident, of course, but there's always the chance that the police may view it differently."

"He's got a bad record, you know. And they never got on together. Of course," she added, "I knew he wasn't my father —my real father, that is."

"Your mother told you, did she?" I was thinking that it was odd she should have told her daughter and not her son.

"Oh, no," she said. "She never told me. But it's something you know by instinct, sort of."

"Then why in heaven's name didn't your brother know?" I said.

"Oh, well, boys are so slow, you know. And it's not something you can just blurt out, is it, Mr. Grant? I mean, it's something you feel, deep inside, and it's sort of secret." And then she said: "What will he do, do you think? Was he serious when he said he'd kill him? I wasn't there, you see. But Mother is convinced he meant it."

"Kill who?" I said.

"His—my father. Colonel Whitaker. He swore he'd kill him, didn't he? That's what Mother says. You were there. Did he say that?"

"Well, yes." I nodded. "But I didn't take it very seriously. It had all come as a bit of a shock to him. Besides," I added, "there's not much he can do about it at the moment, even if he were serious. And by the time he's released, he'll have had a chance to get used to the idea."

She stared at me. "You haven't heard, then?"

"Heard what?"

"David's escaped."

"Escaped?" So that was why she was here. The stupid, crazy young fool! "How do you know he's escaped?"

"The police just phoned. They said he'd escaped from a police car and that it was our duty to inform them if he returned to the house. That's why I came to see you. Mother's almost out of her mind. You see, it isn't only David she's worrying about. It's this Colonel Whitaker—my f-father. I don't understand after the way he treated her, but I think she's still in love with him . . . always has been, probably. And now she doesn't know what to do for the best." She came closer to me then, touched my arm in a gesture of entreaty. "Please, Mr. Grant, you've got to do something. You've got to help us. I'm scared to death Mother will go to the police and tell them what David said. That's what she wanted to do, right away. She said it was her duty, but I knew it wasn't that. She's just about out of her mind as a result of what David's done already. And he does have a bad record, you know. So I said I'd come to you, and she promised she wouldn't do anything until I got home." And she stood back, drained, her large eyes staring at me expectantly.

I didn't know what to say. There was nothing I could do. No

point in my going out and searching the city for him. A filthy night like this the whole police force would have their work cut out to track him down. "Where was it he escaped?"

"Somewhere along the Cowbridge Road, they said."

"And your father—have you any idea how I can get in touch with him?"

Her eyes brightened for a moment. "Oh, if you could!" But then she shook her head. "I've no idea where he is now. Mother doesn't know. Did she show you the book of press-cuttings?"

"No."

"No, of course not, it was still lying there on the floor. The place was an awful mess." And then she said: "I checked myself because I had the same idea. But the last cutting she got was three years ago. I don't know whether he's been in the papers since then. Dad found out, or maybe he knew all the time—anyway, he made her stop them. That last cutting was a picture taken in Basra. But he may have retired by now. He was getting on—over fifty. And if he's retired, then he'd probably be in England somewhere, wouldn't he? That's what all these people who've lived all their lives abroad do when they retire. Do you think perhaps David knows where he is?"

"No," I said. "He tried to get the address out of me." No point in telling her that he might have the same idea that I had and try to check the newspaper files. "In any case," I told her, "he'll have his work cut out to elude the police. I think you can set your mother's mind at rest. The police will pick him up and . . . and time will do the rest. Your mother can see him in prison, talk to him; in no time at all he'll have accepted the situation."

She thought that over for a moment and then nodded. "Yes. That makes sense." And then she said: "Do you think that's why he escaped? . . . I mean, did he really want to kill Colonel Whitaker, do you think? His own father?"

"At the moment, perhaps." There was no telling what the boy had in his mind. He might simply have been jealous of his mother's affection for an old love. But I couldn't tell her that. "In my opinion, it was the shock," I said. "A perfectly natural reaction. When he's had time to think it over, get used to the idea—"

"But why did he escape? He's never done that before. He's been arrested twice, you see, but he never tried to escape." And when I didn't say anything, she gave a little shrug. "Oh, well, it'll all come out in the wash, I expect." She smiled briefly, but the smile didn't extend to her eyes, which were sad and suddenly without lustre. "It was silly of me to come, really." She started for the door, hugging her coat round her. "I should have known there was nothing you could do. It's Mother I'm worried about. David's in enough trouble. . . ." She moved her shoulders as though bracing herself. "I think perhaps I'll go and see Dr. Harvey. Maybe he'd give her a sedative, something to make her sleep so she doesn't keep going over it in her mind and getting silly ideas in her head." She turned and held out her hand. "Goodbye, Mr. Grant. And thank you. I feel a bit better now anyway."

I took her back through the empty office to the street door, and as she wheeled her bicycle out she asked me to telephone her if I had any news. "During the day you can always get me at the Infirmary if it's important. I'd rather you didn't phone my mother. Promise?"

"Of course," I said.

Shortly after she'd gone Andrews came in with the map. By the time I had dealt with the conveyance and finished my other work, it was almost seven thirty. Time enough to call in at the police station on my way down to the docks. What the boy needed was to be given some purpose in life.

I was thinking about this as I pulled on my coat, wondering at the chance of birth, how some people are born to parents happily married, and others . . . My own childhood hadn't been all that happy. I shrugged my shoulders. Life was a battle anyway. Sex, money, happiness—it was all a struggle, like trying to build up this decrepit business. It took all the guts, all the energy you'd got sometimes just to make some sense out of life, and when things didn't work out . . . I set the guard carefully in front of the dying fire, feeling sorry for the boy, sorry for myself.

I suppose I was tired. It had been a frustrating week, and now it was Friday and the week-end stretching ahead. I was feeling the need of a drink. There was a pub I went to sometimes in the dock area, a rowdy place, but virile and full of masculinity and talk of far places, a seamen's pub that always gave me the illusion of islands just beyond the horizon. With a few Scotches, imagination could soar, leaping the tawdry problems of money and piddling lawyer's briefs.

I went out, closing the door of my office behind me, following the white beam of my torch through the empty outer office with its clumsy mahogany counter and frosted-glass panels. I had reached the street door and my hand was on the latch when I remembered the package for Captain Griffiths. I had left it propped up on the mantelpiece so that I shouldn't forget it.

I went back to my office, my footsteps sounding hollow on the bare boards. He'd never forgive me if I let him sail without his dream of the future all set down in the mumbo-jumbo of legal phraseology. A man needed a dream, something to aim at. You couldn't go through life without a goal. For him it was retirement and that little whitewashed cottage looking out over the sweep of Rhossilly Bay; for me it was just a solicitor's office with new paint, new furniture, and clients tumbling over each other for my services. My hand reached out for the handle of the door, and then, suddenly, there was the tinkle of glass falling. The sound came from beyond the door, startlingly loud in the empty stillness.

I switched off my torch and eased the door open a fraction, every nerve in my body tensed and expectant. I heard the scrape of the window latch, the scrabble of boots on the sill, the rustle of the curtains as they were pushed aside. A burglar? But nobody but a fool would expect to find cash lying around loose in a solicitor's office. Perhaps he was after some particular document? But I could think of nothing I was handling at the moment sufficiently important to warrant breaking and entering. I heard him stumble against my chair and then I could hear his heavy breathing coming nearer as he crossed the room to the door. I guessed he'd be making for the light switch, and I flung the door wide and at the same time switched on my torch again.

David Thomas stood there, checked in the white beam of it. His fair hair was plastered down by the rain. His face was

streaked with blood from a gash on his forehead, the left cheek
bruised and filthy with mud. There was mud on his clothes, too
—black, wet patches of it that clung to the sodden cloth. His
jacket was ripped at the shoulder and one trouser leg was torn
so badly that the flesh of his leg showed through the rent. He
was breathing heavily as though he'd been running.

"What the hell are you doing here?" I said and switched on
the light. His face was ghastly white, his eyes unnaturally wide.
He looked scared out of his wits. "Well, I don't expect they'll
think of looking for you in my office." I closed the door and
walked past him and put the curtains straight. Then I took the
guard from the fire and put some more coal on, poking it till a
flame showed. And all the time I was conscious of him standing
there, watching me in silence, too surprised, too scared probably, to move. I pushed the old armchair reserved for clients
close to the hearth. "All right," I said. "Take your jacket off and
come and sit by the fire and dry yourself out." He did as I told
him, too startled to have any initiative of his own left. "Now," I
said, "just tell me what in God's name made you do such a
damn-fool thing."

For a moment I thought he was going to close up on me the
way that sort of kid does when things go wrong and people start
asking questions. The sullen tough-boy look had come back into
his face. "Take your time," I said. "There's no hurry. You've got
all evening if you want it." I thought I'd try flattery then. "Not
many chaps manage to get away from the police so soon after
being taken in charge. How did you do it?"

The tight lips relaxed slightly, a ghost of a smile. "Luck," he
said. He was shivering and I poked the fire again, coaxing it
into a blaze. "They'd got a car to take me to one of their bloody
jails. Said I'd feel more at home in the nick." His tone was a
sneer.

"And you made a break for it."

"Yeah. That's right. There was only one of them in the back
with me, and I made a dive for it when they were driving down
the Cowbridge Road. I hit the pavement and just about knocked
myself out. They nearly had me then. But there was a pub I
knew, and I dived in there and got away out the back." And he

added: "I said I'd see you in your office." There was a touch of bravado in the way he said it.

"Your sister was here a little while back," I told him.

"Sue? What did she want?" He was on the defensive immediately.

"Wanted me to help you."

"Help me?" He gave a derisive laugh. "The only way you can help me is by giving me that address. That's what I came for."

"Your mother's worried sick," I told him.

"So what?"

I lost patience with him then. "Can't you get it into your thick head that your actions affect other people? Stop being so damned irresponsible. The police phoned your mother that you'd escaped, and now she's half out of her mind. . . ."

But he wasn't interested in the heartbreak he was causing other people. "She should have thought of that before she wrote me that letter," he said. "She was half out of her mind then. Did Sue tell you I'd two more months to do in a Borstal Institute?"

"No."

"Well, I had. Two more months and I'd have been out and in the clear. And then I got this letter threatening she's going to commit suicide. Your Da's driving me to it, she said, and I can't stand it any more. And then to come home and find she's been holding out on me all the time, kidding me I was that drunken old fool's son. Christ! And you talk about being irresponsible."

"It isn't an easy thing for a woman to tell her son."

"She'd nineteen years. In nineteen years she ought to have been able to screw up her courage. Instead, she drives the old man to fling it in my face." He stared at the fire, his shoulders hunched, his face bitter. "Does Sue know?" he asked at length. "Does she know she's illegitimate?"

"Yes."

"And what does she feel about it?"

"She said she'd known for a long time—deep down."

"Then why the hell didn't she tell me?"

"I said, deep down. Her mother didn't tell her. She just knew."

He looked sulky then. "We never kept anything from each other before."

"It's not the sort of thing you want to share with anybody else," I said.

"Too right, it isn't." He suddenly beat his fist against the arm of the chair. "Christ! If I'd only known before."

"It wouldn't have helped you," I told him.

He thought about that for a moment and then he nodded. "No, I guess you're right." And he added: "I always wondered why the old man hated my guts." He leaned suddenly forward, picked up the poker, and jabbed at the fire. "Guess I hated his guts, too," he said viciously.

"Well, he's dead now," I said. "Did you know that?"

He nodded and let go of the poker so that it clattered into the grate. "Yep. They told me that. Croaked on the way to hospital, blast him."

His attitude to the man's death shocked me. "For God's sake!" I said. "Haven't you any compassion for the man who was a father to you?"

"He wasn't my father," he cried. "I told you that before."

"He was your father in the eyes of the law."

"Then the law ought to be changed, oughtn't it? You can't make chalk cheese by a legal declaration."

"He supported you all the time you were growing up," I reminded him.

"All right, he supported me. But he hated me all the same. I always knew that. When he took a strap to me, he enjoyed it. He hasn't been able to do that for a long time now. But he'd other ways of getting at me, jeering at me because I read a lot, and at my Arab friends. Do you know what he'd done whilst I'd been in Borstal? I went up to my old room after you'd left. All my books on Arabia, every damn one of them, he'd pulled out and torn to pieces. The only books he hadn't destroyed were the technical ones. I'd a lot of them on oil—geology, seismology, geophysics. He left me those because he didn't think I cared about them." He stared at me. "Now he's dead, and I'm glad. Glad, do you hear?" His voice had risen, and suddenly the tears were welling up into his eyes and he began to cry. "I didn't mean to kill him," he sobbed. "Honest. I didn't mean to." He broke down completely then, sobbing like a child, and I went over to him and gripped his shoulder.

"It was an accident," I said, trying to steady him.

"They don't believe it."

"Did they prefer a charge?"

"No, but they think I killed him. I know they do." And he burst out: "I haven't a chance with them."

"You certainly haven't made it any better by making a break for it like that." I was wondering whether I could persuade him to come with me to the police station and give himself up. I hesitated and then walked over to the phone, but he was on his feet immediately.

"What you going to do? Ring the police?" There was panic in his voice.

"No," I said. "I'm going to ring your home—get your mother down here, your sister, too."

"What for? What good'll that do?"

"If your mother makes a statement, explaining exactly how it happened . . ."

"It's no good," he said. "She wouldn't do it. She'd rather have me hanged. . . ."

"Oh, don't be childish," I said.

"It's true," he cried. "She told me so herself—after you'd gone." He had followed me to the desk and his voice was intense, very serious. "She thinks I'm going to kill Whitaker if I ever lay my hands on him. And she loves him. After all these years, she still loves the man. I don't understand it, but that's how it is. You'd think after the swine had treated her like that, after he'd left her flat . . ." He pulled a blood-stained handkerchief from his pocket and blew his nose. "When I got back this afternoon the old man was giving her hell. I could hear it out in the street. He was calling her all sorts of names. I suppose he was drunker than usual. He had that book of press-cuttings in his hand, and when I told him to shut his mouth, he taunted me with being a bastard, said he'd had all he could stand of another man's whelps. And then he turned on my mother and added: 'And all I can stand of another man's whore. After all I've done to cover up for you,' he said, 'you creep off as soon as I'm out of the house to mope over your lover's pictures.' And he flung the book at her. That's when I went for him." He paused, staring at me, his eyes over-bright. "That book was full of press-cuttings of him—pictures, some of them. I've grown up with that book, grown up with the man himself. I know him, know his way of life, everything about him. It's like I told you—he was a sort of god to me. I wanted to be like him, tough, independent, an adventurer in far places. I tried to get a job as a seaman on ships going out that way from Cardiff docks, but at first I was too young, and then there was the union. I even tried to stow away once. And now I find he's no more than a rotten, dirty little sham who'd leave a woman to bear her twins alone. I told Ma I'd kill him if I ever laid hands on him. Remember? You were there when I said it."

I nodded.

"Well, she believed me. She's convinced I really will kill him if I ever catch up with him."

"And you didn't mean what you said—is that what you're trying to tell me?"

He walked back to the fire and stood staring at it for a moment. Then he slumped down in the chair again, his body limp. "I don't know," he murmured. "Honest, I don't know. All I do know is that I have to find him."

"And that's why you came here, to search my office for his address?"

He nodded. "I knew you'd have it somewhere in your files."

"Well, I haven't." I hesitated. But, after all, the boy had a right to know where his father was. "Will you promise me something? Will you promise me that if you find him, you'll remember that he's your father and that blood is something you just can't rub out with violence?"

He looked at me and was silent a long time. At length he said: "I can't promise anything. I don't know how I'd act." He was being honest at least. "But I'll try to remember what you've just said." And then on a sudden, urgent note: "I've got to find him. I've just got to find him. Please, please try to understand."

The need of that kid . . . It was the thing that had been lacking for him all his life. It was his mother's need reflected and enlarged. The sins of the fathers . . . Why in God's name should a sense of insecurity lead to violence, in people and in races? "All right," I said. "I accept that." And I passed on to him what Griffiths had told me. "But then you know the sort of man your father is. Anyway, there it is, he's still out there. And if you want to contact him, I imagine a letter to the Gulfoman Oilfields Development Company—"

"A letter's no good. I wrote him already—twice. He never answered." He looked up at me. "This Captain Griffiths, is his ship the *Emerald Isle*? She sails regularly to the Persian Gulf." And when I nodded, he said: "That was the ship I tried to stow away on. I was fourteen then, and a year later I tried to sign on. She's in port now, is she?"

"Yes."

"When is she sailing?"

"Tonight."

"Tonight?" He looked up at me, suddenly eager, like a dog being offered a walk. "Tonight. When? What time?" He had jumped to his feet, all the tiredness falling from him. "For Christsake, what time?"

I hesitated. It was no part of a lawyer's job to get involved in a criminal case. My duty was plain. "The sensible thing would be for you to give yourself up to the police."

He didn't hear me. His eyes had fastened on the envelope I had left propped up on the mantelpiece. "Were you taking this down to the ship tonight?"

I nodded, and his hand reached out for the envelope, clutched at it. "I'll deliver it for you." He held it as though it were a talisman, his eyes bright with the chance it represented. "That's all I need. The excuse to go on board. And they wouldn't catch me this time, not till we were at sea." He glanced at the window, balanced on the balls of his feet, as though about to take off the way he had come. But then I suppose he realized I should only phone the police. "Will you let me take it?" His voice was urgent, his eyes pleading. "Once on board the *Emerald Isle* . . . Please, sir."

That "sir" was a measure of his desperation.

"Please," he said again. "It's the only hope I got."

He was probably right at that. And if I didn't let him take it, what other chance would he ever get in life? He'd escaped from Borstal. He'd escaped from the police. With that sort of record he'd be lucky to get away with three years for manslaughter. After that he'd be case-hardened, a criminal for life. And there was the sister, too. A nice girl, that. I sighed. "I'm supposed to be a lawyer," I reminded him . . . or maybe I was reminding myself. "Not a travel agency for boys who've escaped from the police."

"But you'll let me deliver it, won't you?"

What the hell can you do when faced with youth in all its shining innocence and eagerness. "All right," I said. "You can try it, if you like. But God knows what Griffiths will do."

"All I want is the chance to meet up with my father."

I realized then that his mind had leap-frogged all the obstacles; he was already mentally sailing the coast of Arabia in search of his father. "All I'm giving you," I warned him, "is the excuse to get on board that ship. She sails at nine thirty. And those documents have got to be delivered into Captain Griffiths's hands, understand?"

"I'll give them to him. I promise."

"You know your way about the ship?"

"I knew every corner of her once. It'll come back to me as soon as I get on board."

"Well, kindly remember that I'm a solicitor. When you're caught, as you will be eventually, don't implicate me. Shall we say you walked into my office to get legal advice, saw the envelope I had forgotten, and took it on the spur of the moment? Is that understood?"

"Yes, sir."

"I'll take you down to Bute East Dock now," I said. "After that you're on your own." I hesitated. It wasn't much of a chance I was giving him. He'd no clothes other than what he stood up in, no money probably, nothing, not even a passport. But at least I'd have done what I could for him—what I'd have hoped somebody would do for a son of mine if he'd got himself into a mess like this. But then I hadn't a son; I hadn't anybody. "Better clean the blood off your face," I said and showed him where the wash-place was. "And you'll need something to hide your torn clothes."

I left him in the lavatory and went through the office to the cupboard under the stairs. There was an old overcoat that had been there ever since I'd taken over the place, a black hat, too. He tried them on when he'd finished cleaning himself up. The coat wasn't too bad a fit, and with the sweatband padded with strips from an old conveyance the hat was passable. I wondered what my uncle would have said if he knew to what use these sartorial relics of his were being put. And because I wanted him to realize how slender his chances were, I said: "If you're caught before the ship sails, don't try and bluff it out with Captain Griffiths. Tell him the truth and say you want to give yourself up to the police."

He nodded, his face bloodless, his pale eyes almost fever-bright with the nervous tension that was building up in him. The dark coat and the black hat accentuated his pallor, accentuated, too, his beaky nose and the strong jaw. In the old lawyer's cast-off clothes he looked much older than his nineteen years.

There was a back way out of the office, and I took him out by that. It was still sleeting, and there was nobody in the street where I parked my car. We drove in silence down Park Place and across Castle Street, and then we crossed the railway and were in the maze of little streets that edge the docks. I slowed in a dark gap between street-lights and told him to climb into the back and lie on the floor with the rug I kept for my dog pulled over him.

It was fortunate that I took this precaution, for the police at the dock entrance had been alerted and there was a constable there who recognized me; a fortnight before, he had given evidence in a case I'd defended. I told him my business and he let me through. I hadn't expected the police to be watching the docks already and my hands were sweating as I drove on across the slippery steel of the railway tracks.

The *Emerald Isle* was at the far end of the Bute East Dock, close to the lock. She had completed loading and she had steam up, smoke trailing from her single stack. The cranes along the quay were still, their gaunt steel fingers pointed at the night. I stopped in the shadow of one of the sheds. The sleet had turned to snow and it was beginning to lie, so that the dock looked ghostly white in the ship's lights. "Well, there you are," I said. "That's the ship."

He scrambled out from under the rug. "Couldn't you come with me?" he asked, suddenly scared now that the moment had arrived. "If you were to have a word with Captain Griffiths . . ."

I didn't reply to that, but simply handed him the package. I think he knew it was out of the question, for he didn't ask me again. A moment later the rear door opened and I heard him get out. "I—I'd like to thank you," he stammered. "Whatever happens—I won't let you down."

"Good luck!" I said.

"Thanks." And then he was walking across the dock, not hesitantly, but with a firm, purposeful tread. I watched him mount the gangway, saw him pause and speak to one of the crew, an Arab; and then he disappeared from sight through a door in the bridge deck.

I lit a cigarette and sat there, wondering what would happen now. I didn't think he'd much of a chance, but you never know; he was a resourceful kid.

I finished my cigarette and lit another. I was thinking about the constable on the gate. I ought to have realized that that would be one of the first things they'd do following his escape. And the man had recognized me. I tried to analyse my motives in doing such a crazy thing, but I couldn't sort them out. The cold crept into the car as I waited, and still nothing happened, except that the snow thickened and the dock turned dazzling white. A tug hooted out in the river, a lost, owl sound in the winter night. It was twenty minutes past nine.

Ten minutes later a whistle sounded from somewhere high up on the *Emerald Isle* and two men came quickly out of a hut at the end of the dock. They manhandled the gangway ashore and then stood by the warps. Another whistle and the for'ard warp went slack, fell with a splash into the dock. Black smoke belched from the funnel, and as the stern warp was let go, a gap opened up between the ship's side and the quay. I switched the engine on then, turned the heater up, and sat there smoking as the *Emerald Isle* locked out into the River Taff. And when her lights had finally disappeared behind the whitened shoulders of the loading-sheds, I drove back to the solitude of my flat, hoping to God I'd done the right thing.

The story of what happened to him after that I got partly from Captain Griffiths on his return and partly from a letter David wrote me. When he left me on the dock there and went on board the *Emerald Isle* there was no clear-cut plan in his mind. He knew the layout, of course. She was the only ship trading regularly out of Cardiff to Arabian ports, and she had exercised a fatal fascination for him since he was old enough to wander in the docks. It was the Somali steward and not a deck hand who met him at the top of the gangway, and on the spur of the moment, almost without thinking, he inquired whether the passenger accommodation was fully booked. The steward told him no: there were six cabins and only three were occupied. Feeling suddenly more confident, he asked to see the Captain.

Captain Griffiths was in his cabin on the port side of the bridge-deck housing, and when David was shown in he was seated at his desk checking the Mate's trim figures. He took the packet, glanced at it, and then looked up at David. "You work for Mr. Grant, do you?"

"I—I run errands for him."

"Office boy, eh? Well, you're only just in time. We sail in quarter of an hour." Griffiths peered up at him from under his bushy brows. "What's the matter with your face, boy? Been in a fight?"

"No. No, sir. I—I had a fall."

"Must have been a bad one. You're as white as a sheet." He bent down, pulled open a drawer of his desk, and came up with a bottle of whisky. "I'll give you a drink for your pains." He gave that high-pitched cackling laugh, filled the glasses half full, and handed one of them to David. "Well, young fellow, you can wish me luck, for it's a Welsh landowner I am now." And he slapped the packet of documents with unconcealed pride. "There's times, you know," he confided as he swallowed his drink, "when I feel like the Wandering Jew himself, doomed to ply from one silt-laden port to another, right through to Eternity. This," and his hand touched the packet again, "this may help me to preserve my sanity when the temperature's over the hundred and the humidity's so thick your lungs feel as though they're stuffed full of wet cotton wool and will never breathe clean air again; when conditions are like that, then I'll take these documents out and read them through just to convince myself that I really do have a little place on the Gower Peninsula where rain washes the air clean of dust and heat and the damned, Godforsaken, everlasting flies."

"That's the Persian Gulf you'll be referring to, isn't it? Then maybe you'll know where Colonel Whitaker lives now?" He hadn't intended to ask that question, but the unaccustomed liquor had overlaid his nervousness.

Griffiths glanced up at him quickly. "Funny thing," he murmured. "Grant asked me that same question only this afternoon. Is Colonel Whitaker one of the firm's clients?"

"I—I don't know, sir."

"Then what made you ask about him?"

David hesitated. But if he were to succeed in stowing away on board, there was no harm in telling Captain Griffiths the truth right now. "He's my father."

"Your father!" The blue eyes stared. "Good God! Didn't know the Bedouin was married."

"My natural father, sir."

Griffiths's eyes suddenly crinkled at the corners. "Natural father, you say? Well, by God, that's a good one." And he lay back in his swivel chair, pointed his beard at the steel deck above, and cackled with laughter. And then he stopped suddenly. "I'm sorry, boy. You're sensitive about it, I can see. Have you ever met your father?"

"No, sir."

"Well, if you had, you'd know why I laughed. Bedouin sons —and daughters. There's gossip enough about him, but never a whisper of a son in Wales, you see. I'll tell him, next time he's aboard—I'll say to him casually . . ." But David was spared the rest, for the bridge communicator buzzed and a voice said: "Tug coming alongside now, sir."

"Very good, Mr. Evans." Griffiths got to his feet. "I'm needed on the bridge." He paused in front of David, staring up at his face. "Yes. I can see the likeness now. Any message you want me to give him?" And when David shook his head dumbly, he patted him on the arm. "Well, I'll tell him I saw you when next he comes aboard. And now you'd better get off the ship quick or you'll find yourself in Arabia with a deal of explaining to do." And he went off, cackling with laughter, to the bridge above.

David found himself standing alone outside the Captain's cabin. An alleyway ran athwartships. Numbered mahogany doors led off it on either side. He listened, every nerve taut. He could hear voices on the bridge and down below in the saloon, but the deck on which he stood seemed utterly deserted. Treading softly, he walked the length of the alleyway to the starb'd side, as far away from the Captain's cabin as possible. The first door he tried was locked, the second opened to a glimpse of heavily labelled baggage and the startled face of a man lying prone on his bunk with a book. A tug blared so close alongside that he jumped. Cabin Number Four was empty, and he slipped inside and locked the door. And after that he stood for a long time, quite still and breathing heavily, listening to the sounds of the ship, waiting tense for the sudden outcry that would inevitably follow the discovery that he had not gone ashore.

That period of waiting, ten minutes at the most, seemed the longest he had ever known. And then a whistle sounded. It was so like the shrill of a police whistle that he reached for the handle of the door, instinctively seeking escape in movement. But then the engine-room telegraph rang from the bridge overhead and the ship suddenly came to life, a gentle throbbing against the soles of his shoes. He knelt on the unmade bunk then and cautiously pulled back the curtain that covered the porthole. He could see the deck rail and beyond it a flat expanse of water with the snow driving across it. And then the water was swirling to the bite of the screws and he knew the ship was moving.

He took off his hat and coat then and lay down on the bunk under a ship's blanket, listening with his ears attuned to every sound. A gong sounded for the evening meal and there was movement in the next cabin, the gush of a tap, the bang of a

suitcase. The shrill of the whistle on the bridge was answered
a moment later by the tug's farewell blast on her siren. The beat
of the engines increased, and later, after they had slowed to
drop the pilot, the ship began to roll.

He slept during the night, rolled from side to side of the
narrow bunk. But when daylight came, he lay awake, tense
and hungry. Footsteps sounded in the alleyway, cabin doors
slammed, somewhere a loose porthole cover rattled back and
forth. The hours of daylight seemed endless, but nobody came,
nobody even tried the handle of the cabin door. It was as
though he didn't exist, and, perversely, he felt deserted, lost and
forgotten in this strange world he'd been thrust into by events.
He had no watch, so that he'd no idea of the time. The sky was
grey with a low wrack of cloud, no sun. The violence of the
movement was exhausting, and towards nightfall he was sick,
retching emptily into the washbasin. Nobody seemed to hear
the sound of his misery, nobody seemed to care. The seas, thud-
ding against the bows of the ship, made her tremble, so that
everything rattled, and each time she buried her bows the noise
of the impact was followed by a long, shuddering movement
that seemed to run through his tired body as though he were
himself being exposed to the onslaught of the gale.

Night followed the day at last and he slept; and then it was
day again. Darkness and light succeeding each other. He lost
count of the days, and when the sun came out and the sea subsided, he knew he was too weak to hold out alone in that cabin
any longer. The moment had come to face the future.

Just above his head, within easy reach of his left hand, was
a bell-push. He lay half a day, staring at the yellow bone button
embedded in its wooden orifice, before he could summon the
courage to press it, and when the steward came he told the
startled Somali to take him to the Captain.

Griffiths was seated at his desk so that to David's bemused
mind it seemed like that first time he'd met him, except that
now the cabin was full of sunlight and they were off the coast of
Portugal. The Somali was explaining excitedly and Griffiths's
small blue eyes were staring up at him. The Captain silenced
the man with a movement of his hand. "All right, Ishmail. You

can leave us now." And as the steward turned to go, his eyes rolling in his head, Griffiths added: "And see you don't talk about this. The passengers are not to know that a stowaway has been hiding in their accommodation." And when the door closed and they were alone, he turned to David. "Now, young man, perhaps you'd explain why the devil you stowed away on my ship?"

David hesitated. It was difficult to know where to begin, though he'd had four days of solitude to think about it. He was scared, too. The little man in the worn blue jacket with the gold braid on the sleeves was more frightening to him than either of the judges who had sentenced him, for his future was in the Captain's hands. "Well, come on, man, come on." The beard waggled impatiently, the blue eyes bored into him.

I would like to think that he remembered my advice then, but more probably he was too weak and confused to invent a satisfactory story. At any rate, he told it straight, from the receipt of his mother's hysterical letter and his escape from Borstal, right through to the tragedy of his return to the house in Everdale Road. And Griffiths listened without comment, except that halfway through he took pity on David's weakness, for he was leaning on the edge of the desk to support himself, and told him to pull up a chair and sit down. And when finally he was asked to account for his possession of the documents that had been his excuse for boarding the ship, he stuck to the explanation we'd agreed on.

But Griffiths was much too sharp for him. "So you took the packet from Mr. Grant's office and decided to deliver it yourself?"

"Yes, sir."

"You say you found the door of Mr. Grant's office open. That means he'd only gone out for a moment. When he came back and found the packet gone, the natural thing would be for him to come down to the ship and give me some explanation. You're lying, you see."

There was nothing he could do then but tell Captain Griffiths the truth, and the blue eyes, staring into his, began to crease at the corners. By the time he had finished, Griffiths was leaning back in the swivel chair and roaring with laughter, his mouth so wide open that David could see the movement of his uvula in the red hollow of his gullet. "Well, I'll be damned!" Griffiths said, wiping his eyes. "And Grant an accessory . . ." And then he started in on a cross-examination that seemed to go on and on.

Finally he got up and stood for a long time staring out of the porthole at the sunlight dancing on the waves made by the ship's passage through the water, whilst David sat there, numbed and hopeless. "Well, I believe you," Griffiths said, still staring out at the sea. "You could never have made all that up." There was a long silence. "You got Grant to help you—and how you did that I don't know, considering he'd never met your father. He was risking his reputation, everything. You've no passport, of course? That means you can't land in the normal way. And you've never had word from your father, which means he doesn't care to acknowledge your existence—right?"

And when David didn't say anything, Griffiths swung round from the porthole, his beard thrust aggressively forward. "And you stow away on my ship, expecting me to get you into Arabia. How the devil do you think I'm going to do that, eh?"

"I don't know, sir."

"Perhaps Grant suggested something?" But David shook his head unhappily and Griffiths snapped: "A lawyer—he should have had more sense." And he stumped across the cabin and stood peering down at David's face. "Is your father going to acknowledge you now, do you think? How old are you?"

"Nineteen."

"And do you think Colonel Whitaker's going to be pleased to have a bastard he sired nineteen, twenty years ago, suddenly turn up with no passport, nothing—and a jailbird at that?"

David got to his feet then. "I'm sorry, Captain Griffiths," he said stiffly. "I didn't realize . . ." The words didn't come easily, and his mouth felt dry and caked. "I've always dreamed of this, you see—of getting out to Arabia. I suppose it's in my—bastard blood." He said it with bitterness, for he was convinced now that the world was against him, as it always had been—as it always would be. "I'll work my passage," he added wearily, "and when we get to Aden you can hand me over to the authorities."

Griffiths nodded. "That's the first sensible suggestion you've made. And it's exactly what I ought to do." He turned away and stood for a moment lost in thought. "Your father did me a good turn once. I owe him something for that, but the question is would I be doing him a good turn . . ." He gave a quick shrug and subsided into his chair, chuckling to himself. "It has its humorous side, you know." And David watched, fascinated and with a sudden feeling of intense excitement, as Griffiths's hand reached out to the bridge communicator. "Mr. Evans. Come down to my cabin for a moment, will you?" And then, looking at David: "Well, now, for the sake of Mr. Grant, whom I wouldn't have suspected of such lawlessness, and for the sake of your father, who's going to get the shock of his life, I'm going to sign you on as a deck hand. But understand this," he added, "any trouble at Aden and I hand you over to the authorities."

David was too relieved, too dazed to speak. The Mate came in and Griffiths said: "Stowaway for you, Mr. Evans. Have the galley give him some food and then put him to work. I'm signing him on. And see the passengers, at any rate, don't know how he came aboard. His name is—Whitaker." David caught the glint of humour in the blue eyes.

"Thank you, sir," he mumbled, but as he turned away all he could think about was that name, spoken aloud for the first time. Whitaker. Somehow it seemed to fit, as though it had always belonged to him; it was a symbol, too, a declaration that the past was gone, the future ahead.

All down the Mediterranean and through the Suez Canal, the life of the ship, the sun's increasing warmth, the sight of places all dreamed about and now suddenly come to life absorbed him completely, each day bringing the promise of Arabia twenty-four steaming hours nearer. But when they entered the Red Sea, with the water flat like a mirror and the desert hills of the Hejaz shimmering to port, he knew they were getting close to Aden. And at Aden the police might be waiting for him.

It was night when the anchor was let go off Steamer Point, and as he stood on the foredeck directing a stream of water on to the hawsehole, he could see the lights of Crater and the black shape of the volcanic hills behind towering against the stars. His first Arabian port. It touched his nostrils with a breath of sun-hot oil waste. But instead of excitement, all he felt was fear.

Customs and Immigration came aboard. He stood by the rail, in the shadow of one of the boats, and watched them climb the side from a launch. His work was done and he'd nothing to think about now but the possibility of arrest. A subdued murmur came to him from the town, strange Arab cries drifting across the water. Another launch glided to the ship's side. The agent this time. And later two of the passengers were climbing down into it, followed by their baggage. The officials were leaving, too, and he watched the launches curve away from the ship, two ghostly arrow-tips puttering into the night. He breathed gently again, savouring the warm, strange-scented air . . . and then the steward called his name. "Captain want you in cabin."

Slowly he went for'ard to the bridge-deck housing. Captain Griffiths was seated in the leather armchair, his face a little flushed, his eyes bright, a tumbler of whisky at his elbow. "Well, young fellow, it appears that you're in the clear. Nobody is in the least bit interested in you here." And he added: "Doubtless you have Mr. Grant to thank for that. I'm sorry I can't send him a message; the man must be half out of his mind, considering the chance he took."

"I'll write to him as soon as I can," David murmured.

The Captain nodded. "Time enough for that when you're safely ashore. But it's only fair to tell you that if I fail to contact your father, then you'll complete the voyage and be paid off at Cardiff." And having delivered this warning, he went on: "I'll be going ashore in the morning and I'll cable Colonel Whitaker care of GODCO—that's the Gulfoman Oilfields Development Company. It may reach him, it may not. Depends where your father is, you see; he's not an easy man to contact. Meantime, I am instructing Mr. Evans to give you work that will keep you out of sight of the passengers. We have two oil men with us on the voyage up the coast, also an official from the PRPG's office—that's the Political Resident Persian Gulf. See to it that you keep out of their way. If you do get ashore, then I don't want anybody saying afterwards that they saw you on board my ship." And with that David found himself dismissed.

He saw Captain Griffiths go ashore next morning in the agent's launch. All day they were working cargo, the winches clattering as they unloaded Number One hold into the lighter dhows alongside and filled it again with a fresh cargo. In the evening four passengers came aboard, all white, and a dhow-load of Arabs bound for Mukalla who strewed themselves and their belongings about the deck. And then the anchor was hauled up and the ship shifted to the bunkering wharf. The *Emerald Isle* sailed at midnight, steaming east-northeast along the southern coast of Arabia, the coast of myrrh and frankincense, of Mocha coffee and Sheba's queen.

It was a voyage to thrill the heart of any youngster, but David saw little of it, for he was confined to the bowels of the ship, chipping and painting, and all he saw of Mukalla, that gateway to the Hadhramaut, was a glimpse through a scuttle—a huddle of terraced Arab houses, so white in the sunlight that it looked like an ivory chess set laid out at the foot of the arid mountains. Only at night was he allowed on deck, and he spent hours motionless in the bows of the ship, drinking in the beauty and the mystery of the Arabian Sea, for the water was alive with phosphorescence. From his vantage point he could look down at the bow wave, at the water rushing away from the ship in two great swathes as bright as moonlight, and ahead, in the inky blackness of the sea, great whorls of light like nebulae were shattered into a thousand phosphorescent fragments as the ship's passage broke up the shoals of fish—and, like outriders, the sharks flashed torpedo-tracks of light as they ploughed their voracious way through the depths. And every now and then a tanker passed them, decks almost awash with oil from Kuwait, Bahrain, and Dahran.

They passed inside the Kuria Muria Islands at night, and to get a better view of them he ignored his orders and crept up to the boat deck. He was standing there close beside one of the boats when the door of the passenger accommodation opened and two figures emerged, momentarily outlined against the yellow light. They came aft, two voices talking earnestly, as he shrank into the shadow of the boat, bending down as though to adjust the falls.

". . . the last time I was at the Bahrain office. But even in Abu Dhabi we've heard rumours." The accent was North Country.

"Well, that's the situation. Thought I'd warn you. Wouldn't like you to back the wrong horse and find yourself out on your ear just because you didn't know what was going on."

"Aye; well, thanks. But the Great Gorde . . . It takes a bit of getting used to, you must admit. He's been the Company out here for so long."

"I wouldn't know about that, old man. I'm new out here, and, as far as I'm concerned, Erkhard is the man."

The voices were no more than a whisper in the night. The two oil men were leaning over the rail at the other end of the boat, and David was just going to creep away when he heard the name of his father mentioned. "Is it true Colonel Whitaker's the cause of the trouble? That's the rumour." He froze into immobility, listening fascinated as the other man gave a short laugh. "Well, yes, in a way; the Bloody Bedouin's got too big for his boots. And that theory of his, a lot of damned nonsense. He's not thinking of the Company, only of his Arab friends."

"Oh, I don't know. The Company owes him a lot."

"Concessions, yes—and a string of dry wells. The man's a dangerous amateur. I'm warning you, Entwhistle—you talk like that when Erkhard visits you at Abu Dhabi and you'll be out so damn quick—"

"It's Gorde I deal with."

"Okay. But you can take my word for it that it'll be Erkhard who does the next tour of inspection of the development sites. And unless you've got something to show him . . ."

The voices faded as the two men moved away, walking slowly and in step back towards the deck housing. David moved quickly, slipping down the ladder to the main deck, back to his position in the bows. He wanted to be alone, for that brief overheard conversation had given him a strange glimpse of the world on which he had set his heart.

The ship stopped at Masira Island with stores for the RAF, and then on again, rounding Ras al Hadd at night and ploughing northwest into the Gulf of Oman. On the afternoon of the seventh day out from Aden she anchored at Muscat, in a cove so narrow and rocky that David could scarcely believe his eyes; it might have been the Pembrokeshire coast of Wales except that a white, sun-drenched Arab town stood close by the water's edge at the head of the inlet. On either side the rocks bore the names of visiting ships with dates going back to the 1800's, all painted in foot-high letters. Long, double-ended boats of palm wood, their broad planks sewn together with thongs, swarmed round the ship, paddled by Arabs whose faces shone black in the sun.

They were there twenty-four hours, and in the night David thought more than once of diving over the side. The shore was so near. But, once ashore, what hope had he? There was no-where for him to go. In a halting conversation with one of the crew, a coast Arab from a fishing village to the north called Khor al Fakhan, he learned that Muscat was backed by volcanic mountains of indescribable brutality. They were almost fifty miles deep, with every route through guarded by watch towers; and beyond the mountains was the desert of the Rub al Khali —the Empty Quarter. He knew it was hopeless, and so he stayed on board, and the next afternoon they sailed.

He was having his evening meal when he was told to report to the bridge. Captain Griffiths was there, seated on his wooden stool, staring out over the bows to the starlit sea ahead. The only other man on the bridge was the Arab helmsman, standing immobile, his eyes fixed on the lit compass card in its binnacle, only his hands moving as he made small adjustments of the wheel.

"Ah, there you are." Griffiths had turned his head. "When I went ashore at Muscat last night there was a slave from Saraifa waiting for me with a message from your father. You'll doubt-less be relieved to know that he's willing to take you off my hands." And as David mumbled his thanks, the lips smiled be-hind the beard. "I may say I'm just as relieved as you are." And he added brusquely: "There's an Arab *sambuq* waiting now off Ras al Khaima to pick you up. Tonight we shall pass through the Straits of Hormuz into the Persian Gulf. With luck we should sight the *sambuq* about an hour after dawn. Now, you speak Arabic, I'm told."

"A little," David admitted. "But it's not easy to make myself understood—it's the different dialects, I think."

"Well, do you think you can pass yourself off as an Arab?" And without waiting for a reply, Griffiths added: "It's the passengers, you see. They'll talk if they see a white member of my crew being put aboard a dhow." A few words of briefing and then the Captain's hand gripped his arm. "Good luck now, man. And a word of advice before you go—tread warily. It's no ordinary man you've got for a father, indeed it isn't. He's the devil of a temper when he's roused. So go easy and watch your step." And with that he dismissed him and turned again in his seat to stare through the glass at the lights of a ship coming up over the dark horizon.

David left the bridge, dazed and almost reluctant, for now the future was upon him—unknown, a little frightening. At dawn he would leave the ship and the companionship of the men he'd lived with for the past few weeks, and that last link with the home he'd known all his life would steam away, leaving him alone in a strange country, amongst strange people. It surprised him that he felt no excitement, no exhilaration—only loneliness and a sense of desolation. He didn't know it then, but it was in this moment that he said goodbye to his boyhood.

The Mate found him sitting on his bunk, staring vacantly into space. "Here you are, Whitaker." And he tossed a bundle of clothing down beside him. "Ali Mahommed sold them to me—*kaffyah, agal,* robe, sandals, the lot, even to an old brass *khanjar* knife. Three pounds ten, and I've deducted it from your pay." He placed some East African notes and some silver on top of the clothes. "The Old Man told you what to do, did he? Okay, so long as you greet the *naukhuda* with a *salaam alaikum* and a few more words of Arabic. And get along to the paint-shop and put some stain on your face and hands. Your face is about as pink as a white baby's bottom."

Dressing up as an Arab for the first time in his life helped to pass the time, but still the long hours of the night stretched ahead. He lay awake a long time thinking about what the morrow would bring and about the man he hadn't known was his father till that tragic day. And then suddenly it was light, and almost immediately, it seemed, one of the Arab crew came down to tell him the *sambuq* had been sighted. He listened then, waiting, tense and expectant. And then the pulse of the engines slowed and finally died away. This was it—the moment of irrevocable departure. His hand touched the brass hilt of the great curved, flat-bladed knife at his girdle. He checked the *kaffyah,* made certain that the black *agal* was in its place, circling his head. He went quickly up to the after well-deck and waited in the shelter of the main-deck ladder. The rope ladder was over the side opposite Number Three hatch, one of the crew waiting there to help him over. The faint chug of a diesel sounded in the still morning air, coming slowly nearer. He heard the bump of the dhow as it came alongside, the guttural cry of Arab voices, and then the man by the ladder was beckoning him.

He went out quickly with his head down, hidden by his *kaffyah.* A dark-skinned hand caught his arm, steadied him as he went over the bulwarks. Glancing quickly up, he caught a glimpse of the Captain leaning with his elbows on the rail of the bridge wing and below, on the boat deck, a short, tubby man in a pale dressing-gown standing watching. And after that he could see nothing but the ship's rusty side.

Hands reached up, caught him as he jumped to the worn wood deck of the dhow. He called out a greeting in Arabic as he had been told and at the same moment he heard the distant clang of the engine-room telegraph. The beat of the *Emerald Isle*'s engines increased and the hull plates began to slide past, a gap opening between himself and the ship. He turned away to hide his face and found himself on a long-prowed craft built of battered wood, worn smooth by the years and bleached almost white by the torrid heat of the Persian Gulf. A single patched sail curved above it like the dirty wing of a goose hanging dead in the airless morning. The sea around was still as a mirror and white like molten glass, and then the swirl of the ship's screws shattered it.

There were three men on the *sambuq* and only the *naukhuda,*

or captain, wore a turban as well as a loin-cloth. He was an old
man with a wisp of a grey moustache and a few grey hairs on
his chin, which he stroked constantly. The crew was composed
of a smooth-faced boy with a withered arm and a big, barrel-
chested man, black as a Negro, with a satin skin that rippled
with every movement. The *naukhuda* took David's hand in his
and held it for a long time, whilst the other two crowded close,
staring at his face, feeling his clothes—six brown eyes gazing at
him, full of curiosity. A flood of questions, the old man using
the deferential *sahib,* legacy of India. Whenever David said
anything, all three listened respectfully. But it was no good. He
couldn't seem to make himself understood.

At length he gave it up and, judging that it would be safe
now to turn his head to take a last look at the *Emerald Isle,*
he was appalled to find that she had vanished utterly, swallowed in the humid haze of the day's beginning. For a time he
could still hear the beat of her engines, but finally even that was
gone and he was alone with his three Arabs on a flat calm sea
that had an oily shimmer to its hard, unbroken surface.

He felt abandoned then, more alone than he'd ever been in
his life before. But it was a mood that didn't last, for in less
than an hour the haze thinned and away to port the vague outline of a mass of mountains emerged. A few minutes later and
the sky was clear, a blue bowl reflected in the sea, and the mountains stood out, magnificent, tumbling down from the sky in
sheer red cliffs to disappear in a mirage effect at the water's
edge. Ahead, a long dhow stood with limp sail suspended in
the air, and beyond it the world seemed to vanish—no mountains, nothing, only the endless sky. For the first time he understood why men talked of the desert as a sea.

Twice the *sambuq's* aged engine petered out. Each time it
was the boy who got it going. The *naukhuda* sat dreamily at
the helm, steering with the toes of his right foot curled round
the smooth wood of the rudder bar. A charcoal fire had been
burning on the low poop ever since David had come on board,
and the big cooking-pot above it eventually produced a mess of
rice and mutton, which they ate in their fingers. A small wind
stirred the surface of the sea, increased until it filled the sail,

and the engine was switched off. In the sudden quiet, the sound of the water sliding past the hull seemed almost loud. The mainsheet was eased out and the *sambuq* took wing. "Ras al Khaima." The *naukhuda* pointed across the port bow. At the very foot of the mountains and low on the horizon, David made out the dun-coloured shape of houses, the tufts of palms. And shortly after that the coast ahead showed up, low and flat, a shimmering line of dunes.

The sun was barely halfway up the sky when they closed that dune coast. A line of camels marched sedately along the sand of the foreshore, and close under the low cliffs a Land Rover stood parked, a lone figure in Arab clothes standing beside it. He thought then that this was his father and braced himself for that first meeting, wondering what he would be like. But when the *naukhuda* paddled him ashore in the *sambuq's* dugout, it was an Arab who waded into the shallow water to meet them.

Again the difficulty of trying to make himself understood. The Arab's name was Yousif and he spoke a little English. "Coll-onell Sahib not here. You come Saraifa now." The word Saraifa was shouted at him several times as though he were deaf.

"How far is Saraifa?"

The man stared at him as though he were mad. He was a very dirty-looking individual, his greasy turban trailing one end over his shoulders, a torn and very filthy European jacket worn over his Arab robes. His dark face was smudged with oil; this and the little black moustache below the curved nose gave him a sinister appearance.

David tried again: "Saraifa . . . ten miles, twenty?" He held up his fingers.

"Saraifa no far in machine of Coll-onell Sahib." The gap-toothed smile was clearly meant to placate. "Me driver to Coll-onell Sahib. Drive very quick." That seemed to exhaust his fund of English, for he turned to the *naukhuda* and launched into a guttural flood of conversation. At length the *naukhuda* stepped forward, kissed his hand, and touched it to his heart with a little bow. David gave him one of the notes the Mate had handed him and found his hand held in the other's horny palm whilst the old man made him a long farewell speech.

Then at last he was in the Land Rover and they were roaring
along the sand of the foreshore, the driver bent over the wheel
like a rider urging on his horse, with the stray end of his filthy
turban streaming out behind him. A mile or two further on they
left the sea's edge by a camel track that climbed the shallow
cliffs. Looking back, David got a last glimpse of the dhow that
had brought him to the Arabian shore, and then they were
bouncing past the Bedouin caravan he had seen moving along
the sands. The camels stared with supercilious gaze, padding
effortlessly through the sand under their mountainous loads.
The men, wild and bearded, raised their hands unsmilingly in
desert salutation. The silver mountings of their old-fashioned
guns winked in the hot sun, and David caught the wicked gleam
of *khanjar* knives and the brass of cartridge belts. He was seeing
for the first time the desert world that was to be his home.

II

Enquiries of an Executor

The account of his actual arrival in Arabia was contained in the letter he dispatched to me almost immediately after he had reached Saraifa. For that reason, I suppose, it told me little about the actual meeting between himself and his father. Scribbled in pencil on scraps of paper, it had been written mostly on board the *Emerald Isle*. Except for the final page, it had been completed at a waterhole somewhere in the desert where he and Yousif had spent the night. The final page was nothing more than a hastily written postscript: *Saraifa at last, but I arrived at a bad time—my father was with the Sheikh and an oil director and his pilot, and he leaves with them in the morning for Bahrain. He seemed angry at first, but it's all right now, I think. The Sheikh's son, Khalid, is to look after me whilst he is away, and I am to go on a hunting expedition with him to get to know desert ways. My father is a great man here, with a bodyguard and a mud fort or palace where I am writing now. He has only one eye and a black patch over the other, which makes him a bit terrifying at first, and everybody seems afraid of him. Men keep coming into this room for one reason and another, but really to stare at me. It is all very strange—but exciting. Thank you again. David.*

At the end of the year he sent me a Christmas card. It was a Gulfoman Oilfields Development Company card and was post-

marked Basra. He was at an oil school studying geology and
seemed happy. That was the last I heard of him until I received
the news, three years later, that he was missing in the Rub al
Khali desert, the Empty Quarter.

By then I was involved in his father's affairs. It was a strange
business and one that was causing me considerable concern—
though at the outset it had seemed straightforward enough. In
fact, I wasn't in the least surprised when he asked me to act
for him. A lawyer's business is a very personal one and tends to
grow through personal contact. *What my son has told me about
you, and the fact that your firm acted for me for many years in
the matter of the settlement to his mother, leads me to place
complete confidence in your discretion and in your ability to
use your own initiative when required.* He wanted to consoli-
date his financial affairs, he said, and he sent me power of at-
torney and gave me authority to collect all monies, meet any
accounts that became due, and generally manage his business
interests. There was nothing particularly unusual about this, except that I was on no account to attempt to communicate with
him in any way once the arrangement was working.

My correspondence with him lasted over several months. His
letters were all hand-written, and the only address he gave was
his bank in Bahrain. Shortly after it was all agreed, money began to flow in from all over the Middle East, from Arab merchants and bankers, from traders, from a firm of stockbrokers
in Cairo, and a large sum from the cashier of the London office
of the Gulfoman Oilfields Development Company. This went on
for about a year. Some of it was in kind—pearls from a dealer in
Bahrain, even a box full of Maria Theresa dollars and another
full of silver, presumably gifts from the local sheikhs.

Finally the flow had dried up, and, presuming that the operation was against his retirement, I invested the money for him,
mostly in local industry of which I had personal knowledge.
The market, of course, was a restricted one, but it never occurred to me that he would almost immediately want large sums
in cash. And then in May of the following year accounts began
to come through for settlement—for stores, equipment, vehicles;
the largest single item was almost £5,000 for a second-hand seis-

mological truck, complete with geophones and all the necessary equipment for a geophysical survey, and there had been a shipping agent's account for freighting it down from Basra to Muscat on the *Emerald Isle*.

It was clear that he was embarking on a program of oil exploration on his own, expecting it to be financed by the nominee account, and it worried me, for I'd no means of knowing where it was going to end. I ignored my instructions then and wrote him several times, care of his bank, but received no reply. And in the New Year I received another batch of accounts, this time for fuel and stores and drilling-pipe. I was by then thoroughly alarmed about the whole situation. He obviously didn't realize that there were restrictions on bank lending, and I was reluctant to sell securities on a weak market. I was able to meet the immediate accounts, but I had to know what his future plans were. On March 5 I received an account for the hire of a complete drilling-rig. I phoned an oil man I knew in Milford Haven, and he gave me figures for the probable cost of drilling, even with a hired rig, that staggered me. I wrote to Whitaker then, stating that unless he sent me a statement of his plans and the probable cost by return, I should have no alternative but to fly out at his expense to discuss the whole situation.

That was the position on the morning of March 24 when I came into the office and found an airmail letter with a Bahrain stamp amongst my post. I thought it was the reply I was expecting, but when I opened it I found it was from Susan Thomas. Apparently she was now working as a nurse at a hospital in Dubai. She enclosed a copy of a cable she had received from the offices of the Gulfoman Oilfields Development Company in Bahrain. I read it through twice before my mind was able to take in and accept what the words meant, so great was my sense of shock.

NURSE SUSAN THOMAS THE HOSPITAL DUBAI FROM GODCO— MARCH 18: REGRET INFORM YOU YOUR BROTHER DAVID WHITAKER MISSING DESERT RUB AL KHALI SINCE FEBRUARY TWENTY-EIGHT STOP TRUCK NOW DISCOVERED ABANDONED SOME FIFTY MILES WEST NORTHWEST OF SARAIFA OASIS STOP EXTENSIVE GROUND SEARCH WITH AIR CO-OPERATION RAF IN DIFFICULT

DUNE COUNTRY HAS REVEALED NO TRACE ALSO UNREPORTED
NOMAD TRIBESMEN STOP SEARCH NOW RELUCTANTLY CALLED
OFF MUST BE PRESUMED DEAD STOP COMPANY OFFERS DEEPEST
SYMPATHY YOU AND YOUR MOTHER—ERKHARD.

Presumed dead! It was hard to believe. Dealing as I had been
for the last two years with his father's affairs, I had often thought
about him, wondered how he was getting on, what he was doing. I had even thought of writing to him to ask him about his
father's plans. And now this. My own sense of disbelief was
echoed by Susan's letter—a purely intuitive reaction. *We were
twins, as you know, yet all this time, whilst they have been
searching, I knew nothing, felt nothing. If David is dead, then
surely I would have known.* And then, a little further on in the
letter: *Early last month he came to see me, very late at night.
He was in some sort of trouble. But what it was he wouldn't
say. He seemed withdrawn and he had a rather wild look. I felt
he was in danger, but I still cannot believe he is dead.* And then
the words: *He told me then that if anything were to happen to
him I was to write to you at once.* In the final paragraph she
apologized for being a nuisance and added: *But please, please
contact the London Office of the Company and try to persuade
them to have the search resumed.* The letter was signed simply
Susan, as though I were an old friend.

I was due in Court at ten o'clock and still had the rest of my
post to go through; I put the letter aside and didn't get back
to it until late that afternoon, when I rang the London office of
the Gulfoman Oilfields Development Company. But of course
they knew nothing. A thin, cultured voice informed me that all
local administration was dealt with by the Bahrain office. "The
cable is signed Erkhard, you say? Then I think you may take it
that everything possible has already been done and the facts are
as stated. Mr. Erkhard is our General Manager out there and
in charge of all developments." However, he took my name and
address and promised to pass on my observations to Bahrain.

I cleared my desk and then got my car and drove down to
Grangetown to break the news to Mrs. Thomas; not a very pleasant task, but one that I couldn't very well avoid, since Susan
had written: *This is something I cannot bring myself to do in*

a letter. It would be so much kinder if you would do it—more personal, and you can explain the circumstances better. Tell her I will write later.

Mrs. Thomas had aged, of course, but more so than I would have expected. Her hair was completely grey now, no longer drawn back tightly from her forehead, but hanging untidily in wisps. The dress she wore was none too clean, and the eyes looked almost furtive as they flickered from one thing to another, never at rest and never looking directly at me. At the same time, the lines of strain had gone; her face seemed to have filled out, become smoother.

She invited me into the parlour, where the couch was still in the same place, the roll-top desk still littered with books on racing form. She was nervous, and she was talking all the time as we stood there, almost in the same positions, like actors cued to their places, talking about David, about Sue, about her life and how lonely it was now. "But Dafydd is a great comfort to me. He was never much of a letter writer, but since he went to Arabia . . ." Her eyes flicked to my face. "Is it about Dafydd you've come, Mr. Grant?" But then they had fled to another part of the room and she was saying: "I'm expecting a letter from him soon. He doesn't write regularly, of course. He's in such strange places. But such a picture he gives me, I can almost see it, you know . . . the Bedouin men and the camels and the heat; like a dream it is and me twenty again and waiting for letters." She gave a little hurried laugh, almost a titter. "I get confused sometimes. Over two years it is now since Sue went out there. I've been alone ever since, you see, and the mind plays tricks. . . ."

"When did you last hear from David?" I asked her.

"Oh, recently. Quite recently. And I'll have another letter from him soon. Any day now, I expect . . ." And then, sheering away from the subject, she said: "You've never seen his room, have you? All his books. I'd like you to see his room." And without waiting for a reply, she bustled out of the room as though anxious to escape from me. "I've kept it just as it was, you know."

She led me up the ill-lit stairs to a little room at the end of a short landing. The place smelt musty and had the chill of long abandonment. A flick-knife lay on the painted top of a

chest of drawers like a warrior's trophy from some forgotten war,
and above the bed was a shelf full of books. "He was a great one
for reading," she said. "Anything about Arabia. I did my best
to get him interested in other things, but there . . . I knew he'd
go there sooner or later. It was in the blood, as you might say."

There were about fifty books there, most of them books on
Arabia, including expensive volumes like Doughty's *Arabia
Deserta*—all damaged, but stuck together with loving care. It
was a strange glimpse of a young man's yearning. "I believe
Colonel Whitaker once wrote a book about Arabia," I said. "I
tried to get a copy, but it was out of print."

She nodded. "It's a long time since anybody could get a copy.
It wasn't very successful, you see. But there is one here somewhere." She leaned her weight against the bed and ran a work-
coarsened finger along the bookshelf. And then she took down a
book and handed it to me. The title was *Wanderings by Camel
through the Empty Quarter*. "Signed it is, you see," she said
proudly. "He gave it to me before he left." And she added wist-
fully: "It was the only present he ever gave me."

The book, of course, brought back memories to her. She
smiled at me shyly—almost coyly. "You know it was whilst he
was home writing that and getting it published that I came to
know him. I was in service then at Llanfihangel Hall. That was
his family's place." She hesitated. "I suppose he was bored,
really." The coy little smile had spread to her eyes, so that her
whole face was strangely transfigured. "But we enjoyed ourselves." She said it with a happy little sigh, and then she added:
"Ah, well, you only live once, Mr. Grant. That's what I tell myself whenever I'm feeling lonely. You've had your fun, Sarah,
I say. You've had your fun and you've paid the price. Are you
married, Mr. Grant?"

"No."

"And no illegitimate children?" She gave a queer laugh as I
shook my head. "Well, there you are. People like you miss a
great deal in life." And she added with surprising perception:
"You shouldn't always live at second hand, you know. Rummag-
ing about in other people's lives . . ."

"We do our best to help," I murmured uncomfortably. And

then I asked her if I could borrow Whitaker's book for a few days. I thought it might help me to understand the sort of man he was. She looked at me in surprise. "No," she said quickly, her eyes darting to the book. "No, I don't think I'd like any one to borrow that." And she took it from me and put it quickly back in its place. "I'll make you some tea if you like," she said as she took me back down the stairs.

At the bottom, under the light, there was a faded photograph of a pretty girl in a high-necked frock. "That was taken just about the time I met the Major," she said as she saw me looking at it. "He was a major then, you see—from the Kaiser's War. You didn't recognize it as me, I suppose?" She smiled. "I was considered very pretty then, you know—though I didn't look so pretty when he'd finished with me and I was bearing twins; more like a balloon, you know. Now, won't you stay and have a cup of tea, Mr. Grant, and you can tell me how you managed to get Dafydd out to his father. I should have thanked you for doing that, shouldn't I, but at the time I thought it might . . ." She hesitated. "You see, I've always been afraid of what would happen when they met. And then Dafydd started to go wrong —all those Arab friends of his. . . ." We had reached the parlour again, and she said: "I shall never forget that afternoon. Mr. Thomas lying there on the couch, and Dafydd—" She pointed towards the spot where he had stood. "And Dafydd standing there and swearing he'd kill his own Da. But there . . ." She gave me a weak, uneasy smile. "They're together now. And nothing has happened, has it? It was silly of me to take a young boy so seriously." And she added almost violently: "But it scared me at the time. It scared me silly."

"You say they're together *now?*"

"Oh, yes—in a place called Saraifa. That's an oasis—"

"What was the date of that last letter you had?"

"I—I don't remember." Her mouth was suddenly trembling. "It was quite recent, Mr. Grant."

"Could I see it, please?"

She hesitated, her eyes wandering round the room. And then finally she went to the roll-top desk and took a single sheet of paper from the top of a neat little pile of similar sheets. "August it was," she said almost in a whisper. "August the twenty-third."

Seven months ago. "And you haven't heard from him since?"

She shook her head, her hand trembling as she stared down at the letter.

"And he was at Saraifa; does he say what he was doing there?"

"He'd been on a gazelle hunt with Sheikh Makhmud and his son. . . ."

"What sort of work, I mean?"

"No, he doesn't mention work. But it would be something to do with oil. He's a geologist, you see, and works for one of the oil companies." She was reading the letter to herself again, her lips forming the words which I was certain she knew by heart. "He writes beautiful letters, you know—all about the country and the people he meets. He writes so I can almost imagine I'm out there with him." She put the letter back on the pile. "That was my dream once, that I'd go out there to live." She stood there smiling to herself and staring out at the dingy street. "Just a dream," she repeated. "But with the books and the maps I can see it all from his letters. I'm a Welsh woman, you see. I have the gift of imagination." And then with a sudden edge of bitterness to her voice: "You need imagination sometimes in a hole like this."

How could I tell her the boy was dead? "Have you heard from his father at all?"

She shook her head. "No, I've never heard from the Major—not once in all these years." There was a catch in her voice, and she moved quickly away towards the door. "I'll make you some tea."

"Please don't bother," I said. "I have to go now."

But she was between me and the door, her hands fumbling at her dress, her eyes searching my face. She had finally screwed herself up to the pitch of facing the implication of my visit. "What's happened, Mr. Grant?" she asked. "What's happened between them? As soon as I saw you standing there on the door-step . . ."

"Nothing has happened between them. According to my in-formation—"

But she didn't let me finish, wasn't even listening. "I knew they should never have met," she cried. "They're alike, you see. They've the same nature—obstinate, very obstinate." She was almost sobbing for breath. "I knew what it would mean. It's in their stars. They're both Sagittarius, you see. And he was such a fine man when I knew him. Such a fine man—and lusty, so full of fire and vitality." She was wringing her hands, and a sound came from her lips like the sound of keening. "Known it I have, always. Oh, God!" she whispered. And then, staring straight at me: "How did it happen? Do you know how it happened?"

There was nothing for it then but to let her know the facts, such as they were. And because it was easier I handed her the copy of the cable her daughter had sent me. She read it through slowly, her eyes widening as the shock of it went home until they became fixed, almost vacant. "Dafydd!" She murmured his name.

"He's reported missing, that's all," I said, trying to comfort her, to offer her some hope.

But she didn't seem to take that in. "Dead," she whispered. And then she repeated his name. "Dafydd?" And her tone was one of shocked surprise. "I never thought it would be Dafydd. That's not right at all." The fixed stare was almost trance-like. "It was never Dafydd that was going to die." And a shiver ran through her.

"I'll write to your daughter. No doubt she'll let you have any further information direct." She didn't say anything, and her eyes still had that fixed, trance-like look as I took the copy of the cable from her nerveless hand. Her behaviour was so odd I didn't like to leave it with her. "Don't worry too much. There's still a chance. . . ."

"No." The word seemed to explode out of her mouth. "No, better it is like this, God rest his poor soul."

Appalled, I hurried past her, out into the fresh evening air. The stars—what a thing to be believing in at a time like this. Poor woman!

But as I drove away, it was the father I was thinking about, a sense of uneasiness growing in my mind, fostered by the violence of her strange reaction. Going back to that house, to that poor woman driven half out of her senses by an old love she

couldn't discard; it was all suddenly fresh in my memory—her
fears and the way he'd sworn to kill his father. What had happened between those two in the intervening years? Or was this
just an accident—one of those things that can happen to any
young man prospecting out there in the remote deserts of
Arabia?

Back at the office I got out the Whitaker file and read that
postscript to David's letter again. But there was nothing in it
to give me a clue as to how his father had reacted. The words
might have been written by any youngster plunged into new
and strange surroundings, except that he had described his father as though he were looking at him with the eyes of a complete stranger. But then that was what he was. Right at the
bottom of the file was the dossier Andrews had produced from
press-cuttings in the library of the Welsh edition of a popular
daily, and I read it through again:

> Charles Stanley Whitaker, born Llanfihangel Hall near Usk,
> 1899. Joined the Cavalry as a trooper in 1915, served with
> Allenby in the offensive against the Turks, and rose to the
> rank of major. After the war, he stayed on in the Middle
> East. Policeman, trader, dhow-owner; he adopted the Mos-
> lem religion, made the pilgrimage to Mecca, has lived with
> the Bedouin. His book on his crossing of the Rub al Khali
> desert was published in 1936. By then he had already be-
> come something of a legend. Following publication of his
> book, he went back to the Middle East, and after three
> years with Gulfoman Oilfields Development, he joined
> Wavell's staff on the outbreak of war with the rank of colo-
> nel. Awarded the V.C. for gallantry, wounded twice, served
> with Wingate and later with Wilson. Was still a colonel at
> the end of the war. He then rejoined Gulfoman Oilfields
> Development as political representative.

There was a picture pinned to the dossier which showed him
in Arab dress standing beside a Land Rover on a desert airstrip.
The black patch over the right eye was plainly visible; so, too,
was the prominent, beak-like nose. He was slightly stooped, as
though conscious of his height; he was a head taller than the
other two men in the picture. This and the beard and the black

patch over the eye gave him a very formidable appearance, and, though the picture wasn't a very clear one, looking at it again, I couldn't help feeling that he was a man capable of anything, and I could appreciate the impression he had made on a Welsh servant girl all those years ago. He would have been thirty-six then, a good deal younger, and I suppose he had taken her the way he would have taken a slave girl in a Bedouin encampment; but for her it had been something different, an experience so out of the ordinary that she had thought of nothing else for the last twenty-five years.

I wondered whether she still possessed that album full of press-cuttings. I would have liked to look through it and also through the letters from her son, but I couldn't face the thought of going back to the house. I returned the file to its place and wrote to Susan advising her to make the journey to Bahrain and see Erkhard. *Nothing can be done, it appears, at this end,* I told her. *Erkhard seems to be the only man who has the authority to order the search to be resumed.*

Two days later the news of David's death was in *The Times*— a rather guarded account, it seemed to me. It was clearly based on a Company handout, but it did include a brief description by one of the RAF pilots who had flown the search.

> Flight-Lieutenant Hill described the truck as similar to those used by oil companies for seismological work, though no company markings showed on either bonnet or sides. It was halfway up the side of a big sand dune, as though it had stalled or bogged down in an effort to surmount this obstacle. It was hardly surprising, he said, that he had flown several times over the area without seeing it; high winds— the local *shamal*—had piled the sand up on one side of it. He had only sighted the truck because the sun was low and it was casting a shadow.

It was less a news story than a short article, and most of it was about Colonel Whitaker—*that strange, half-Arab figure, so prominent in the search for Gulf oil during the past twenty years.* It was "From Our Own Correspondent," and I had a vague sense as I read it that there was something behind the piece, something that he was not in a position to reveal but that was nevertheless there for those who could read between the lines. Such phrases as: *The fascination of this man who has maintained his theory about oil in the face of persistent failure;* and *Whether he is another Holmes or not, whether the oil company he served for so long will live to regret his departure, only time will tell.* Finally there was this: *It appears there is some foundation for the rumour that his son, though employed by GODCO, was on loan to him for some private purpose, presumably connected with prospecting for oil.*

The suggestion that David had been on loan to his father at the time of his disappearance did nothing to allay the uneasiness that had resulted from my visit to Mrs. Thomas. And then the following morning Captain Griffiths walked into my office and I knew for certain that there was something more to the boy's death than the Company had so far revealed.

Griffiths had docked at first light and was still in uniform, having come straight from his ship. "I promised to deliver this personally into your hands." He put a fat envelope down on the desk in front of me. "Personally, you understand. He wouldn't risk it through the post."

"Who's it from?" I asked. But the address was handwritten, the writing familiar. I knew it was from David before he answered my question. "Young Whitaker," he said and sat himself down in the chair opposite my desk.

I was too startled to say anything for a moment, for the boy had been alive when he'd handed this to Griffiths. I picked it up, staring at the address as though that would give me some clue as to what was inside. "When did he give you this?"

"Well, now . . ." He frowned. "It was Sharjah, and we were anchored about a mile off—"

"Yes, but what was the date?"

"It's the date I'm trying to remember, man." His little beard bristled. "Without my log I can't be sure. But we left Basra on January twenty-third and we called at Kuwait, Bahrain, Doha, Abu Dhabi, and Dubai before we anchored off Sharjah; it would be about the middle of the first week in February."

And David had been reported missing on February 28. Griffiths must have been one of the last people he saw before he went out into the desert—perhaps one of the last of his own race to see him alive.

"Still the same offices, I see." Griffiths had pulled his pipe out and was busy filling it. He didn't know the boy was dead.

"The trouble is the clients don't pay their bills," I said and slit the packet open. The old rogue had never settled my account, though he'd admitted that Whitaker had made him a present of fifty quid for getting the boy out to Arabia. Inside was a hand-written letter folded around another envelope that had GODCO, BAHRAIN, printed on the flap. Across the front of it he had typed: DAVID WHITAKER—TO BE OPENED ONLY IN THE EVENT OF MY DEATH.

Those words—they came as a shock. I stared at them, wondering how he could possibly have known he was going to die. Or was it just a coincidence?

"What's the matter?" Griffiths asked. "What's he been up to?"

I suppose he thought he was in some sort of legal trouble. "You haven't seen *The Times* then?"

"Of course not. I only got in this morning. Why?"

"David Whitaker is dead," I said. And I told him about the truck they'd found abandoned and the description of it given in *The Times*. "You must have been one of the last people to see him alive."

"I see."

His acceptance of it might have surprised me, except that my mind was still on that envelope. "It's almost uncanny," I murmured.

"What is?"

"Your coming here, with this." I turned the envelope round so that he could see what was typed across it. "He must have had some sort of premonition. . . ."

Griffiths nodded his head slowly. "That explains it." And he added: "May his soul rest in peace, the poor devil." He said it quietly, with reverence, as though he were on the deck of his ship and consigning the boy's body to the deep.

"Explains what?" I asked him.

"The circumstances . . ." He hesitated. "Very strange they were." And then he looked at me, his gaze very direct. "I don't think you quite understand, Mr. Grant. That boy risked his life on a filthy night with a *shamal* blowing to get that packet to me without any one knowing."

"Risked his life?" I was reading through the covering letter, only half listening to him.

"Yes, indeed, for he came off in one of those fisherman's dug-outs and just an Arab boy with him. It was a damned foolhardy thing to do. There was a wicked sea running. He needed a lawyer, he said, somebody he could trust."

"Why? Did he say why he needed a lawyer?"

"No." Griffiths shook his head. "No, he didn't say why, and it's something I've been asking myself ever since I put that envelope away in the ship's safe. What would a young geophysicist want with a lawyer out there in the middle of Arabia?"

I finished reading the letter and then I put it down on the desk. Griffiths was lighting his pipe, his head cocked on one side. "Well, he's dead now, you say." He was eying the unopened envelope the way a thrush eyes a worm.

"Perhaps you'd tell me just what happened?" I suggested.

"Well . . ." He hesitated, his eyes still on the envelope. "It was night, you see. We had finished unloading and the deck lights had been switched off about an hour when one of my Arab crew reports a dugout alongside and a white man in it called Thomas asking for me. Well, I couldn't recall his name—how should I? I have so many passengers; they come and go along the coast—oil men, Locust Control, Levy officers, Air Force personnel, Government officials. How should I remember his name, even if he was another Welshman? It was four years since he'd used it anyway. And then he came stumbling into my cabin and I recognized him at once, of course."

I thought he was going to stop there, but after a moment's silence he went on: "Only the previous voyage I'd had him on board as a passenger, from Bahrain down to Dubai. He'd changed a great deal in those six months; all the vitality of youth seemed to have been whipped out of him, his skin burned almost black by the sun and the hard, angular bones of the face showing through. But it was the eyes, man. They weren't the eyes of a youngster any more; they were the eyes of a man who'd looked the world in the face and been badly frightened by it."

"Who was he afraid of?" I was thinking of the father then.

"I didn't say he was afraid of anybody."

"Did he talk to you at all—about himself?"

"Oh, yes, indeed. He was talking all the time. To be honest, Mr. Grant, I thought he might be going round the bend. Some of them do that, you know . . . the heat and the sand, and if it's lonely work—"

"Yes, but what did he say?"

"Nothing very much. Nothing that I can remember, that is. He was talking very fast, you see, the words tumbling over themselves—about his job and where he'd been."

"And where had he been? Had he been to Saraifa?"

But Griffiths shook his head. "I can't remember," he said. "I don't think he mentioned Saraifa. It was talk for the sake of talking, you know—for the sake of hearing the sound of his own voice and having somebody listen to it. He'd been in some wild places, I think, and mostly on his own, nobody with him but Arabs."

I asked about the packet then. "Did he talk about that at all?"

"No. He sat at my desk and wrote that covering letter. And when he'd finished it, he borrowed an envelope from me, sealed the whole thing up, and asked me to put it in my safe and deliver it to you personally the moment I docked."

"Didn't you ask him why it was so urgent?"

"Of course I did. I was damned curious about the whole thing. But his manner was so odd—"

"He didn't say anything about it being political dynamite, then?"

"Political dynamite?" Griffiths's bushy eyebrows lifted. "No, he didn't say anything like that." A wary look had come into his eyes. "Is that what he says in that letter?"

I nodded. "Where's Colonel Whitaker now? Can you tell me that?"

But he didn't know for certain. "Probably in Saraifa," he said. "Why?" His tone was suddenly cautious, as though he were a witness under cross-examination, and since I had no intention of telling him the reason for my interest in Whitaker, I asked him about the previous voyage when he'd had David on board as a passenger. "Was he going to join his father, do you know?"

But he couldn't even tell me that. "All he said was that he was going down into the Rub al Khali." He took out his watch and glanced at it. "It was a hell of a time to be going down into the Empty Quarter," he added as though glad to escape into generalities. "That time of the year the sand is hot enough to burn the tires off a truck and the soles off your boots."

"It was summer?"

He nodded. "Early July it would have been."

And that was the month I'd received the shipping agent's account. "Did you have a seismological truck on board?"

"Yes." He stared at me curiously, surprised that I should know about it. "It was deck cargo, and we shipped it down to Muscat. I remember that because we had a devil of a job getting it ashore; had to lash four of the local boats together and bridge them with planks."

"You don't think it could be the same truck—the one that was found abandoned?"

But of course he couldn't tell me that.

"Did you know he was on loan to his father? Did he say anything about that?"

He shook his head and got to his feet.

"Did he talk about his father at all?"

"No, he didn't mention him." He said it flatly, as though to discourage any further questions. "I must be going now, Mr. Grant. Just docked—a lot of things to see to, you know."

I was reluctant to let him go. "One more question, Captain Griffiths." I was standing facing him then. "You said once that you heard all the gossip out there. Have you heard any rumours about Saraifa?"

"Rumours?"

"That Colonel Whitaker is prospecting for oil there."

He started to say something, but then he seemed to think better of it and shook his head. "A man like that, you never know what's true and what isn't. And Saraifa is a long way from the coast. A trouble spot, too." He glanced uneasily at his watch again.

I read him the *Times* correspondent's report, the paragraph about David being on loan to his father. But all he said was: "The Whitaker Theory. It crops up whenever anybody writes about that man." And then he was moving towards the door. "Well, I've done what I promised, and that's that." He held out his hand. "Sad about David Whitaker, very sad. Good boy—lots of character." He shook my hand briefly, cast a quick glance at the envelope still lying unopened on my desk, and then went to the door. His last words to me as I saw him out were: "It's a tricky business, oil. Lot of money involved; politics, too. And if he was operating anywhere near the Hadd-Saraifa border . . . Well, you'd understand if you'd ever been out there." He said it in a fatherly way, as though he were giving me some sound advice.

I was reluctant to let him go. That little Welsh sea captain was stuffed full of all the gossip of the Gulf if I could only have wrung it out of him. But I don't think he wanted to talk, and anyway I was anxious to find out what that envelope contained. The covering letter had given me no real indication.

You helped me once long ago. Now I'm asking you to help me again. He mentioned the envelope then and asked me to put it in a safe place and only open it in the event of his death. *You're the only man I feel I can trust with a thing like this.* And he added: *I should warn you that it's political dynamite, and if anybody knew it was in your possession it might lead to trouble.* He concluded with apologies for bothering me with his affairs, and then these words: *Thank you again for helping me to a life that has suited me and that I have enjoyed.* It was signed: *Yours gratefully—David.*

I read it through again, standing at my desk, and there was no escaping the significance of those final words. For some reason he had believed he was going to die. Had he been ill, suffering from some terrible disease? But that didn't fit Griffiths's description of him. Nervous, wrought up, even frightened—yes; but not ill. And why the secrecy anyway?

I picked up the envelope and slit it open. Inside were a type-

written letter, his will, and two envelopes—one addressed to Sir
Philip Gorde at the London office of GODCO, the other marked:
Location and Sketch Map. Location of what? But it wasn't difficult to guess, for what else but the discovery of oil could be
described as political dynamite in the deserts of Arabia?

The letter didn't say so in so many words, but it made it pretty
clear. And because it gives some indication of his frame of mind
—and also because it formed the basis of my subsequent actions
—I give it here in full. It was dated December 29 of the previous
year, and above the date he had typed: *Somewhere in the
Sheikhdom of Saraifa.*

Dear Mr. Grant,

The time has come to put my affairs into the hands of
somebody I know and can trust. I am working here on an
old survey. It was carried out a long time ago and the man
who did it is dead now. If my own results confirm his report
—and I shall know very shortly—I shall try and catch Captain Griffiths at Sharjah when the *Emerald Isle* stops there
about the end of next month. I cannot explain to you why it
is necessary. All I can say is that this is a forbidden zone
and that I am working against time and without authority.
Everything is against me—almost like it was when I came
to you last. I've always been a bit of a rebel at heart. But
outside of the pack, you're on your own. And whatever happens to me, I'm determined that Saraifa shall have the
benefit of my efforts. The oasis fights a losing battle with
the desert. Without money it is doomed. And I spent six of
the happiest months of my life there.

When you read this I shall be dead. Please then take the
following action: Contact Sir Philip Gorde, who is on the
board of directors of GODCO, and give him the envelope
I have addressed to him. It contains a document which is
correctly phrased and is a copy of other concession agreements. It will also contain my survey report, but without
the locations. The locations will be contained in a separate
envelope, together with additional copies of my survey report. This envelope is only to be handed over after Sir
Philip Gorde has signed the concession agreement and le-
gally bound the Company, to your satisfaction, to drill *four*

test wells at the locations indicated. [The *four* had been written in in ink, presumably later.]

In the event that Sir Philip Gorde refuses to sign, then you will please take whatever action you think best in the interests of Saraifa. Khalid, the Sheikh's son, knows what I am doing and you will find he fully understands what is at stake so far as the oasis is concerned. It is essential that somehow you get the concession taken up. Saraifa needs oil desperately and if you succeed you will not find Khalid lacking in appreciation, or Sheikh Makhmud for that matter. You may, of course, make what use you can of the circumstances of my death, my parentage, and my past to achieve publicity and so attract the interest of other oil companies.

Enclosed also is my Will. I have appointed you my Executor and after making the necessary arrangements with my bank in Bahrain, you will please draw on the account for fees and expenses. Please understand that I would not again involve you in my affairs if I were not desperate. In the event of my death I have instructed my sister to contact you immediately.

David Whitaker

It was an unusual communication for a solicitor to receive, most unusual; and, reading it through again, I was struck by the fact that he made no mention of his father. In the whole of that document there wasn't one reference to Colonel Whitaker. *Everything is against me.* There were other phrases, too. I was greatly disturbed about the whole thing, particularly as I knew that Whitaker was engaged in an operation that must run counter to the interests of the company he had served and which David was serving at the time of his death.

However, there was no point in speculating. His instructions were clear, and I picked up the phone and rang the London office of GODCO. And whilst I was waiting for the call to come through I had a look at the will. He had typed it himself, but it was a perfectly legal document even though the witnesses to his signature were two Arabs. It appointed me executor and his sister, Susan, sole legatee with instructions to take care of their mother. Again no reference to his father.

This and the letter and the fact that he had made such careful provision against the possibility of death gave a strange quality of isolation to his activities, as though he were operating alone in a hostile world. I think it was then that I seriously considered the possibility that his disappearance was no accident.

My call to GODCO came through and I was put on to the same thin, cultured voice. No, Sir Philip was not available, would not be for some time. He was on a tour of the Company's Middle East properties and not expected back for at least a month. I could contact him through the Bahrain office if the matter were important.

I put the phone down and sat there for a long time, considering. But I don't think there was ever any real doubt in my mind. I hadn't heard from Whitaker, and, quite apart from his son's death, the necessity for a meeting with him was urgent. It was just that the Persian Gulf was a long way away and I had got out of the habit of travelling. Fortunately, I now had an arrangement with another firm of solicitors which enabled me to get away when necessary, and in the end I put a call through to a local travel agency. BOAC flights direct to Bahrain were weekly, leaving on Thursdays at 1000 hours and arriving 0305 hours Friday. That just gave me time to make all my arrangements, get visas, and clear my desk of the more urgent matters. I told them to book me out on the next flight, locked the contents of the envelope in the safe, and went out for a drink. I needed to think, for I was beginning to realize what it was he'd landed on my desk. *Political dynamite!* If he was a good geophysicist, then what I'd locked away in my safe might well be the location of a new oilfield.

Three days later I flew out of London Airport in a storm of rain and wind. March going out like a lion; but at Rome it was hot, and all down the Mediterranean we had bright sunshine. And I sat in my seat with an empty feeling inside me, for the day before I'd left Cardiff a man had come to see me, a tired-looking, hard-faced man with a skin like leather who'd refused to give Andrews his name or state his business.

Even when he was alone with me in my office he went about it in such a tortuous way that it only gradually dawned on me what he was after. It was cleverly done—a hint here, a hint there, and the abyss gradually opening up at my feet. He knew David had boarded the *Emerald Isle* off Sharjah, knew, too, that Griffiths had delivered that packet to me. He'd been down to see him at his cottage in the Gower. He'd been to the police, too; had talked with Sergeant Mathieson and had checked the files. He knew the boy's real name, his whole background, everything, and what he wanted from me was that packet.

He smiled when I told him I couldn't discuss my client's affairs. "Professional etiquette? Your professional etiquette, Mr. Grant, is somewhat elastic, if you follow me." It was a cat-and-mouse game, for he knew I'd helped the boy to get out of the country. "There are several charges outstanding and a warrant."

"The boy is dead," I reminded him.

But it made no difference. He had his instructions, he said. These were to take possession of the packet. "You can hand it to me or forward it to the Company—one or the other." I asked him what authority he had for making such an outrageous proposal, but all he'd say was that it was in the country's interests. One knows, of course, that there are men like that employed by Government and by large companies, but one doesn't expect to come across them. They belong to a half-world that lies outside the experience of ordinary citizens.

"In your own interests, I suggest you hand it to me. Nobody need know anything then."

It was blackmail, and by then I was sweating, for I was beginning to realize what I was up against. Politics and oil—the Middle East; the scope of a provincial lawyer doesn't cover that sort of world. . . . I just hadn't the right sort of pull, the contacts, the friends in high places.

"You can go to the devil," I told him.

He got to his feet then. "I had hoped for your co-operation." And he added: "Think it over, Mr. Grant. The police have an interest in this, and if they began an investigation . . . It could be very unpleasant for you. A man in your position, a lawyer . . ." He left it at that and picked up his hat.

I wondered then whether he knew I was leaving for Bahrain in two days' time. The Foreign Office had my passport. They could still refuse to grant me the necessary visas. "All right," I said. "I'll think it over."

And the next day, in London, I found I had been granted a visa for Bahrain, but not for either Dubai or Saraifa. A note pinned to my passport stated that for *any further visas you should apply to the office of the Political Resident Persian Gulf in Bahrain.*

Darkness fell, the port light showing red. I woke to the touch of the air hostess's hand on my shoulder and the sighing sound of the flaps going down. The sliver of a new moon had risen, reflected with the stars in the still surface of the sea coming up to meet us, a steel mirror suddenly patterned with the arrowheads of fish traps as we skimmed the shallows. A moment later we touched down in Bahrain. And at three thirty in the morning the air was still heavy with the day's heat. It came at us as soon as the door was opened, suffocating in its humidity.

The squat, white-fronted coral houses of Muharraq were without life as the airport bus drove us across the long causeway to the main island and the town of Manama. A solitary dhow was putting to sea, the curve of its sail a thing of ghostly beauty against the blackness of the water; all the others lay dormant in the mud or bare-poled against the coral hards with sails furled.

Only the BOAC Hotel showed any sign of life at that hour. It was down an empty side-street, the airline's bluebird insignia standing out against the drab of concrete; lights were burning against our coming. I was given a room with a balcony that was full of the sounds of a late-night party, laughter and the clink of glasses. There was a lot of coming and going in the passage outside, and I went to sleep to the sound of a girl's voice harsh and loud and slightly drunk.

Sunlight woke me four hours later, the hard sunlight of a hot country. An Arab boy brought me tea, and I drank it, lying naked on the bed, a stale feeling at the back of the eyeballs and my body hot and without energy. Getting up, shaving, having breakfast—it was all an effort. And this was only April. I wondered what it must be like in midsummer.

When I enquired at the desk for the offices of the Gulfoman

Oilfields Development Company, I was told that they were several miles out of town on the Awali road. A fat man in a tropical suit of powder blue was asking about a taxi he'd booked for Awali. He was an Italian who had joined the flight at Rome, and I asked him whether he would give me a lift. "*Sì, sì, signore.* Of course."

His name was Ruffini and he was a journalist. "You are in oil?" he asked as we drove past the Customs Quay crowded with dhows. And when I said no, he looked surprised. "But you 'ave an appointment at GODCO, no?"

"A matter of an estate," I told him. "A client of mine has died."

"So!" He sighed. "A lawyer's business—always to concern itself with death. Is depressing for you, no?" He offered me an American cigarette. "Who do you see at this Company? Is none of my business," he added quickly, seeing my hesitation. "But though I am never in Bahrain before, I 'ave contacts—introductions, you say. If I can 'elp you . . ." He left it at that, reaching into his breast pocket for a pair of dark glasses. And because he was being helpful I told him who it was I'd come to see.

"You know anything about this Sir Philip Gorde?" he asked.

"He's a director of the Company in London."

"But not the most important man out here, I think." And he leaned forward and asked the driver, a pock-marked Bahraini with a lot of gold teeth. "Who is the big man at GODCO?"

"Is Meester Erkhard."

Ruffini nodded. "Alexander Erkhard. *Bene.* That is also my information."

"Many years," the driver added, turning to face us. "Many years it is Sir Gorde. Not now." The car touched the road verge, sending up a cloud of dust. "Ten years now I have taxi and am driving down the Awali road, sir, with men from BAPCO, GODCO, ARAMCO. I speak not well Eenglish, but understand plenty, get me? I look after the boys good, very bloody good. They all friends of Mahommed Ali. That my name, sir." He was looking over his shoulder again. "You want something, you find my car outside BOAC Hotel."

"When did Mr. Erkhard come out to Bahrain?" I asked.

"Five, six years ago, sir. Before I get this Buick."

"And Sir Philip Gorde was the big man then?"

"That's right, sir. He is here before Awali, before I am born—a friend of the Ruler, of all Arabs. Very great man, Sir Gorde. But then he is sick and this Mr. Erkhard, he come to Bahrain. Everything different then. Not friend of Ruler, not friend to Arabs." And he spat out of the open window. "Here is GODCO office now."

We turned left with a screech of tires. The dusty date gardens were left behind and a white building stood at the end of a tree-lined road. Beyond it lay the sea, a blue line shimmering on the horizon. "*Ecco!*" Ruffini gripped my arm, pointing away to the right, to a litter of small mounds. "Tumuli. *È molto interessante.* There is a Danish man who dig in those tumuli. The oldest burial ground in Arabia per'aps."

The brakes slammed on and the car stopped with a jerk. I got out. "I will see you at the 'otel. Per'aps we 'ave a drink together, eh?" I thanked him for the lift and he waved a pudgy hand. "*Ciao!*" The taxi swung away and I went in through the double glass doors. It was like walking into a refrigerator, for the place was air-conditioned to the temperature of a London office. Glass and tiled walls, steel furniture, and the girl at the reception desk cool and immaculate. But when I asked for Sir Philip Gorde she frowned. "I don't think Sir Philip is back yet. Have you an appointment?"

"No," I said. "But I've flown out from England specially to see him."

She asked me my name and then got on the phone. A white-faced electric clock ticked the seconds away on the wall above her head. Finally she shook her head. "I'm sorry. It's as I thought. Sir Philip is still in Abu Dhabi."

"When will he be back?" I asked. Abu Dhabi was the first of the Trucial sheikhdoms and at least a hundred and fifty miles from Bahrain.

She started talking on the phone again and I lit a cigarette and waited. At length she said: "Could you tell me the nature of your business with Sir Philip, please?"

"If he's in Abu Dhabi," I said, "there's not much point, is there?"

She cupped her hand over the mouthpiece. "If it's urgent, then I think they'd contact him for you. I told them you'd come out from England specially."

I hesitated. But there was no point in concealing what I'd come about. "It concerns David Whitaker," I said. "I'm a lawyer."

"David Whitaker." She repeated it automatically, and then the name suddenly registered and her eyes widened. "Yes," she said quickly. "Of course. I'll see what I can do."

I leaned on the desk and waited, watching her as she talked into the phone. There was a long pause while she just stood there holding it, and occasionally glancing at me with an expression of curiosity she couldn't conceal. And then I heard her say: "Yes, of course, sir. I'll send him up right away." She put the phone down and came back to the desk. "Mr. Erkhard will see you himself." She said it on a note of surprise. "If you'll go up to the first floor, his secretary will be waiting for you."

I thanked her and went up the stairs. Erkhard's secretary proved to be a man, neat and immaculate with a copy-book smile of greeting. "Mr. Grant? Will you come this way, please?" He took me along a cool corridor and into an office that looked out across the tumuli. "Mr. Erkhard's very busy and you've come unexpectedly without an appointment. If you'd keep it as short as possible."

"I didn't ask to see Mr. Erkhard," I said, and that seemed to upset him.

"No, no, of course. I understand." He paused at the communicating door on the far side, a discreet little pause that gave emphasis and importance to the moment. Then he opened the door. "Mr. Grant, sir."

The room was dove-grey, the furniture black steel. The big window looking out across the tumuli was a single sheet of flawless glass fitted with plastic Venetian blinds. The desk at which Erkhard was seated filled most of the far side of the room, and all the wall behind him was taken up with a relief map of Arabia dotted with flags. He didn't rise to greet me, but simply waved me to the chair opposite his desk.

"You're a lawyer, I understand?"

I nodded and sat down.

"And you're out here on account of young Whitaker's death?"

"I'm his executor."

"Ah, yes." There was a peculiar softness about his manner, a smoothness almost. It was something to do with the roundness of his face and the way the lips were moulded into the suggestion of a smile. He was sitting perfectly still, watching me— waiting, I felt. It was disconcerting, and I found him a difficult man to place, probably because he wasn't a type I had met before. In a weaker man that half-smile might have appeared ingratiating. But there was nothing weak about Erkhard. And the eyes were cold as they stared at me, unblinking. "Have you seen the young man's family?" There was an accent, but so slight it was barely noticeable.

"The mother," I told him. "I haven't seen the sister yet."

"She's out here in Dubai—a nurse."

I nodded. "You cabled her the news. She sent me a copy."

"Yes. A very unfortunate business. It's not often we have a casualty." There was a long pause, and then he said: "Why are you here, Mr. Grant? Are you hoping to persuade us to resume the search? I had a message, something to that effect from London Office." And he added: "I assure you it would be quite useless."

"Perhaps if I had a full account of the circumstances," I suggested.

"Of course. There is a report of the search. I'll see that you're given a copy before you leave." Another long pause. "You were asking for Sir Philip Gorde, I understand. Why?" And when I didn't answer, he added: "I signed that cable to Nurse Thomas and you've been in touch with London. You know perfectly well that I gave the order for the search to be abandoned." He stared at me. "Perhaps you would care to explain?"

"There's nothing to explain," I said. "It happens that I have to see Sir Philip on a private matter."

"Connected with Whitaker?"

"Yes."

He got suddenly to his feet. "I'm the General Manager in

Arabia, Mr. Grant. Whitaker was employed by me. His death is my responsibility, not Sir Philip Gorde's."

"I appreciate that."

"Then your correct approach was surely to ask for an interview with me?"

It seemed to worry him, and I wondered why. He was staring down at me, waiting for an answer. Finally he turned away and stood looking out of the window at the brown, dried-up landscape. His light tropical suit was obviously tailored in London and the silk shirt was monogrammed with his initials. "Sir Philip is in Abu Dhabi." He said it quietly as though he were speaking to himself. "Tomorrow, or perhaps the day after, he will be going on to Sharjah. That's another of the Trucial sheikhdoms, further to the east. He will not be back here for at least a week, perhaps a fortnight." He turned then and looked directly at me again. "How do you propose to contact him? Have you thought of that?"

"I only got in this morning," I said.

"Have you visas for the Trucial sheikhdoms?"

"No. I have to apply to the Political Resident's office—"

"Mr. Grant." He was smiling again. "I don't think you understand. It isn't easy to get visas for the Trucial Oman. The PRPG is very naturally extremely reluctant. . . ." He gave a little shrug. "This is Arabia, you know, not Europe. The political situation is far from stable and there is a great deal at stake; enormous sums of capital have been sunk in this area." He paused there to give me time to consider. "Of course, we could help you. Not only in the matter of your application for a visa, but in transport, too. We have flights going east along the coast to our various development projects. In fact, I think there is one going to Abu Dhabi tomorrow. But," he added, "in order to help you we should have to know the exact purpose of your visit."

He was taking a lot of trouble over this. "I'm sorry," I said. "Beyond saying that my business with Sir Philip concerns the estate—a matter of a signature—I cannot disclose . . ."

"You have a document for him to sign?" He sounded puzzled, and when I refused to be drawn, he gave a little shrug and returned to his desk. "Since it is a private matter and not the concern of the Company, I'm afraid I can't help you, Mr. Grant. I'll send Gorde a personal note, of course, to tell him you're here." A fractional hesitation and then with that little smile that never remotely touched his eyes: "And if you'd care to communicate with him direct, then I've no doubt we could arrange for a letter to be delivered to him by tomorrow's plane." His hand reached out to the onyx bell-push on the desk.

"One moment," I said. I wasn't sure how to handle it, but I knew that once I was out of that office, the opportunity to question him would be gone for ever. "I wonder . . . Perhaps you would be good enough to clear up one or two points for me?" I said it tentatively. "Whilst I'm here," I added.

There was a momentary hesitation whilst his hand still hovered on the bell-push.

"I'm a little puzzled about certain aspects of the boy's death," I murmured.

The hand moved back from the bell-push, reluctantly. And then he smiled and leaned back in his chair. "Of course."

"You say he was employed by you at the time of his death?"

"He was employed by the Company, yes."

I hesitated. The devil of it was I didn't know what I was after. Something . . . but what? The map, towering behind him, caught my eye. "Could you show me exactly where it was his truck was found?"

He got up at once, almost with relief, I felt. The position he indicated was well to the southwest of Buraimi Oasis, a position where three dotted lines met. Peering over his shoulder, I saw that these marked the boundaries of Saudi Arabia, the sheikhdom of Saraifa, and the emirate of Hadd. His finger rested on a point inside the Saudi Arabian border. The whole area was shaded with little dots. "The sands of the Rub al Khali," he explained. "Dune country. It's called the Empty Quarter."

"You've no concession in Saudi Arabia, have you?"

"No."

"Then what was he doing there?"

"That's something we should like to know, Mr. Grant."

"He was there without your authority, then?"

"Of course." His nod was very emphatic.

"If he was carrying out a survey, then presumably he had a survey crew. What happened to them?"

He hesitated and the quick glance he gave me suggested that this was something he didn't want to go into. But in the end he said: "He had an Arab crew. They were picked up by askari of the Emir of Hadd. However, the men have been interviewed. It appears they became nervous. Hardly surprising in that area. Anyway, they downed tools, took the Land Rover, and left Whitaker there on his own."

"In Saudi Arabia?"

"No, no."

"Where, then?"

He glanced at me quickly again, his eyes narrowing. "They wouldn't say. At least . . . they couldn't give the exact location."

"Was it somewhere on the Hadd border?" I asked, remembering what Griffiths had said.

He ignored that. "Doubtless they could have led us to the place, but the Emir refused to allow them outside the Wadi Hadd al-Akhbar." He gave a little shrug. "The Emir is very difficult." And he added: "But of course this is hardly a matter that concerns you."

"On the contrary," I said sharply, "it's important that I know exactly where the boy was supposed to be operating at the time of his death. Until I know that . . ."

But he shook his head. "Best leave it at that, Mr. Grant."

"Because of the political aspect?" I was convinced now that the locations in my briefcase would show that David had been operating somewhere along the Hadd-Saraifa border.

"Politics come into it, yes. They always do in Arabia."

"And particularly where oil is concerned?"

He nodded agreement, and I asked him then whether he thought there was oil in that area.

He looked at me very tight-lipped and said: "We've no reason to imagine so."

"Then what's the political problem?"

He hesitated, and then half turned to the map again. "Those borders," he said. "They're all three in dispute. Particularly the border between Hadd and Saraifa."

"Would you describe that as 'political dynamite'?" His eyes narrowed and I pushed it further: "If oil were discovered there?"

"Yes," he said, and turned back to his desk. "I think, Mr. Grant, we are getting a long way from the purpose of your visit."

"I don't think so." He wanted to terminate the interview. Equally, I wanted to continue it. "Did David Whitaker submit a survey report to you at any time during, say, the two months before his death?"

"No."

I stared at him, wondering whether that was the truth. And then I decided to play the thing I'd been holding in reserve. "Suppose I told you that I have in my possession the locations he was working on at the time of his death?"

He affected disbelief. But it lacked something, the quickness of spontaneity, the sharpness of genuine surprise. And suddenly my mind clicked. "Four days ago," I murmured, "in my office in Cardiff . . . I was visited by a gentleman who attempted by threats to get those locations from me." He didn't say anything, and I let the silence drag out. "He didn't get them, of course," I said quietly. I was staring at him, but he kept his eyes on the desk.

"I don't think this concerns me." The silence had forced it out of him. His hand reached for the bell-push.

I waited, and he hesitated. Curiosity had won. He turned to me and said harshly: "David Whitaker was employed by us. We should know the locations he was surveying. We have a right."

"Have you?" I asked.

"Yes. And I'll add this: I find it very difficult to understand why you should have been given this information whilst the Company has been left in the dark."

He was facing me, and after what seemed a long time his eyes fell away to the desk again. He was puzzled. A little frightened, too. I thought he'd every reason to be both.

"David Whitaker knew he was going to die." I said it slowly and with emphasis. And before he had time to recover from the shock of what I'd said, I shifted my ground. "Does Colonel Whitaker know his son's dead?"

"I really cannot say." He was still considering the implication of what I'd told him, and I was convinced it was something he hadn't known before.

"We regarded the sister as the most suitable person to inform." And he added: "The boy was illegitimate, you know." It was a mistake, for it confirmed something I had come to suspect—that David's background was known to the Company. But he didn't seem conscious of it. Nor did he seem conscious of the drift of my questions. "I think you will agree, when you've read the report of the search, that everything possible was done."

"But they didn't find his body?"

"No. And if you knew the sort of country it is there, that wouldn't surprise you." He seemed anxious to reassure me on this point. "It's big-dune country and the sand is moving all the time. It obliterates everything. Even his truck was half buried when they located it."

"It was a seismological truck, I believe?"

He nodded.

"One of yours?"

He didn't answer immediately and there was a sudden stillness in the room. And when he spoke he chose his words carefully. "I've already told you he was employed by the Company at the time of his death."

"Oil-company trucks are usually marked with the name of the company, aren't they?"

"What are you implying?"

"There were no markings on this particular truck."

"How do you know?"

"There was a report of the search in *The Times*."

"Oh, so you've seen that." He hesitated. "Not every truck, you know, is marked with the Company's name."

"That doesn't answer my question," I said. "Was that truck a Company truck or not?"

I thought he was going to evade the question. But then he said: "No. No, it wasn't one of our trucks."

"Whose truck was it, then?"

But he'd had enough. "I'm not prepared to discuss the Company's affairs. The truck has no bearing on the boy's death."

"I think it has," I said, as his hand reached for the bell-push again. And I added: "One final question. Can you tell me where I'll find Colonel Whitaker?"

"Whitaker? I thought it was Gorde you'd come to see?"

"Whitaker, too," I told him. "David may have been employed by you, but he was on loan to his father at the time of his death."

"Quite untrue. *The Times* is in error." And he pressed the bell. The interview was at an end.

As though he had been waiting for his cue, the secretary came in immediately.

"See that Mr. Grant has a copy of the report on the Whitaker search, will you, Fairweather? He can take it away with him." Erkhard turned to me. "Have you a taxi waiting?" And when I shook my head, he told his secretary to arrange for a Company car to drive me back to Manama.

"You haven't told me where I'll find Colonel Whitaker," I said as I got to my feet.

He couldn't very well refuse to answer me in front of his secretary. "In Saraifa, I imagine." And he added: "But if you're thinking of going there, I should remind you that you will not be granted a visa."

Did that mean he'd use his influence to prevent me getting one? I hesitated, glancing up at the map. The flags had names on them, and because it might be the only opportunity I'd have, I went across to it and had a close look at them. There were only two anywhere near the Saraifa-Hadd border and the names on them were Ogden and Entwhistle.

"That map is confidential, Mr. Grant." It was the secretary, at my side now and quite agitated.

"You needn't worry," I said. "I know nothing about oil, so it doesn't tell me anything. Who did the ground search?" I asked Erkhard.

"Entwhistle," he answered without looking up.

"I'll give you that report now," the secretary said.

Erkhard didn't look up as I left, determined to give me no excuse for further questions. In the outer office I asked if I could write a note to Sir Philip Gorde. The secretary gave me a sheet

of Company notepaper and I wrote it at his desk with him more
or less standing over me. I marked the envelope *Personal,* but
I was careful to say nothing in it that Erkhard didn't know already. The secretary promised to see that it went out by the
next plane. "If there is a reply, I'll send it down to your hotel."
He gave me a duplicated copy of the report of the search and
showed me out.

I read that report in the car driving back to Manama. It told
me very little that I didn't already know. The truck had been
discovered by nomads of the Rashid tribe, who had passed the
news on to some Harasis going down to the Gulf of Masira.
The *naukhuda* of a dhow had brought the news across to Masira
Island, and the RAF station there had radioed it on to RAF HQ,
Aden. A Valetta, landing at Masira on the milk-run up from
Kormaksar, had begun the aerial search on March 11, and the
abandoned truck had been located after a three-day search.
Erkhard had then ordered Entwhistle, who was operating about
seventy miles away, to break off his seismological survey work
and proceed at speed to the area.

Due to a broken spring, Entwhistle had not reached the abandoned truck until three days later. He had then carried out a
systematic search, but had found no trace of David, and the
few nomads he encountered knew nothing about him. After four
days, lack of supplies had forced him to retire. Meantime, the
Valetta, supported by a plane chartered by GODCO, had carried out an intensive air search. This had been abandoned on
March 16. Everything had then depended on the ground
search, but the rough going had put Entwhistle's radio out of
action and it was not until he joined up with Ogden's outfit on
March 24 that he was able to report his failure to find even the
body.

It was obvious that no blame attached to the Company. As
Erkhard had said, everything possible had been done. I put the
report away in my briefcase. The only man who could tell me
anything more was Entwhistle, and, remembering the position
of his flag on Erkhard's operations map, I knew there wasn't
much chance of my having a talk with him.

We were approaching the town now, the twin minarets of

the Suq al-Khamis Mosque standing slender against the sky, and I told the driver to take me to the Political Resident's office. "The PRPG, sir?" He slowed the car. "Is not in Manama. Is out at Jufair by the Naval Base." He hesitated. He was a very superior-looking Bahraini. "You wish me to drive you there?"

"Please."

He turned right and we reached the Jufair road by the National Cinema. "Have you a pass, sir? Everybody need a pass to enter Jufair Naval Base." But the native sentry on the gate knew the car and he let us through without question. We were close to the sea then with a frigate lying white as a swan on the oily-calm water. The road curved amongst the trees, the Government blocks standing discreetly back in semblance of a country estate. It was all manifestly English, and so, too, was the Passport Control Office with its forms. Purpose of visit . . . what did I put for that? I handed my passport to the clerk, together with my application for visas.

"Abu Dhabi, Dubai, Sharjah, and Saraifa. That's quite a tour." He shook his head doubtfully, turning over the pages of my passport. "The first three, they're Trucial sheikhdoms—they may be possible. But Saraifa—that's quite out of the question."

"Isn't that for the Ruler to decide?" I asked. "I understand it's an independent sheikhdom."

The suggestion seemed to strike him as a novel one. "We decide who goes to Saraifa," he said stiffly. And he added: "If you'll come back later . . ."

"This afternoon? I want to leave for Abu Dhabi tomorrow."

"This afternoon?" He sounded doubtful. "Well, perhaps . . ."

I drove to the BOAC office then, only to discover that if I wanted to fly to Abu Dhabi I should have to charter a plane. Gulf Airways ran a service to Sharjah, but not to Abu Dhabi. It was my first experience of the difficulties of communication in the country. Back at the hotel in time for lunch, I was hailed by Ruffini, sitting alone like a pale-blue toad in front of a tall glass. "You like a beer?"

He had seen one of the chief executives of BAPCO—the Bahrain Petroleum Company—out at the oil town of Awali, and then had an interview with Erkhard. "This afternoon I go to

Jufair, but I do not think they tell me anything." He leaned towards me across the table. "You puzzle me, Signor Grant," he said. "A lawyer, always with your briefcase. You say you are not interested in oil, yet your business is with two of the most important oil men in the Gulf."

The boy brought my drink. "Salute!" Ruffini raised his glass. "That girl at the reception desk—she is new to GODCO and she talk. This morning when you ask for Sir Philip Gorde and he is not there, Erkhard immediately sees you 'imself. Why?" His eyes were fixed on my face, full of curiosity. "Why are you so important? What is in that briefcase of yours, signore?" He shook his head and gave a mock sigh. "You will not tell me, of course. Not yet." His face creased in a smile and he gulped down the rest of his drink. "Let's go and eat."

Over lunch he told me why he was in Bahrain. He worked for a newspaper group in Milan and he'd had a tip-off from one of Italy's leading oil men. "I think he is right," he said. "There is trouble. But where?" He had been up since six, talking in the bazaar, to Indians chiefly. A squadron of Bren-gun carriers of the RAF regiment was rumoured to have been sent to Sharjah, and two RAF reconnaissance planes had been fitted with long-range tanks. There was talk, too, of additional transport allocated to the Trucial Oman Scouts, and the G.O.C. Persian Gulf was known to be on a tour of inspection. "If there is trouble 'ere," he said, "then it mean only one thing—oil." And suddenly, without warning, he said: "What about this David Whitaker, eh?" He smiled at me. "Now you are surprised. But that little girl knew him and you told her your business is about this boy who is missing." He stared at me. "But you don't want to talk about it, eh?"

"There's nothing to talk about," I said. "I'm his executor, that's all."

"An' you 'ave to see Sir Philip Gorde, who is four years ago one of the most important men in the Gulf, but not any more— who is also the life-long friend of Colonel Whitaker, the boy's father. An' you 'ave nothing to tell me, eh?" He shook his head sadly. "Per'aps you do not know it, my friend—but I think maybe you are sitting on the story I want." He stared at me a moment, and then very seriously: "You will think I am being very stupid now, but walk with care. I like you. I like men who 'ave a sense of duty. That is why I am warning you."

"You sound very serious." I wanted to laugh it off. But he said: "I am very serious. Oil is big money. And in a country like this it is also political dynamite." Probably he misread the shock his choice of words gave me, for he added quickly: "You don't believe that, eh? Well, I will take a bet with you. You will not get to Abu Dhabi or to Sharjah. Saraifa is closed anyway. You will, in fact, not be allowed out of Bahrain. And you will be got out of 'ere somehow before Sir Philip Gorde returns. Have you got your visas yet?"

"I have to go back to Jufair this afternoon."

"Okay," he said. "You can come with me. But you will not get any visa."

He was right there. They were very apologetic about it down at Jufair, but the only man who could deal with my application had unfortunately been called away on urgent business. Perhaps if I came back tomorrow. There was no point in arguing. The brick wall of officialdom can't be battered down unless you have the right contacts, and I'd no contacts at all. I went for a walk along the naval jetty. There was a wind blowing off the anchorage, but it was a hot wind and did nothing to refresh me.

Half an hour later Ruffini joined me. "Do you get your visas?" He gave me a wicked smile. He knew I hadn't got them.

"Did you get the low-down on the political situation?" I asked him.

He gave a fat chuckle and shook his head. "The same thing. Nobody is saying anything. What is more," he added, "you and me, we are in the same boat. No visas for Ruffini also. He is to stay 'ere and mind his bloody business." He hoisted himself on to the sea wall. "Officials can be very stupid. If I have to stay on in Bahrain and write my story from 'ere, then I have to guess at what goes on, and maybe I guess wrong." He was staring out across the anchorage, his eyes screwed up against the dazzle of the water. "That gunboat, for instance . . ." He nodded towards the frigate, which was slowly fetching up to her anchor, the clatter of her winch coming to us very clear across the water. "An exercise, they tell me. Routine. Maybe that is all it is and they are speaking the truth. But 'ow do I know?"

We stayed and watched her steam out of the anchorage, and then Ruffini heaved himself down off the wall. "Do you ever 'ear of the Emir of Hadd?" he asked as we walked back to the taxi. "The Emir Abdul-Zaid bin Sultan? Well, no matter." He wiped the perspiration from his face. "But try shooting that name at the political people 'ere and see 'ow their faces go blank. I tell you," he added, "this country is worse than a Sicilian village, full of old vendettas and not a clear boundary anywhere to mark the finish of one sheikh's piece of sand and the beginning of the next."

He took me back to the hotel and I lay and sweated on my bed till dinner-time, wondering how I was to contact Gorde and thinking about Ruffini. Was there really trouble brewing? But it all seemed remote—as remote as Colonel Whitaker out there in Saraifa and utterly inaccessible. And next day, after a full morning's work, I was no nearer either of my objectives.

I rang the Passport Office, but nothing had been decided. And when I checked on transportation I found that even if I were willing to charter a plane, there was none available with sufficient range to fly direct to Saraifa, and in any case flights there were prohibited. I went to the bank then and settled David's affairs as far as I was able. It was the same bank that his father dealt with, and the manager was helpful. He confirmed that Colonel Whitaker was living in Saraifa, this contrary to his very strict instructions. But he could tell me little else, and I went back to the hotel and had a drink with two RAF officers and a civilian pilot, a Canadian named Otto Smith. After lunch we all went down to the Sailing Club for a bathe.

Half the English colony was there, for it was Saturday, and amongst them was the girl from the GODCO reception desk sprawled half naked on the cement of the old seaplane jetty. "So you're off to Sharjah, Mr. Grant?" And when I told her I was having visa trouble, she smiled and said: "I think you'll find it's all right."

"How do you know?"

"Oh, I know everything." She laughed. "No, I happened to see your name on the flight list for tomorrow's plane."

She was perfectly right. When I got back to the hotel that evening I found my passport waiting for me, stamped with visas for Sharjah and Dubai. There was also a message, signed by Erkhard's secretary, informing me that "owing to the Company's desire to help you in every possible way" free passage was being granted to me in a Company plane leaving for Sharjah at 1030 hours the following morning, Sunday. The message added that accommodation would be available at the Fort and it was not anticipated that I should have to wait long before Sir Philip arrived from Abu Dhabi.

There was no doubt in my mind that Erkhard had intervened to get me the necessary visas. But why? The day before, he had made it clear that he didn't intend to help me. And after the way I had cross-examined him I hadn't expected it. And yet here he was giving me a free ride on a Company plane. I sat on my bed and smoked a cigarette whilst the hot evening breeze blew in through the open window, and the only conclusion I came to was that they had sent my note to Gorde and he had given the necessary instructions. Whatever the reasons, it was a great relief to me, and I got up and started to pack.

I had just closed the larger of my two suitcases when there was a knock at the door. It was one of the house-boys to say there was a young Arab asking for me at the desk. "It is a boy from the bazaar, sir. From the al-Menza Club." And he grinned at me.

I had a wash and then dressed. The boy was still there when I got down quarter of an hour later. He was little more than an urchin and none too clean, and when he realized I didn't speak Arabic, he seized hold of my wrist, pulling at me and hissing the words "al-Menza" and "girl-want." Girl-want seemed to be the sum total of his English, and I told him to go to hell. He understood that, for he grinned and shook his head. "Girl-spik. Spik, sahib."

I got hold of the house-boy then and he said the boy had been sent by one of the girls at the al-Menza Club. "She wishes to speak with you, sir." This time he didn't grin. And he added with a puzzled frown: "It is a personal request. This boy is from the house where she lives."

I didn't like it. "Tell him no," I said and I went over to an empty table and ordered a beer. It took two house-boys and a lot of argument to get rid of the boy. I drank my beer and then went in to dinner, a solitary, dreary meal. I had just finished when the waiter came to tell me a taxi-driver was waiting outside for me. It was Mahommed Ali. "There is a boy in my taxi," he said. "Is wishing you to go to the al-Menza to meet a girl."

"I've already told him I'm not interested."

"You should go, sir. She 'as something to tell you."

I hesitated. But, after all, the man was a taxi-driver attached to the hotel. "You'll drive me there, will you?"

"Okay, sir."

It wasn't far to the bazaar area and we finished up in a side-street that was barely wide enough for the car. The al-Menza was sandwiched between a cobbler's shop and a narrow alley, the door guarded by a turbaned Sudanese. I told the driver to wait, and the boy took me by the hand and hurried me down the alley and through the black gap of a doorway into a dark passage. He left me there and a moment later footsteps sounded, high-heeled and sharp, and then a girl's voice, low, with a peculiarly resonant quality, almost husky. "*Monsieur.*" She took my hand, her fingers hard, not caressing. "Through 'ere, pleez."

A door was pushed open and there were soft lights and the faint beat of Western music, a jive record playing somewhere in the building. A beaded curtain rattled back and we were in a little room no bigger than a cell. The floor was bare earth with a rug and a few cushions. A naked light-bulb dangling from the ceiling showed me my companion.

I don't know quite how to describe that girl. She certainly wasn't beautiful, though I suppose that is a matter of taste, for she was obviously Arab; Arab mixed with something else—European, I thought, with a touch of the real African. She stood very straight with a lithe, almost animal grace. She was the sort of girl you could picture at the well drawing water and striding away across the sand with a pitcher on her head. She was that, and she was the other sort, too; the husky voice—dropped a shade, it would be totally erotic, a vicious invitation. No point in dramatizing; she was just a Middle Eastern tart, but I'd never met one before and it made an impression.

We sat cross-legged on the cushions, facing each other. She wore a queer sort of dress and I had a feeling that at the touch of a secret button she'd come gliding out of it like a butterfly out of a chrysalis. Her hands were pressed tight together and she leaned forward, her eyes, her lips devoid of invitation, hard almost and urgent.

"You know why I ask you to come 'ere?"

I shook my head.

"You do not guess?" There was the ghost of a smile on her half-open lips. But when I said "No," she snapped them shut. "If you are not the man," she blazed; "if you 'ave come 'ere because it is the sort of place . . ." At that moment she didn't look at all nice. "All right," she said, biting on her teeth. "You tell me now—is it because of David you come to Bahrain or not?"

David! I stared at her, beginning to understand. "Did David come here, then?"

"Of course. He was an oil man and this place is for oil men. They 'ave the same devil in them as other men where the sun is 'ot—but David was nice, a vair nice boy." She smiled then and the hardness went out of her face, leaving it for a moment like a picture of Madonna-with-child, despite the slightly flattened nose, the thickened lips. It was a queer face, changeable as a child's.

"How did you know I was here on account of David Whitaker?" I asked. "It is David Whitaker you're talking about?"

She nodded. "One of the men from the GODCO office is 'ere las' night. He tol' me about you." She didn't say anything after that, but sat staring at me with her big, dark eyes as though trying to make up her mind about me. "You like some coffee?" she asked at length.

"Please." I needed time, and I think she'd guessed that. She was gone only a few moments, but it gave me a chance to collect myself and to realize that she was perhaps the one person in Bahrain who could tell me what sort of man David had become in the four years since I'd seen him. She put the coffee

down between us, two small cups, black and sweet. I gave her
a cigarette and sat smoking and drinking my coffee, waiting for
her to start talking. I had that much sense. If I'd rushed her,
she'd have closed up on me.

"Have you seen his sister?" she asked finally.

"Not yet." It wasn't the question I'd expected.

"But you 'ave 'eard from her, no? Does she think he is dead?"

I sat there, quite still, staring at her. "What else could she
think?" I said quietly.

"And you? Do you think he is dead?"

I hesitated, wondering what it was leading up to. "His truck
was found abandoned in the desert. There was a ground and
air search." I left it at that.

"I ask you whether you think he is dead."

"What else am I supposed to think?"

"I don' know." She shook her head. "I jus' don' know. He
is not the sort of boy to die. He believe too much, want too
much of life."

"What, for instance?"

She shook her head slowly. "I don' know what he want. Is a
vair strange boy, David. He have moods; sometimes he sit for
hours without saying nothing, without moving even. At such
times he have a great sense of—of *tranquillité*. You understand?
I have known him sit all night, cross-legged and in silence, without moving almost a muscle. At other times he talk and the
words pour out of him and his eyes shine like there is a fever in
him."

"What did he talk about?"

She shrugged her shoulders. "So many words. I don' understand half of what he say. About the desert mostly, and the
Bedou. Water, too; he loved water—much more than oil, I think.
And the *falajes;* he often talk about the *falajes* and about Saraifa
—how the desert is moving into the oasis."

I asked her what the word *falaj* meant, but she couldn't explain it. "Is something to do with water; tunnels, I think, under
the ground because he say it is vair hot there, like in a Turkish
bath, and there are fishes. And when you look up you can see
the stars." She frowned. "I don' know what it is, but he say once

it is like the wind-towers at Dubai—something brought from
Persia. But I have never seen the wind-towers at Dubai," she
added.

"And this was in Saraifa?" I asked.

"*Oui*. Saraifa. With David it is always Saraifa. He has a—a
folie for that place." She said it almost sadly, and she added:
"He wish to prove something there, but what I do not know—
'imself per'aps." For a while she sat quite still and silent, and
then she said very softly: "He was a man with a dream." She
looked up at me suddenly. "And dreams don' die, do they? Or
are men's dreams like the seed in a place like this—all barren?"

I didn't know what to answer. "You loved him, did you?" I
asked gently.

"Loved?" She shrugged. "You want everything black and
white. What is love between man and woman—and in a place
like this?" Her shoulders moved again, slight and impatient.
"Per'aps. But sometimes he could be cruel. He had a vein of
cruelty in him—like the Arab. At other times . . ." She smiled.
"He showed me a glimpse of what life could be. And when he
talked about his dreams, then he is near to God. You see," she
added, her voice suddenly tense, "he is important to me. The
most important thing in my whole life. That is why I cannot believe he is dead."

I asked her when she had last seen him and she laughed in
my face. "You don' see a man when is lying in your arms. You
feel—feel . . . if you are a woman." She stared at me and then
she giggled like a girl. "You look so shocked. Have you never
been with a woman like me before? But no, of course, you are
English. I forget. You see, I am Algérienne, from Afrique Nord.
All my life I am accustomed to Frenchmen—and Arabs." She
spat the word "Arabs" out as though she hated them. "I should
have been still in Algérie, but when the Indo-China war is on,
they send us out to Saigon, a whole planeful of women like me.
We come down at Sharjah because of engine trouble and we
are there in the Fort for two weeks. There I met a merchant from
Bahrain, so I don' go to Saigon, but come 'ere to Bahrain, and
later I am put into the al-Menza Club as hostess. That is 'ow I
come to meet David."

"Yes, but when did you last see him?" I asked again.

"In July of las' year. And it was not 'ere, but at the place where I live."

"That was just before he sailed for Dubai?"

"*Oui.*" Her eyes were searching my face. "He was—how you say?" She hesitated, searching for a word. But then she shrugged. "Vair sad, I think. He say that there is only one man in the 'ole world that 'e can really trust and that this friend is in England."

"Didn't he trust his father?" I asked.

"*Le Colonel?*" She moved her shoulders, an expressive shrug that seemed to indicate doubt. "When I see him that las' time he trust nobody out here—only this friend in England. You are from England and yesterday you are at the Company's offices enquiring about David." She leaned forward so that the deep line between her full breasts was a black shadow. "Tell me now, are you this friend?"

"Didn't he tell you his friend's name?"

"No, he don' say his name—or if he do, I 'ave forgot."

"Well, I'm his lawyer. Does that help?"

"A man of business?"

"Yes. His executor, in fact. That means that I carry out his instructions when he is dead."

"And now you carry them out? That is why you are 'ere in Bahrain?"

"Yes."

"Are you never his friend—before?"

"Once," I said. "Four years ago." And I told her how I'd helped him to get away in the *Emerald Isle.* Evidently she knew this story, for she nodded her head several times and her eyes were bright with the memory of his telling of it.

"Yes," she said when I had finished. "Now I know you are the man." And then she leaned forward and gripped my hand. "Where you go now—after Bahrain?" she asked. "You go to find him, yes?" And she added: "You will give him a message, pleez? It is important."

I stared at her. Her dark face was so intense, her belief in his immunity from death so tragic.

"Pleez." Her voice was urgent, pleading. "It is vair important."

"He's dead," I reminded her gently.

She dropped my hand as though she had hold of a snake. "His truck is found abandoned in the desert. That is all." She glared at me as though challenging me to destroy her belief. "That is all, you 'ear me? Pleez." She touched my hand again, a gesture of supplication. "Find 'im for me, *monsieur*. There is trouble coming in the desert and he is in danger. Warn him, pleez."

There was no point in telling her again that he was dead. "What sort of trouble?" I asked.

She shrugged. "War. Fighting. What other trouble do men make?" And when I asked her where the fighting was going to break out, she said: "In Saraifa, I think. That is the rumour in the bazaar. And that boy who bring you 'ere, Akhmed; he is the son of a famous pearl-diver. He know the *naukhudas* of all the dhows, and there is talk of *sambuqs* with arms coming across the sea from Persia. I don' know whether it is true or not, but that is the talk. And 'ere in Bahrain we hear all the talk. That is why I ask to see you, to tell you that you must warn him. He is in great danger because of 'is father."

"What's Colonel Whitaker got to do with it?" I asked.

"He is drilling an oil well in Saraifa. Oh," she said angrily, "the greed of you men! Money, money, money—you think of nothing else and you must cut each other's throats to get more and more. But with David it is different. He don' want money. He want something . . . I don' know. I don' know what he want. But not money. He don' care about money."

It was extraordinary, this girl telling me what Colonel Whitaker was doing, confirming what I had already guessed. "How do you know Colonel Whitaker is drilling for oil?" I asked.

"How? I tell you, this place is for oil men. They 'ave their intelligence, and because they are 'omesick and half dead with ennui, they talk." She gave a little laugh. "There is so much talk in this 'ouse that I can almost tell you what each oil man eat for breakfast from Doha right down the Gulf to Ras al Khaima."

I sat for a moment thinking about the rumours she'd heard, remembering what Ruffini had said out there on the Jufair jetty.

"You will tell him what I say. You will warn him?"

"Of course." What else could I say?

"Do you go to Saraifa? If you go there, pleez, you should talk with Khalid. He is the sheikh's eldest son. He and David hunted together when he is first in the desert. They are like brothers, he always say."

I gave a little shrug. How would Khalid know? How would anybody know what had happened? The boy was dead. "I'll see his father," I said. "If I can."

"*Non, non.*" There was urgency, a sense almost of fear, in her voice.

I stared at her hard. "Why not?" But if she knew anything, she wasn't saying. And because I didn't like the way my thoughts were running, I asked her where David had been going that last time she had seen him."

"To Dubai," she answered. "By ship."

"The *Emerald Isle?*"

She nodded.

"And after that—after Dubai?"

Again that slight, impatient movement of the shoulders. "He don' say. He don' tell me where he go."

"Was it Saraifa?"

"Perhaps. I don' know."

"There's some suggestion that he was on loan to his father, that he was doing a survey for Colonel—"

"*Non, non.*" Again the urgency, the leap of something stark in the wide dark eyes. "*C'est impossible.*" She shook her head emphatically.

"Why is it impossible?"

"Because . . ." She shook her head again. "He cannot go to work with him. I know that now." And she added under her breath: "*Que le bon Dieu le protège!*" I felt I had to know the reason, but when I pressed her for it, she shied away from the subject. "I must go now." She got to her feet in one easy, balanced motion. It was as though my questions had started an ugly train of thought—as though to admit that he'd gone to Saraifa to join his father was to admit the fact of his death. And as I stood up I was remembering again the nagging suspicion that had been in my mind that day Griffiths had come to see me in Cardiff.

"*Au revoir.*" She held out her hand and I was conscious again of the steel grip of those thin fingers. "You are his friend. I know that now. And when you find him you will warn him?" I nodded, not saying anything. "And you can give him my love also," she said with a sudden flash of gaiety. And then serious again: "The boy Akhmed will be waiting each morning for you at the 'otel. I have arranged it. He knows many people and he can help you if you wish. And remember, please," she added, "this is an island very close to the great deserts of Arabia—much closer than Algérie is to the Sahara. And the desert is Arab. Your Eenglish officials and the oil men, they know only what 'appen on the surface. They can see the bees swarm, but they do not know when the old queen die. You understand?" And with that she pulled back the bead curtain and I was out in the passage again, where the dance music sounded faintly. She took me as far as the alleyway, where the boy was waiting, and then with a final touch of those fingers, a flash of white teeth, she was gone.

It was only after I was back in the car that I realized I didn't know her name. I got it from the boy—Tessa; a very European name for a girl of her mixed parentage. Later I learned that it was a shortened form of Tebessa, the town on the Algerian-Tunisian border where she had been born.

I lay awake a long time that night wondering about David, about what had really happened. Three women—his mother, his sister, and now this girl Tessa—all convinced he was alive. And the picture she had sketched of him, the warning of trouble brewing . . . I went to sleep with the unpleasant feeling that I was being caught up in the march of events. And in the morning Mahommed Ali drove me to the airport.

III

The Empty Quarter

We took off

shortly after ten, skimming low over sand flats that ran out into
the shallows where fish stakes stood in broad arrows. The white
coral buildings of Muharraq vanished behind us, and after that
the waters of the Gulf stretched away on either side, a flat sea
mirror shimmering in the heat, and the colours were all pastel
shades.

The plane was piloted by the Canadian I had swum with the
previous day—Otto Smith. He had joined me on the apron just
before take-off and, realizing that I'd never seen what he called
"this Godforsaken country" before, he had offered to make it a
low-level flight. We flew, in fact, at less than a thousand feet. A
white-winged dhow swam like a child's toy on the sheet-steel
surface below, and where the water shallowed to islands banked
with sand it was translucent green, the sand-banks sugar white.

We crossed the Qattar Peninsula: a glimpse of an oil camp, the
airstrip marked out with oil drums, the camp a wheel of con-
centric buildings and the rig a single lonely tower. A sheikh's
palace standing on an empty beach, square like a military fort,
the mud of its walls barely discernible against desert sand. The
palm-frond shacks of a *barasti* fishing village, and then the sea
again, until the white of gypsum appeared on the starboard side
and miniature buttes of sand standing out of the water marked
the mainland coast of Arabia.

The plane was full of equipment and stores bound for an oil

camp along the coast towards Ras al Khaima, beyond Sharjah.
There were only three passengers besides myself—an officer of
the Trucial Oman Scouts and two oil men who were straight out
from England and could tell me nothing. I sat in silence, in a
mood of strange elation, for the sight of the desert so close below the plane gave me the illusion at least that Saraifa was
within my reach.

We followed the coast all the way. Shallow sand dunes re-
placed the glare of gypsum flats, the coast became dotted with
palms, and here and there a pattern of nets spread out on the
shore to dry marked a fishing village. About an hour and a half
out Otto Smith called me for'ard to look at Dubai. "The Venice
of Arabia," he shouted to me above the roar of the engines. A
broad estuary dog-legged through the sand-banks, dwindling
amongst the town's buildings, which crowded down to the
waterfront, capped by innumerable towers, slender like *cam-
panili*—the wind-towers that Tessa had talked of, a simple system of air-conditioning brought from Persia by the pirates and
smugglers of the past.

Ten minutes later we reached Sharjah: another estuary, but
smaller and with a sand-bar across the entrance, and the mud
town crumbling to ruin. We came in low over a camel train
headed south into the desert, the glint of silver on guns, the
flash of white teeth in dark faces, and a woman, black like a
crow, with a black mask covering her face, riding the last camel.
Watch-towers stood lone sentinels against the dunes, and far
away to the east and southeast the mountains of the Jebel were
a hazy, dust-red wall. We came to rest close by the white glare
of the Fort, and behind it lay the camp of the Trucial Oman
Scouts.

Sharjah Fort was like any desert fort, only now it was an air-
lines transit hotel. Two rusty iron cannon lay in the sand on
either side of the arched entrance, and all the interior was an
open rectangular space with rooms built against the walls. Otto
took me to the lounge and bought me a beer. The room was
large, the walls enlivened with maps and coloured posters, the
tiled floor gritty with blown sand. "How long are you going to
stay here?" he asked me. And when I said I was waiting for

Gorde, he looked surprised. "Well, you're going to have a darn long wait," he said.

"How do you mean?"

"Didn't they tell you? He sent a radio message through yesterday to say he'd changed his plans. He's being flown back to Bahrain tomorrow."

So that was it . . . that was why Erkhard had changed his mind. A free ride in a Company plane and I'd be in Sharjah by the time Gorde got back to Bahrain. "Thank God you told me in time," I said.

"In time? Oh, you mean you want to ride back with me." He shook his head. "Sorry, fellow. I got a full load from Ras al Khaima. And not to Bahrain either—to one of the off-shore islands." And he added: "It's too bad. They should have told you."

I sat, staring at my beer, momentarily at a loss. "Is there any way I can get to Abu Dhabi from here?"

"Today?" He shook his head. "Anyway, you haven't a visa, have you?"

That was no good, then. "When's the next flight back to Bahrain, do you know?"

"Civil? Oh, there'll be one through in a day or two. The manager will have the flight schedules."

I asked him then who would be flying Gorde back to Bahrain, but he didn't know. "Might be Bill Adams, might be me." He took a long pull at his beer. "Probably me, I guess. He likes to have me fly him. Reminds him of the old days when he was boss out here and we flew everywhere together." And he began telling me about an old Walrus they'd flown in the early days just before the war. "One of those push-prop amphibians. Boy! We had fun with that old kite. And Gorde didn't give a damn; he'd let me slam it down any old place."

"Could you give him a message?" I asked, for I was quite certain now that the note I'd left with Erkhard's secretary would never be delivered.

"Sure, what is it?"

I hesitated. "Perhaps I'd better write it."

"Okay. You write it. Then whoever picks him up tomorrow can give it to him." His freckled face crinkled in a grin. "You might've been waiting here for weeks. Not that there aren't worse places than Sharjah to be marooned in. This time of year the bathing is wizard. Know what I think? I think that in a few years' time this coast will be one of the world's great winter playgrounds." I finished my note whilst he was extolling the tourist attractions of the Persian Gulf, and then he began talking about the strange places he had landed in.

"Have you ever been to Saraifa Oasis?" I asked him.

"Saraifa? Sure I have. We had a concession there once."

I asked him how far it was to Saraifa and he said something over two hundred miles. A long way across the desert, but less than two hours by plane. "Has it got an airfield?"

"Sure. You don't think I walked, do you? But that was four years ago," he added. "I'm told the sand has moved in since then. Funny thing." He glanced at me quickly. "You're out here on account of young Whitaker; his lawyer—that right?"

I nodded.

"Well, that last time I flew Gorde into Saraifa, it was the day David Whitaker arrived there. It was about the last thing Gorde did before he handed over to Erkhard and went home on sick leave. We flew in to Saraifa to break it to Sheikh Makhmud that the Company wasn't going to renew the concession. They were arguing about it all evening, with that one-eyed devil *Haj* Whitaker sitting there like an Arab and swearing by the Koran that he'd get even with Erkhard. Has anybody mentioned the Whitaker Theory to you?"

I nodded.

"Oh, well, you'll know what it meant to the old Bedouin, then. Saraifa was his baby. He'd negotiated the concession, and if it hadn't been for Erkhard they might have been drilling there now. But Erkhard was the new broom, and if Whitaker could have got at him that night I swear he'd have killed him with his bare hands. It was as elemental as that. Now, of course," he added, "it's a different story. Erkhard's under pressure, and *Haj* Whitaker . . ." His navigator called him from the doorway. "Okay, Eddie. Be right with you." He swallowed the rest of his beer and got to his feet.

"You were saying you were there in Saraifa when David Whitaker arrived?" I said.

"Oh, yes. Well . . . I was just there, that's all. He was dressed in Bedouin clothes; he was very young and he looked scared stiff. Couldn't blame the poor kid. He'd never been in Arabia before, never met his father before, and that black-hearted bastard just stared at him as though he wished the floor would open up and swallow him. He even introduced the boy to us as David Thomas. It seemed like he didn't want to acknowledge him as his own son, which wasn't very clever of him, for the boy had the same cast of features—the nose, the jaw, the heavy eyebrows. Well, I must go now." He held out his hand for the envelope. "Don't worry. I'll see Gorde gets it. And I'll come and rescue you sometime during the week if you haven't flown out by Gulf Airways." A wave of the hand and he was gone, out through the screen door. I was alone then with the posters and the lazy circling flies and the old magazines.

It was siesta-time and after the departure of the plane the Fort went back to sleep. I was allotted a room, and after I'd had a shower, I went up on to the terrace that ran like a broad firing-step round the inside of the walls and sat there in a pair of shorts and sun-glasses staring at the shimmering line of the mountains. Down there to the south, where the high volcanic peaks disappeared below the sand horizon, lay Saraifa. Two hundred-odd miles, Otto had said. I remembered Griffiths's description of conditions in summer: *hot enough to burn the tires off a truck and the soles off your boots.* The heat came up at me with a furnace fierceness, and the flat expanse of the airfield lay in mirage-pools of water.

But if I'd been manoeuvred clear of Gorde, and Whitaker was inaccessible, there was at least one person available to me here. And as the sun sank and the breeze came up, damp off the sea, I dressed and made enquiries about getting to Dubai. A lieutenant of the Trucial Oman Scouts, who was in the lounge having a drink, offered to take me in after the evening meal.

It was just over twelve miles to Dubai, out past the sheikh's palace with its string of fairy lights and the hum of its generator, and along a winding road beaten out of the *sabkhat.* The road

was as black and hard as macadam, and all to the right of us
were salt flats running out into the sea—a thin, baked crust,
treacherously overlying a slough of mud that was as lifeless as
the surface of the moon. To the left the desert sand was humped
like the waves of a petrified sea, and far in the distance the
mountains of the Jebel, purple and remote, stood sharp-etched
on the earth's rim.

As we drove through this empty world I asked the lieutenant
whether his outfit was expecting trouble in the interior. He
laughed. "We're always ready for trouble. That's what we're
for." And when I mentioned the rumours circulating in the bazaars of Bahrain, he said: "Oh, you don't want to worry about
them. Bahrain's always buzzing with rumours." He had a soldier's contempt for civilians, and I think he thought I was
scared.

The hospital was a mile or two outside Dubai, a solitary building sprawled over a sand hill. The last glow of the sun had
gone, the sky fading to darkness, and the building stood black
against the sand. Night was falling fast. "Give Doc Logan my
salaams and tell him I'll come over tomorrow and help him drink
his Scotch," my lieutenant said and roared off in his Land Rover
towards the distant wind-towers of Dubai.

The hospital was a ramshackle building, part mud, part wood
—a strange place to meet a girl I hadn't seen for four years.
She came to the little waiting-room dressed in apron and cap,
and at the sight of me she stopped and stared in surprise, for
nobody had bothered to enquire my name.

"Mr. Grant! I—I can't believe it." She came forward and shook
my hand.

"Well, you're not the only one," I said. "I can hardly believe
it myself."

Her hand was smooth and dry and firm. Her face looked
thinner, and the fat of youth had been worked out of her body;
her blond hair was bleached almost white by the sun, her skin
tanned. She looked fit, and the shine of youth was still in her
eyes. It was a strange meeting, and for me—and I think also for
her—it brought a feeling of relief, for there was that bond between us, and from that moment neither of us could feel entirely

alone any more. It was also to have the effect of making me determined, somehow, to get to Saraifa.

"We can't talk here," she said. "I'll be b-back in a minute." Still that slight attractive hesitation in her speech.

When she returned she had removed her cap and apron and wore a light coat. We left the hospital and strolled north whilst the sand turned from brown to silver and the stars came out. I held her arm because I felt her need and mine for the touch of companionship, and the wind was warm on my face.

She had received my letter, but she hadn't been to Bahrain, hadn't even written to Erkhard. "What was the use?" She seemed at first to have accepted the fact of her brother's death and she was quite willing to talk about him. And as she talked, the picture that emerged was of a man I had only just begun to guess at.

She had come to Dubai two years ago, not so much to be near him—she had had the sense to realize that she would very rarely see him—but because of his fascination for Arabia, which he had somehow managed to convey to her. "I was here almost three months before I saw him, and then he came without warning. He was straight out of the desert, from a survey down by the Liwa Oasis, and I didn't recognize him at first. He was dressed as an Arab, you see. But it wasn't that," she added. "And he hadn't changed, not really."

She paused there, as though collecting the details of that meeting from the recesses of her memory. "I can't explain it," she said finally. "He was just different, that's all. He had become a man, and there was a remoteness about him. Do you read the Bible, Mr. Grant? Those descriptions of the prophets. There was something of that about him. He always had enthusiasm, a sort of inner fire, but now it seemed to have depth and purpose."

She had only seen him four times in the two years she had been out there, but each time her reaction had been the same. "It was as though he had become dedicated."

"Dedicated to what?" I asked. But she couldn't tell me, not in so many words. "To a way of life," she said, and went on to talk about the influence his father had had on him. The relationship hadn't been at all easy at first. "They started off on the

wrong foot, you see. When David arrived at Saraifa, Sir Philip
Gorde was there with his pilot. The driver should have taken
David to his father's house; instead he was brought straight to
Sheikh Makhmud's palace. It meant, of course, that his arrival
was immediately known to two Europeans. It complicated the
whole thing, particularly as David was virtually smuggled into
Arabia. His father thought it due to wilful disobedience, and he
was furious." She smiled at me. "I think they hated each other
at first. They were too much alike, you see."

I asked her whether she'd met Colonel Whitaker, and she
nodded. "Once, just over a year ago." He'd come to the hospital
to see her. "It was just curiosity," she said. "There's no feeling
between us—not like there is between him and David. David's
got much more of his father in him than I have. And anyway,"
she added, "after being so long in Arabia he has the native attitude to girls—necessary for the procreation of the race, but useless otherwise. Being a nurse, I know. They'll go to any lengths
to get a sick boy to the hospital, but a girl child—she can die or
not, just as she pleases."

I asked her then what impression she had got of her father,
and she gave a slight shrug. "There's no love lost between us, if
that's what you mean."

"Yes, but what's he like?" And I explained that I was looking
after his financial affairs and had come out partly in the hope of
meeting him.

She didn't answer for a moment, as though she had to think
about it. "It's odd," she said at length. "He's my own father. I
know that. I think we could both feel that in our bones. But it
meant nothing." She hesitated. Finally she said: "My only impression is one of hardness, almost of cruelty. It's the desert, I
think; the desert and the Moslem faith and the Arabs he's lived
with so long. He's a little terrifying—tall, one-eyed, imperious.
He's like an Arab, but the sheikhs I've met are much softer,
gentler men, more guileful. He has a strange quality of command, the sort of quality I imagine some of our kings once had
when they believed implicitly in the Divine Right. You could
never be easy in his company. His whole personality, it radiates

. . ." She paused, at a loss for words. "I can't explain it, but he frightens me."

"What about David?" I asked. "Did he feel the same way?"

"At first. Later he came under his spell, so that he looked upon him as something akin to God." He had been, she said, under the spell of his father when he had first come to see her. He had had six months at Saraifa, living the life of an Arab, and a year at an oil school, learning to become a geophysicist. He had come to her straight from his first experience of field work and was then going on leave to Saraifa. "He talked a lot about Saraifa—about the way the desert was moving in on the oasis, slowly obliterating the date-gardens. He could be very emotional about it." She smiled gently. "He was like a woman at times, the way he wanted to defend Saraifa."

"Defend it?" I thought for a moment she was referring to the rumours of trouble.

"From the Rub al Khali," she said. "From the sand. He dreamed of taking a seismological outfit there and proving his father's theory. Oil, he said, was the only hope. If he could prove there was oil there, then the concession would be renewed and there would be money to rebuild the *falajes*."

That word again. I asked her what it meant, but all she said was: "It's some system for bringing water to Saraifa, and it has largely been destroyed." She sighed and sat down on the sand, her hands clasped about her knees. I gave her a cigarette and she sat there smoking, remembering, I suppose, the last time they had been together.

"Did he ever take a seismological truck into Saraifa?" I asked her.

She looked at me quickly, her eyes big and round in the starlight. I think she had forgotten for the moment that I was there. "I don't know," she said. And after a long silence she added softly: "I know so little about him, really. I don't know what he was doing, or why he was so depressed; and the truck abandoned like that. I know so little." And then she looked at me again and said with great emphasis: "But I know he was a man —a real man; and also that he would endeavour to the limit for something he believed in."

"Saraifa?"

She nodded. "Perhaps—for Saraifa."

"Because of his father?"

She didn't answer for a while. At length, she said: "No. Not because of his father."

"What, then?"

"The people, his friend Khalid—the sand killing the place. I don't know. The sand, probably. That was something physical. He was always fascinated by physical things. He likes action."

"But he was a dreamer, too?"

She nodded. "Yes, he was a dreamer, too. He was always a rebel in the world he knew. When we were kids . . . he'd escape into a world of his own. A m-mental world, you see. It was always much larger than life. He'd invent games—just for the two of us. And then, later—well, the gang life attracted him for the same reason. It was a form of escape."

"And you think his father's world—Saraifa—was an escape?"

She shrugged. "Escape or reality—what does it matter? It was real to him. I remember the second time he came to see me. He took me to dinner at the Fort at Sharjah and he was full of plans, bubbling over with them. He was going to take over from a man called Entwhistle, who was sick. And after that he was going on a month's leave—to Saraifa. A busman's holiday; he was going to run a survey for his father. He was so full of it," she said a little sadly. "And so bloody optimistic," she added, almost savagely.

"Where exactly in Saraifa was he going to try for oil?"

"I don't know. What does it matter?"

"Was this in July of last year?"

She nodded, a glance of surprise. "He had his own ideas—something he'd unearthed in some old geological report. I couldn't follow it all. When he's excited he talks nineteen to the dozen and I'm never certain what is fact and what he's made up. He seemed to think he could do in a month what GODCO had failed to do the whole time they'd had the concession. He was always like that. He could build a whole kingdom in five minutes—in his mind." She gave a little laugh. "Once, you know, he ran a tramp shipping line out of Cardiff. It got so big that every ship that came into the docks belonged to him. That was the first time he got into trouble. He beat up a night watchman for telling him to get off the bridge of an old laid-up Victory ship." She sighed. "That was the sort of boy he was."

"And after he'd been to Saraifa?" I asked. "Did he come and see you?"

"No, he flew straight back to Bahrain. I didn't see him until December."

She didn't seem to want to talk about it, for I had to drag it out of her. Yes, he had been going to Saraifa again. She admitted it reluctantly. He'd been loaned to his father.

"Are you sure?" I asked.

"I can't be sure about anything, but that's what I understood."

So the *Times* correspondent had been right. And I remembered how Erkhard had skated round the question.

"It was all so strange," she murmured. "I thought it was what he'd been wanting all along. Instead he seemed—I don't know how to put it—almost appalled at the prospect. He was in a most extraordinary state of nervous tension. . . ."

"Had he seen Erkhard?" I asked. "Was it Erkhard who had loaned him to his father?"

"I don't know. He wouldn't talk about it. He just came to tell me where he was going and what he was doing. He didn't stay long. In fact," she added, "it was a rather awkward meeting and I had the feeling he'd only come because he'd felt it was his duty."

But I was barely listening to her, my mind on Erkhard and this extraordinary arrangement. If it was true, then it could only mean one thing—that Erkhard and Whitaker had some sort of an arrangement . . . an improbable combination, if Otto was to be believed. "And this was in December?"

She nodded.

"You said you'd seen him four times," I said. "When was the fourth?"

"The fourth?" She stared at me and her face looked very pale. "It was in February." She couldn't remember the date, but it was early in February. I knew then that he'd come to her after he had boarded the *Emerald Isle*, probably that same night,

because she said she was called out well after midnight by an
Arab boy and had found him sitting alone on the sand. "Somewhere near here," she said, looking about her.

"Did he talk about his father?"

"No," she said. "Though . . ." She hesitated. "I think they'd
had a row. I can't be sure. It wasn't anything he said." And she
added: "He wasn't very communicative, you see."

I asked her how he'd behaved. "Was he scared at all? Did he
behave as though he was in fear of his life?"

She looked at me quickly, her eyes searching my face. "No,"
she said slowly. "No, I don't think he was scared. More . . ."
She shook her head. "I can't explain. He just behaved strangely,
that's all—very strangely." In fact, most of the time he'd been
with her he'd sat in absolute silence. "David could do that. As
a kid I got used to those silences. But . . . I don't know. This
seemed deeper, somehow, as though . . ." But she couldn't put
it into words. "He didn't talk much," she reiterated. "There was
a moon, and I remember his eyes riveted on my face. It was as
though he couldn't look at me enough. I felt . . . it was as
though he wanted to capture an impression, take a sort of mental
picture with him. It was a very strange, uncomfortable feeling
—and he looked so like his father in the Arab clothes he was
wearing."

"Did he tell you what he was doing?"

"No. He wouldn't tell me anything, but I had the feeling that
it was dangerous. He was terribly thin, nothing but skin and
bone, and his eyes, staring at me, looked enormous and very
pale in the moonlight. When he left he kissed me, not with
warmth, but as though he were kissing a priestess who held the
key to the future in her hands. And just before he left me, he
said a strange thing. He said: 'Whatever you hear of me, Sue,
don't believe it.' And he added that if anything happened to
him, I was to write to you. And then he left me, walking quickly
across the sand without looking back."

We were sitting on a little rise and the sand fell away from
us, sloping gently to a *barasti* settlement, the dark shapes of the
palm-frond huts barely visible, for the moon was new and only
just risen. Nothing stirred and the only sound was the bleat of a

goat. "I can't believe he's dead," she said. "I won't believe it."

And because it was what she wanted to believe I told her about the girl in Bahrain and about her mother's reaction. "Yes," she said. "Mum did everything she could to discourage his interest in Arabia. But too late. When we were small she shared her thoughts with us, and her thoughts were of the man she called our 'Uncle Charles.' That album of press-cuttings—they were almost the first pictures I ever remember looking at. And now here we are, the two of us, in Arabia."

"And your father?" I asked. "Did he talk to you about Saraifa?"

"To me?" She smiled and shook her head. "I'm only a girl. He wouldn't talk to me about what he was doing."

"You say David was loaned to him by GODCO," I prompted.

She nodded, and when I pressed her for the reason, she said almost sharply: "Oh, his father is doing what he's always done out here—dabbling in oil." And then almost gently: "It's rather sad, really. One by one the concessions he negotiated for GODCO have been abandoned. He was once a great figure out here—a sort of Lawrence." She had pity for him, even if she had no love.

"And now?" I asked.

"Now?" She shook her head. "I don't know. David wouldn't talk about him, not that last time. But there are all these rumours. He had this theory, you know. Some say it's crazy, but I've met others who believed he was right."

I asked her whether she'd met Entwhistle. I thought perhaps he might have been to see her. But she shook her head.

"What about these rumours?" I said.

"They're just rumours." She shrugged. "I don't know whether they're true or not. Nobody I've met has ever been to Saraifa. With the border in dispute, nobody is allowed to go there. It's just . . . well, the desert is like the sea used to be, you know—exaggerated stories are passed on by word of mouth."

I pressed her then to tell me what the stories were, and she said: "He's supposed to be drilling on his own account—with an old broken-down rig operated entirely by Bedouin. The oil boys I've talked to all say that's nonsense, that uneducated desert

Arabs couldn't possibly operate an oil rig. But I don't know.
Though I'm scared of him and have no feeling for him, I know
he's a remarkable man, and you've only got to talk to the officers
here to realize that the Bedouin are very quick to pick up a
working knowledge of machinery."

She threw the stub of her cigarette away and got to her feet.
"I wish to God I knew what had happened." Her voice trembled;
she was very near to tears. There was a lot more I suppose she
could have told me about him, but I didn't press her. I thought
there was plenty of time and that I'd see her again. For her sake
I steered the talk to other things. We passed a watch-tower,
standing like a lonely border keep, and she told me they were
still manned, the guard climbing in through the hole halfway up
the tower's side every night and pulling the ladder up after him.

"It looks so peaceful here," I said.

She laughed. "It is—on the surface. But who knows what is
going on underneath? Certainly not our people. Some of these
young English boys who are sent out here to advise . . ." She
shook her head. "Sometimes I wonder. What must the sheikhs
think? This desert way of life, it goes right back to Hagar and
Ishmael, racially and culturally hardly changed. They know human nature the way these youngsters out from England will
never know it. They're full of guile and intrigue; the Pax Britan-
nica, even the oil, is just an incident in time. It's only a few years
back, you know, that the Sheikh of Dubai fell upon an Abu
Dhabi raiding force, killing over fifty of them. It wasn't very far
from here."

Back at the hospital, she asked me whether I had arranged
transport to get me back to Sharjah. "I can walk," I said. But
she wouldn't hear of it. "You'd lose your way in the dark. You'd
either wander into the desert or else into the *sabkhat*. Step
through the crust of that and nobody would ever see you again."
She insisted that I stay at the hospital.

They had a small guest room, and I spent the night there,
and in the morning she arranged a lift for me in a TOS truck
going back to Sharjah. She looked cool and very matter-of-fact
as she said goodbye to me. "Come and see me again before you
leave. And if you have any news . . ." She left it at that, and I

sat and watched her from the back of the truck as we drove away, a solitary figure in white standing motionless outside the hospital. She hadn't moved when I lost sight of her behind a shoulder of sand.

It was that lack of movement; I became suddenly, instinctively aware of a loneliness that matched my own, and my heart went out to her. And as the truck roared along the packed mud surface of the Sharjah track, it wasn't of the girl who had walked with me in the moonlight on my first night on the edge of the Arabian desert that I was thinking, but of that other girl—the girl who had come to my shabby office in Cardiff to plead for help for her brother. She was a woman now, and though she might not like her father, I felt he had given her something of himself that made her, like him, an unusual person. She had courage, loyalty, and a strange aura of calm, an acceptance of life as it was. They were qualities both restful and disturbing, and, remembering every detail of that walk in the sands, the watch-tower and her perceptive comments on the desert world, I knew I didn't want to lose her, knew that somehow I must discover what had happened to David and set her mind at rest. I was half in love with her. I knew that before ever the truck reached Sharjah, and all that morning I walked, filled with a restlessness that was the restlessness of frustration. But you could walk for a day and still have no sense of progress in the merciless emptiness of the sea of sand that stretched away to the south.

I had my lunch in the company of a German commercial traveller and two American tourists staying the night on their way to India. The German could talk of nothing but the fact that his product had been copied in Karachi and was on sale in almost the identical wrapping in the bazaars of Dubai. The Americans were from Detroit, plaintive and unable to see any attraction in the untamed beauty of the desert, faintly disturbed by the condition of the Arabs, nostalgic for a hotel that would give them the built-in sense of security of a Statler.

The sound of aircraft coming in low interrupted the desultory conversation. Ten minutes later the screen door was flung open and Otto came in with his navigator. "Hi!" He waved his hand

and came over to me. "Fairy godfather, that's me. Anything you want, Otto produces it. The Old Man's in the manager's office right now."

"Gorde?"

He nodded. "But watch out. He's hopping mad about something."

"Thanks," I said and went across to my room and got my briefcase.

The manager's office was by the arched entrance, and seated opposite him in one of the big leather armchairs was a much older man with a yellowish face that was shrivelled like a nut. He had a tall glass in his hand, and on the floor at his side lay a rubber-ferruled stick. Small bloodshot blue eyes stared at me over deep pouches as I introduced myself. He didn't say anything, but just sat there summing me up.

I was conscious at once that this was a very different man from Erkhard. He looked as though he belonged in the desert, a man who had had all the red blood baked out of him by the heat. He wore an old pair of desert boots, khaki trousers, and a freshly laundered cream shirt with a silk square knotted round his throat like a sweat rag. A battered brown trilby, the band stained black by the perspiration of years, was tipped to the back of his grizzled head.

"You got my message," I said.

He nodded. "Yes. I got your message. But that wasn't what brought me." His voice was dry, rasping, the words staccato as though life were too short for conversation. "Should be in Bahrain now." He gave the manager a brusque nod of dismissal, and when we were alone he said: "There's a newspaper on the desk there. That's why I'm here. Read it. I've marked the passage."

It was the airmail edition of a leading London daily. The marked passage was on the foreign-news page. It was headed: NEW OIL DISCOVERY IN ARABIA?—*Desert Death of Ex-Borstal Boy Starts Rumours.* It was written "by a Special Correspondent," and besides giving a full and graphic account of David Whitaker's disappearance and the search that had followed, it included his background; everything was there, everything that

I knew about the boy myself—his escape from the police in Cardiff, the fact that he was Colonel Whitaker's son, even the details of how he'd been smuggled into Arabia on a native dhow. The story ran to almost a column with a double-column head, and about the only thing it didn't give was the location he'd been surveying immediately prior to his death.

"Well?" Gorde rasped. "Are you responsible for that?"

"No."

"Then who is?"

That was what I was wondering. Whoever had written it had access to all the information that I had. "I don't know," I said.

"You're David Whitaker's solicitor. His executor, in fact, Otto tells me."

"Yes."

"And just over two days ago you were in London."

"Nevertheless, I'm not responsible for it."

"A young kid just out of oil school and operating in an area he'd no business in . . . A criminal, to boot." He glared at me, his fingers drumming at the leather arm of the chair. "The Political Resident had that paper specially flown down to me at Abu Dhabi. The Foreign Office has teleprinted him that half the London press have taken the story up. He's furious."

"The facts are correct," I said.

"The facts!" But he wasn't thinking of the boy's background. "You know where his truck was found abandoned? Inside the borders of Saudi Arabia," he almost snarled. "A story like that —it could spark off another Buraimi, only worse, much worse." He paused then, staring at me curiously. "Your note said you wanted to see me. You said it was urgent, something about this boy—a communication."

I didn't answer at once, for I'd read through to the end of the newspaper story, to the editorial footnote that had been added at the bottom: *The London Office of the Gulfoman Oilfields Development Company issued a statement yesterday denying that there was any truth in rumours that the Company had made an important new oil strike. Asked whether David Whitaker had made a confidential report prior to his death, an official*

*of the Company stated categorically that nothing was known in
London about any such report. Despite the Company's denials,
GODCO shares went ahead yesterday in active dealings on the
London Stock Exchange.*

"Well?"

"Suppose there's something in it?"

"Suppose pigs had wings," he snarled. "Well, come on, man.
What was it you wanted to see me about?"

For answer I opened my briefcase and handed over the envelope David had addressed to him. "Have you seen Colonel
Whitaker since you've been out here?" I asked.

"What's that got to do with it?" He was staring down at the
envelope, and when I started to explain, he cut me short. "Oh,
I've heard the talk, if that's what you mean. But it's nothing to
do with the Company. If Charles Whitaker likes to waste his
money trying to prove a theory . . ." He grunted. "It's just
damned awkward, that's all. The boy's death makes a colourful
story, and coming on top of his father's activities . . ." He gave
a little shrug and slit open the flap of the envelope with his
finger. "Erkhard was trying to keep it quiet—and rightly. Saraifa
is a trouble spot. Always has been. And the political chaps are
touchy about it."

"That doesn't explain why he should try to prevent me seeing
you."

He had taken out a letter and two wads of foolscap. "What's
that? What are you talking about?" He reached into his pocket
for his glasses.

I told him then how I'd been given facilities for Sharjah as
soon as it was known that he had changed his plans and was
flying back to Bahrain.

"What are you suggesting?" he demanded.

"That Erkhard didn't intend us to meet."

"Nonsense. What difference could it make to him?" He put
on his glasses, and after that he didn't talk as he read steadily
through the contents. Finally he said: "Do you know what this
is, Mr. Grant?" He tapped one of the foolscap sheets. "Do you
know what he's trying to get me to do?"

"Sign some sort of undertaking, but I don't know exactly—"

"Undertaking!" he rasped. "If I sign this—" He waved the sheet of paper at me. "It would commit the Company to drilling four test wells at locations to be supplied by you." He took his glasses off and stared at me. "Is that right? You hold the locations?"

"Yes," I said. "They're in a separate envelope. If you sign that document, then I'm instructed to hand it across to you."

"But not otherwise?"

"No."

"And you've got it with you?"

I nodded. "It's here in my briefcase."

"And if I don't sign . . . What do you do then?"

"In that case I imagine my actions wouldn't concern you."

"No?" He laughed. And then he was looking down at the document again. "I see here that you will be acting as agent for Sheikh Makhmud and his son Khalid in this matter. Have you ever met Sheikh Makhmud?"

I shook my head.

"And you know nothing about the Middle East." He was staring at me and his eyes had the suggestion of a twinkle. "It has its humorous side, you know. The boy must have thought you a most remarkable lawyer." He went back to the document again. "Further, it commits the Company to the payment of an advance of a hundred thousand pounds in respect of oil royalties of fifty per cent, provided always that Sheikh Makhmud and his son agree to grant to the Company the sole concession from date of signature to the year two thousand. Well," he said, "there's your undertaking. The boy must have had a touch of the sun when he typed that." And he tossed it across to me. "Read it yourself and tell me what you think of it—as a lawyer."

I glanced through it quickly, wondering what he expected me to see in it. "It looks perfectly legal," I said.

"Exactly. That's what makes it so damned odd. He'd taken the trouble to look up all the legal jargon for that sort of a document." He leaned suddenly forward. "He couldn't have got that in the desert, could he? It means he looked it up before ever he went out there, before he'd even run his survey."

"What are you suggesting?"

"That his report's a phony. I'm not a fool, Grant. That boy's been got at, and I can guess who's got at him. Here. Take a look at the survey report." He thrust it at me. "He used his own typewriter for that. The other's different, probably an office machine. He typed that document and then went out into the desert—"

"David lost his life as the result of that survey," I reminded him.

"Did he? How do you know what caused his death?" He glared at me. "You don't, and nor do I. Nobody knows—or even what's happened to him. Has any one mentioned the Whitaker Theory to you?"

"I know about it," I said. "Is that why you think he's been got at?"

He nodded. "Way back in the thirties Charles Whitaker began claiming that we'd find the oilfields continuing down from the Gulf here between the sand seas of the Empty Quarter and the coastal mountain ranges to the east. It seemed a possibility, and, remembering how Holmes's theory had finally been proved right in Bahrain, I took a chance on it and moved some of my development teams in from the coast. It was an expensive business, and Buraimi was about the limit, from the practical point of view. I was operating partly in the Sharjah sheikhdom and partly in Muscat territory, and after I'd burned my fingers, even the big companies like Shell and ARAMCO wouldn't look at his theory."

"That was a long time ago now," I said.

"Yes, before the war."

"What about Saraifa? Did you do any development work there?"

"No, it was too far from the coast. I sent a geological party in in 1939, but the initial reports weren't very encouraging, and then the war came and the chap in charge of the survey was killed. We didn't try again, though Charles was always pressing us to do so. He had a political appointment for a short time after the end of the war, but when he rejoined the Company in 1949 he was still just as convinced that he'd be proved right in the end." He shook his head. "Poor fellow! It had become an obsession—Saraifa in particular; he wanted us to try again there. The

wartime development of desert transport made it a practical
proposition, but the political situation between Saraifa and
Hadd was worsening, and anyway I'd lost faith in his theory by
then." He stared at the foolscap sheets in my hand. "If that
survey report had been turned in by one of our most experi-
enced geophysicists, I wouldn't touch it."

"Because of the political factor?"

"No. Not just because of the political factor."

"What, then?"

He hesitated. "Because it doesn't fit in with the reasons I'm
out here." He stared at me then, his eyes narrowed above the
tired pouches of flesh. "The fact is," he said, "the Company's
been spending too much money in the Gulf area and getting
too little in return. Nobody is supposed to know this yet—not
even Erkhard, though I think he's guessed. My instructions are
to carry out a thorough investigation of all our development
projects in the Gulf with a view to cutting down our commitments. It amounts to a reassessment of the value of each project,
and those that show no real promise of yielding results are to be
abandoned. So you see . . ." He gave a little shrug, his hands
spread out. "This is hardly the moment for me or anybody else
to involve the Company in new commitments."

"I see." There was really nothing more to be said, and I folded
the papers and put them in my briefcase.

"It's a funny thing." He was leaning back in his chair, his eyes
half closed, chuckling to himself. "The Company did this once
before. They sent Alex Erkhard out, and because I was sick and
hadn't the energy to fight him, he got my job. And now, four
years later, I'm back with the same powers he had and the
knowledge that he's made more mistakes that I did and lost the
Company a lot of friends." Again that dry, rasping chuckle, and
then his eyelids flicked back. "What I've told you is in the strict-
est confidence, you understand. You've been put to a lot of trouble to contact me. I thought it only fair to explain the situation
to you. If it's any satisfaction to you, I'd add that a report like
that isn't conclusive. Seismology never is; it's simply an indication. The only way to be sure you're sitting on an oilfield is to
drill down and find out."

"And suppose Whitaker's doing just that?"

"Hmm. To know the answer to that, we'd have to know the locations the boy was surveying and where his father's drilling." He stared at me. "Well, there it is. You've got your instructions. . . ."

I nodded. There was no point in continuing the discussion. "You're going back to Bahrain, I take it, Sir Philip?"

"Bahrain? Oh, you'd like a lift in my plane, is that it?"

I nodded. "Please."

He seemed to hesitate. But then he said: "All right." He picked up his drink. "You know my pilot—Otto Smith? Perhaps you'd be good enough to get him for me." He tapped his leg. "Can't move about like I used to."

"I'll get him," I said. And I went out and left him there, leaning back in the chair with his eyes half closed as though exhausted.

I had some difficulty in finding Otto, but eventually I ran him to earth in the showers, sitting naked, smoking a cigarette and gossiping with his navigator. I waited whilst he dressed and then went back with him to the manager's office.

Gorde was in the same position, but now he had my briefcase open on his lap and he was peering down at a sheet of paper he held in his hand.

I can't remember what I said to him—I was too angry. I think I called him some pretty unpleasant names, but all he said was: "What did you expect me to do?" His tone was mild. Almost he seemed amused. "If I'd asked you to let me see the locations, you'd have refused. Quite rightly." And he added: "I just wanted to check them against the position where his truck was found."

"But you'd no right—"

"Of course I'd no right," he said. "But yelling at me and getting yourself into a muck sweat won't alter the fact that I now have them. Do you know where they are?" he asked, peering up at me.

"No," I said. "I haven't had an opportunity—"

"On the Saraifa-Hadd border. Right bang on the bloody border." He glared at me. "I suppose you'll tell me you didn't know that the border was in dispute?" The way he said it implied that I'd tried to put something over on him.

Angrily I told him that I didn't have the advantage of his lack of scruples. "I kept strictly to my instructions and refrained from opening the envelope until I'd seen you."

"All right," he said. "We'll talk about it in a moment." He levered himself round in his chair. "Is the plane refuelled yet, Otto?"

"I don't know, sir. I'll check, if you like. Are you wanting to leave right away?"

"Yes, right away. But first I want you to check that your tanks are full. A personal check, please. You've got to have enough fuel on board to fly to the Saraifa border and back."

"I'm afraid we have to have authority to fly to Saraifa, Sir Philip."

"Since when?"

Otto hesitated. "I don't know exactly. Since the trouble there, I guess. It was just after you left; a border clash between Saraifa and Hadd. They had to send the Trucial Oman Scouts in, and since then nobody has been allowed to go to Saraifa."

Gorde gave a little sigh. "Let's not argue about it, Otto. I intend to have a quick look at these locations. Now then, how do we go about it without some little clerk reporting my movements to the PRPG, eh?"

Otto thought for a moment. "I think the best thing would be to say we're doing a recce of certain areas, taking a look at a seismological outfit we've got operating at the foot of the Jebel, possibly landing at Ras al Khaima if we've time, otherwise returning here. If we make it vague like that, I guess it'll be all right. That is, so long as you don't want to land at Saraifa."

"I don't know what I want to do," Gorde grumbled. "Haven't had time to think about it yet." He poked around in my briefcase until he found a sheet of plain paper. "Communications here still functions for civilian messages, doesn't it?" And when the other nodded, he pulled a gold pencil from his pocket and began to write. I watched him as he signed his name and read it through. I was more curious than angry now; he'd taken mat-

ters out of my hands, and for the moment my only concern was
to get on this flight.

"Have Communications send that off right away." He held
out the message. "Then check your fuel. Oh, and Otto," he
added as the pilot was leaving. "We'll be flying on to Bahrain
tonight." The door closed and he turned to me. "I suppose you
think I owe you an apology, hm?" He handed me back my briefcase. "Well, maybe I do. But I spent a lot of my time in Saraifa,
and anyway I'm an oil man. We've no built-in moral code like
you boys when it comes to things like locations." He folded the
foolscap sheet and put it back in its envelope and sat there tapping it against his thumbnail, lost in thought. "It's just possible,
I suppose. . . ." He said it softly, speaking to himself.

"That Colonel Whitaker's drilling in one of these locations?"

But he shook his head. "In that area? He wouldn't be such
a fool." Silence again, and the rhythmic tapping of that envelope. "However . . ." The small, bloodshot eyes peered at me
curiously, and then he began to chuckle. "A provincial lawyer
—and it's just possible you might have got hold of the thing the
Company has been searching the Gulf for during almost thirty
years." The rasp of that chuckle seemed to threaten to choke
him. "You and Charles Whitaker. God Almighty!" he gasped.
"And that boy . . . he'd never have dared operate on that border
on his own."

"You think they were together, then?"

"How the hell do I know?" He handed me the envelope. "I
don't know where Charles is drilling any more than you do. I'm
not even certain he is drilling. It's just rumours." He reached
for his stick and dragged himself to his feet. "But I mean to
find out," he said. "If Charles is drilling on these locations . . ."
He let it go at that, and since he seemed to take it for granted
that I was going with him, I stuffed the envelope into my pocket,
picked up my briefcase, and followed him to the door. As he
pulled it open, he said to me over his shoulder: "Prove Whitaker's theory correct, and on that border, and you'll be in
politics so deep, my friend, that you'll wish you'd never been
born. But I can't believe it," he added, limping out into the
bright sunshine. "Pig-headed, proud, revengeful . . . He still

couldn't be such a bloody fool." And he stumped off across the courtyard, shaking his head and muttering to himself.

We took off ten minutes later, and by then I'd had an opportunity to glance at the contents of that envelope. There were several foolscap sheets headed: REPORT OF SURVEYS CARRIED OUT ON SARAIFA TERRITORY; and it was subheaded: *Basis on which an Immediate Program of Test Drilling is Recommended at Points A, B, C, & D.* Pinned to it were four sheets of graph paper covered with figures and diagrams. There was also a sketch map giving his survey points, a whole series of them, each with the position pin-pointed in latitude and longitude. A number of Arab names were given, but none that I could recall from my brief examination of the map in Erkhard's office. Points A, B, C, and D were marked in red ink; they were very close to each other, in a little huddle at the eastern end of the line of his survey. There was no covering letter. Just the report and the sketch map.

I read the report through carefully as we flew south into the desert. It was typewritten, highly technical—quite beyond my comprehension. For this reason I do not intend to give the details. But there were several references to the "Whitaker Theory," and right at the beginning there was a paragraph that read: *It should not be imagined that I stumbled on this by accident. If anything comes of it, the credit must go to Henry Farr. He surveyed the area in the very early days of the war. The Saraifa Concession was fairly new then and Farr's outfit was the only survey team in the area. Moreover, he made his report at a time of crisis in the Middle East; it was pigeonholed away in the Company's headquarters and shortly afterwards he died fighting in Abyssinia. I was fortunate enough to come upon this report when searching old surveys for anything that had a bearing on Saraifa. . . .*

I leaned back in my seat, thinking about the war and how that old report had got lost in the files. Colonel Whitaker had fought in Eritrea. The same area. I wondered whether he and Farr had ever met. I was thinking about that when Gorde leaned across to me. "Well?" he said. "What are you going to do about that report when you get back to Bahrain?" He was smiling, tight-lipped. "The boy's like his father," he grunted. "A dreamer. The same dream, too."

"The dreams of youth sometimes come true," I said. I was remembering how Sue had talked of him.

His eyes clouded and he looked away from me, staring out of his window towards the mountains. "Ah, yes, the dreams of youth." He gave a little sigh. "But the boy's dead and Charles isn't a young man any more."

"And what about Farr?" I asked.

He shrugged. "He's dead, too."

"You don't think they could be right?"

"The Whitaker Theory?" He gave a snort. "Charles had a nose for oil, a sort of instinct for it, like Holmes. But he didn't know a damn thing about geology. That nose of his cost the Company a lot of money. We struck oil, but never in large enough quantities. I should know," he almost snarled. "I backed him, and it cost me my job out here. And I loved it," he added quietly. "I loved this country. Look at it!"

He leaned across, pointing to the desert that lay below the wing-tip, a corrugated dune sea stretching to the mountains that lay all along the horizon. "Clean and hard and cruel. I had twenty years of it. I know it better than I know my own country, and it calls to me the way the sea calls to a sailor—and I'm stuck in a damned office in London; I haven't been out here for almost four years." And he relapsed into silence, staring out of his window.

But a moment later he touched my arm and pointed downward. A great sweep of dunes thrust eastward, narrowing like a finger till the tip of the yellow sand touched the red rock wall of the mountains. Right below us a black line wound like a thread across the dunes—a camel caravan going south and leaving a faded snail-like smudge behind it in the sand. "The Ramlah Anej," he said in my ear. "We're crossing the eastern edge of the Rub al Khali." And he added with a sort of boyish delight: "I'm one of the very few men who've crossed the Empty Quarter by camel. Charles and I did it together. We said we were looking for oil, but that was just an excuse." He was smiling and his eyes were alight with the memory of it, so that through age and illness I got a glimpse of the young man he'd once been.

After that he fell silent and left me alone with my thoughts as the aircraft roared steadily south, the mountains always away to the left, always marching with us, a moon-mad landscape of volcanic peaks, sometimes near, sometimes receding to the lip of the earth's surface. And below us the sun marked the desert floor with the imprint of our plane, a minute shadow dogging our course.

It was just after four when the navigator came aft and woke Gorde, who had fallen asleep with the curtain drawn across his window and his battered hat tipped to shade his eyes. "Jebel al-Akhbar coming up now, sir. Otto wants to know whether you'd like to fly over Hadd or make a detour."

"May as well have a look at the Emir's hide-out," Gorde murmured, rubbing the sleep out of his eyes. "Long time since I last saw it." He got to his feet and motioned me to follow him.

The view from the flight deck was a blinding glare made bearable only by the green shade above the pilot's head. All away to the right of us was sand as far as the eye could strain, a petrified sea corrugated by the action of the wind. But from the left, mountains were closing in, bare, black, lava-ash mountains marked by patches of a livid, chemical green. They swept round ahead of us in a long curve, terminating abruptly at the sand sea's edge in a bold headland topped by a pinnacle of bare rock. "Jebel al-Akhbar," Gorde said, nodding towards it over the pilot's head. "There's an old stone fort on the top of it, and the town of Hadd is right underneath. Remarkable place. There's a saying amongst the Arabs of this part: 'Who holds al-Akhbar holds Hadd.' You'll see in a minute."

Otto was pushing the control column forward, and as we lost height the headland began to come up fast. "See the fort?" Gorde's hand gripped my arm. "I got a gazelle there once. The Emir invited us hunting and a seluki bitch named Adilla cornered it for me right under the walls there. My first visit to Saraifa," he added. "The time we signed the original concession."

I could see the fort clearly now, a biggish place, crumbling into ruin, with an outer ring of mud-and-rock walls and in the

centre a single watch-tower perched high on a pinnacle of rock.
We skimmed it with about a hundred feet to spare, and on the
farther side the hill dropped sheer to a valley shaped like a
crescent moon and half ringed with mountains.

The valley floor was flat, a patchwork quilt of cultivation;
date-palms, grey with dust, stood thick as Indian corn in mud-
walled enclosures, and there were fields of millet green with
new growth. In the further reaches of the valley, where cultivation dwindled into grey, volcanic ash, a solitary sand-devil
swirled a spiral of dust high into the air.

"Hadd." Gorde stabbed downward with his thumb, and,
peering over his shoulder, I caught a glimpse of a mud town
that seemed built into the rock below the fort. Right below us
a *mêlée* of men and goats and camels stood transfixed beside a
well. Mud walls towered above them, and, looking back, I saw
the town of Hadd climbing into its rocky cleft, with a great
fortified palace built on many levels facing towards the desert.
A green flag fluttered from a flagpole. "Always reminds me of
the Hadhramaut," Gorde shouted in my ear. "They build like
that in the Wadi Duan. Well-sited, isn't it?" He might have
been a soldier, his interest was so professional.

Otto half turned in his seat. "I'm setting course now for the
position given in the search report, that okay?" And when
Gorde nodded he banked the plane so that I had a last glimpse
of the Wadi Hadd al-Akhbar, a little oasis of green set against
a nightmare backdrop of volcanic rock. And then it was gone
and the arid, lifeless desert stretched out ahead of us.

Gorde produced the slip of paper he'd used for making notes
and handed it to the navigator. "Those are the fixes for the
Saraifa-Hadd border locations. Plot them now. We'll be flying
over them as soon as we've had a look at the spot where he
abandoned his truck."

We flew on in silence then, and gradually the gravel plain
gave place to sand, the dunes getting higher, their shadows
longer, until they were towering crescent-shaped downlands
stretching into infinity. The navigator passed Otto an alteration
of course and the shadow of the plane came ahead of us, growing imperceptibly bigger, as we lost height.

"Have we crossed the border?"

The navigator nodded. "Just crossing it now."

Gorde's hand gripped my elbow. "That's the trouble with this damned country," he said. "The borders are nothing but map references. Nobody cared so long as it was just a waste of desert sand. But you try explaining map references to an Arab sheikh once he's dazzled by the prospect of oil."

The navigator leaned across and made a circling movement with his hand. Otto tipped the plane over on the port wing-tip and we searched the glaring dunes below us. We circled like that, slowly, for several minutes, and then suddenly we straightened out, swooping down towards the humped back of a dune, and there, halfway up it, was the truck, almost obliterated by sand. I never saw such a desperately lonely-looking object in my life, a piece of dead machinery lying there like a wrecked boat in the midst of an ocean of sand.

We slid down on to it like a hawk stooping to its prey. It was a big closed-in truck, old and battered-looking and patched with rust. There were no markings on it, and as it rushed away beneath us Gorde echoed my own thoughts. "What was the fool doing, driving that truck alone into these dunes?" he demanded. "Do you know?" He was glaring at me, and when I shook my head, he grunted as though he didn't believe me. "A good twenty miles west of the survey locations," he growled. "He must have had some reason."

Otto banked steeply so that the truck was there, just beyond the port wing for us to stare at. But looking at it couldn't explain its presence on the slope of that dune, and in the end Gorde gave instructions for us to proceed to the locations David had surveyed and motioned me to follow him back into the relative quiet of the passenger cabin.

"Well," he said, dropping into his seat, "what do you make of it, eh?" But I could see he didn't expect an answer. He was slumped in his seat, an old man lost in thought. "Doesn't make sense, does it?" he grumbled. "The boy dead somewhere down there below us and his father not caring a damn and busy drilling a well . . ." He turned to me. "How did they get on, those two, do you know? What were their relations just prior to the boy's death?" And when I didn't say anything, he snapped: "Come on, man. You must know something. You've come all the way out from England; you wouldn't have done that unless you knew a little more than you've told me." He stared at me angrily. "Have you seen his sister?"

I nodded.

"Well, what does she say about it? He must have talked to her."

"She'd like to think he's still alive."

"What, in this country—and the truck lying there on that dune for almost two months?"

"She's never been into the desert."

"No, of course not." He asked me again what she had said about him, and whilst I was telling him the desert below gradually changed, the dunes altering shape until they were long ridges like waves with gravel flats in the troughs.

I was just telling him about the last visit David had made to his sister when the plane gave a lurch, the port wing tipped down, and over Gorde's shoulder I caught a glimpse of tire marks running straight, like the line of a railway, along the length of a flat stretch between two dunes. A pile of rusted tins, the black trace of a fire, the remains of a dug latrine—they were there for an instant and then the plane straightened up and we flew on, following the tire marks that had scored a straight line wherever the sand was soft.

Gorde got up then and I followed him forward. Indications of another camp came up at us, swept by beneath the plane. We were flying very low, the line of the dunes on either side closing us in. And then, straight ahead, the black shadow of a truck. It was stationary and we came up on it fast, belly to the gravel flat, roaring over it so close that I could read the black lettering on its side—G-O-D-C-O—and could see the drill at its rear turning.

It was the same sort of truck as the one we had seen abandoned a short while back, and as we turned and came down on it again, a figure in khaki shorts and an Australian bush hat waved to us. There were Arabs moving about by the drill, and close by the truck was a Land Rover with G-O-D-C-O painted across its bonnet.

Gorde swung round on me. "What the devil's a seismological truck doing here? Did you know it was here?"

"Of course not." For one wild moment I thought those three women might be right, and I almost tore the glasses from Gorde's hand. But the khaki figure was broad and thick-set, the round, brick-red face covered with ginger hair.

Gorde tapped Otto on the shoulder. "Can you land here?" he demanded. "I want to talk to that man. Who is it? Do you know?"

"Looks like Jack Entwhistle," Otto answered, and he swung the plane over again, circling back with the wing-tip almost scraping the top of the dunes. He was flying with his eyes glued to his side window, searching the ground. "Looks okay," he said. "No big stones, no wadis that I can see. I guess I can get down. Don't know how it will be taking off again."

Gorde didn't even hesitate. "Then put her down," he said. His face had gone a sickly yellow. He was furious.

"Hold tight, then." The plane banked again, came in level over the flat gravel pan, and I felt the drag as the flaps and undercarriage went down. He flew about half a mile with the ground so close that we might have been in a car, then he gave her full throttle, lifted her up and round in a turn that left my stomach behind me. We came back on to the line of the gravel, slow and dropping this time with the truck standing bang in our path. The wheels touched, bounced once on a rough patch, and next time we stayed down, bumping heavily over the rough surface, stones rattling against the outside of the fuselage, until the brakes came on and we slowed to a halt.

We were about three hundred yards from the truck, and the man who had waved to us was already in the Land Rover coming towards us. By the time the navigator had got the fuselage door open the Land Rover was drawing up alongside. The air that came in through the open door was hot with the glare of sun on sand. There was no wind, and the heat seemed trapped between the dunes. Gorde moved awkwardly down the fuselage, supporting himself with his hands on the backs of the seats.

He looked tired and old and very grim as he faced the man who came in from the desert.

"Entwhistle, isn't it?"

"That's right, Sir Philip." The man was North Country, square and stocky, the eyes grey in the red, dust-filmed face. He looked pleased. "It's grand to see you out here again, sir. How are you?" He wiped his hand on the seat of his shorts and held it out.

Gorde ignored the hand, ignored the warmth and friendliness of the other's tone. "Who gave you orders to run a survey here?"

Entwhistle hesitated, dropped his hand. He looked momentarily off balance, uncertain of himself.

"Was it Erkhard?"

"No, sir. To be honest, Sir Philip, nobody gave me orders."

"Then what the hell are you doing here? You're a hundred miles from your survey area."

"Aye, I know that." He ran his hand a little nervously over his face. "It isn't easy to explain. You see . . ." He hesitated. "I was the chap who carried out the ground search for David Whitaker. You know about that, do you?"

Gorde nodded. "Go on," he said, his voice flat. "And make it short. I haven't any time to waste."

But Entwhistle wasn't the sort of man to be brow-beaten. "If it comes to that, Sir Philip, I don't have any time to waste myself. I want to run this survey and get the hell out of here as fast as I can." His tone was obstinate. "This isn't what you'd call a healthy place. I got here two days ago and we hadn't been camped twenty-four hours before we had a visit from a bunch of Bedou. They didn't behave like nomads; more like the Emir's men. Though we're still in Saraifa here."

"The Saraifa concession was abandoned four years ago," Gorde said sharply. "You've no right here. None whatever."

"I'm well aware of that, Sir Philip."

"Then why are you here?"

Entwhistle hesitated, rubbing gently at a desert sore that showed red and ugly beneath the sweat stain of his right armpit. "You never met David Whitaker, did you, sir?"

"What's that got to do with it?"

"Oh, well . . ." He hesitated, and then, unable apparently to put it into words, he sought refuge in facts. "I couldn't exactly say it in my report of the search. It would have put the Company on the spot, if you see what I mean. But there was something fishy about that truck stuck there on a sand dune across the border into Saudi. There was nought wrong with it mechanically, you know. It was just out of fuel, as though he'd driven it straight into the Empty Quarter until he'd no more petrol. And if you'd known David . . ." Again the hesitation, and then a quick shrug. "He knew the desert—knew it a damn sight better than I'll ever know it. What was he doing there, that's what I'd like to know? If he'd been scared out of here by the Emir's men, why didn't he head for Saraifa?"

"Come to the point," Gorde said impatiently. "I want to know why you're here."

"Aye. Well, I went over every inch of that truck. I thought if there'd been foul play or anything like that, he'd have left some clue, something that a chap like myself, a fellow geophysicist, would understand. The only thing I found was an old attaché case full of correspondence and copies of survey reports. One of those reports concerned this area."

"I don't seem to remember reading that in the account you sent to Erkhard."

"No."

"You thought you'd keep it to yourself, eh? Thought you'd check on his findings on the quiet?"

Entwhistle scratched uncomfortably at the sore. "He was on loan to his father, you see. It didn't concern the Company, exactly. And he seemed so sure he'd—"

"It never occurred to you, I suppose, that there's a political factor?"

Entwhistle's grey eyes stared at Gorde without flinching. "David Whitaker was a good bloke. I don't know whether he sent a copy of that survey report to the Bahrain office or not; and I don't care. Nobody had done anything about it. Not even his father. He was out on his own and he thought he was on to something. I spent the better part of a week searching the desert for his body, and it seemed to me if I couldn't give him a headstone, I might at least see if he was right and we could name an oilfield after him. Maybe it sounds a little crazy to you, Sir Philip," he added almost belligerently, "but I just felt it was up to me to do something. I don't like to see a good chap's life thrown away for nothing. And if Erkhard kicks me off the Company's pay-roll as a result, I shan't cry my eyes out."

Gorde didn't say anything for a moment. He seemed lost in thought. "How far have you got with the check?" he asked at length.

"There are four locations given as probable anti-clines in the report. I've done a check on the most southeasterly—Location D, he called it. Now I've just begun drilling the first shot-hole on Location C. If you care to come to the truck, I can show you David Whitaker's report. Or has Mr. Erkhard already shown it to you?"

"No, he hasn't. Nevertheless," Gorde added, "I've seen a copy. Grant here was kind enough to show it to me." This on a note of irony, and he introduced me then. "A lawyer. Like you, he wants to know what young Whitaker was doing across the border into Saudi." He turned to me. "I don't suppose you've ever seen a seismological truck, have you?" And when I shook my head, he said: "Well, if you want to see the sort of work David Whitaker was engaged on, I'm sure Entwhistle would show you over his vehicle." He turned back to Entwhistle. "No point in stopping you in the middle of drilling a shot-hole. You can finish the check on your Location C. Then you're to pull out. Understand?"

"Yes, sir." Relief and something akin to affection showed for an instant on Entwhistle's face.

"Results to be sent direct to me. And now take Grant to your truck and show him how it works. Meanwhile, I'll write a letter for you to Sheikh Makhmud, just in case. I don't doubt he knows you're here." He stood back from the door. "Ten minutes," he said to me. "All right? And then I want to find Charles Whitaker's rig; find out why he isn't drilling here if his son was so damn sure."

I nodded. I didn't even hesitate. I was being given the opportunity of ten minutes alone with Entwhistle. I jumped out of the plane and it was like jumping into the full glare of an open-hearth furnace. Entwhistle remained a moment talking to Gorde, and when he joined me in the Land Rover he glanced at me curiously, so that I wondered what Gorde had told him about me. Stones rattled against the rusted mudguards as we batted over the gravel towards the truck, which seemed to be standing in a pool of water. The mirage only lifted when we were within a hundred yards of it.

I was more interested in Entwhistle than in the mechanics of his seismological equipment, and as soon as we were in the shade of the truck's interior I asked him what he thought had happened to David. "I suppose there's no chance that he's still alive?"

It didn't seem to surprise him that I'd made the suggestion. "Did you see my personal report to Erkhard, or was it some sort of a composite thing rehashed by the Bahrain office?" he asked.

"It was a general report," I told him.

"Aye, I thought so. They'll be letting the dust collect on mine in some pigeonhole. Can't blame them. I made it pretty plain what I thought." He hesitated, rubbing his hand across the ginger stubble on his chin. "A rum do, and no mistake. There was that truck half buried in sand and about forty miles from the nearest water-hole. And nothing wrong with the damned thing but lack of petrol. Even the spare jerry cans were empty."

"What are you suggesting?" I asked.

He hesitated. "I don't rightly know," he muttered, eying me cautiously. "But I know this," he added with sudden violence; "a chap like David doesn't drive into waterless desert with empty fuel cans. And to run out of juice just there . . . Except for the centre of the Empty Quarter, he couldn't have picked a spot that was much further from water." He stared at me and I think we were both thinking the same thing, for he said: "I'd like to know what his father thinks about it. In fact, when I've finished here I intend to drive over to Saraifa and see if the old Bedou knows . . ." He stopped and cocked his head on one side, listening. Faint through the noise of the drill came the distant sound of an engine. I didn't understand at first, but then it grew louder, overtopping the noise of the drill, and in a sudden panic of realization I dived for the door, just in time to see the plane become airborne.

It passed so low over the top of the truck that I instinctively ducked, and as I straightened up I was cursing myself for a fool. I should have known. I should have realized Gorde might want to get me out of the way. I turned furiously on Entwhistle, who was standing in the doorway of the truck looking slightly uncomfortable. "You knew about this?"

"Aye, he told me." He smiled a little doubtfully. "He asked me to give you his apologies for any inconvenience."

"God rot the old man!" I muttered savagely. To be caught like that, to be fooled into thinking he was just trying to be helpful, and all the time . . .

I stared at the plane, which was rapidly dwindling to a speck, feeling suddenly helpless, isolated out here in an oven-hot world that I didn't understand.

"A day or two, he said," Entwhistle murmured apologetically. "That's all. I'll try and make it as pleasant as possible."

The plane had altered course. I saw it circle once and then it was heading back towards us, and for a wild moment I thought perhaps he'd changed his mind. It came in low, flying slowly with the flaps down. But the undercarriage remained up. As it bumbled close over our heads something white fluttered down from the pilot's window. And then it turned and disappeared low over the dunes, and the sound of it was lost again in the noise of the drill.

Entwhistle was already running to retrieve the object they had dropped to us. He came back with a cigarette packet and a crumpled sheet of paper. "All right. You can stop drilling," he shouted. He repeated the order in Arabic, and as the drill slowed to an abrupt silence he handed me the paper. On it was written in pencil: *Stop drilling and proceed at once to Saraifa. Concentration of armed tribesmen camped in the dunes two miles north of you. Warn Sheikh Makhmud and give him my salaams. Philip Gorde.* A chill feeling crept up my spine as I read that message, and Entwhistle's comment did nothing to restore my morale. "Bit of luck, the Old Man flying down here."

He flipped the coin that Otto had used to weight the packet. "Mightn't have seen the sun rise tomorrow otherwise."

It came as a shock to me to realize that he was perfectly serious. "They would have attacked you?" I asked.

"Slit our throats, probably." He sounded quite cheerful.

"But—" I looked about me, at the dunes asleep in the heat of the day, the furnace-hot world of the desert all around me, quiet and peaceful. It was hard to believe. "But you're still on Saraifa territory," I said.

He shrugged. "The Emir would dispute that. And the political boys, all those bloody old Etonians—they don't want any trouble. My name's going to be mud." He stared down at the coin in his hand. And then he put it in his pocket and set about organizing the packing up of the outfit, leaving me standing there, feeling slightly lost, a stranger in a strange world.

IV

The Doomed Oasis

His crew were all Arab
and they went about the business of breaking camp noisily but
efficiently. They had done it many times. In fact, it seemed a
natural process out there amongst the dunes. They were mostly
young men, a colourful mixture of race and dress, their teeth
flashing white in their dark faces as they fooled around, making
light of the work. They were fit and full of life and laughter;
they had a football, which they kicked at each other periodically, the guttural Arab tongue coming in staccato bursts from
their lips.

There was nothing for me to do and I sat perched on the Land
Rover's mudguard, watching them and looking around me at the
surrounding country. There was a dune, I remember, that ran
away into the distance like the Prescelly Hills north of St.
David's. I was looking at it, thinking of holidays I had spent in
that part of Wales, and suddenly my eyes became riveted on a
dark speck that showed for an instant on its back. It vanished
almost immediately, so that I thought my eyes had played me
a trick. In that shimmering heat it was difficult to be sure. And
then it showed again, nearer this time. I could have sworn it was
a man moving below the crest of the dune. I was just on the
point of telling Entwhistle that he had a visitor when I was
jolted off my seat; the clang of metal against metal was followed
instantly by the crack of a rifle, and I was looking down at a hole
the size of my fist in the side of the Land Rover's hood.

For an instant everything was still. There was no sound, no

movement; Entwhistle and his Arabs just stood there, shocked into immobility, staring at that hole in the side of the Land Rover. Then Entwhistle shouted something. Rifles cracked from the top of the dune, little spurts of sand were kicked up round us. A bullet ricocheted off the truck's drill and went whining past my head. Entwhistle flung himself at the Land Rover. "Jump in!" he shouted. His crew were running for the truck. Another bullet smacked into the Land Rover, so close that the wind of it fanned my trouser legs, and then I heard shouts, saw men running towards us from the line of the dunes. The engines burst into life, drowning all other sounds. I dived for the seat beside Entwhistle as he slammed the Land Rover into gear. Two Arabs landed almost on top of me as the vehicle jerked forward. Behind us the truck was moving, too, and beyond its lumbering shape I caught a glimpse of long-haired tribesmen dropping on to their knees, aiming their rifles. But I never heard the shots. All I could hear was the revving of the engine as Entwhistle ran through the gears.

A moment later and we were clear, out of their range. The two Arabs sorted themselves out and I turned to Entwhistle. His foot was hard down on the accelerator and his lips were moving. "The bastards!" he was saying. "The bloody bastards!" And then he looked at me. "Dum-dum bullets." His face was white under the sunburn. "They cut them across to make them soft-nosed. Blow a hole in you the size of a barn door." It was this rather than the attack that seemed to outrage him.

"Who were they?" I asked and was shocked to find that I hadn't proper control over my voice.

"The Emir's men. They must have seen the plane turn back and realized we were being warned of their presence." He turned to make certain that the truck was following. "Fine introduction you've had to desert life." He grinned, but not very certainly. He shouted something in Arabic to the two men perched on the baggage behind and they answered him with a flood of words. Shortly afterwards he pulled up. The truck drew up beside us, its engine throbbing, excited Arab faces looking down at us, all talking at once.

He got out then and spoke to the driver, walked all round

the truck, and then came back and lifted the hood of the Land Rover. "Look at that," he said. I got out and my legs felt weak as I stared at the hole that first bullet had made. Little bits of lead were spattered all over the engine. "Bastards!" he said and slammed the hood shut. "Well, it might have been worse, I suppose. Nobody's hurt and the vehicles are all right."

It was only after we'd got moving again that I realized the windscreen in front of me was shattered. Little bits of glass were falling into my lap. I kept my eyes half closed until I had picked out all the bits. "How far is it to Saraifa?" I asked him.

"Not much more than forty miles by air." I gathered it was a good deal more the way we'd have to go, for the dunes ran southeast and we had to get east. "Might make it shortly after dark if we don't get bogged down too often."

It was just after four thirty then. We kept to the gravel flats between the dunes, travelling at almost thirty miles an hour. The air that came rushing in through the shattered windscreen was a hot, searing blast that scorched the face. The ground was hard as iron, criss-crossed with innumerable ridges, over which the Land Rover rattled in an endless series of back-breaking jolts.

In these circumstances conversation wasn't easy; the wind of our movement, the noise of the engine, the rattle of stones— we had to shout to make ourselves heard. And Entwhistle wasn't a talkative man. He'd lived on his own too much. Besides, he had a North Countryman's lack of imagination. He even used the word "humdrum" when I asked him about his job. And yet I got the impression that he loved it. But it was the job, not Arabia, he loved. He'd no feeling for the country or its people. More than once he used the contemptuous term "wogs" when speaking of the Arabs. But though he wouldn't talk about himself much, he was quite prepared to talk about David.

He had met him three times in all, once in Bahrain and then later when he was sick and David had relieved him. "Queer chap," he said. "Fact is, I didn't like him much when he came out to take over my outfit. But then," he added, "you don't like anybody very much when you're suffering from jaundice."

"But you felt differently about him later?" I prompted.

"Aye. Got to know him a bit better then. We were two days

together whilst we moved to a new location. Then he went off to Saraifa. He'd got some leave due and he was going to spend it mucking around with an old seismological truck his father had got hold of." I asked him what had made him change his mind about David, and he said: "Oh, the way he talked. He was a great talker. Mind you," he added, "he was still too chummy with the wogs for my liking, but you couldn't help admiring the chap. Wanted to make the desert blossom and all that."

"Water?" I asked.

He nodded. "That's it. He'd got a bee in his bonnet about it. Talked about Saraifa being doomed. Well, of course, it is. I've only been there once, but—well, you'll see for yourself. A few more years . . ." He didn't talk for a while after that, for we had come to soft sand; he took it fast, his foot pressed hard down on the accelerator, and we bucketed through it like a small boat in a seaway.

We came off the sand on to a hard gravel pan that scintillated with a myriad diamond gleams. "Mica," he shouted. The glare of it was dazzling. "You interested in geology?"

I shook my head.

"Pity." He seemed genuinely sorry. "Damned interesting country." For him there was nothing else of interest in Arabia. We bucked another stretch of sand ridged into shallow waves, and then he told me what had decided him to check David's survey report. Amongst the papers in that attaché case he had found Farr's report. "Didn't tell the Old Man. Thought I'd keep it in reserve. God knows where David dug it up. It was twenty years old, the paper all faded; the typing, too. Could hardly read the damned thing."

"Have you got it with you?" I asked.

"Aye." He nodded. "I wasn't going to leave that behind. I'll show it to you later. Can't think why the Company didn't do something about it."

"There was a war on," I said. "And Farr was killed in Abyssinia."

"You know about it, then?" He seemed surprised.

"David referred to it in his report."

"Oh, yes, of course."

We hit another patch of sand, a solid vista of it that stretched interminably ahead of us. We didn't talk much after that. It was soft sand and the going was tough. Twice the seismological truck got bogged down and we had to lay sand-mats. The sun sank slowly down into the desert behind us as we ploughed on, engines roaring, radiators steaming. We were in big-dune country that was like a huge, petrified sea, the waves coming up one after the other, yet never moving, always motionless, and the shadows lengthening behind them. It had an eerie, still quality; and it left me with a sense of awe, for it had a certain majesty, a cruel, lost quality that was unnerving. Once I shouted: "Is it like this all the way to Saraifa?"

"Christ! I hope not," he yelled back.

"But don't you know?" I asked.

"How the hell should I? Never been here before."

The sun set, a brick-red ball of fire hazed, it seemed, with dust. Here and there we came upon the derelict remains of trees, gnarled and twisted in a life-long struggle against crippling odds. Dusk descended swiftly and the light faded out of the dunes. Behind us they stood like downlands etched sharp against the sky's last light. Above us the stars suddenly appeared. Again the truck behind us became bogged and we dug the sand-mats down in front of the wheels and pushed and strained to gain a few yards. And when at last we got it moving there was no light left and it was dark.

"Will you be able to find Saraifa in the dark?" I asked Entwhistle.

"*Inshallah,*" he said, and we pushed on.

How he did it I don't know, but about an hour later the dunes became smaller, the stunted tree-growth more noticeable, and then suddenly we ran out on to hard gravel again. And shortly after that the headlights picked up the first of the date-gardens, a sad relic of a once fertile place, the walls no longer visible, just the starved tops of the palms sticking up out of the sand.

We passed between two of these ruined gardens and then we joined a well-worn track where the sand had been ground to a fine powder; there were the marks of tires, the droppings of camels. The headlights picked out the round bulk of a watch-tower with men running from it, their guns gleaming with silver furnishings. Entwhistle slowed as they stood barring our path. They wore turbans and long white robes, and strapped across their shoulders was a sort of harness of leather studded with the brass of cartridges; stuffed into their belts were the broad, curved-bladed *khanjar* knives, the hilts of silver glinting wickedly. As we stopped they came swarming over us, enveloping us with their harsh guttural speech, all talking at once, white teeth flashing in villainous dark faces.

"What do they want?" A black-bearded ruffian had the muzzle of his gun jammed against the side of my neck, and though I tried to keep my voice under control, I don't think I was very successful.

"All right, all right," Entwhistle was shouting at them. "One at a time, for God's sake." He didn't seem the least bit scared. Finally, after a long conversation with my bearded friend, he said: "It looks like trouble. We're more or less under arrest." He spoke to the bearded Arab again and then he was ordering men on to the Land Rover and others to the truck behind. "It seems," he said as we moved off, "that Sheikh Makhmud sent a party out in two Land Rovers this afternoon to arrest my outfit and bring me back to Saraifa for questioning." And he added: "This could be the sort of thing David came up against. They're scared stiff of the Emir and frightened to death of any activity on the Hadd border."

"Didn't you know that before you decided to run a survey there?" I asked.

"Of course I did. But I was reckoning to run the survey and get out before any one discovered I was there." He crashed the gears savagely. "I took a chance and it didn't come off, that's all."

We skirted the crumbling wall of a date-garden. The palms were green here, the gardens uninvaded by the desert sand. And then suddenly we were in the open, driving on hard gravel, and straight ahead of us, a black bulk against the stars, was the shadowy shape of the Sheikh's palace standing like a fortress on its hill. The wooden gate of the arched entrance was closed, but it opened to the cries of our guards, and then we were inside, in a great courtyard packed with men and camels and lit by the flames of cooking-fires. In an instant we were surrounded, lapped round by a tide of men, all shouting and brandishing their weapons.

A big, portly man appeared, his face black as a Sudanese. "The Sheikh's secretary," Entwhistle said to me. He looked like a eunuch, fat and soft, his manner almost feminine. He gave orders for the care of the men and then escorted us into the palace, along dark corridors sparsely lit by smoking lamps made out of old cans, to a small room that looked out on to a central courtyard. Here the earthen floor was carpeted with rugs, the walls lined with cushions; an Arab rose to greet us. He was a compact, stocky man with almost black eyes and a proudly curved nose. The *khanjar* knife stuck in the girdle of his finely woven robe was a beautiful example of the silversmith's craft. "Sheikh Makhmud," Entwhistle whispered.

I found my hand held in a firm grip. "You are welcome to Saraifa," the Sheikh said in halting English. "My house is your house." He had an air of command, yet his voice was gentle. But the thing that surprised me most was the fact that he wore glasses. They were silver-rimmed glasses and they drew attention to the blackness of his eyes. His clean-shaven face was long and tired-looking. He was a man about Gorde's age, I suppose. The other occupant of the room had also risen, a thin man with a greying moustache and a little pointed beard, his eyes heavily made-up with *kohl*. He was Makhmud's brother, Sultan.

We sat cross-legged on the cushions and there was nothing in the Sheikh's manner to indicate that we were anything but honoured guests. Polite conversation was made, partly in the Arab language, partly in English. Slaves came with a silver jug and a silver ewer. We washed our hands, and then they brought in a simple dish of rice and mutton. "You eat with your right hand," Entwhistle whispered to me, and I tried to copy his practised movements.

I was hungry enough not to care that the meat was stringy and over-fat. We ate almost in silence, and when we had finished, the hand-washing was repeated and then coffee was served in little handleless cups, poured by a slave from a silver pot of intricate native design. And with the coffee came the questions. Sheikh Makhmud's voice was no longer gentle. It had a harsh, imperious quality, and Entwhistle was soon in difficulties with the language, lapsing periodically into English as he tried to explain his presence on the Saraifa-Hadd border. In the end he passed Sheikh Makhmud the note Gorde had written.

Entwhistle had just launched into an account of the attack that had been made on us when a young man entered. He was short, well-built, and beneath his brown cloak he wore an old tweed jacket. But it was the features that caught the eye; they were delicate, almost classic features, the nose straight, the eyes set wide apart, with high cheekbones and the full lips framed by a neatly trimmed moustache that flowed round the corners and down into a little pointed beard. He looked as though he had just come in from the desert, and I knew instinctively that this was Khalid, the Sheikh's son; he had an air about him that showed he was born to command.

He greeted his father and his uncle, waved us to remain seated, and folded himself up on a cushion against the wall. The brass of cartridge belt, the silver of *khanjar* knife gleamed beneath the jacket. He sat in silence, listening intently, his body so still that I was given the impression of great muscular control—a hard-sinewed body below the Arab robes.

There was a long silence when Entwhistle had finished. And then Sheikh Makhmud made what sounded like a pronouncement, and Entwhistle exclaimed: "Good God! I'm not going to do that." He turned to me. "He wants us to go to the Emir and explain that we were on the border without authority."

"You go freely," Sheikh Makhmud said in English. "Or you go with escort. Which you prefer?"

Entwhistle didn't say anything. His face was set and pale.

"Is very difficult, this situation," the Sheikh said almost apologetically. "Very dangerous also. You must make the Emir understand, please."

"Very dangerous for us, too," Entwhistle muttered angrily.

"I don't want any trouble."

"You want oil, don't you?"

"Colonel Whitaker is already drilling for oil."

"Then what was his son doing on the Hadd border?" Entwhistle demanded. "He ran a survey there. He wrote a report. And then he vanished." There was no answer. "Khalid. You were his friend. What happened to him?"

But Khalid was staring out into the courtyard.

In the silence I heard myself say: "He got a letter through to me just before he disappeared. He knew he was going to die." I felt them stiffen, the silence suddenly intense. I looked at Khalid. "Did he die a natural death?" His eyes met mine for a moment and then fell away. "Somebody here must know how he died—and why."

Nobody answered, and the stillness of those three Arabs scared me. It was the stillness of unease. "Where's Colonel Whitaker?" I asked.

The Sheikh stirred uncomfortably. "You are full of questions. Who are you?"

Briefly I explained. I was still explaining when there was a sudden uproar in the passage outside and a man burst into the room, followed closely by the Sheikh's secretary. A staccato burst of Arabic and they were all suddenly on their feet. I heard the world *falaj* run from mouth to mouth, saw Khalid rush out, quick as a cat on his feet. His father followed more slowly, the others crowding behind him.

"What is it?" I asked Entwhistle. "What's happened?"

"One of the *falajes*. I don't know exactly, but for some reason the water has stopped."

We were alone now. Everybody had forgotten about us. It was as though that word had some sort of magic in it. "What exactly is a *falaj*?" He didn't seem to hear me, and I repeated the question.

"*Falaj*?" He seemed to drag his mind back. "Oh, it's the water system on which the date-gardens depend. The water comes from the mountains of the Jebel anything up to thirty miles away and it's piped into Saraifa by underground channels."

"And the underground channels are the *falajes*?"

"Yes, that's it. They're centuries old—a Persian irrigation system. In fact, they're the same as the Persian *qanats*." He went to the passage and stood listening. "Bit of luck," he said, dropping his voice to a whisper. "If we can get hold of the Land Rover . . ." He grabbed hold of my arm. "Come on."

I followed him down the dimly lit mud corridors and out into the courtyard. The cooking-fires still smoked. The camels still crouched in a shapeless, belching huddle under the walls. But in the whole courtyard there wasn't a single Arab to be seen.

"Look! Even the guard on the gate has gone."

"But why?" I asked. "Why should that word—"

"Water. Don't you understand?" He sounded impatient. "Water is life here in the desert."

"But they can't depend on one channel. There must be many to irrigate a place like this."

"Five or six, that's all." He was searching the courtyard. "There used to be more than a hundred once. But tribal wars . . ." He gripped my arm. "There's the Land Rover. Over by the wall there." He pointed. "Come on! There's just a chance. . . ."

"What's the idea?" I asked.

"Get out whilst the going's good. Hurry, man!" His voice was high-pitched, urgent. "I'm not risking my neck on a mission of explanation to that bloody Emir." He had seized hold of my arm again. "Quick!"

I started to follow him, but then I stopped. "I'm staying," I said.

"Christ, man! Do you want to get killed?"

"No, but I want to find out why that boy was killed."

He stared at me. "You think it was like that—that he was murdered?"

"I don't know," I said. I didn't know anything for certain. "But I'm not leaving here until I've seen Colonel Whitaker."

He hesitated. But then he shrugged his shoulders. "Okay. It's your funeral, as you might say. But watch your step," he added. "He's a tricky bastard, by all accounts. And if what you're suggesting is true and David was murdered, then your life wouldn't be worth much, would it?"

"I'll be all right," I said.

"Aye, I hope so. But just remember you're right on the edge of Saudi Arabia here and the British Raj is worn a bit thin in these parts." He hesitated, looking at me, and then he started towards the Land Rover.

I stood and watched him, certain I was being a fool, but equally certain that I wasn't leaving. I saw him jump into the driving-seat, heard the whine of the starter, the roar of the engine. And then the Land Rover was moving and he swung it round and came tearing towards me. "Jump in, Grant," he shouted as he pulled up beside me. "Hurry, man! Hurry!"

"No," I said. "I'm not leaving." My voice was like the voice of a stranger to me. "You get out whilst you can. I'll be all right." And I added: "I'll make your excuses to the Sheikh for you." I meant it to be a jocular, carefree remark, but my voice sounded hollow. He was still hesitating and I said quickly: "Good luck to you!"

He stared at me hard and then he gave a little nod. "Okay. I expect you'll be all right. I'll notify the authorities, of course." And he slammed in the gear and went roaring across the courtyard and out through the empty gateway. The cloud of dust he'd raised gradually settled, and I walked to the gate and stood there watching his headlights threading a luminous trail through the date-gardens. And when they finally disappeared in the open desert beyond, I went slowly down the hill, heading for the murmur of voices, the glimmer of lights amongst the palms beyond the village.

I was alone then—more alone than I'd ever been in my life before.

The moon was just risen, and with the stars the village was lit by a soft translucence. The mud buildings were pale and empty, the open square deserted save for the hens nested in the dust and a solitary sad-looking donkey. Beyond the village I followed the crumbling wall of a date-garden until I came out into the open again. All Saraifa seemed gathered there, the men bunched together like a crowd at a cock-fight, the women dark bundles flitting on the edge of the crowd or squatting like hens in the sand. Everybody was talking at once, a thick hubbub of sound that seemed to lose itself instantly in the great solitude of the desert that stretched away to the east, to the dim-seen line of the mountains.

Nobody took any notice of me as I skirted the crowd. It was thickest close by the date-garden. Out towards the desert it thinned, and here I found a raised water channel built of rock and spanning a hollow aqueduct that might have been built by the Romans. It was my first sight of a *falaj,* and it was empty. I leaned over it, touched the inside with my fingers. It was still damp, and in a little puddle of water at the bottom tiny fish flashed silver in the starlight as they gasped for breath. Clearly, the water had only recently ceased to flow, turned off as though by a tap.

Fascinated, I crossed the hollow to the far side. For perhaps twenty yards the *falaj* was open, a neat, vertical-sided trench running a black shadow line across the sand. It was about two feet across and the same deep. I walked along it to the point where it was roofed over. For a hundred yards or so I could trace the outline of it, but after that the sand swallowed it up entirely. From a slight rise I looked towards the mountains. Anything up to thirty miles, Entwhistle had said, and they were the source of the water.

I walked slowly back along the line of the *falaj* to the point where it broke surface, and at the sight of the empty trough with the little fish gasping out their lives I could understand the calamity of it, the sense of disaster that had seized upon the people of this channel-fed oasis. A dry *falaj* meant a ruined date-garden, the beginnings of famine. Only five or six left out of more than a hundred, tribal wars . . . The place was as vulnerable as an oil refinery fed by a desert pipeline. Cut the *falaj* and Saraifa ceased to exist.

The sound of male voices died away, leaving only the high-pitched chatter of the women; there was a stillness of decision as I approached the crowd gathered about the *falaj* channel where it entered the date-garden. In the centre stood Sheikh Makhmud and his brother Sultan. Khalid was facing them, arguing fiercely. His features had no trace of effeminacy in them now. From the skirts of the crowd I saw Sheikh Makhmud turn impatiently away from his son. He called a man forth by name —Mahommed bin Rashid, a fierce, hawkfaced man with a black beard, the one who had stopped us as we entered Saraifa. He

gave him an order, and a long "*A-a-agh*" of satisfaction issued
from the throats of the crowd. Instantly all was confusion. Men
brandished their weapons, calling on Allah, as a dozen or more
of them were singled out and went hurrying back to the palace.
Sheikh Makhmud turned and with his brother and his secretary
followed them slowly.

It was the signal for the crowd to break up, and as they strag-
gled away from the empty *falaj* Khalid was left standing there
alone. A few men only remained, a little, compact group of silent
followers ranged behind him. They were different from the rest
in that their arms were without any silver trappings; they carried British service-pattern rifles.

He stood for a long time without moving, staring after his
father and the crowd that followed him, noisy now with the excitement of action. And when they had disappeared from sight
he turned to his men with a gesture of dismissal and they, too,
moved away, but still silent, still in a compact group. He was
completely alone then, staring down at the empty water channel, lost in his own thoughts. Even when I approached him he
didn't stir. I don't think he knew I was there, for when I asked
him whether he spoke English, he turned to me with a start of
surprise.

"A little English—yess." His speech was slightly sibilant, his
features marred when he opened his mouth by long, widely
spaced teeth. "I am at Bombay University, my education." He
was staring up the hill towards the palace, his mind still on
what had happened. "They think they are being brave and that
I am afraid. They don't understand." His tone was bitter and
angry. "Their guns are very much old, and the men of Hadd
will be waiting for them."

I asked whether it was Hadd who had stopped the water
supply, and he said: "Yess. They perpetrate it once before. Then
the British help us. Your people send soldiers with automatic
guns and mortars. But not now. This time we are alone." He
turned and I saw his dark eyes, sad in the starlight. "The *falajes*,
you understand, sir, are very much vulnerable." He had ac-
quired the Indian penchant for long words. And he added with
great determination, speaking slowly as though stating some-

thing to himself: "We must fight for them now. But not like this. This way is to die." He began to walk slowly towards the palace.

There were many things I wanted to ask him, but this didn't seem the moment, and I walked beside him in silence, conscious of his preoccupation. His head was bent and he moved slowly, his sandals dragging in the sand. He was only two years older than David. I learned that later. Yet his manner was that of a man upon whom the whole responsibility for this desert community rested.

"Do you know Arabia much, sir?" he asked suddenly. And when I told him this was my first visit and that I'd only arrived a few days ago, he nodded and said: "You are from a town called Car-diff, yess? David speak of you sometimes."

That mention of Cardiff, the knowledge that this young Arab knew who I was . . . Saraifa seemed suddenly less remote, my position here less solitary.

"When David first come here, he is like you; he speak Arabic a little, but he don't understand our customs or the way we live here in the desert. The *falajes* mean nothing to him and he has never seen the big dunes when the *shamal* is blowing." He had stopped and he was smiling at me. Despite the wide-spaced, fang-like teeth, it was a gentle smile. "I am glad you come now." He offered me his hand and I found my wrist gripped and held in a strong clasp. "You are David's friend, and I will see that no harm come to you."

I thanked him, conscious that he had given me the opening I needed. But already I was becoming vaguely aware of the subtlety of the Arab mind, and this time I was determined not to make the mistake of asking direct questions. Sue's words came unconsciously into my mind: *David wanted to defend Saraifa, too.* I saw his face soften as he nodded, and I asked: "What was it about this place that so captured his imagination? His sister said he could be very emotional about it."

"His sister?" He smiled. "I have seen his sister once, when I am taking a plane at Sharjah. She is with the doctor, and I do not speak. A very fine person, I think."

I knew then that David had spoken of Sue to Khalid. "What is there about Saraifa," I said, "that he fell in love with it the way other men do with a woman?"

He shrugged. "He came here for refuge and we made him welcome. Also his father live here. It became his home."

But that didn't explain it entirely. "It was something more than that," I said.

"Yess." He nodded. "Is a very strange chap. A *Nasrani*—a Christian. He live very much by your Book, the Bible." That surprised me, but before I could make any comment, he added: "I should hate him because he is an infidel. Instead, I love him like my own brother." He shook his head with a puzzled frown. "Perhaps it is because I have to teach him everything. When he first come here, he knows nothing—he has never hunted, never owned a hawk; he does not know how to ride a camel or how to make a camp in the desert. For six months we are living together, here in Saraifa, in the desert hunting, up in the mountains shooting wild hare and gazelle. But he is very good with machines, and later, when he is on leave from the oil company and we are working for the reconstruction of one of the old *falajes*, then he spend all his time down in the underground channels with the family who specialize in that work. You see, sir, this oasis is one time very much bigger, with very many *falajes* bringing water to the date-gardens. Then Saraifa is rich. Richer than Buraimi to the north. Richer perhaps even than the Wadi Hadhramaut to the south. It is, I think, the richest place in all Arabia. But nobody can remember that time. Now it is . . ." He stopped abruptly, his head on one side, listening.

And then I heard it, too—the soft pad-pad of camels' feet on gravel. Down the slope towards us came a bunch of camels moving with that awkward, lumbering gait. A dozen dark shapes swayed past us, the riders kneeling in the saddles, their robes flying, their rifles held in their hands. For an instant they were like paper cut-outs painted black against the stars, beautiful, balanced silhouettes. Then they were gone and the pad of their camels' feet faded away into the sand as they headed towards the mountains.

"*Wallahi, qalilet-el-mukh!*" Khalid muttered as he stared after them. And then to me: "That man, Mahommed bin Rashid. You heard him when my father give the order. *Inshallah*, he said, we will kill every harlot's son of them. But he is more like to die himself, I think." And he turned away, adding as he strode angrily up the hill: "Allah give him more brain in the world hereafter."

The sight of that handful of men riding east into the desert along the line of the *falaj* had changed his mood. He was preoccupied, and though I tried to resume our conversation, he didn't speak to me again until we reached the gates of the palace. Abruptly he asked me what sleeping quarters I had been allotted. And when I told him none, he said: "Then I arrange it. Excuse my father, please. He is very much occupied." He asked about Entwhistle. "Good," he said when I told him he'd gone. "He is not a fool, that man. He knows when it is dangerous." And he added: "It would have been better perhaps if you had gone with him."

"I'm not leaving here," I said, "until I know what happened to David."

There was a moment then when he hesitated as though about to tell me something. But all he said was: "Is best you talk to his father—*Haj* Whitaker."

"I intend to," I said. And when I asked him whether Colonel Whitaker was in Saraifa, he replied: "I don't know. He has his house here, but is most times at the place of drilling."

"And where's that?"

"To the south of 'ere, about ten miles towards Sheikh Hassa's village of Dhaid."

We had entered the great courtyard. A man sidled up to us, made his salaams to Khalid. He was dark and toothy, with a ragged wisp of a turban on his head, and his eyes watched me curiously as the two men talked together. My name was mentioned, and finally Khalid turned to me. "Now all is arranged. Yousif speak a little English. He will show you where you sleep." His hand gripped my arm. "Ask *Haj* Whitaker why he goes to see the Emir of Hadd almost two moons past. Ask him that, Meester Grant." It was whispered to me, his lips close against my ear and a hard, angry glint in his eyes.

But before I could question him he had drawn back. He said something to Yousif and with a quick *salaam alaikum* he left

me, moving quickly through the camp-fires, the only man in all
that throng who wore a European jacket.

"Come!" Yousif seized hold of my hand. Heads were turned
now in my direction, and here and there a man got up from
the fireside and began to move towards us. I had no desire to
stay there, an object of curiosity. Yousif guided me through dark
passages and up to a turret room by a winding staircase where
the plaster steps were worn smooth as polished marble by the
tread of many feet. The floor was bare earth, the roof beamed
with palm-tree boles. A slit of a window no bigger than a firing-
embrasure looked out on to the flat, beaten expanse of the village square. I was in one of the mud towers of the outer wall,
and here he left me with no light but the glimmer of moonlight
filtering in through the embrasure.

Strange, disembodied sounds drifted up to me on the warm
night air: the murmur of Arab voices, the grunt of camels, a
child crying—and in the distance the weird chuckle of a hyena.
I knelt on the firing-step, peering down. Beyond the mud houses
I could see the darker mass of the palms. Bare feet sounded on
the turret stairs and the yellow light of a hurricane lamp appeared; the room was suddenly full of armed men bearing bed-
ding, which they laid on the floor—a carpet, some blankets, an
oryx skin, and a silken cushion. "May Allah guard you," Yousif
said, "and may your sleep be as the sleep of a little child."

He was halfway through the door before I realized what that
long speech in English must mean. "You're Colonel Whitaker's
man, aren't you?"

He checked and turned. "Yes, sahib. Me driver for Coll-onell."
He was staring at me, his eyes very wide so that the whites
showed yellow in the lamplight. "I tell Coll-onell you are here
in Sheikh's palace." He was gone then.

There was no doubt in my mind that he'd been sent to find
me. Whitaker was in Saraifa, and Khalid had known it as soon
as Yousif had sidled up to us. I sat down on the silken cushion,
staring blindly at that cell-like room. There was nothing to do
now but wait. I felt tired; dirty, too. But I'd no water with which
to wash. No soap, no clothes—nothing but what I was wearing.
Yousif had left me the hurricane lamp, and its light reached

dimly to the palm-wood rafters. A large desert spider moved among them with deliberation. I watched it for a long time as it went about its unpleasant business, and finally I killed it, overcome with a fellow-feeling for the flies caught in its web. And then I put out the lamp and rolled myself up in a blanket.

It was hot, but I must have fallen asleep, for I didn't hear Yousif return; he was suddenly there, his torch stabbing the darkness, almost blinding me.

"Coll-onell say you come."

I sat up, glancing at my watch. It was past eleven thirty. "Now?"

"Yes, now."

Down in the courtyard the fires were almost out, the Sheikh's retainers lying like corpses wrapped in their robes. A few stirred as we crossed to the gate, now barred and guarded; a brief argument and then I was in a battered Land Rover being driven at reckless speed across the deserted village square, down into the date-gardens. Behind us the palace fort stood bone-white in the moonlight, and then the palms closed round us.

Whitaker's house was an old mud fort on the far side of the oasis. Most of it seemed to be in ruins, the courtyard empty, the mud walls cracked and crumbling. There was sand everywhere as we hurried through a maze of passages and empty rooms. The place seemed dead, and I wondered that a man could live alone like this and retain his sanity, for he seemed to have no servants but Yousif and to live in Spartan simplicity in one corner of this vast, rambling building.

We came at last to a room where old portmanteaus and tin boxes stood ranged against the walls, and then I was out on a rooftop that looked out upon the desert. He was standing against the parapet, a tall, robed figure in silhouette, for there was no light there, only the moon and the stars. Yousif coughed and announced my presence.

Whitaker turned then and came towards me. His face was in shadow, but I could see the black patch over the eye. No word of greeting, no attempt to shake my hand. "Sit down," he said and waved imperiously to a carpet and some cushions spread on the floor. "Yousif. *Gahwa*." His servant disappeared,

and as I sat down I was conscious of the stillness all about us
—no sound of Arab voices, none of the tumult of the Sheikh's
palace, no murmur of the village below the walls. The place
was as isolated, as deserted as though we were the only people
in the whole oasis.

He folded himself up, cross-legged on the carpet facing me,
and I could see his face then, the beard thinning and grey, the
cheeks hollowed and lined by the desert years, that single imperious eye deep-sunken above the great nose. "You had a good
journey, I trust." His voice was oddly pitched, hard but unusu-
ally high, and he spoke the words slowly, as though English
were no longer a familiar language.

"It was interesting," I said.

"No doubt. But quite unnecessary. It was clearly understood
between us that you would make no attempt to contact me direct. And though I admit the financial situation must have
seemed—"

"I came about your son," I said.

"My son?" He looked surprised. "Your letter merely said you
were worried about the amount of money I was spending."

"Your son appointed me his executor."

He moved his head slightly, the eye glinting in the moonlight, bright and watchful. He didn't say anything. Behind him
the low parapet hid the desert, so that all I could see was the
great vault of the night studded with stars. The air was deathly
still, impregnated with the day's heat.

"I'm not convinced your son died a natural death." I hadn't
meant to put it like that. It was his stillness, the overpowering
silence that had forced it out of me.

He made no comment and I knew that this was going to be
more difficult than my interview with Erkhard, more difficult
even than my meeting with Gorde, and some sixth sense warned
me that this man was much more unpredictable. The clatter
of cups came as a distinct relief. Yousif moved, silent as a
shadow, on to the rooftop and poured us coffee from a battered
silver pot. The cups were handleless, the Mocha coffee black
and bitter.

"Does his mother know he's dead?" It surprised me that Whitaker should think of her; and when I told him that I'd broken the news to her myself, he asked: "How did she take it?"

"She didn't believe it at first." And because I had an overwhelming desire to break through his strange aura of calm, I added: "In fact, she seemed to think it was your own death I was reporting."

"Why? Why did she think I was dead?"

"The stars," I said. "She believes in astrology."

He sighed. "Yes, I remember now. I used to talk to her about the stars." And he added: "It's a long time ago. A long time."

"Do you believe in astrology, then?" I asked.

He shrugged, sipping noisily at his coffee. "Here in the desert we live a great deal by the stars. It is very difficult not to believe that they have some influence." And then, abruptly changing the conversation: "How did you get here? It's not easy to get to Saraifa." I started to tell him, but as soon as I mentioned Gorde, he said: "Philip Gorde? I didn't know he was out here." It seemed to upset him. "Did he tell you why he was here?" He mistook my silence. "No, of course not. He'd hardly tell you that." He shook his cup at Yousif to indicate that he'd had enough, and when I did the same the man departed as silently as he had come, leaving a dish of some sticky sweetmeat between us. "*Halwa*. Do you like it?" Whitaker made a vague gesture of invitation.

"I've never tried it."

We were alone again now and the silence between us hung heavy as the thick night air, a blanket through which each tried to gauge the other. I let it drag out, and it was Whitaker who finally broke it. "You were telling me about your journey." He stared at me, waiting for me to continue. I broke off a piece of the *halwa*. It was cloying on the tongue and it had a sickly-sweet taste. "You arrived here with Entwhistle, one of the Company's geologists. What was he doing on the Hadd border, do you know? The fellow had no business there."

"He was checking your son's survey," I said.

There was a sudden stillness. "I see." He said it quietly. And then, in a voice that was suddenly trembling with anger: "On whose orders? Not Philip Gorde's, surely?"

"No."

"Erkhard?"

"You seem very worried about this."

"Worried!" The word seemed forced out of him. "Don't you understand what's happened here tonight? The thing I've been dreading . . . The thing I've been trying to avoid ever since I knew . . ." He checked himself. And then in a quieter voice: "No, you're new out here. You wouldn't understand. One of the *falajes* has been stopped. And all because of this blundering fool Entwhistle running a survey on the Hadd border." His voice had risen again, trembling with anger.

"He was doing what David was doing at the time he disappeared," I said quietly.

But it didn't seem to register. He had withdrawn into his own thoughts. "Twenty years . . ." His voice sounded tired. And then his eye was staring at me again. "How would you feel if the thing you'd worked for over a period of twenty years was in danger of being ruined by young fools too impatient to understand the politics of the desert?" He turned his head and stared for a moment into the night. "The air is heavy. There'll be a storm soon." He gathered his robes about him and rose to his feet, crossing to the parapet and leaning against it, staring out into the desert like some Biblical figure from the distant past. "Come here, Grant." And when I joined him, he stretched out his arm. "Look, do you see those dunes?" He gripped my arm, pointing west into the desert.

Standing on that rooftop was like standing on the bridge of a ship lying anchored off a low-lying island. To the left lay the dark-treed expanse of the oasis, and beyond the date-gardens I could see the village and the squat bulk of the Sheikh's palace standing on its gravel rise. But to the right, where his arm pointed, was nothing but desert. Dim in the moonlight the dunes stretched away into infinity, a ridged sea of sand, pale as milk.

"When you've seen a storm here you'll understand. Then all the desert seems in motion, like the sea beating against the shore of the oasis, flooding into the date-gardens. The dunes smoke. They stream with sand. They're like waves breaking; the whole great desert of the Empty Quarter thundering in, the sand flowing like water." He turned to me and his grip on my arm tightened. "The only thing that stands between Saraifa and destruction is the camel thorn. Out there—do you see? Those trees. They're like a breakwater holding the sand sea back, and they're dying for lack of water."

"The *falajes?*" I asked, and he nodded. "Entwhistle said there used to be around a hundred of them."

"Yes. We've traced them from aerial photographs."

"Your son was very much concerned about—"

"Oh, yes, concerned . . . But he lacked patience. He was like a young bull. No subtlety. No subtlety at all." And he added: "What's been done tonight can be quickly repaired. There's an open well every mile or so along the length of the underground channel of the *falaj*. They've blocked one of these wells with sand and stone. It can be unblocked almost as quickly. But the old *falajes* . . ." He shook his head. "The wells are fallen in, the underground channels collapsed. Restoring them is a lengthy and costly business. Sheikh Makhmud has managed to restore just one in the fourteen years he's been Sheikh of Saraifa. It took two years and cost more than twenty thousand pounds. If Saraifa is to survive . . ." He gave a little shrug. "We need a dozen new *falajes*, not one."

"And only oil will pay for them?"

He nodded. "Yes."

"David took the same view," I said. "That's why he was prospecting on the Hadd border." And I added: "What happened, Colonel Whitaker? What happened to your son?"

He turned and looked at me. "You think I should know?"

"I've come a long way," I said, "in the certainty that you must know."

His eyebrows lifted, the single eye stared at me, not blinking. "The certainty?"

"Yes," I said. "The certainty." And I added: "He was on loan to you at the time he disappeared. It was the seismological truck you purchased in Basra last June that he left abandoned on the side of a dune twenty miles inside the borders of Saudi Arabia.

And just before he disappeared, you visited the Emir of Hadd.
You must know what happened."

"Well, I don't." He said it flatly, and it was difficult not to
accept it.

"Then why did you visit Hadd?"

"Who else could do it?" And he added: "David was on the
Hadd border against my orders—against Sheikh Makhmud's orders, too. Somebody had to try and convince the Emir there
wasn't any oil there."

"Because the border's in dispute."

"Yes. There's been trouble there ever since the Company was
first granted a concession to prospect in Saraifa. As you probably
know, Saraifa is an independent sheikhdom. Unlike the Trucial
States, it's not even in treaty relation with the British Crown,
though it's generally considered to be a part of the British sphere
of influence. Hadd is different again. It's independent in theory
and in fact, and during the last few years it has strengthened its
ties with Arab countries. Some years back we were finally driven
to sending troops in, to keep the peace, and they occupied the
fort of Jebel al-Akhbar overlooking the town of Hadd. But we
couldn't do that now. It would be much too dangerous." He
hesitated, and then he added: "The risk would only be justified
if vital interests of our own were involved."

"What sort of vital interests?" I asked. But I knew the answer
before he gave it.

"Oil," he said. "From a Western point of view—as you'd
know if you'd been out here any length of time—everything in
Arabia comes back to oil."

"Your son's death, too?" I asked. He looked at me, but didn't
say anything. "When did you first hear he was missing?"

"Towards the end of February."

"Could you give me a date?"

He frowned and for a moment I thought he wasn't going to
answer that. But then he said: "I can't be certain. Your calendar
doesn't mean very much to us out here in the desert. But by the
moon it would be about the beginning of the last week in February."

Almost a week before the abandoned truck had been found

by the Bedouin, more than three weeks before his disappearance had been reported to the Company. "You didn't notify Erkhard."

"No."

"Why not? David was in the Company's employ, even if he was on loan to you."

He didn't say anything. He seemed suddenly to have withdrawn inside himself. I think perhaps he was waiting for my next question, knowing it was coming.

"The truck was discovered abandoned on February twenty-eight," I said. "Yet you say you knew he was missing almost a week before that. How did you know?"

There was a long pause. At length he said: "Some askari were dispatched from Saraifa. When they reached his camp they found it deserted, not a soul there; the truck and the Land Rover had gone, too."

"Askari?"

"Members of Sheikh Makhmud's bodyguard. Their orders were to arrest him and bring him back to Saraifa."

"Alive?"

"Of course." He stared at me angrily. "What other instructions do you imagine they would be given? They were dispatched by Sheikh Makhmud—at my request. That was immediately after my return from Hadd." And he added: "It was done for his own good—and because it was necessary. The Emir was in a very dangerous mood."

So that was how it had been. "And you didn't want Erkhard to know that he'd been operating on the Hadd border?"

"I didn't want Erkhard to know and I didn't want the political boys to know. As I've said, David was there against my express orders. God Almighty!" he breathed. "The impatience of youth! They want the moon for breakfast and the sun for lunch." He leaned on the parapet, staring down to the white sand below. "I blame myself," he said quietly. "I should have packed him off back to Cardiff. Instead, I let him stay. More, I tried to think of him as my son, as God's gift from my loins, a prodigal given back into my hands." He shook his head. "I should have known it wouldn't work."

He paused there and I didn't say anything, for I felt his isolation here might trap him into some self-revelation if I didn't try to force it. He looked at me again, the desert lines deep-etched by the moon, a long, sad, solitary face. "As you know, I'm a Muslim. I wanted him to become a Muslim, too. I wanted him to make the desert his home and to carry on where I left off in due course." He sighed softly. "I forgot the boy was already nineteen, and only half mine . . . and that half as obstinate as the devil." He smiled. In that harsh face it was a smile of extraordinary tenderness. "I turned him into a Christian instead." He said it with bitterness, adding: "In the end I think he came to hate me."

"Why?"

The question was out before I could stop myself, and I saw him freeze and close up on me. "People get at cross-purposes, you know." His tone was casual now. "It's one of the sad things about human relationships. But there . . . No point in talking about it now. The boy's dead, and that's that."

"You can't be sure of that," I said.

He stared at me, his eye blazing in the darkness. "What do you mean? I had all the chaps I could spare out looking for him. Khalid was searching, too, and Makhmud had men hunting for him all over Saraifa. The one place we never thought of searching was west into the Empty Quarter." And he said, with gentleness, softly to himself: "The desert is like the sea. No man can disappear into it for two months and come out alive."

"All right," I said. "He's dead. But if you haven't discovered what happened to him, what do you think happened to him?"

His eye looked into mine. "Have you ever been frightened?"

"Yes, once," I said. "In Tanganyika."

He nodded. "Then you'll understand me when I say no man knows how he'll react to fear until he's faced with it. Especially when he's alone. And David was alone. His Arab crew had deserted him. We found that out later. They panicked."

"And you think David did the same?"

He shrugged. "It's a cruel place, the desert. And solitary as hell. Empty, too. Even in company the Bedou sing to keep their spirits up." It was much what Griffiths had said, and it seemed

plausible enough. He took my arm and led me back to the carpet. "You were telling me about your journey. . . ."

I told him as much as I thought he'd a right to know—about
the package Griffiths had brought me and my meeting with Erkhard. But it was Gorde he was really interested in—Gorde and
Entwhistle and the fact that the two of them had been together
at the locations David had been surveying. It seemed to worry
him, and he questioned me closely about Gorde's reactions—
what had he said, where was he going when he'd left me there
with Entwhistle? And then he asked me what it was that had
decided Entwhistle to check David's survey. "He must have
known he was risking his life there on that border. What made
him think it was so important?"

I hesitated. He was sitting there, watching me, very still, very
tense, and I knew suddenly that this was what the whole interview had been leading up to and that he was deeply concerned.
"When Entwhistle searched the abandoned truck," I said, "he
found all David's papers. They included his own survey report
and also the report of a much older survey run just before the
war. I think it was that report—"

"Whose report?" The question was shot at me out of the dark.
"Was it Henry Farr's report?"

I stared at him. "You know about that?"

"Of course. Henry sent me a copy of it. He was well aware of
my interest in the area. Later we had a talk about it—just before
he went into Abyssinia."

"But if you knew about it . . ." It seemed so incredible. "In
his letter to me David said he found it in the Company's files.
You never told him about it?"

"No."

"Why ever not? You must have known how he felt about
Saraifa, his desperate urge to—"

"He was employed by the Company—by Erkhard." His voice
was taut and hard, a note almost of hostility.

"But . . . I don't understand," I said. "All these years . . .
And Khalid says you're drilling to the south of the oasis. That's
at least forty miles from David's locations."

"Exactly. Just about as far from the Hadd border as it's pos-

sible to get and still be in Saraifa." He got to his feet and began
pacing up and down, seeking relief in movement from the nervous tension that I now realized had existed inside him from the
first moment of our meeting. "It's not easy to explain. You don't
understand the situation." He stopped suddenly and faced me.
"For twenty years I've had to sit on this, convinced that my
theory was right, that the oil-bearing strata continued from the
Gulf down into Saraifa, between the Empty Quarter and the
mountains you can see there to the east." His voice was sharp
and bitter with frustration. "I had to find some way. . . ." He
paused, standing there over me, and he was silent a long time,
as though reaching for a decision. Finally he said: "You know
so much. . . . You may as well know the rest. Erkhard's coming
here tomorrow, flying down from Sharjah. He's under pressure,
as I think you'll have guessed from your conversation with Philip
Gorde. With God's help I'll get him to sign the concession, and
once the Company's involved . . ." He turned and resumed his
pacing. "There was no other way. No company would sign a
concession with Saraifa if they knew it involved drilling on the
Hadd-Saraifa border. No company would dare. But once they're
committed . . ." He beat his fist against the palm of his hand.
"I've seen it happen before. The technical men come in. They're
not concerned with politics. They ride roughshod over everything, and in the end the Government is forced to support them."

"So there isn't any oil where you're drilling?"

"No, not as far as I know."

It was a strange business. He'd spent all that money, almost a
year of desperate effort to lure the Company into becoming involved again in Saraifa. It was clever, but . . . "And you think
Erkhard will sign the concession agreement?"

"I think so, yes. In the four years he's been General Manager
he hasn't been very successful. His position isn't as strong as
it was when he came out here."

"But why didn't you tell David what you were doing?"

"How could I? He was Erkhard's man." And he added: "I
still have contacts in the Bahrain office. According to them, he
was under orders to report on everything I was doing."

"And he agreed?"

"They knew his background. After that, of course, I couldn't trust him."

"Then why was he on loan to you?"

"Erkhard offered him to me. I'd had him here before; I couldn't very well refuse." And then sadly: "I didn't dare tell him. Besides, he lacked patience. He always approached things head-on, wanting to force the issue. If I'd thought he'd have been guided by me . . ." He shrugged. "Well, it can't be helped now."

He turned to me, his manner suddenly matter-of-fact. "You must be tired, and I've a long day ahead of me. You're fixed up all right, I take it, at the Sheikh's palace?"

I nodded and got to my feet. "But I still don't understand why you did nothing about the Farr report—after the war when the Company had the concession."

"Various reasons," he answered. "Most of them political. All the time the Company had the concession there was spasmodic fighting on the border. The Emir, you see, was determined to grab any oil there was for himself. And when we finally sent in troops to keep the peace, it was too late for me to do anything about it. The concession had lapsed, Philip Gorde had gone home sick, and Erkhard had taken over. Erkhard would have dealt with the Emir or anybody else. He'd no feeling for Saraifa, the way Philip had." He turned abruptly and shouted for Yousif. And then, looking at me very hard, he said: "You've come at a strange moment, Grant, and I've told you things I've told no other man. I've had to, or you'd have caused more trouble. By the mere fact of coming out here . . ." He hesitated and I knew he was thinking of Gorde. "What did Philip say? Was he surprised when he discovered where I was drilling?"

"I don't think he knows," I said. "He wasn't even sure you were drilling."

"Oh, he knows. A plane passed over the rig this afternoon. I thought for a moment it must be Erkhard arriving a day early, but when it circled and turned away I began to wonder." He was looking out into the desert again and his face showed the strain he was under. "I could have wished it had been anyone but Philip Gorde. He's the only man in the whole Company who knows enough to guess what I'm up to. But there's nothing I can do about it now."

Yousif had appeared, and Whitaker held out his hand to me. "You're a lawyer, Grant. You've been involved in our affairs for a long time. I rely on you not to talk." He held my hand gripped in his. "We have two enemies here in Saraifa—the Emir and the sands." He gestured towards the white expanse of the dunes and added softly: "Tomorrow, with God's help, I'll lay the foundations of victory over them both." It was said with great intensity, his eye fixed on my face.

I left him then, standing alone as I had found him on that rooftop, a strange, almost fanatical figure against the backcloth of endless desert. Even when I got back to my turret room, the memory of him was so clear in my mind that I felt he was still with me. But I was too exhausted to think clearly about that extraordinary meeting. I fell asleep and dreamed instead of women crying over children dead of thirst.

I woke in the small hours to the reality of their cries, a queer, keening sound coming up from the square below. The palace, too, was alive with voices, and though they were muffled by distance and the thickness of the walls, I caught the vibrant note of disaster.

It was quite chill as I flung off my blanket and went to the embrasure. The village square was ghostly pale in moonlight, empty save for a little group immediately below me, a dozen women and some children huddled like rags around the dead body of a man. He had been shot in the face and he wasn't a pretty sight there in the moonlight. Nearby a camel lay in a pool of blood.

It was just after four by my watch and already the sky was paling in the east. I put on my shoes and went down into the courtyard. The place was in an uproar, fires smoking and men standing in little groups, all talking at once. The nearest fell silent as they saw me and the word *"Nasrani"* passed from mouth to mouth, a whisper of fear, perhaps of hate. I beat a hasty retreat to the seclusion of my turret cell.

Sleep was impossible after that, and I sat huddled in my blanket and watched the dawn break over the Jebel Mountains, the grey light of it creeping across the palm tops, heralded by the brazen sound of an ass braying. The keening ceased, and when I went to the window embrasure there was no sign of the dead man and the camel's carcass had gone. It might have been a bad dream, for as daylight flooded the square it was full of the sound of children and their carefree laughter.

There was a *shireeya,* or open water-hole, a short distance from the tower, and young Arab girls were driving goats towards it. There were boys there, too, with their asses, filling goat-skin bags and dripping a dark trail of the precious fluid as they took it to houses in the village. Skinny, undersized fowl pecked in the dirt; a shapeless bundle of womanhood passed, her face hideously concealed by the black mask of the *burqa.* And when the sun lifted its glaring face above the distant line of the mountains, the palms, the sand, the mud houses were all miraculously suffused with colour, as though I were looking at the scene through rose-tinted glasses. Exhausted, I lay down again and was instantly asleep.

I woke to the cry of *"Gahwa"* and a barefoot attendant pouring coffee for me, his gun slung across his back, the brass of his cartridge belt gleaming in the light from the embrasure. It was eight thirty, and the flies crawled over the dates he left for my breakfast.

I ate the dates slowly, for time hung heavy on my hands and I didn't dare venture out alone after what had happened. My eyes felt tired, my body lethargic. My mind wandered in weary circles as the heat of the desert grew in intensity, invading the room. It was almost eleven when Khalid came for me. A brief salaam, a polite hope that I'd slept well, and then he said: "My father holds a *majlis.* He desires your presence, sir." His face looked grave, and the eyes, deep-sunk and shadowed, spoke of a sleepless night. "The Emir of Hadd has sent one of his sheikhs to make demand for a new border." His voice sounded weary, too.

"What happened last night?" I asked. "There were women crying and a dead body in the square."

"They waited in ambush by the fourteenth well. Mahommed

bin Rashid is dead and two of his men also. Three are wounded. Come! My father waits for you."

I asked him if I could wash first, but he said there was no time. "You must explain now, please, to the Emir's representative why you and Meester Entwhistle are on the border." And then urgently: "Tell Sheikh Abdullah there is no oil there."

"I'm not a geologist."

"He don't know that. He thinks you work for the oil company."

"Well, I don't." I spoke sharply, irritable with lack of sleep. "I'm a lawyer, and all I'm interested in is what happened to David Whitaker."

His dark eyes stared at me hard. "Is better you don't talk about David at this meeting," he said quietly.

"Why?" Angry and tired, I didn't stop to think what I was saying. "Because your father sent some of his bodyguard to arrest him?"

"You saw *Haj* Whitaker last night. You know why they were sent. He was on the Hadd border against my father's orders."

"Against Whitaker's orders, too, I gather."

"Yes. If he had been a Muslim instead of a *Nasrani* . . ." He gave a little shrug. "The Prophet has taught us that the word of the father is as a law and that the son must obey." And he added: "My father is wishing to avoid trouble. He does not believe that a few miles of desert sand is worth fighting for."

"And you do?"

Again the little shrug. "My father is an old man and he has known *Haj* Whitaker many years now. He is guided by him in these matters. And I—I also am not a geologist."

"Who did your father send with the soldiers?" I asked. "Was it you?"

"No. Mahommed bin Rashid." He turned abruptly. "Come, please. My father is waiting." And as I followed him down the turret stairs, he said over his shoulder: "Please. You will not speak of David." He said it fiercely, with great urgency.

He led me through passages that were cool in semidarkness and up to a rooftop by another staircase. The *majlis*, or audience, was being held in an open room with arches that looked out across the rooftop to the oasis. Sheikh Makhmud didn't rise to greet me. His face looked tired and strained, sullen with anger. He was also, I think, a little frightened. Beside him sat the representative of Hadd, a bearded, sly-eyed, powerfully built man with an elaborately embroidered cloak and a headdress that was like a turban of many colours.

Sheikh Makhmud motioned me to sit facing him. I was thus in the position of the accused facing a Court, for all the notables were there, seated cross-legged and grave on silken cushions ranged round the inner walls of that airy room. On a carpet in the centre were bowls of camel milk and tinned pears. Nobody touched them except the flies. The atmosphere was tense, almost electric.

The situation was distinctly unpleasant, for it was obvious as soon as Sheikh Makhmud began to question me in halting English that he regarded me as responsible for the situation that had developed. Entwhistle's absence didn't help, and though I answered the questions truthfully, I could see from Sheikh Abdullah's manner that he didn't believe me. He listened to the translation with a lack of interest that he didn't bother to conceal.

In the end I lost my temper with him. I scrambled to my feet, and, standing over the man, delivered myself of the sort of broadside I occasionally indulged in in the Courts. My action might have been dictated by expediency, for attack was undoubtedly the best method of defence. But, in fact, my nerves were on edge. "Your men attacked us without warning and without cause!" I shouted at him. And I described how the soft-nosed bullet had slammed into the hood of the Land Rover, how the fusillade of shots had raised spurts of sand all around us. He looked suddenly uncomfortable. "Only a few years ago," I said, "my country had to send troops here to keep the peace. Now you break it again. Why? What explanation do you wish me to give when I return to Bahrain?"

My words translated, the crafty eyes slid from my face to the assembled men and he licked his lips as though suddenly uncertain of himself. "You have no answer," I said, and with that I gave Sheikh Makhmud a quick bow and made my exit. I

couldn't go far, for armed retainers barred the staircase leading down from the roof. But I had made my point and felt better
for it, even though I was now forced to remain out in the full
glare of the sun. I sat myself down on the oven-lid heat of the
mud parapet and pretended to be absorbed in watching a camel
caravan being loaded at a huddle of *barastis* close by the date-
gardens. Behind me I could hear the guttural sound of the men's
talk as they continued to deliberate.

Coffee was served and Khalid came over and joined me. "Is
no good," he said. "The Emir listens to Cairo Radio and he believes he has powerful friends. It has made him bold. Also he
has many new rifles. They have come up from the Yemen, I
think. From the coast also." And he added: "Only if we have oil
here in Saraifa will your people give us their full support. We
know that."

"Mr. Erkhard is seeing Colonel Whitaker today," I said.

He nodded. "My father will not make a decision until he hears
from *Haj* Whitaker. He is full of hope."

"And you?" I asked, for the way he said it suggested he didn't
share his father's optimism.

He shrugged. "I also hope, but *Haj* Whitaker is old, and he is
tired and sick."

"Sick?"

"Sick here." And he touched his heart.

I asked him then what exactly Sheikh Abdullah was demanding. "A new border," he said and drew it for me in the sand of
the rooftop floor with the toe of his sandalled foot. It meant that
all the area David had surveyed would belong to Hadd.

"And if your father refuses?"

Again that fatalistic shrug. "Then Sheikh Abdullah say they
will destroy another *falaj,* and another and another, until we
have no water for the dates, no water for our beasts, none for
ourselves even. We die then of thirst and starvation." He was
staring out across the oasis. "I am young yet. I had thought to
rebuild the *falajes,* one by one, until Saraifa is like a garden
again and the desert at bay. That is my dream."

"And David's, too."

"Yes, it is the dream we share since we first hunt the gazelle together." His eyes had a far-away look, his voice sad with the loss of that dream. His father called to him and he finished his coffee and went back to his place. The conference was resumed, and, looking at the faces of the men gathered in that room, I knew he was right. They were in no mood to fight, and if Whitaker didn't save them, then they would accept it as the will of Allah and agree to the Emir's demands.

The camel caravan down by the palm-tree fringe finished loading. I watched the heavily laden beasts move off through the date-gardens, headed north into the desert. The whole oasis shimmered in the heat, and beyond it stretched the sands, a golden sea thrusting yellow drifts amongst the palms. The sun climbed the sky. The heat became unbearable, the talk spasmodic, and Sheikh Abdullah sat there, his heavy eyelids drooping, not saying anything, just waiting.

I was half asleep when I saw the dust trail of the vehicle. It was coming through the date-gardens from the south, driven fast, and when it emerged into the open I saw it was a Land Rover packed with Arabs, all shouting and waving their guns in a frenzy of excitement. And as it reached the outskirts of the village they began firing into the air.

A few minutes later Yousif burst through the retainers standing at the head of the stairs. He went straight up to Sheikh Makhmud, interrupting the deliberations with that extraordinary lack of respect that seems a contradiction almost of the feudalism of the Bedou world. He was excited, and Arabic words poured from him in a flood as he handed the Sheikh a folded slip of paper.

As soon as Sheikh Makhmud had read it his whole manner changed. His eyes lit up. He became revitalized, a man suddenly in command of the situation. He said a few words, speaking softly and with great control. The name of Allah was repeatedly mentioned, presumably in praise. And then he rose to his feet. The effect was remarkable. The place was suddenly in an uproar, everybody on his feet and all talking at once. There was a general movement towards the stairs, and Sheikh Makhmud swept out ahead of his elders, moving fast and with a light, soundless tread, so that he seemed to flow like water from the rooftop.

Khalid followed him, the others crowding after them, and in a moment there were only myself and the Emir's representative left. He looked unhappy, his arrogance undermined by this development which had clearly affected his embassy. I smiled at him, waving him to the staircase ahead of me, and was amused at the childish way he turned his back on me in a huff.

From the rooftop I could see men running. The news seemed to have spread round the oasis in a flash. And south, beyond the palms, another dust trail moved across the desert. By the time I had found my way down to the great courtyard the whole male population of Saraifa seemed gathered there. And when the Land Rover, driven by Colonel Whitaker himself, turned slowly through the gateway, forcing a passage through the crush to where Sheikh Makhmud stood waiting, a great shout went up: *"Haji! Haji!"* In the passenger seat beside Whitaker sat Erkhard, as cool and neat and spotless as when I had seen him last.

The greetings over, the Company's General Manager was taken into the palace. I had a glimpse of Whitaker's face as he walked beside Sheikh Makhmud, towering over him and all the Arabs around him. He wasn't smiling and yet it expressed his elation—a secret, almost violent emotion. Twenty years was a long time, and this the culmination of his life, the moment of victory. It seemed a pity David couldn't be here to share it.

Nobody took any notice of me now. I walked out through the main gate, down into the shade of the palms, and sat by the steaming waters of the *shireeya*. Gorde, Whitaker, Erkhard, Entwhistle . . . those three women . . . My brain reeled with the heat. Unable to fix any pattern to my thoughts, I returned finally to my turret room. It was cooler there, the shadowed interior peaceful, and I took my siesta to the lazy buzzing of flies, the distant murmur of people wild with joy.

I must have slept heavily, for when I woke the sun was low and there was a little pile of freshly laundered clothes beside me—a tropical suit, shirt, tie, pants, socks. There was also a note from Whitaker: *The concession is signed and there is a feast to celebrate. I thought you might like a change of clothes. Yousif will call for you at sunset.*

As soon as I started to put them on I knew the clothes weren't his, for he was much taller and these fitted me reasonably well. They were obviously David's, and it seemed to me strange that I should be attending this feast in his clothes.

The acrid smell of wood smoke permeated the room, and the hubbub of sound from the village square drew me to the embrasure. The whole beaten expanse was full of people and cooking-fires. The carcasses of sheep and goats hung by their hind legs, their slashed throats dripping blood into bowls. Chickens were being prepared, and blackened pots of rice simmered over the fires. Half Saraifa was in the square, and there was a great coming and going of the Sheikh's armed retainers, who carried the cooked dishes into the palace. The sun sank and the sky blazed red for an instant and then died to purples and light greens.

"You come now, sir, please."

Yousif stood at the head of the stairway, almost unrecognizable in clean clothes and spotless turban, a curved *khanjar* knife gleaming silver at his waist. He took me down to a central courtyard that I hadn't seen before. It was packed with retainers, the silver and brass of guns and cartridges gleaming in the shadows. The Sheikh and his guests were already gathered in the long, colonnaded room on the far side, and dishes lay in lines in the dust.

Khalid came forward to greet me. He was beautifully clad in long robes of finest cashmere, a brown cloak gold-embroidered, and his eyes, newly made-up with *kohl*, looking enormous, his beard shining and silky with some scented lotion. Whitaker was seated on one side of Sheikh Makhmud, Erkhard on the other. And next to Whitaker sat Sheikh Abdullah of Hadd. "You sit with me," Khalid said.

As I passed Erkhard, he looked up. "Grant!" I couldn't help being amused at his surprise. "They told me in Sharjah that you'd left with Gorde, but I didn't expect to see you here." He frowned. "Where is Gorde, do you know?"

"I think he flew back to Bahrain."

He nodded. "Good."

As I took my place beside Khalid, retainers were already moving amongst the guests with ewers of water. We rinsed our hands, and the first great platters were moved forward on to the rugs. The occasion was very formal. Nobody talked unless the Sheikh himself was talking. The result was that conversation went in disconcerting leaps—one moment bedlam, the next a silence in which the only sound was the coming and going of the retainers in the courtyard.

The feast was a monstrous, gargantuan affair—mutton, goat's flesh, young camel, chicken, gazelle. The platters came on and on and kept on coming, the meat nestled on piled-up heaps of rice, eggs floating in a spiced gravy like little yellow balls, omelettes piled in tiers, flat and leathery like griddle cakes, flat disks of bread, liquid butter and cheese. Half the dishes never got beyond the colonnades, but remained outside in the dust, enough to feed an army. Like all Bedouin feasts, it was intended as a meal for the Sheikh's bodyguard, who were waiting on us, for all the palace retainers, and finally for the people of Saraifa themselves so that they would all feel they had shared in the event.

The cooking was rough desert cooking, the meat overdone and swimming in fat, the dishes lukewarm at best. But I was so damned hungry I scarcely thought about what I was eating. Khalid kept plying me with delicacies—the tongue of gazelle, I remember, and something that I popped into my mouth and swallowed whole, hoping it wasn't what I thought it was. An old man sat in a corner playing intermittently on what I can only describe as a lute. The palace poet, I was told. Later he would unburden himself of a poem in praise of the guests and of the occasion. "It will be a long poem," Khalid said and his eyes smiled whilst his face remained quite serious. There was a sudden silence and into it the man next to me tossed a belch of impressive loudness. There was a great deal of belching. It was a mark of appreciation, and before we were halfway through the meal I found myself doing the same, so quickly and easily does one fall into other people's conventions. Also my stomach was by then very full.

Outside in the courtyard Sheikh Makhmud's falconers paraded their birds. He was very proud of his falcons, and, seeing them, talons gripped around wooden perches spiked into the sand or around the leather-gauntleted arms of their keepers, I found myself glancing at Whitaker, noticing the same quick, predatory look, the same sharp, beaky features. Our eyes met for a moment and it seemed to me that the mood of exhilaration had drained out of him, as though success had a sour taste; or perhaps it was the clothes I was wearing, reminding him of his son.

The main dishes had all been removed now. Lights were brought, for the sun had set and it was growing dark. They were modern, chromium-plated pressure lamps, and they were hung on nails in the walls, where they hissed and glared and had to be constantly pumped to maintain the pressure. And with the lamps came dishes of every sort of tinned fruit. There was *halwa*, too. Coffee followed, and at a sign from Sheikh Makhmud the poet moved into the centre. He sat facing the guests and began plucking at his lute, chanting a ballad—the story, Khalid said, of Saraifa's need of water and *Haj* Whitaker's long search for oil. It had the effect of intensifying the mood of excitement that gripped all the Arabs . . . all except Sheikh Abdullah, who sat staring stonily into space.

And then suddenly the stillness was shattered by the noise of an aircraft flying low. The ballad-singer faltered, the sound of the lute ceased; the story came abruptly to a halt, unfinished.

The sound swept in a roar over the palms. I thought I caught a glimpse of a dark shape against the stars, and then the engine died. It was coming in to land. Sheikh Makhmud called to his secretary, and a guard was dispatched to escort the visitors. Everybody was talking at once, and Erkhard leaned across to me and hissed: "Who is it? Do you know?"

I didn't answer, but I think he must have guessed, for his eyes were coldly bleak and there was a tightness about his mouth. I looked past him to where Whitaker sat. His face was expressionless, but his body had a stillness that was without repose.

After what seemed a very long wait Gorde and Otto were escorted into the courtyard.

It was a strange moment, for Gorde walked straight in on the feast, limping and leaning on his stick, the sweat-stained trilby jammed firmly on his grizzled head, his battered features set in grim lines. He didn't greet Sheikh Makhmud. He didn't greet any one. He stopped in the middle of the centre archway and stared in silence at the gathering, my briefcase tucked under his arm. It was an effective entrance, and I knew by his aggressive manner that he had intended it to be. Impressive, too, for he was dressed exactly as I had last seen him, and behind him crowded the bodyguard, all armed to the teeth. It was impressive because of the contrast: the man so small, so completely at the mercy of the armed men behind him, and yet so dynamic, so completely in command of the situation.

He ignored Sheikh Makhmud's greeting. "What's the feast for?" That harsh voice seemed to cut through the room.

Nobody moved. Nobody spoke. Even Sheikh Makhmud seemed stunned into silence.

"Mister Erkhard." The "Mister" was a calculated slap in the face. "I take it you've signed a concession agreement? There's nothing else for Saraifa to celebrate at this moment." And then, without giving Erkhard a chance to reply, he turned to Sheikh Makhmud. "I hope you're not a party to this—that you signed in ignorance of the true situation."

"I don't understand." Sheikh Makhmud's hands fluttered in a way that suggested dark moths endeavouring to cope with the intrusion of unwelcome thoughts. Slipping into Arabic, he began a speech of welcome.

Rudely, Gorde cut him short. "Have you got the concession agreement on you? I'd like to see it, please." He held out his hand, and such was the driving force of the man's personality, the absolute conviction that men would obey him, that Sheikh Makhmud slipped his hand into the folds of his robe and brought out the document. Meekly he handed it over. "I think you find everything is all right." The soft words, the gentle voice gave no sign of doubt or tension.

Gorde called to one of the bodyguard to bring him a light. A stillness hung over the scene as he unfolded the document and glanced quickly through it. Then he raised his head and looked directly at Erkhard. "And you signed this on behalf of the Company."

The note of censure brought an immediate reaction from Erkhard. "As General Manager, I'm entitled to sign concession agreements." His voice was thin, a little venomous as he added: "You should know that. You signed enough of them in your day."

"But never one like this." And, slapping the document with his hand, he added: "This isn't our normal agreement. Our normal form of agreement simply gives the Company the right to prospect. This makes it a legal charge upon the Company to do so. Moreover—" and his gaze fastened on Whitaker—"it doesn't limit it to the area south of here where your rig is. It covers the whole of Saraifa, including the area in dispute on the Hadd border."

"Philip." Whitaker had risen to his feet. "I'd like a word with you."

"And I'd like a word with you," Gorde said sharply.

"In private."

"No. We'll settle this thing here and now. I just want a straight answer to a straight question. Is there or is there not oil where you're drilling?"

"We're only down to three thousand-odd feet."

"That doesn't answer my question." Gorde stared at him coldly. "There isn't any oil, is there? There never was any oil there, and there never will be."

"I don't believe it." Erkhard, too, was on his feet.

"It doesn't matter whether you believe it or not, Alex," Gorde rapped back. "It's the truth."

"But he's drilling with his own money. He's invested every penny he's got. Ask Grant. He handles his financial affairs, and Whitaker admits he's out here partly because his money is almost exhausted. A man doesn't put all his savings first into a thorough seismological survey and then into a drilling program . . ."

"Bait." The tone of Gorde's voice brought Erkhard up short. "He was baiting the trap."

"I don't understand."

"Of course you don't. You'd never in a thousand years understand a man like Charles Whitaker. You ride him out of the
Company and it never occurs to you that he'll get his own back
some day. If you hadn't been so intent on trying at the last
minute to rectify your position . . . And you thought you were
getting an oilfield on the cheap, for the price of his development costs plus fifty per cent on royalties. Well, you ask him.
You just ask him whether there's any oil there."

But it wasn't necessary. One glance at Whitaker's face told
Erkhard all he needed to know. It was drawn and haggard, the
colour of putty, and though the mouth moved, no words came.
Erkhard crossed to Gorde, took the document from his hand,
and tore it across and across and dropped the pieces in the dust.

There was a deathly hush. All eyes were turned on Sheikh
Makhmud, waiting for his reaction. His face was the colour of
clay, a shocked, almost old-womanish face, and his hands were
trembling in the wide sleeves of his robe. "Sir Philip." He had
some difficulty in controlling his voice. "Your Company has
signed an agreement. To tear up the paper is not to say the
agreement does not exist."

"You can take us to Court," Erkhard said. "But if Gorde's
right, you'll lose your case."

Sheikh Makhmud waved his hands to signify that he had no
intention of taking the Company to Court. He ignored Erkhard,
addressing himself to Gorde. "I have always trusted the British.
And you also; you have been my friend."

"I am still your friend," Gorde said.

"Then, please, you will honour the agreement."

"There is no agreement." His voice held a note of pity now.
"Mr. Erkhard has done the only thing possible in the circumstances." He turned to Whitaker. "For God's sake, Charles, did
you have to raise their hopes like this?" It was clear from his
words that he didn't like the role he was being forced to play.
"The truth was bound to come out in the end."

"What is the truth?" The pale eye was fastened on Gorde
in an aloof stare. "Do you know it? Are you so sure there's no
oil in Saraifa? For twenty years now I have searched . . ."

"To hell with your theory," Gorde snapped. "Just answer me this, a simple yes or no. Is there oil where you're drilling?"

"I've told you, we're only down to just over three thousand feet. Erkhard could have waited—"

"You know damn well he couldn't wait. You're not such a fool that you haven't guessed why I'm out here risking my health on another tour of the Gulf."

"You thought my theory sound enough at one time. Remember?"

"And I backed you," Gorde rasped. "I backed you because you'd got faith in yourself. But now I wonder. Now I think you've lost that faith. I don't think you believe in your theory any more."

"What makes you say that?" Whitaker's voice was sharp, unnaturally high, and his face looked shocked.

Gorde leaned his squat body forward. "Because," he said, "if you'd any faith in your theory, you'd have backed your son. Instead, you left him to die out there on his own—alone, deserted." Each word punched home in that rasping voice. It was a terrible indictment. And he added: "Didn't you understand that he was attempting to do what you'd no longer the guts to even try and do—to find oil, real oil? Not this sham, this clever, crooked dodge to trap us into signing—"

"Philip!" It came from Whitaker's mouth as a strangled cry. "I want to talk to you—alone."

It was an appeal, the call of past friendship. But Gorde ignored it. "I've nothing to say to you, Charles." The words came bleak and cold. "Except perhaps this: if there is any oil in Saraifa, then my guess is that it's right there on the border where your son was prospecting. But," he added, turning to Sheikh Makhmud, "I have to tell you that there's absolutely no question of our Company—or any other company, for that matter —undertaking exploratory work there at the present time. I was with the Political Resident for two hours this morning. He made the Government's attitude very clear. And now that I know what happened here last night, simply because one of our geologists was inadvertently on that border, I think he's right."

There was silence then, and for a moment Colonel Whitaker

continued to stand there as though shocked into immobility. Knowing what I did, I felt sorry for him. Gorde had misinterpreted his motives, but there was nothing he could do about it at that moment. Whitaker knew that. Abruptly he gathered his dark, embroidered cloak about him. "I'm sorry you had to come when you did, Philip." His tone was bitter; his manner arrogant, unbending, aloof. "You'll live, I hope, to regret the words you've said and your hasty judgement. I did what I thought best for Saraifa, and Makhmud knows it." He walked past Gorde then, his one eye staring straight ahead of him as though on parade; a beaten, proud old man. The ranks of the bodyguard parted and he walked through them, magnificent and solitary.

With his departure the whole place became a babel of sound. It was as though Whitaker alone had held down the safety-valve of the crowd's temper. Violence quivered on the sultry air, and I got up quickly and went over to Gorde. "I think you ought to see Whitaker," I said. "As soon as possible. Tonight."

"Why?"

But the place had suddenly become quiet. Sheikh Makhmud was on his feet making a speech, presumably of explanation. "I can't tell you here. But I think it's important you should see him."

"It's true, is it—you look after his financial affairs?" He stared at me, his face tired now, leaning heavily on his stick. "Where's Entwhistle?" I told him and he nodded. "Sensible fellow. This is no place to be just now." He glanced at the sea of faces that packed the courtyard beyond. "It all looks very feudal, doesn't it? But there's an element of democracy in these desert states. The sheikhs rule by consent, not by right. Just bear that in mind." He was turning away, but then he checked. "Here's your briefcase." He handed it to me. "You'll find all the papers there."

Again I pressed him to see Whitaker, but he shook his head. "It wouldn't serve any purpose after what I've said. And anyway I don't intend to. He's the pride of the devil, has Charles."

"Go and see him," I said. "And take these papers with you." I held the briefcase out to him.

He looked at the case and then at me. "I took them along with me when I went to see the PRPG this morning. I thought

I might persuade him . . ." He gave that little shrug of his. "If he could have given us the All Clear politically, I think I might have taken a chance on that boy's survey and backed Erkhard. But he didn't. More, he gave me a direct order that the Company was to keep clear of the area."

It was final, and as though to emphasize the point, he said: "I'll be leaving tomorrow morning as soon as it's light. No doubt Charles will take care of you, but if you want a lift out . . ." Sheikh Makhmud stopped talking and the courtyard was in an uproar again. Gorde's hand gripped my arm. "Hope turned to despair makes men dangerous," he said, his small, bloodshot eyes looking into mine. "There's going to be trouble here, and these people are in an ugly mood."

He turned abruptly away from me, and in the midst of the noise and confusion I heard him saying casually to Sheikh Makhmud: "Mind if we have something to eat? I'm damned hungry."

Immediately Sheikh Makhmud was the solicitous host, courteous and hospitable. "*Faddal! Faddal!*" He waved Gorde to the place vacated by Whitaker, found room for Otto, called for food to be brought. Khalid was in the courtyard now, pacifying the tribesmen, shepherding them out. He was quick, decisive, a born leader, but they went sullenly.

I returned to my place, feeling nervous and ill at ease. I didn't need to be told that they were in an ugly mood. I could feel it all around me. It was like an electric charge. And the uproar had spread from the feasting-place into the great courtyard beyond and out into the village of Saraifa. The sound of their voices murmured on the night air, a continual angry buzzing as the whole population swarmed about the palace. Men came in and out to stand and stare, and it seemed to me that their eyes in the lamplight blazed with a wild, fanatical hate. Erkhard felt it, too, for he leaned across to me and said: "It's all very well for Gorde to say he'll leave at daybreak. He's got his plane here. Mine is ten miles away beside that rig." And he added: "Damn the man! A Moslem. I should have guessed he'd be up to every sort of trickery."

"Did you have to turn him against his son?" I said angrily.

But it didn't register with him. "Greed," he said. "It's an Arab failing."

I thought that was good, coming from an oil man with his reputation. But I didn't have a chance to reply, for Yousif was suddenly bending over me. "Coll-onell want you come," he whispered. "Very important, sahib."

I hesitated, unwilling to leave the protection of Sheikh Makhmud's presence or to lose contact with Gorde and his promise of a lift out. But I couldn't very well refuse. "All right," I said and got to my feet. Courtesy demanded that I pay my respects to Sheikh Makhmud before leaving. He didn't rise, and his eyes regarded me coldly from behind their glasses. No doubt he held me partly responsible for what had happened. His face looked haggard, the line of his mouth bitter beneath the grey wisp of his beard. I turned to Gorde. "I'm going to see Whitaker now," I said. "But I'd like to accept your offer of a lift."

He had just taken a piece of meat from the dish in front of him and he looked up, licking the grease from his fingers. "First light," he said. "And watch it, Grant. Charles has lost face, and anything can happen to a man that's been hit as hard as he has."

Yousif's hand was on my arm, and as I turned I saw Sheikh Abdullah's dark eyes fixed on me. The men in the courtyard fell back from me, suddenly silent, as we made our way out. Their eyes followed me, gleaming in the lamplight, and once again I caught the whisper of that word: *"Nasrani."* There was no mistaking the significance of it this time. They were hating us all that night.

V

The Quicksands of the Umm al Samim

Whitaker was waiting
for me on that same rooftop overlooking the desert, but this
time he was pacing up and down it. His movements were caged
and restless. He checked only momentarily as I entered. "Will
Philip Gorde come and see me, do you think?" he asked, and
when I told him no, he resumed his pacing. "After all these
years, to talk to me like that!"

It was too dark for me to see his face, but I could tell from
the stooped outline of his shoulders, the lowered head, above
all, the nervous quickness of his movements, the way he spoke,
that his mood was one of desperation. "All my life I've had to
use subtlety. It's been part of my job out here. Always the need
to find my way through the maze of Arab politics. Never a
straight course. Always the devious approach. These oil men out
from England—stupid men like Erkhard who don't understand
the Arab mentality—they don't realize the problems of these
Bedou sheikhs, the feuds, the vague boundaries that didn't matter so long as it was desert sand and nothing more. History,
culture, race—they go back three thousand years and more, virtually without change, untouched by Western civilization. It's
a culture in which the individual is still dominant, personality
and human emotions the overriding factors governing men's actions. And over all this are the outside factors—international

politics, the Foreign Office. Even Philip doesn't really know the Arab—though he likes to think he does."

It was the fact of having somebody with him of his own race. The words came out of him in a pent-up torrent. But what he said was said for his own benefit, not for mine; an attempt to justify his actions. But when he'd said it all, he turned and faced me, suddenly almost humble: "Suppose I go to Philip myself?"

There was no point in raising his hopes. "I don't think it would do any good." And I told him about Gorde's visit to the PRPG.

His head came up. "In other words, I was right. The Company's not allowed to enter into any agreement involving the Hadd border." There was relief in his voice, but it was overlaid by the bitterness of frustration. And he added acidly: "Nice of the Political Resident to confirm my own assessment of the situation so exactly." His shoulders sagged; he turned his face towards the desert. "Then I've no alternative now. . . ." He said it to himself, not to me, standing very still, looking out to where the stars met the hard line of the sands. "Over thirty years I've been out here, Grant. I'm practically a Bedou. I think like them, act like them. . . . I'm over sixty now and I know more about the Arab and Arabia . . ." He stopped there, and in the stillness I could hear the breeze rattling the palms. He turned slowly and stared at me. "All those years out here, and a boy of twenty-four sees it clearer than I do." His voice was harsh, his face grim, the lines cut by sand and sun so deep they might have been scored by a knife.

"It's a pity you didn't reach that conclusion earlier," I said.

He took a step forward, the eye bulging, his body taut, gripped in a sudden blaze of anger. But all he said was: "Yes, it's a pity." He turned and resumed his pacing, the shoulders stooped again. "Heredity is a strange thing," he murmured. "If we'd been less alike . . ." He shrugged and added: "In that case, I don't suppose he'd have gone back to the locations against my orders." He fell silent again then. The breeze was from the east and it brought with it the murmur of Saraifa, like the beat of the surf on a distant shore.

"You wanted to see me," I reminded him. The sound of that distant crowd made me anxious to get back to Gorde.

"Yes, about finances." He kicked a cushion towards me and told me to sit down. "Just what have I got left?" he demanded, folding himself up on the floor beside me.

I was glad Gorde had returned my briefcase then. I could have told him the position more or less from memory, but all the papers were there and it made it easier. He shouted for Yousif to bring a light, and for the next ten minutes I went over the figures with him. He hadn't much left. But there were some shares I hadn't sold and they'd appreciated quite considerably, and, after repaying bank loans, I thought he'd have just enough if he lived quietly. I thought he'd decided to go home, you see —to leave Arabia and retire. It seemed reasonable for a man of his age. "I'm sorry it's not more," I said, putting the papers back in their folder.

He nodded. "I'll have to borrow, then."

"It would be better," I said, returning the file to my briefcase, "if you could arrange to live within your means."

He stared at me, and then he burst out laughing. But the laughter was without humour. "So you think I'm beaten, do you? You think I'm turning tail and heading for home like a village cur. . . ." The fury building up in him seemed to get hold of his throat, so that the words became blurred. "That's what they'll all be thinking, I don't doubt—Gorde, Makhmud, that man Erkhard." And then in a voice that was suddenly matter-of-fact: "I take it you'll be going back in one of the Company planes?"

"Gorde has offered me a lift."

"Good. I'll have letters for you to various merchants in Bahrain. A list of things to order, too. Would you like to wait here whilst I write them or shall I send Yousif up with them later? When is Philip leaving, by the way?"

"First light." And because I wanted to make certain I didn't miss the flight I asked him to have the letters sent after me.

He nodded. "That gives me the night in which to think this thing over." He summoned Yousif and gave him instructions to take me back to the palace. "By the way," he said, as I got to my feet, "you mentioned a package Griffiths had brought you, something David took to him on board the *Emerald Isle*. Was that his survey report?"

I nodded.

"Based on Henry Farr's old report?"

"Yes."

"I take it Entwhistle was running a check on David's locations. You don't know with what result, I suppose?"

"No. He didn't say."

He had risen to his feet and, standing close to me, he seemed to tower over me. "I'd like to see my son's survey report. Have you got it with you in your briefcase?"

I realized then why he'd considered his finances inadequate. "Good God!" I said. "You're surely not going to start drilling operations on that border. . . ." I was staring at him, remembering what Gorde had said. But there was nothing wild-eyed about him. He was bitter, yes. He'd been humiliated, deeply shocked by the behaviour of a man he'd always regarded as his friend, but the eye that met mine was level and unflinching, and I knew that he hadn't yet crossed the borderline into madness. "You haven't a hope of succeeding now," I said. "The Emir will be watching that border, and the instant you start drilling . . ."

He smiled thinly. "I'm not afraid of death, you know. Being a Muslim makes one fatalistic." He turned away, leaning his body on the parapet and staring out across the dunes, grey now with the first light of the risen moon. "I don't know what I'm going to do yet. I haven't made up my mind." He hesitated and then turned to me. "But if I should decide to go ahead, then I'd like to have David's report. He gives the locations, I take it?" And when I nodded, he said: "Do they coincide with Henry Farr's?"

"I don't know."

"No, of course not. I ran a check survey myself, you know. That was a long time ago now, when I had a bodyguard of more than a dozen men, all on the Company's payroll, and the use of the Company's equipment. In those days—quite soon after the war—I reckoned my chaps could hold the Emir off if it came to a showdown long enough for me to pull out with my equip-

ment. But it never came to that. I got away with it without the
Emir knowing. But I knew I couldn't do that with a drilling-
rig."

"Then how do you expect to get away with it now?" I demanded.

He shrugged. "I don't know that I can." He was smiling softly
to himself. "But I've been out here a long time, Grant. I know
that little Emir inside out. I've had spies in Hadd sending me
back reports, and I think I know enough now. . . ." He gave
a little shrug and the smile was no longer soft; it was hard, almost cruel. "I'm outside the Company now. It makes a difference. And it's just possible I could get away with it where the
Company couldn't." He straightened up. "Well, what about it?
Are you going to let me have David's report?"

It wasn't ethical, of course. He hadn't been mentioned in his
son's will. But then I'd failed with Gorde and I could now regard myself as free to take what action I liked. Also I thought
that, had David known what I now knew, he would have
wanted his father to have the locations. I gave him a copy of
the survey report and, after writing the location fixes out on a
slip of paper, I gave him that, too.

He glanced at it and then slipped it into the folds of his
cloak. "Thank you." He held out his hand. "You've come a long
journey. I'm sorry it didn't have a pleasanter ending. I'll send
Yousif with the letters in a few hours."

I hesitated. But I knew he wasn't a man to take advice. "In
that case, you'd better let me know what I'm to tell Gorde."

"Nothing," he said. "Nothing at all."

I left him then, standing alone on that rooftop with the desert
clean and white behind him, and followed Yousif out to the
battered Land Rover. It was cooler now and I felt almost relaxed. In a few hours I should be able to have a bath and a
change and sit back with a long, cool drink. And yet, riding
down the palm-shadowed track between the date-gardens, I
found myself filled with a strange nostalgia for the place. It had
an appeal I found difficult to define, a sort of poetry, and the
dim-remembered lines of a poem came into my mind, something
about being "crazed with the spell of far Arabia" and stealing

his wits away. I was beginning to understand what this place
had meant to David, to a boy who'd never had a real home
before and who was wide open to the strange beauty of it and
as impressionable as any Celt.

I was still thinking about this when we ran out from the
shadow of the palms and saw the square, black with the mass
of men standing there. The roar of their voices came at us in a
wall of sound. Yousif eased his foot off the accelerator, hesitating, uncertain whether to drive straight to the main gate or not.
And then three figures rose from beside the *shireeya* and stood
blocking our path.

"Sheikh Khalid's men," Yousif said, and there was relief in
his voice as he braked to a stop. They clambered on to the mudguards, talking urgently in the hard, guttural tongue that is
always associated in my mind with flies and sand. "We go a different way. Is much better." Yousif swung the Land Rover
round, circling the gravel rise and approaching the palace from
the rear through a litter of *barastis,* all apparently deserted. We
stopped finally at a small door with an iron-barred grille set in
an otherwise blank wall.

Khalid's three men closed round me as I got out, and when
I told Yousif I wanted to be taken straight to Gorde, he said:
"You go with them now, sahib. Sheikh Khalid's orders." And
he drove off, leaving me there.

Eyes peered at us through the grille. The door opened and
I was hustled through the dark passages of the palace and up
to my turret room. There my three guards left me, and, standing
at the embrasure, I looked down on what was obviously a very
explosive situation. The crowd was being harangued by a man
on a rooftop opposite, and another was shouting to them from
the back of a camel. The whole square was packed solid. Every
man and boy in the oasis must have been gathered there, and
many of them were armed.

Camels were being brought into the square and men were
mounting on the outskirts of the crowd. And all the time the
agitators shouting and the crowd roaring and the tension growing. The air was thick with menace, and then somebody fired
a rifle.

The bullet smacked into the mud wall not far from my embrasure. It was all that was needed to set that crowd alight. Other guns were fired, little sparks of flame, a noise like firecrackers, and a great shout; the crowd became fluid, flowing like water, moving with the sudden purpose of a river in spate. Men leaped to their camels, mounting on the arches of their lowered necks, driving them with the flood tide down the slope to the dark fringe of the date-gardens.

In a moment the square was deserted, and with the murmur of the crowd dying to silence, the dark walls of my room closed in on me. I had a sudden, overwhelming need then to find Gorde and the others, and I picked up my briefcase and felt my way down the black curve of the stairs. A light showed faint in the passage at the bottom. A figure stirred in the shadows. Thick Arabic words and the thrust of a gun muzzle in my stomach halted me. It was one of Khalid's men, and he was nervous, his finger on the trigger. There was nothing for it but to retreat to my room again. In the mood prevailing in the oasis, it was some comfort to know that I had a guard. I lay down and tried to get some rest. The sound of the crowd was still faintly audible. It came to me through the embrasure, soft as a breeze whispering through the palm trees. And then it died and there was an unnatural quiet.

It didn't last long, for the shouting started again. Shots, too. It was a long way away. I got up and went to the embrasure, peering out at the empty square and the dark line of the palms shadowed by the moon. A glow lit the night sky to the east. It grew and blossomed. Then suddenly an explosion, a great waft of flame and smoke beyond the date-gardens. And after that, silence, the flame abruptly gone and the palms a dark shadow-line again in the moon's light.

Voices called within the palace, the sound muffled by the thickness of mud walls, and then for a while it was quiet. But soon the crowd was ebbing back into the square, flowing into it in little groups, silent now and strangely subdued. I was sure that it was Gorde's plane I'd seen go up in smoke and flame, and I stayed by the embrasure, watching the tide of humanity as it filled the square, wondering what they'd do now—hoping to God their passions were spent.

Bare feet sounded on the stairs. I turned, uncertain what to expect, my mouth suddenly dry. The beam of a torch probed the room, blinding me as it fastened on my face. But it was only my three guards back again, jabbering Arabic at me and gesturing for me to accompany them. I was hurried along dark passages, past gaping doorways where men sat huddled in dim-lit rooms, arguing fiercely. The whole palace was in a ferment.

We came finally to a low-ceilinged room lit by a pressure lamp, and in its harsh glare I saw Khalid sitting surrounded by robed figures. They were mostly young men and they had their guns resting across their knees or leaning close at hand against the walls. He rose to greet me, his face unsmiling, the bones sharp-etched in the lamplight. "I am sorry, sir, for the disturbance you have been given." A gesture of dismissal and the room quietly emptied, the conference broken up. "Please to sit." He waved me to a cushion on the carpeted floor and sat down opposite me, folding his legs neatly under him with the ease of a man who has never known a chair.

"What happened?" I asked. "Did they set fire to Gorde's plane?"

"Is a mistake. They are angry and they fire some bullets into it." He was very tense, coiled up like a spring too tightly wound. Somewhere a child was crying and I heard women's voices, soft and comforting. "You 'ave been to see *Haj* Whitaker, is not so?" And when I nodded, he said: "I understand you are concerned in the management of his affairs?"

"His financial affairs." I didn't want him to think I was responsible for anything that had happened out here. His manner, his whole bearing had changed, the surface layer of a university education gone entirely. I glanced over my shoulder. My three guards were still there, squatting in the open doorway.

Khalid was staring at me out of his dark eyes. The *kohl* had worn off. Lacking that artificial lustre, his eyes looked sad and sombre. "I have spoken with my father. I understand now what it is *Haj* Whitaker try to do for Saraifa. Unfortunately, I am not before tonight in my father's confidence." And he added with a trace of bitterness: "Better if he had told me. Better also if *Haj* Whitaker explain to David what he is doing." He paused there and I was conscious again of the strain he was under, of the tension building up in him. He leaned suddenly forward. "What will he do now?" he asked me. "Now that Meester Erkhard don't honour the concession he sign. What will *Haj* Whitaker do?"

"That's his affair," I said. I didn't want to become involved in this.

"Please, Meester Grant. I must know."

"I don't think he's made up his mind yet."

He stared at me. "Do you think he may leave Saraifa?" And when I didn't answer, his eyes clouded and he seemed to sag. "We have very much need of him now," he said quietly. "He has the ear of many sheikhs, of some of his own people also." And he added: "Since ever I am a small boy I have known about this great man *Haj* Whitaker. I can remember the feast to celebrate the original concession. He is young then and full of fire. But always, always the people here—my father and myself also —we have looked to *Haj* Whitaker. He is known from the Persian Gulf to the Hadhramaut, from Muscat on the Indian Sea to the water-holes of the Rub al Khali and the Liwa Oasis, as a great man and the friend of all the Bedou. Particularly he is known as the friend of Sheikh Makhmud. If he desert us now . . ."

"I'm sure he's no intention of deserting you."

But he didn't seem to hear me. "There must be some reconciliation. It is altogether vital." He leaned suddenly forward, staring at me hard. "Meester Grant. There is something I must know. It is if I can trust you."

"That's up to you," I said, wondering what was coming. And I added: "I've been virtually a prisoner since I returned from seeing Colonel Whitaker."

He gave me a quick, impatient shrug. "Is for your own safety."

But I wondered. "Where's Sir Philip Gorde?" I didn't want to be involved in this any further. "I'd like to be taken to him now."

"First you will listen, please, to what I have to tell you." He seemed to consider, his dark eyes fixed on me, searching my face. "I think you are a friend to David before you work for his father, is not so?"

"It was because I befriended David that Colonel Whitaker asked me to look after his financial affairs."

"Yess. Yess, I believe that." But his eyes still searched my face as though he wasn't sure.

"What is it you want to tell me?" I wanted to get this over. Presumably Gorde and Otto would be leaving with Erkhard, and I wanted to be on that plane, away from the dark feuds of this desert world.

He didn't answer at once. But then he suddenly seemed to make up his mind. He leaned forward. "David is alive," he said.

I stared at him, too astounded for the moment to utter a word. "Alive?" Those three women . . . but, remembering their attitude, I remembered Whitaker's too. "What do you mean?" I was suddenly extremely angry with Khalid. "How can he be alive?" And when he didn't say anything, I added: "It's more than six weeks since your father sent an armed guard to arrest him and they found his camp deserted."

"I know. But is alive." He said it very seriously.

"Where is he, then?" I still didn't believe him. I thought it was a damned stupid lie he'd thought up to try and keep Whitaker in Saraifa. As if Whitaker, with all his experience of the desert, would believe it. "You tell me where he is and—"

"No." His voice was flat and decisive. "No, I don't tell you —not yet. But is alive. That I promise, Meester Grant." I suppose he realized that just stating it wouldn't convince me, for he went on quickly: "When *Haj* Whitaker is gone to visit the Emir, I am much disturbed for David's life. He is already on that border almost two moons with the truck that was brought by his father across the Jebel Mountains from Muscat. He is altogether alone, and his father I believe to be hating him for things he has said."

"What sort of things?"

He shrugged. "He don't tell me. But he is very much unhappy, I know that. He come here to this room to see me before he leave, and he warn me there is no oil where *Haj* Whitaker is drilling, that the only place there is any probability of oil is on that border. He says also that his father is an old man now and has lost faith in himself and that he is drilling to cheat the Company, for revenge against this Meester Erk-hard and nothing more."

"And you believed him?"

"He is as my brother. He don't lie to me." And then he told me how he'd taken two of his men and a spare camel and had ridden to the border as soon as he knew David was to be arrested. He'd found David alone, deserted by his crew. After emptying the spare cans from the seismological truck, David had driven it into the Rub al Khali desert until it had run out of petrol on the side of that dune. "Then he leaves the truck and rides on with us. It is all as we arrange it together."

"You mean you planned it in advance?"

"Yess. It is all arranged between us because I am afraid for this emergency."

The details fitted. They fitted so well that I was forced to accept what he'd told me as the truth. But he wouldn't reveal where David was hidden. "He is with my two men—Hamid and a boy called Ali. They are of the Wahiba and altogether to be trusted."

"Why have you told me this?" I asked.

"Because everything is gone wrong, everything David planned—and now I need your help. You are David's friend, and also you work for his father. I think per'aps only you can bring reconciliation between them. And without reconciliation . . ." But he seemed reluctant to put his fears into words. "What do you think now, sir?" he asked abruptly. "Is reconciliation possible? How will *Haj* Whitaker act when he finds David is alive?"

"How would you react if you thought your son were dead?" But I realized I'd no idea what Whitaker's reaction would be. I didn't know enough about their relationship, how he'd come to regard his son in those last months. If Sue were right and they really had been close at one time . . . "It'll come as a hell of a shock to him."

"Yess, but is it possible—a reconciliation?"

"Of course. Particularly now that Colonel Whitaker . . ." I
hesitated, wondering whether I ought to tell him what was in
Whitaker's mind. But I thought he'd a right to know that Whitaker was considering drilling on his son's locations. After all, it
was what David had wanted. They'd be able to work on it together now.

With this thought in mind, I was quite unprepared for the
violence of Khalid's reaction when I told him. "Is imbecility!"
he cried, jumping to his feet. "He cannot do that now. Is altogether too late." He was pacing up and down, very agitated
and waving his arms about. "Sheikh Abdullah has already left
to return to Hadd. He will report to the Emir all that has occurred here. If then *Haj* Whitaker remove his oil rig to the border . . ." He turned to me, still in great agitation, and said:
"It will mean war between us and Hadd. War, do you understand? For my father is guided by *Haj* Whitaker. The Emir
knows that. And if *Haj* Whitaker himself is on that border, then
the Emir will know there is oil there and that my father will
concede no revision of the boundaries between Hadd and
Saraifa. You understand? You will help me?" He didn't give me
time to answer, but summoned my escort. "We leave at once,
for there is little time. Excuse, please. I go to my father now."

He left then and I was alone with my three Arab guards. The
child had stopped crying. There was no sound of women's
voices. The palace slept, and, sitting there, thinking about David, convinced now that he was still alive, I gradually became
resigned to the fact that I wasn't going to get away in the plane
that morning.

Khalid was gone about ten minutes. When he came back his
face was pale, his manner subdued. "I tell my father I am going
to Dhaid to gather more men."

"Did you tell him about Whitaker?"

"No. I don't tell him. And I don't tell him about David either
—not yet. Is very much disturbed already. Come!"

"Is David at Dhaid?" I asked.

"No. But Sheikh Hassa holds that village for us. He will give
us camels, and perhaps Salim bin Gharuf is there. I don't know.
We have to hurry." He gave an order to my escort and I was

hustled out of the palace into the great courtyard where his
Land Rover stood. The escort piled in behind us, and as we
drove down into the date-gardens it was difficult to believe that
the people of this peaceful place were threatened with extinction, that they had been so roused that night that they'd set
fire to an oil-company plane. The breeze had died and the whole
world was still. Nothing moved. And when we ran out into the
desert beyond the palms, it was into a dead, white world, for
the moon was high now. We headed south, Khalid driving the
Land Rover flat out, bucking the soft sand patches, eating up
the flat gravel stretches at a tearing speed.

We were held up for a time by a choked petrol feed, and
the first grey light of dawn was taking the brightness from the
moon when a needle-tip of latticed steel showed above the grey
whale-back of a dune. It was Whitaker's oil rig, a mobile outfit
—the sort they call an "A" rig, truck and drill combined. It stood
up out of the desert floor like a steel spear planted in the sand
as a challenge to the vast wastes of emptiness that surrounded
it. Beside it was a *barasti*, two Bedou tents and some tattered
wisps of black cloth that acted as windbreaks.

As we neared it we heard the sound of the diesel, could see
the Arab drilling-crew busy drawing pipe. Other Arabs were
loading a second truck with lengths of pipe. Early though it
was, the place was humming with activity, and when Khalid
stopped and questioned them, he learned that Yousif had arrived just over an hour before with orders for them to prepare
to move.

Whitaker had made his decision. He was moving his rig to
the Hadd border, and up in my empty turret room there were
doubtless letters waiting for me to take to Bahrain. "Is crazy!"
Khalid cried, jumping back into the driving-seat. "Why does he
do this now? He should do it before or not at all." He drove on
then, passing close below the derrick. It looked old and battered,
the metal bare of paint and burnished bright in places by the
drifting sands. The derrick man was up aloft stacking pipe, his
loin-cloth smeared with oil, his turbaned head a bundle of cloth
against the paling sky.

Dawn was coming swiftly now, and beyond the shallow slope

of a dune I saw the tinsel-gleam of Erkhard's aircraft. It stood
at the far end of a cleared stretch of gravel, and the sight of it
brought back to me my urge to escape from the desert. But
when I demanded to be taken to it, Khalid took no notice except to give an order to the Arabs in the back. I reached for the
ignition key. A brown hand seized my arm, another gripped my
shoulders, and I was held pinned to my seat whilst we plunged
at more than thirty miles an hour into a world of small dunes,
and the plane vanished beyond my reach.

After that the going was very bad for mile after weary mile.
And when finally we came out of the little-dune country, it was
on to a gravel plain ribbed by crumbling limestone outcrops. A
few dried-up herbs, brittle as dead twigs, bore witness to the
fact that it had rained there once, many years ago. The land
was dry and dead, flat as a pan, and as dawn broke and the
sun came up, I lost all sense of horizon, for the whitish surface
reflected the glare in an endless mirage.

All the way from the rig the going was bad. We had more
trouble with the petrol feed, and it was past midday before we
caught sight of the low hill on which Dhaid stood. It throbbed
in the heat haze, looking like the back of a stranded whale surrounded by pools of water. The crumbling mud walls of the village were merged in colour and substance with the crumbling
rock on which they were built, so that it wasn't until we stopped
at the foot of a well-worn camel track that I could make out the
shape of the buildings. There was a single arched gateway, and
we had barely started up the track on foot when the villagers
poured out of it and rushed upon us, leaping from rock to rock,
shouting and brandishing their weapons.

Khalid showed no alarm, walking steadily forward, his gait,
his whole bearing suddenly full of dignity. And then they were
upon us, engulfing us: a wild, ragamuffin lot, teeth and eyes
flashing, dark sinewy hands stretched out to us in the clasp of
friendship. They were dirty, dusty-looking men, some with no
more than a loin-cloth, and they looked dangerous with their
black hair and bearded faces and their animal exuberance; and
yet the warmth of that unexpected welcome was such after that
empty, gruelling drive that I greeted them like brothers, their

horny, calloused hands gripped around my wrists. It was the beginning of my acceptance of desert life.

Sheikh Hassa followed behind the rest of the villagers, picking his way sedately over the rock, his gun-bearer just ahead of him carrying his new BSA rifle, which was his pride and joy. He was a short, tough-looking man with a shaggy black beard that gave him an almost piratical appearance. He greeted Khalid with deference, touching his hand with his fingers, carrying them to his lips and to his heart. "*Faddal.*" And we went up the track and through the gateway into the village. A crowded square pulsating in the heat, a cool, darkened room spread with a rug, camel milk in bowls still warm from the beast's udder, and talk—endless, endless talk. I leaned back on the cushions, my eyelids falling, my head nodding. The buzz of flies. The buzz of talk. Not even coffee could keep me awake.

And then Khalid called to me and introduced me to a sinewy old man who stood half naked in the gloom, a filthy loin-cloth round his waist and his head-cloth wound in a great pile above his greying locks so that he looked top-heavy. This was Salim bin Gharuf. "He is of the Duru," Khalid said, "and he knows the place." I asked him what place, but he ignored that. "Is better now that you wear these, please." He produced a bundle of Bedou clothing, holding it out to me.

They were cast-off clothes and none too clean. "Is this really necessary?" I demanded.

He nodded emphatically. "Is better you look like one of us now."

"Why? Where are we going?"

"I tell you later. Not here. You will change, please." He helped me off with my European clothes and wound the loin-cloth round my waist; the long, dusty robe, the length of cloth twisted about my head, sandals, too, and an old brass-hilted knife for my belt. Sheikh Hassa watched me critically. I think the clothes were his. Men came and peered, and the crowded room resounded with their mirth. Khalid sensed my annoyance. "They don't mean any disrespect, sir. And you are going where no *faranji* has been before—save David."

It was meant to mollify, but all it did was rouse my curiosity

again. "Well, if you won't tell me where he is," I said, "at least
tell me how long it will take us to reach him."

"A day and then half a day if we travel fast. Perhaps two
days. I don't know. There is possibility of a storm."

I think perhaps he might have told me more, but at that moment a man burst into the room shouting something, and instantly all was confusion. The room emptied with a rush that
carried me with it out on to the white glare of a rooftop. Below
us a single camel climbed wearily up the track, urged on by its
rider.

Khalid pushed past me. "Is one of my father's racing camels,"
he said.

Five minutes later he returned with the rider, a thick-set man
with long hair twisted up in his head-cloth. Khalid talked for a
moment with Sheikh Hassa and then with Salim. Finally he
came to me. "The oil men have left, and at dawn this morning
several large raiding parties from Hadd crossed our borders.
My father orders me to return."

My surprise was occasioned less by the news than by the realization that the camel must have made the journey in less time
than we had taken in the Land Rover. But Khalid's next words
jolted me into awareness of what it meant to me personally.
"You go now with Salim."

"But . . ."

"Please, Meester Grant." His face looked old now beyond his
years, haggard after the long drive, the sleepless night. His eyes,
staring at me, burned with an inner fire. "Is altogether important now. Tell David what has happened, that his plan has
failed and that there is no hope now of the oil concession. He
must go to his father immediately."

But my mind was on the practicalities. "That's all very well,"
I said, glancing uneasily at the old man. "But Salim doesn't
speak any English. And I don't know the country." I looked
about me quickly. Khalid's bodyguard was behind him, Sheikh
Hassa right beside me. There was no escape. "Where am I supposed to go, anyway? Where is David?"

"You go to the Umm al Samim."

Sheikh Hassa leaned his black beard forward, and his harsh

voice repeated the words "Umm al Samim" on a note of surprise. And then he looked at me and rolled his eyes up into his head and laughed and made a strangling sound.

"What's he mean by that?" I demanded. "What's he trying to tell me?"

Khalid's hand gripped my arm. "The Umm al Samim is quicksands. But there is a way," he added quickly, and I glanced at Hassa and knew that he'd been telling me that I was going to my death. "I tell you there is a way," Khalid said fiercely. "Salim knows it as far as the first good ground. He will guide you as he guided us when we make original exploration two seasons past."

"And what about the rest?"

"You will find by testing with a stick. Perhaps when you call, David or the Wahiba will hear you." His grip on my arm tightened. "You will go?"

"Suppose I refuse?"

"Then I take you with me back to Saraifa." He was looking me straight in the face. "This is what you want, isn't it correct—to find David? Now you find him." And he added, staring at me hard: "Are you afraid to go?"

"No, I'm not afraid." I saw him smile. He knew after that I'd hardly refuse. "All right, Khalid," I said. "I'll go. But what do you want me to do? A boy hiding out in some quicksands isn't going to help you now."

"He must help us—he and his father. We are at point of desperation now, and it is his fault." He said it without rancour, a statement of fact, and he added: "It was a good plan, the way he visualize it—to go into hiding and, by making appearance he is dead, to draw attention to his survey. He think you will succeed to obtain the signature of Sir Gorde to a concession and that then per'aps we have oil, at least the support of the Company and so of your people. But instead all is turned to disaster. Because he is working on that border the raiders of Hadd are in our territory and the concession *Haj* Whitaker arrange is torn up. We have no Arab friends like the Emir has. We are alone, and everything is in conspiracy now to destroy us."

His words, the intensity with which he spoke, showed me the

tragedy of it—father and son working for the same ends, but
against each other. "Yes, but what can he do?"

"He must ride to a meeting with his father. Salim has good
camels. You and David together—you must persuade *Haj* Whitaker to stop drilling on the Hadd border and to go to Bahrain,
to the Political Resident. If they don't send soldiers, then please
to send us modern weapons and automatic guns so that we can
fight."

"Very well," I said. "I'll do what you say. I only hope it works
out."

"Tell David also . . ." He hesitated. "Tell him it is possible I
do not see him again. And if that is happening, then say to him
that he is my brother, and the Emir Abdul-Zaid bin Sultan my
enemy into death."

"What do you mean?" I asked.

"He will understand."

"But you're not going to your death."

"*Inshallah!* I do not know that." His tone was fatalistic. "This
is an old feud, Meester Grant. As old as Saraifa is old, or Hadd.
It goes back many centuries to the days when all the *falajes*
are running with water, a hundred channels making irrigation
for the palms. Then Saraifa is a great garden extenuating many
miles, and the dates go by camel north, to the sea and to India,
across the mountains to the Batina coast, and south to the Hadhramaut—even, some say, to Mukalla and the olden port of
Cana to be carried by dhow to the far places of the world. But
we are always too much occupied with our gardens, and the
people of Hadd are very much envying us for our riches. They
are men of the hills, cruel and hard and altogether without
goodness. So." He gave a helpless little shrug. "So it is that we
are always fighting for our date-gardens and one after another
the *falaj* channels are being destroyed until Saraifa is as you
see it now, open to the desert and soon to die if the *falajes* are
not rebuilt. Do you know, Meester Grant, there is not one man
who can tell me, even when I am a little boy—even by the hearsay of others, his father or his grandfather—what it is like when
there are more than six *falajes* working. Always wars . . . always, until the British come a hundred years ago. And now—"

he spread his hands in a little gesture of helplessness—"now another war perhaps, and if we do not have a victory, then it is finish and in a few months the *shamal* will have blown the sands of the Rub al Khali over our walls and our houses and we shall be like those old lost cities in India. . . . There will be nothing to show that we ever exist in this place." He stopped there, a little breathless because he had put so much of himself and his emotions into foreign words. "You tell him that, please." He turned then and spoke rapidly to Salim. The tattered figure moved towards me. "You go now," Khalid said. "*Fi aman allah!* In the peace of God."

"And you also," I said. The skinny hand of my guide was on my arm, a steel grip propelling me down mud steps out into the shadowed cool of an alley. In a little open space beyond there were camels couched, and at his cries three tall beasts lumbered to their feet. They had provisions already loaded and dark skin bags bulging with water. A boy brought two more camels, and Salim chattered a gap-toothed protest as he realized that I didn't even know how to mount my beast. They brought it to its knees and put me on it, and at a word it hoisted me violently into the air. The old man put his foot on the lowered neck of the other and stepped lightly into the saddle, tucking his legs behind him.

We left Dhaid by a small gateway facing south, just the two of us and the three pack-beasts tied nose to tail. The boy ran beside us as far as the base of the limestone hill and then we were out on the gravel flat and travelling fast, a peculiar, swaying gait. It required all my concentration just to remain in the saddle. Perhaps it was as well, for it left me no time to consider my predicament. Our shadows lumbered beside us, for the sun was slanting towards the west, and Salim began to sing a high-pitched, monotonous song. It was a small sound in the solitude that surrounded us, but though I couldn't understand the words, I found it comforting.

The sun vanished before it reached the horizon, hazed and purple as a mulberry. We camped at dusk where the dusty green of new vegetation spattered the sand between ribs of limestone. The camels were let graze, and Salim built a fire of furze and cooked a mess of rice and meat. One of the pack-beasts was in milk, and we drank it warm from the same bowl. And when he'd looked to his ancient rifle, oiling it carefully, we mounted and went on again.

We travelled all that night without a break. The moon turned the desert to a bleak bone white, and in the early hours a mist came up and it was cold. By then I was too tired to care where I was going, and only the pain of the saddle chafing the insides of my thighs, the ache of unaccustomed muscles kept me awake. The dawn brought a searing wind that whipped the mist aside and flung a moving cloud of sand in our faces. Lightning flashed in the gloom behind us, but no rain fell—just the wind and the driving sand particles.

We stopped again for food, lukewarm and gritty with sand, and then on again until the heat and the moving sand drove us into camp. I laid my head on my briefcase, covering my face with my head-cloth, and slept like the dead, only to be wakened again and told to mount. My nose and mouth were dry with sand, and we went on and on at a walking pace that was relentless in the demands it made on my endurance. Dawn broke and the sun lipped the mountains that poked their rugged tops above the horizon to the east. Salim didn't sing that day, and as the wind died and the sand became still, the heat increased until my head reeled and dark specks swam before my eyes.

By midday we were walking our camels along the edge of a dead, flat world that stretched away into the west, to disappear without horizon in a blur of haze. There was no dune nor any outcrop of rock, no tree, no bush, nothing to break the flat monotony of it. Salim turned in his saddle. "Umm al Samim," he said with a sweep of his hand, the palm held downward and quivering. I remembered the strangled sound Sheikh Hassa had made at the mention of that name, and yet it looked quite innocent: only that unnatural flatness and the dark discolouration of water seepage revealed the quagmire that lay concealed below the crust of wind-blown sand.

We followed the shore of the sands for about an hour whilst the sun beat down on us and the dull expanse shimmered with humidity. And then, by the gnarled remains of some camel thorn, we dismounted and started into the quicksands, leading our camels.

Close inshore there were patches of solid ground, but further out there was nothing that seemed to have any substance, the ground and air both quivering as we struggled forward. I can't remember any sense of fear. Fear is a luxury requiring energy, and I had none to spare. I can, however, remember every physical detail.

It was a *sabkhat* on the grand scale, and beneath the hard-baked crust my feet touched slime. At times it was difficult to stand at all, at others I broke through to the black filth below, and at every step I could feel the quiver of the mud. The camels slithered, bellowing in their fear, in constant danger of losing their legs and falling straddled. We had to drag the wretched beasts, even beat them, to keep them moving. This and the need to be ready to give them some support when they slipped did much to keep my mind from the filthy death that threatened at every step. And whenever I had a moment to look ahead, there was the Umm al Samim stretched out pulsating in the humid glare, innocent-seeming under its crest of sand, yet deadly looking because it was so flat and level—as level as a lake.

And it seemed to have no end. It was like the sea when visibility is cut by haze. But here there were no buoys, no markers that I could see, nothing from which Salim could get his bearings. Yet once I saw the old tracks of camels, the round holes half filled with sand, and whenever I broke through to the mud below, my feet found solid ground before I was in further than my knees; in some way that was not apparent to me Salim was following a rib of rock hidden below the surface of the sand.

Time had no meaning in the pitiless heat, and the sweat rolled dripping down my back. I had a moment of panic when I would have turned and run if it had been possible. But then a camel slipped, and a moment later Salim seized my arm and pointed ahead with his rifle. Little tufts of withered herbs lay limp in isolated clumps, and on the edge of visibility a gnarled thorn tree shimmered like a witch, its gaunt arms crooked and beckoning.

With the first of the withered herbs I felt the ground under my feet. It was hard and firm, and when I set my foot down nothing quaked, there was no gurgling sound, no sound of imminent break-up of the crust. Where the camel thorn stood there was naked rock, and I flung myself down, revelling in the scorched hardness of it.

We were on a little island, raised imperceptibly above the flat level of the quicksands, and it was as far as Salim had ever penetrated. I watched him as he searched for Khalid's tracks, stopping every now and then to call, a high-pitched, carrying sound made with his hands cupped round his mouth. But the steaming heat absorbed his cries like a damp blanket, and there was no answer.

In the end he gave it up and began prodding with his camel stick along the edge of the sands. Twice I had to pull him out, but finally he found firm ground beneath the crust, and, leaving the camels, we started forward again, moving a step at a time, watching the quiver of the crust and prodding with the stick.

Behind us our tracks vanished into nothing. The rock island vanished, too, the white glare swallowing even the bulk of our camels. We were alone then, just the old man and myself in a little circle of flat sand that quaked and gurgled and sucked at our feet.

I don't know how long we were feeling our way like that. Once we saw the faint outline of a camel's pad, but only once. And then suddenly thorn trees throbbed in the haze ahead, looking huge, but dwindling as we approached the firm ground on which they stood. They were no more than waist height, and, standing beside them, Salim cupped his hands and called again.

This time his cry was answered—a human voice calling to us, away to our left where the sands ran flat. I thought it was imagination, perhaps an unnatural echo of Salim's voice, for there was nothing there: an empty void throbbing in the heat, and the air so intensely pale it hurt the eyes.

And then suddenly the void was no longer empty. A man had materialized like a genie out of the heart of a furnace, his face burned black by the pitiless heat, his lips cracked, his ragged beard bleached by the sun, his hair, too, under the filthy headcloth.

He came forward and then stopped, suddenly suspicious,
reaching for the gun slung at his shoulder.

"Salim!" Recognition brought a quick flash of teeth, white in
the burnt dark face. *"Wellah! Salaam alaikum."* He came forward and gripped Salim's wrist in a Bedou handclasp whilst the
old man talked, his words coming fast and high-pitched with
excitement. And then the man turned to stare at me, pale eyes
widening in startled disbelief. It was only when he finally spoke
my name that I realized this strange nomadic-looking figure was
David Whitaker.

"It's a long time," I said. "I didn't recognize you."

He laughed and said: "Yes, a hell of a long time." He reached
out his hand, and his grip was hard on mine. Not content with
that, he took hold of both my shoulders and held them as though
overwhelmed by the need for physical human contact. "I can't
believe it," he said. And again: "I can't believe it."

I could hardly believe it myself. He was greatly changed. As
Sue had said, he'd become a man. But even in that first glimpse
of him I recognized again the quality of eagerness that had first
attracted me to him. "So you really are alive." I don't think I'd
fully accepted the fact until that moment.

"Yes, I'm alive—just." His dark face cracked in a boyish grin.
"Christ!" he said. "It never occurred to me you'd come out here
to look for me. Hell of a bloody journey. How did you know
where I was?" But I suppose he saw I was exhausted, for he
added quickly: "Come up to the camp. You can stretch out and
I'll have Ali brew some coffee." He called to two men who had
materialized out of the weird glare and were hovering on the
edge of visibility. "My companions," he said.

They came forward warily, like dogs suspicious of a new
scent, and they both had service rifles gripped in their hands.
The elder he introduced as Hamid—a big man with long hair to
his shoulders, bearded and impressive like a prophet. The other
was little more than a boy, his face full-lipped and smooth, almost a girl's face, and he moved with the same natural grace.
His name was Ali bin Maktum.

"Now let's have coffee and we'll talk." David took my arm and
led me to where the ground was higher and tattered pieces of

black Bedou cloth had been erected as windbreaks, stretched
on the bleached wood of camel thorn over holes they had
scraped in the soft limestone. *"Faddal!"* It was said with Bedou
courtesy, but with an ironical little smile touching the corners
of his mouth.

He sent Hamid off to look to our camels, and whilst the boy
Ali brewed coffee over a desert fire of sand and petrol, he sat
beside me talking hard about the heat and the humidity and
the loneliness he had been suffering in this Godforsaken place.
I let him run on, for I was tired and he needed to talk. He was
desperate for the company of his own kind. He'd been there
six weeks, and in that time Khalid had made the journey twice
to bring them food and water. "I wouldn't trust any one else.
They might have talked." He was tracing patterns in the sand
then, his head bent, shadowed by the head-cloth. Flies buzzed
in the sudden silence. "Why are you here?" His voice came taut
with the anxiety of a question too long delayed. "Who told you
where to find me—Khalid?"

"Yes," I said. "Khalid." And I added: "There's a lot to tell you."

He misunderstood me, for his head came up, his eyes bright
with sudden excitement. "It's all right then, is it? You saw Sir
Philip Gorde and he signed that concession agreement I typed
out?" The words came breathless, his eyes alight with hope. But
the hope faded as he saw my face. "You did see Sir Philip, didn't
you?"

"Yes," I said. "I gave him the envelope."

"Well, then . . ."

"He didn't sign the agreement."

The effect of my words was to knock all the youth right out
of him. His face looked suddenly old and strained; lines showed
so that he seemed more like his father, and his shoulders sagged.
"So it didn't work." He said it flatly as though he hadn't the
spirit left for any display of emotion, and I realized that all the
weeks he'd been waiting here alone he'd been buoyed up by
this one hope. "I thought if I disappeared completely, so completely that everyone thought I was dead . . . They did think I
was dead, didn't they?"

"Yes," I said. "Everyone, including your father, presumed you were dead." And I added, a little irritably because I was so tired: "You've caused a lot of people a great deal of trouble; and your mother and sister a lot of needless grief."

I thought for a moment he hadn't heard me. But then he said: "Yes, indeed, I realize that. But Sue at least would understand." His face softened. "How is she? Did you see her?"

"Yes," I said. "I saw her." And that, too, seemed a long time ago now. "I don't think she ever quite accepted the idea that you were dead. Nor did your mother or that girl in Bahrain."

"Tessa?" The lines of strain were momentarily smoothed out. "You saw her, too?" He seemed surprised, and he added: "I'm sorry. I'm afraid I've put you to a great deal of trouble." He was staring down at the sand patterns between his feet. Abruptly he rubbed them out. "I was so convinced it was the only way. I had to get past Erkhard somehow. I thought if I could get my report to Sir Philip Gorde. He was the one man. . . ." His voice faded. And then, still talking to himself: "But I couldn't just send it to him. It had to be done in some way that would enable him to override the political objections. I thought all the publicity connected with my disappearance . . . I'd planned it all very carefully. I had a lucky break, too. That night I visited Captain Griffiths on the *Emerald Isle,* there was an agency correspondent in transit to India stopping the night at the Fort in Sharjah. I saw him, told him the whole story—my background, how I'd escaped from Borstal and got myself out to Arabia, everything. I thought a story like that . . ." He darted a quick glance at me. "Didn't he print it?"

"After you were reported missing, when the search had failed and you were presumed dead."

"Yes, I made him promise he wouldn't use it unless something happened to me. But didn't it have any effect?"

"It seemed to cause quite a stir in the Foreign Office."

"But what about the Company?"

"It put the shares up," I said, trying to lighten it for him.

"Hell! Is that all?" He gave a bitter little laugh. "And I've been sitting here . . . waiting, hoping . . ." His shoulders had sagged again, and he stared out into the throbbing glare, his eyes narrowed angrily. "All these weeks, wasted—utterly

wasted." His voice was bleak. He looked weary—weary and depressed beyond words. "I suppose you think now I've behaved
like a fool—disappearing like that, pretending I was dead. But
please try and understand." He was leaning towards me, his
face young and defenceless, his voice urgent now. "I was on my
own and I knew there wasn't any oil where my father was drilling. I ran a check survey without his knowledge; it was an anti-
cline all right, but badly faulted. It couldn't hold any oil." His
voice had dropped to weariness again. He'd been over all this
many times in his mind. "I don't know whether he was kidding
himself or trying to cheat the Company or just doing it to get
his own back on Erkhard. But I wanted the Company to drill
on my locations, not his. I wanted oil. I wanted it for Saraifa,
and I wanted it to be the real thing."

"Your father wanted it, too," I said gently. "And he, too, was
convinced there was oil where you did your survey."

"That's not true. He refused to believe me. Told me I was
inexperienced, that I'd no business to be on that border, and
forbade me ever to go near it again."

"I think," I said, "you'd better listen to what I have to tell
you."

The coffee was ready then, and I waited until Ali had poured
it for us from the battered silver pot. It was Mocha coffee, bitter
and wonderfully refreshing, and as I sipped the scalding liquid
I told him the whole story of my journey and all that had happened. Once whilst I was telling it, he said: "I'm sorry. I didn't
realize." And later, when I came to the point where Gorde had
left me with Entwhistle and we'd been fired on, he apologized
again. "I'm afraid you've had a hell of a time, sir, and all my
fault." That "sir" took me back, for it still didn't come easily
from him.

But it was my account of that first interview with his father
that really shook him. When I had explained to him what his
father had been trying to do, he was appalled. "But, Christ!
Why didn't he tell me? I'd no idea. None at all. And when Khalid
told me he'd been to see the Emir of Hadd . . ." He stared at
me, his face fine-drawn, his voice trembling as he repeated:
"Why the hell didn't he tell me what he was trying to do?"

"I think you know why," I said. "You were employed by the Company, and the Company to him meant Erkhard." And I added: "Erkhard knew your background, didn't he? He used that as a lever to get you to spy on your father."

It was a shot in the dark, but it went home. "He tried to." His tone was almost sullen; he looked uncomfortable.

"And you agreed?" I'd no wish to conduct a cross-examination, but I thought it essential he should see it from his father's point of view if I were to succeed in bringing them together again.

"I hadn't any choice," he said, stung to anger by my question. "Erkhard threatened to turn me over to the Cardiff police."

"And your father knew about that?"

"It didn't mean I was going to do what Erkhard wanted."

"But you'd agreed to do it," I insisted, "and your father knew you'd agreed."

"I suppose so." He admitted it reluctantly. "He's still got his friends inside the Company."

So there it was at last, the basic cause of the rift between them—the thing that girl Tessa had hinted at, that Sue had felt but hadn't been able to explain.

"Christ!" he said. "What a bloody stupid mess! And all because we didn't trust each other like we should have done. How could I guess what he was up to? Though it's just the sort of twisted, devious approach . . ." His voice faded and once more he was staring out into the void. "I got very close to him at one time, but even then I was always conscious of a gulf, of something hidden that I couldn't fathom. He's very unpredictable, you know, Mr. Grant. More Arab than the Arabs, if you see what I mean." He was very much on the defensive then. "After four years I can't say I really understood him. Switching races like that, and his religion, too—it left a sort of gulf that couldn't be bridged. And when Khalid told me he'd been to see the Emir, it made me wonder . . ." He hesitated. "Well, as I say, he's unpredictable, so I decided it was time I put my plan into action and disappeared. Khalid thought so, too. He'd brought Hamid and Ali, two of his most trusted men, and a spare camel. So . . ." He shrugged. "I knew it was hard on Sue. Hard on Tessa, too—

and on my mother. But I was alone, you see. I'd nobody to turn
to, except Khalid. He was the only man in the world who had
faith in me. And I couldn't look to the Company for help. Erkhard had made that very plain. And, anyway, oil companies are
in business for themselves, not for the Arabs. They've been
known to sit on an oilfield for years for political or commercial
reasons. . . ." The sweat was pouring off him and he wiped his
hand across his brow. "Well, go on," he said. "What happened
when Erkhard came to Saraifa—did my father succeed in getting a concession signed?"

But I think he'd guessed that I shouldn't have come here
alone if it were all settled. He listened, silent, not saying a word,
as I told him the rest of my story. Once his eyes came alight
with sudden excitement; that was when I told him of my second
talk with Whitaker and how Khalid and I had seen the drilling-
rig being dismantled for the move up to the Hadd border. The
thought that his father was at last doing what he'd been wanting
him to do for so long gave him a momentary sense of hope. But
it was only momentary, for I went straight on to tell him of the
scene at Dhaid and how the lone rider had brought the news
that Gorde and Erkhard had left and Hadd forces had crossed
the border into Saraifa. "So it's come to that, has it? Open war
between Hadd and Saraifa." His body was suddenly trembling
as though with fever and his voice was bitter. "And Khalid sent
you to me. What did he say before you left? What message did
he give you?"

"He said he thought this time Saraifa had reached the point
of desperation." And I gave him the gist of what Khalid had
said to me. When I had finished he didn't say anything for a
long time, sitting there lost in thought, staring out across the
flat misery of the Umm al Samim. "The only home I ever had,"
he whispered. "Did you see it when the *shamal* was blowing,
with the Rub al Khali like a sea, the dunes all smoking and the
sands pouring into the date-gardens? It's like a flood then." His
father's words—his father's voice almost. "The oasis is doomed,
you see. Doomed to extinction by the desert. But that's a natural
process, something to be fought with the natural resources of
the country. Khalid and I, we were going to rebuild the old

falaj channels with the money from oil royalties. That was our
dream. But this . . ." He stared at me hard, his eyes wide.
"You're sure it's war, are you? It's not just a border raid?"

I gave him Khalid's speech then, as near as I could remember
it word for word.

"So it's my fault, is it?" He said it with deep bitterness, and
after that he was silent for a long time. Finally, he looked at me.
"Unto death, you said. Khalid used those exact words, did he?"
And when I nodded: "So it's not just a raid—it's the real thing
this time." He was almost in tears, he was so deeply moved. And
then sadly: "My father's fault, too—he's made his decision too
late." And he began cursing softly to himself. "Those dung-
eating bastards from Hadd, they'll smash down the last of the
falaj channels. What would have taken twenty years by natural
means will take less than that number of months. The desert
will roll in. Christ Almighty! The bastards!" It was a cry from
the heart, and I was conscious of desperation here, too—a desperation that matched Khalid's. "They can't fight a war against
Hadd. They've nothing to fight it with—only antiquated guns."

He began questioning me then, pressing me for details, many
of which I couldn't give him, for he wasn't interested in his
father now, or Gorde or the Company; his attention was fixed
on Hadd and the way Sheikh Abdullah, the Emir's representative, had behaved, and what had passed between him and
Sheikh Makhmud that morning before Whitaker and Erkhard
had arrived. The sun sank in a blood-red haze and the air became dank. My head nodded, my body suddenly drained of
warmth and shivering with fatigue. "You'd better get some rest
now," he said finally. "We'll be leaving as soon as the moon's
up and it's light enough to see our way through the quicksands."
He seemed to have reached some decision, for his voice was
firmer, his manner less depressed. He brought me a tattered
blanket musty with sand. "I've kept you talking when you
should have been getting some sleep."

"What do you plan to do?" I asked him. "You'll go to your
father, I take it?"

"Yes. He's still got a few of his bodyguard left. A dozen men
and I could create a diversion that would keep the Emir busy

until my father has time to make his influence felt in Bahrain. Khalid's right. We must work together now—my father and I." The mention of Khalid's name seemed to bring his mind back to his friend. "He said he was my brother, didn't he? Unto death?"

"Your brother, yes," I said. "But as I remember it, he used the words 'into death' in connection with the Emir—'my enemy into death.'"

"Well, pray God it doesn't come to that." There were tears in his eyes, and, standing there, staring straight into the flaming sunset, he quoted from the Bible: "*The Lord be between me and thee, and between my seed and thy seed for ever.*"

Dimly I recognized the quotation as the oath sworn by his namesake; I didn't realize it then, but this was the covenant, sworn in the midst of the quicksands of the Umm al Samim, that was to take him to that fort on top of Jebel al-Akhbar and to the terrible final tragedy.

I saw the sun set and the quicksands turn to blood, and then the sky faded to the palest pastel green and the stars came out. Lying there, it was like being stranded on a coral reef in the midst of a flat lagoon. Sometime in the small hours the wind woke me, blowing a drift of sand in my face. The moon was up, but its face was hidden in a cloud of moving sand. There was no question of our leaving, and I lay till dawn, unable to sleep, my eyeballs gritty, my nose and mouth clogged with sand, and when the sun rose all it showed was a sepia haze. We ate in extreme discomfort, the sand whistling like driven spume across the flat surface of the Umm al Samim.

The storm lasted until almost midday, and then it ceased as abruptly as it had started. We cooked a meal of rice and dried meat, and then we started back, collecting our camels on the way and struggling through the quicksands to the solid desert shore. We mounted then and, keeping the Umm al Samim on our left, rode till dusk, when we camped. A meal and a short two-hour rest and then on again, with Salim arguing sullenly.

"The old fool thinks the beasts will founder." David's face was grim. He was in a hurry and he had no sympathy for men or beasts. "Like all the Bedou, he loves his camels more than he loves himself."

We marched all night and there were times when I hoped the camels would founder. My muscles were stiff and aching, and where the wooden saddle chafed my legs, I was in agony. The starlight faded, swamped by the brighter light of the risen moon, and in the grey of the dawning day we reached the big well at Ain. Salim went forward alone to water the camels, for, early as it was, there were others at the well before us. "Men of the Duru tribe, I expect," David said as we sat on the ground with the loads stacked round us, brewing coffee. "Salim will bring us the news."

I dozed, and woke to the sound of the old man's voice. "What's happened?" I asked, for his face was lit by the excitement of some great event. "What's he saying?"

"He's talked with some men of the Rashid, back from selling camels at Saraifa." David's face was grey in the dawn. "They say there's been fighting already—a battle."

"Between Hadd and Saraifa?"

"It's hearsay, that's all. They don't know anything." He didn't want to believe it, but his voice was urgent as he gave the order to mount.

We loaded the camels in a hurry, and as we started out again, I saw that our direction had changed. I asked him where we were going, and he said: "Dhaid. We'll get the news there." And after that he didn't talk. His mood was sullen and withdrawn, his temper short, and he answered Salim angrily whenever the old man protested at the pace of our march.

We rode all day and far into the night, and in the morning the camels were almost done, their pace painfully slow. We reached Dhaid a little after midday. Nobody came out to meet us. Camels dotted the limestone slopes of the hill, and men lay listless under the walls of the village. Inside the arched entrance, the little open place was packed with people; whole families with their beasts and chattels were crowded there in the oven heat that beat back from the walls.

They were all from Saraifa—refugees; the atmosphere was heavy with disaster, the news bad. Two more *falajes*, they said, had been destroyed and a battle fought, out by one of the wells. Khalid was reported dead, his father's soldiers routed.

"Old-fashioned rifles against automatic weapons." David's tone was bitter. "For months the Emir has been receiving a steady trickle of arms. And we've done nothing about it. Nothing at all."

"They're independent states," I reminded him.

"That's what the political boys said when I told them arms were being smuggled in dhows to the Batina coast and brought by camel across the mountains. A perfect excuse for doing nothing. And now, if Khalid is dead . . ." His voice shook. His face looked ghastly, the skin burned black, yet deathly pale. "Sheikh Makhmud's an old man. He can't fight this sort of a war. And the Emir has only to block two more *falajes* and his men can just sit and wait for the end."

We left Salim with the camels and fought our way through the crowd to Sheikh Hassa's house. We found him in the room where I had left Khalid a few days before. He was sitting surrounded by a crush of men all talking at once. The new rifle lay forgotten on the floor. Beside him sat a young man with long features that were tense and pale. "Mahommed," David whispered. "Khalid's half-brother." He'd fled from the battlefield, but he'd seen enough to confirm the rumours we'd heard in the market place. The battle had been fought by the ninth well out along the line of the Mahdah *falaj*, and the casualties had been heavy. Sheikh Makhmud himself had been wounded, and the latest reports of survivors indicated that he had retired to the oasis with the remnant of his forces and was shut up in his palace and preparing to surrender.

David talked to the two of them for about ten minutes, and then we left. "Sheikh Hassa's scared," he said as we pushed our way out into the shade of the alleyway. "All these frightened people flooding into his village . . . It's knocked the fight right out of him. And Mahommed's only a boy. Hassa will hand over Dhaid without firing a shot." He said it angrily, with deep bitterness. And he added: "Fifty resolute men could defend this place for a month—long enough to preserve its independence from Hadd."

"What about Khalid?" I asked. "Did his brother say what had happened to him?"

"No. He doesn't know." His face was grey and haggard. "All this killing and destroying—it's so bloody futile, a lust for oil. Can't they understand the oil won't last? It's just a phase, and when it's past they'll be faced with the desert again; and the only thing that will matter then is what they've built with the oil against the future." And he added angrily: "The Emir didn't care a damn about that border until my father got Gorde to sign a concession. It was just sand, and nothing grew there. And then to cancel it . . . I can still remember the look on Sheikh Makhmud's face that night. God!" he exclaimed. "The callousness of men like Erkhard—Gorde, too. They don't care. These people are human beings, and they're being buggered around by hard-faced men who think only in terms of commerce and money."

We were out of the alley, back in the glare of the crowded market place. He spoke to Salim and gave him money, a handful of Maria Theresa silver dollars poured from a leather bag, and then we settled ourselves in the dust by the entrance gate, leaning our backs against the crumbling mud walls amongst a crowd of listless refugees who watched us curiously. "I've sent Salim to buy fresh camels," David said. "We'll leave as soon as he returns."

"How long will it take us to reach the Hadd border?" I was feeling very tired.

But his mind was on Khalid. "I must find out what's happened to him." He was silent a long time then, tracing patterns in the sand with his camel stick. And then abruptly he rubbed them out with the flat of his palm. "If he's dead . . ." His emotions seemed to grip him by the throat, so that the sentence was cut off abruptly. And then, his voice suddenly practical: "In that case, there are his men. He had more than a score of them, a paid personal bodyguard. Wahiba mostly and some Rashid; all good fighters." He was staring hungrily out into the burning distance of the desert. "I need men," he whispered, his teeth clenched. "Men who'll fight. Not these—" He gestured with contempt at the listless figures around us. "A score of men properly armed and I could put the fear of God into that bloody little Emir."

I didn't bother to ask him how, for I thought it was just wishful thinking and all in his imagination. My eyes were closing with the heat and the weariness of my aching muscles. I heard him say something about getting me to Sharjah as soon as he could, and then I was asleep.

I woke to the voices of Salim and the two Wahiba; they were arguing loudly whilst David sat listening, a tattered Bible propped on the rifle across his knees. Two camels stood disdainfully in front of us. "They've become infected with the mood of this place, blast them!" David closed the Book and got to his feet. A crowd was beginning to collect. He said something to Hamid and the man looked suddenly like a dog that's been beaten. And then David took his rifle from him and handed it to me. "Come on!" he said. "Let's get going." He spoke angrily to the two Wahiba and then we mounted.

The camels were thoroughbred Oman racing camels. I could feel the difference immediately. The crowd parted, letting us through, and we picked our way daintily down the rocks. Out on the flat gravel of the desert below, we moved into an ungainly canter, circling the hill on which Dhaid rested and heading northeast again.

"These people," David said, "they're so damned uncertain—full of guts one minute, craven the next. Salim I didn't expect to come. But Hamid and Ali . . ." He sounded depressed. "My father now, he can handle them the way I'll never be able to." There was admiration, a note of envy in his voice. "They'd never have left him in the lurch." We rode in silence then and at a gruelling pace, the heat very great, so that I was thankful for the water we had got at Dhaid.

We camped at dusk and David had just lighted a fire when he turned suddenly and grabbed his rifle. I heard the pad of camels' feet and then the riders emerged out of the gathering darkness. There were three of them, and David relaxed. "Salim, too," he whispered. He didn't give them any greeting, and they slunk to the fire like dogs. I gave Hamid back his rifle. He took it as though it were a gift and made me a long speech of thanks.

"They're like children," David said. His voice sounded happy.

We had a handful of dates each and some coffee, that was all. And then we rode on.

In the early hours of the morning, with the moon high and a white miasma of mist lying over the desert, we approached the ninth well of the Mahdah *falaj*. Hamid and Ali were scouting ahead on either flank. David and Salim rode close together, their rifles ready-to-hand across their knees. The tension had been mounting all through that night ride, for we'd no idea what we were going to find at the end of it.

For the first time I rode my camel without conscious thought of what I was doing, my whole being concentrated in my eyes, searching the mist ahead. The desert was very still and, half concealed under that white veil, it had a strange, almost eerie quality. From far ahead came a weird banshee howl. It rose to a high note and then dropped to an ugly cough. "Hyena," David said and there was loathing in his voice. The sound, repeated much nearer and to our flank, checked my camel in its stride. It was an eerie, disgusting sound. A little later Salim stopped to stare at some camel tracks. There were droppings, too, and he dismounted, sifted them through his fingers, smelt them, and then delivered his verdict: men of the Bait Kathir, and they had come south the night before with two camels belonging to Saraifa.

"Loot," David said, and we rode on in silence until about ten minutes later Hamid signalled to us. He had sighted the first corpse. It had been stripped of its clothes and there wasn't much meat left on the bones, which stared white through the torn flesh. The teeth, bared in the remains of a beard, had fastened in agony upon a tuft of dried-up herb.

It wasn't a pretty sight with the sand all trampled round about and stained black with blood, and after that the bodies lay thick. They had been caught in ambush and slaughtered as they rushed a small gravel rise where the enemy had lain in wait. There were camels, too, their carcasses bared to the bones and white and brittle-looking like the withered remains of dwarf trees dead of drought. The whole place smelt of death, and things moved on the edge of visibility. Two men slunk away like ghouls, mounted their camels, and disappeared into the mist.

We let them go, for David's only interest was to discover whether Khalid had been killed. Methodically he and Salim checked every corpse, whilst the two Wahiba scouted the edges of the battlefield. David could put names to most of the bodies, despite decomposition and the mutilations of scavengers, and one I recognized myself: the leader of Khalid's escort. He lay face down in the tire marks of a Land Rover, and close beside him were the bodies of three more of Khalid's men, stripped of their clothes and arms.

We hadn't far to go after that. The tire marks lipped a rise, and a little beyond, the burnt-out remains of the Land Rover itself loomed out of the mist. They had sought cover behind it, and their bodies had been ripped to pieces by a murderous fire. Khalid lay with eyeless sockets and half his face torn away. The near-naked body was already disintegrating, and where the stomach had been torn open the rotten flesh crawled with maggots and the blood was dry and black like powder. Four of his men lay near him in much the same state of putrefaction.

"The waste!" David breathed. He was standing, staring down at the remains of his friend, and there were tears in his eyes. "The bloody, senseless waste!" There was a shovel still clipped to the Land Rover, its handle burnt away. He seized it and attacked the ground with violent energy, digging a shallow grave. And when we'd laid what was left of Khalid to rest and covered it with sand, David stood back with bowed head. "He might have saved Saraifa. He was the only one of them who had the vision and the drive and energy to do it." He wiped his face with his head-cloth. "May he rest in peace, and may Allah guide him to the world beyond." He turned his back abruptly on the grave and strode blindly off across the sand towards the gravel rise that had been the scene of the ambush.

Along the back of it ran a ridge of bare rock. Behind it the ground was scattered with the brass of empty cartridges. "War surplus." He tossed one of them to me. "Governments sell that stuff. They never think of the loss of life their bloody auctions will ultimately cause. A pity the little bureaucrat . . ." But he let it go at that, wandering on along the ridge. At four places we came upon the empty magazines of automatic guns; in each case they lay beside the tire marks of vehicles. "They hadn't a chance," he said bitterly and started back to where Salim waited with the camels.

Before we reached them, Ali came hurrying back. He had been scouting to the east, along the line of the *falaj,* and had almost stumbled into a small Hadd force camped by the next well. He said the walls of the well had been thrown down, the whole thing filled with sand and rock. We waited for Hamid. He was a long time coming, and when he did arrive his manner was strange, his eyes rolling in his head as words poured out of him. "He's just buried his father," David said. "The old man's body had a dozen bullets in it." Grimly he gave the order to mount.

I was glad to go. Dawn was breaking and a hot wind beginning to blow from the northwest. I was sick of the sight of so much death. So was David. This, after the lonely weeks he'd spent in that filthy area of quicksands . . . I didn't need the set, withdrawn look of his face, the occasional mumbling of the lips to tell me that he was mentally very near the end of his tether. "Where are we going?" I asked as we rode towards the next well, the wall of which was just visible on the horizon, a little rock turret above the drifting, moving sands.

"Saraifa," he said. "I'll know the worst then." I think he could already picture the misery that awaited us.

Halfway there we met with a family of the Junuba heading towards the mountains with a long string of camels loaded with dates for the coast. They gave us the news. The last *falaj* had ceased to flow that morning. Sheikh Makhmud was said to have died during the night. His brother, Sheikh Sultan, ruled in his place. We purchased some dates from them—we had been unable to buy any supplies in Dhaid—and hurried on.

All the way to Saraifa the traces of disaster were with us: the carcass of a camel, a body sprawled in the sand, discarded arms. But, according to the Junuba, the Emir's men were not in the oasis. "They don't need to attack now," David said. "They can sit on the *falajes* they've destroyed and just wait for the end, like vultures waiting for a man to die." And he added: "Sheikh Sultan will make peace. He's a gutless, effeminate old man, and they know it."

The wind increased in force until it was blowing a strong *shamal* and we never saw Saraifa until the crumbling walls of a date-garden appeared abruptly out of the miasma clouds of wind-blown sand. The palms thrashed in the blinding air as they closed around us.

We passed a patch of cultivation, the green crop already wilted and turning sear. And when we reached the first *shire-eya,* we found it dry, the mud bottom hard as concrete, split with innumerable cracks. The *falaj* channel that supplied it was empty. The skeletal shape of little fish lay in the sand at the bottom of it.

Only when we came to the outskirts of Saraifa itself was there any sign of human activity. Camels were being loaded, household possessions picked over. But most of the *barastis* were already empty, the human life gone from them. Men stopped to talk to us, but only momentarily. They were bent on flight.

It was the same when we reached the mud buildings in the centre of Saraifa. Everywhere there were beasts being loaded. But it was the tail end of the exodus; most of the houses were already deserted. And in the great square under the palace walls the watering-place no longer delivered its precious fluid to a noisy crowd of boys with their asses; the ground round it was caked hard, and the only persons there were an old man and a child of about two.

We circled the walls and came to the main gate. The great wooden portals were closed. No retainers stood guard on the bastions above. The palace had the look of a place shut against the plague and given over to despair. David sat for a moment on his camel, looking down on the date-gardens half hidden beneath the weight of driven sand, and tears were streaming down his face. He turned to me suddenly and swore an oath, demanding that the Almighty should be his witness—and the oath was the destruction of Hadd. "Khalid is dead," he added, and his eyes burned in their sockets. "Now I must do what he'd have done, and I'll not rest till the *falajes* are running again—

not only the five they've destroyed, but the others, too. That I swear, before Almighty God, or my life is worth nothing."

We rode out of Saraifa then, leaving behind us the pitiful sight of a people driven from their homes by thirst, heading into the desert, our heads bent against the wind, our mouths covered. Once David paused, his arm flung out, pointing. "Now you see it. Now you see the Rub al Khali rolling in like the sea." And indeed it did look like the sea, for through gaps in the flying curtain of sand I could see the dunes smoking like waves in the gusts, the sand blowing off their tops in streamers. "That's what Khalid was fighting. Like water, isn't it? Like water flooding in over a low-lying land." And, riding on, he said: "With the people gone, the wells all dry . . . this place won't last long." His words came in snatches on the wind. "How long will they survive, do you think—those families hurrying to go? They're not nomads. They can't live in the sands. They'll die by slow degrees, turned away by sheikh after sheikh who fears they and their beasts will drink his own people out of water. And what can they live on when their camels are gone?"

He was riding close beside me then. "Sometimes I hate the human race . . . hate myself, too, for being human and as cruel as the rest." And then quietly, his teeth clenched, his eyes blazing: "There'll be men die in Hadd for what I've seen today."

It was the strange choice of words, the way he was trembling, and the violence of his manner—I thought he'd been driven half out of his mind by Khalid's death and the tragic things we'd seen.

"All I need is a few men," he whispered to me. "Khalid's are all dead. Half a dozen men, that's all I need."

The sun's heat increased and the wind gradually died. I suffered badly from thirst, for we hadn't much water left and we were riding fast. Towards midday, in a flat gravel pan between high dunes, we came upon the tracks of heavy vehicles. We followed them and shortly afterwards heard the roar of diesels. It was the drilling-rig, both trucks floundering in a patch of soft sand. The big eight-wheeler was out in front, the rig folded down across its back, and it was winching the second truck, loaded with pipe and fuel drums, across the soft patch.

They were working with furious energy, for they'd had refugees from Saraifa through their camp just before they'd pulled out, and they were scared. We stopped with them long enough to brew coffee and give our beasts a rest, and when we rode on, David said to me: "Why's he want to bring that rig here now? What good will it do?" He was haggard-eyed, his face pale under its tan. "They told me he'd requisitioned Entwhistle's seismological outfit—the men as well as the truck. He did that just after the battle, when he knew what had happened. I don't understand it. He must realize it's too late now. . . ."

The shadows of the dunes were lengthening, their crests sharp-etched against the flaming sky. We were working our way across them then, and as the sun finally sank, we came to the top of a dune, out of the shadow into the lurid light of the blood-red sunset, and in the gravel flat below we saw the tracks of vehicles and the blackened circles of camp-fires. "Location B," David said, and we rode down into shadow again.

The camp had been abandoned that morning. So much Salim was able to tell us from the ashes of the camp-fires, and after that we kept just below the dune crests, riding cautiously, with Ali scouting ahead.

We'd only just lost sight of the abandoned camp when the thud of an explosion shook the ground and the sands on the steep face of a dune opposite slid into motion with a peculiar thrumming, singing sound. Our camels stood halted, their bodies trembling, and the singing sound of the sands went on for a long time. There was no further explosion. But almost as soon as we started forward again, Ali called to us and at the same moment there was the crack of a rifle and a bullet sang uncomfortably close.

I don't remember dismounting. I was suddenly stretched on the sand with Salim pulling my camel down beside me. David and Hamid were crawling forward to the dune crest, their guns ready. I thought for a moment we had been ambushed. But then Ali shouted a greeting. He had dropped his rifle and was standing up, throwing sand into the air. It was the Bedou sign that we came in friendship, and in a moment we were dragging our camels down the steep face of the dune and three Arabs were running to meet us, brandishing their weapons and shouting.

We had reached Colonel Whitaker's camp at Location C.

The tents were huddled against the base of a dune, black shapes in the fading light, and out on the gravel flat Entwhistle's seismological truck stood, lit by the glow of cooking-fires. There were perhaps fifteen men in that camp, and they flitted towards us like bats in the dusk. As they crowded round us, one of them recognized David. All was confusion then, a babel of tongues asking questions, demanding news.

David didn't greet them. I doubt whether he even saw them. His eyes were fixed on his father, who had come out of one of the tents and was standing, waiting for us, a dark, robed figure in silhouette against the light of a pressure lamp. David handed his camel to Salim and went blindly forward. I think he still held his father in some awe, but as I followed him I began to realize how much the day had changed him. He had purpose now, a driving, overriding purpose that showed in the way he strode forward.

There wasn't light enough for me to see the expression on Colonel Whitaker's face when he realized who it was. And he didn't speak, even when David stood directly in front of him. Neither of them spoke. They just stood there, staring at each other. I was close enough then to see Whitaker's face. It was without expression. No surprise, no sign of any feeling.

"It's your son," I said. "He's alive."

"So I see." The voice was harsh, the single eye fixed on David. "You've decided to return from the dead. Why?"

"Khalid asked me to come here and talk to you. He wanted us to—"

"Khalid's dead."

"I know that. I buried his body this morning." David's voice trembled with the effort to keep himself under control. "He died because his father hadn't the sense to avoid a pitched battle." And he added: "We passed that rig of yours a few miles back. It's too late now to start drilling on my locations."

"On your locations?"

"On Farr's, then—as checked by me."

"And by me," Whitaker snapped. "Since you've got Grant with you, I presume you now have some idea what I was trying to do. If you hadn't disappeared like that—"

"Don't, for God's sake, let's have another row." David's voice was strangely quiet. "And don't let's start raking over the past. It's too late for that now. Khalid was right. We've got to work together. I came because I need men."

"Men?" Colonel Whitaker stared at him with a puzzled frown. "What do you need men for?"

"I'll tell you in a moment. But first I'd like to know what you're planning to do with that rig. You can't, surely, intend to drill here—not now, after what's happened?"

"Why not?"

"But it's crazy. It'll take you months—"

"You call it crazy now, do you?" Whitaker's voice was hard and pitched suddenly very high. "Last time I saw you, you were raising hell because I wouldn't drill here. Well, now I'm going to try it your way."

"But don't you realize what's happened in Saraifa?"

"Of course I do. Sheikh Makhmud is dead and I've lost an old friend. His brother, Sultan, is Ruler in his place, and you know what that means. Saraifa is finished."

David stared at him in disbelief. "You mean you're going to do a deal with the Emir?" His tone was shocked.

Whitaker's face was without expression. "I've seen him, yes. We've reached a tentative agreement." And then as he saw the look of contempt on David's face, he exclaimed: "*Allah akhbar!* When are you going to grow up, boy?"

"You don't have to worry on that score, sir. I've grown up fast enough these past few months." David's voice was calmer, much quieter. He seemed suddenly sure of himself. "But there's no point in discussing what's gone. It's the future I'm concerned with—the future of Saraifa. Can I rely on you for support or not?"

Whitaker frowned. "Support for what?"

"For an attack on Hadd. I've worked it all out in my mind." David's voice came alive then, full of sudden enthusiasm. "For centuries they've been destroying other people's wells. They've never known what it is to be short of water themselves. I'm going to give them a taste of their own medicine. I'm going to destroy the wells in Hadd."

"Are you out of your mind?" Whitaker glared at him. "Even if you did blow up a well, what good would it do? In a day or at most two they would have repaired it."

"I don't think so," David said quietly. "Just let me have a few men."

"Men? You won't get men out of me for a crack-brained scheme like this." And then in a gentler voice: "See here, David. I realize you've probably been through a lot during the past two months. And if you've been out to the battlefield on the Mahdah *falaj*, as I rather suspect from your attitude, I don't imagine it was a pleasant sight."

"It wasn't a pleasant sight riding through Saraifa and seeing the people there without water and fleeing from the oasis," David answered hotly.

"No. But . . ." Colonel Whitaker hesitated. He'd seen the obstinate look on David's face. No doubt he sensed his mood, too, which was desperately determined. "Come into the tent," he said. "I refuse to continue this discussion out here." He glanced at me. "If you'll excuse us, Grant. I'd like to talk to my son alone for a moment." He pulled back the flap of the tent. "*Faddal.*" It was said quite automatically. A carpet showed red in the glare of the lamplight, some cushions, a tin box, and the two of them were inside the tent and the flap fell.

The outline of the dunes, smooth and flowing like downlands, faded into darkness as I sat alone on the sand, a centre of curiosity for the whole camp. The sky was clouded over, so that there were no stars and it was very dark.

It was about half an hour later that David suddenly emerged out of the night and sat down beside me.

"What happened?" I asked him.

"Nothing," he replied tersely. And after that he sat for a long time without saying a word, without moving. Finally he turned to me of his own accord. "I don't understand him," he said. "It was like talking to a complete stranger." And he added: "I don't think Saraifa means anything to him any more." The bitterness of his voice was overlaid with frustration. "It's tragic," he whispered. "Half a dozen men. That's all I asked him for. But he thinks it's all a dream, that I don't know what I'm doing."

"You told him about Khalid—what he'd said to me?"

"Of course."

"And it made no difference?"

"None."

"What did you talk about, then?"

He laughed a little wildly. "About locations, geological formations, a drilling program. He wasn't interested in anything else." And then, speaking more to himself than to me: "I couldn't get through to him. I just couldn't seem to get through." He beat his fist against the ground. "What do you do when a man's like that?" He stared at me angrily. "I don't understand him. Do you know what he said? He said I was forgiven. He said everything was to be just as it was between us in the early days when I first worked with him. I'm to stay here and help him drill a well. He and I—together; we're going to drill the most important well in Arabia." Again that slightly wild laugh. "And when I mentioned Hadd, he said Hadd or Saraifa, what did it matter now? He'll treat with the Emir, with the Devil himself, so long as he's left in peace to drill his well and prove his bloody theory to the damnation of Philip Gorde and all the rest of the oil boys. God! I wonder I didn't kill him." And he added: "The man's mad. He must be mad."

"Obsessed, perhaps . . ." I murmured.

"Mad." He glared at me. "How else do you explain his attitude, his fantastic assumption that I'd be content to sit here drilling a well after what's happened? For Khalid's sake I'd have agreed to anything. I'd have played the dutiful bastard sitting at the feet of the Great Bedouin. But when I asked him for men . . ." He shook his head. "He wouldn't give them to me. He wouldn't do a damned thing to help. Said I was crazy even to think of it. Me? And all he could talk about, with Makhmud dead and men he'd known for years lying by that well with their guts half eaten out—all he could talk about was his damned theory and how he'd known all along he was right. I tell you, the man's mad." His voice was sharp with frustration. "I wish to

God," he said bitterly, "I'd never come out here, never set eyes on him. And to think I worshipped the man. Yes, worshipped him. I thought he was the greatest man living."

The bitterness in his voice . . . "What are you going to do?" I asked him.

"Take what men I can and get the hell out of here. Do what I planned to do—without his help." His voice had a bite to it, and he slid to his feet. "There's nothing else left for me to do —nothing that means anything, nothing useful." He left me then and hurried down to the dark shapes sitting around the cook-fires, calling to them in their own tongue, gathering them about him. And then he began to harangue them.

A little wind had sprung up, and it chilled the sweat on my body. But it wasn't the drop in temperature that made me shiver. I was caught up in a situation that was beyond my control, isolated here in the desert with two men equally obsessed —the one with oil, the other with an oasis. And then Whitaker's voice close behind me: "Grant. You've got to talk him out of it."

I got to my feet. He was standing there, a dark silhouette against the dunes, staring down at where his son stood amongst the smoke of the fires. "His plan is madness."

But I'd been with David too long not to feel sympathy for him. "He's fighting for something he believes in," I said. "Why don't you help him?"

"By giving him men?" His harsh, beaked face was set and stony. "I've few enough for my purpose as it is." And then in a softer voice: "I had my loyalties, too. But now, with Makhmud dead, I'm free to do what perhaps I should have done in the first place. I've seen the Emir. I've sent Yousif to Sharjah with those letters to merchants there. I'm rechecking the earlier surveys. In a few days we'll spud in and start to drill. And when I've brought in the first discovery well, then all this trouble between Hadd and Saraifa will be seen in perspective, a small matter compared with the vast changes an oilfield will bring to the desert here."

"And your son?" I asked.

He shrugged. "As I told you before, when I thought he was dead, I'd hoped he'd follow me, a second Whitaker to carry on where I left off. Instead, I find myself cursed with an obstinate, stupid youth who's no respect for my judgement and opposes me at every turn." He put his hand on my arm, and in a surprisingly gentle voice he said: "Talk to him, Grant. Try and do for me what I know I can't do myself. His plan is suicidal."

He was looking straight at me and I was shocked to see there were tears running down his cheeks—not only from the one good eye, but welling out from beneath the black patch that concealed the other. "Do what you can," he said softly. And then he turned quickly away and went back to his tent.

Ten minutes later David was back at my side, looking tired and drained. "One man," he said in a bleak voice. "One man will come with me. That's all. Hamid's brother, bin Suleiman. And he's coming, not because he understands my plan, but simply because with him, as with Hamid, it's a blood feud now." He gave a shrug and a quick laugh. "Well, the fewer the better, perhaps. They'll drink less water, and water is going to be our trouble." He called to Hamid and gave the order to load the camels. "We'll leave as soon as I've got the things I need out of Entwhistle's truck."

I started to try and talk him out of it, but he brushed my words aside. "My mind's made up. Talking won't change it." And then he said: "What about you? Are you staying here or will you come with me?" He stared at me, a long, speculative look. "If you should decide to come with me, then I can promise to get you away to the coast with Salim as your guide." And he added: "If you don't come, then I think I may be throwing my life away for nothing. You're my only hope of contact with the outside world, and if the world doesn't know what I'm doing, then it's all wasted."

I asked him what exactly he planned to do, but he wouldn't tell me the details. "You'd have to know the ground or you might agree with my father and think it crazy. But I assure you," he added with great conviction, "that with any luck at all it will work. It's the last thing the Emir will be expecting, and the fact that we'll be a very small party . . ." He smiled. "It makes it easier, really—the first part, at any rate. And I promise you you'll not be involved in the rest. Think it over, will you, sir? I need your help in this—desperately." He left it like that and disappeared abruptly into the night.

I lay on the hard ground, listening to the movement of the camels, the sounds of preparation for another journey. A little wind came in puffs, sifting the sand, and it was dark. A stillness had enveloped the camp. I don't think I'm any more of a coward than the next man, but to seek out death, deliberately and in cold blood . . . You see, it never occurred to me he could succeed. I thought his father was right and that he was throwing away his life in a futile gesture. I remembered Gorde's description of Whitaker—an old man tilting at windmills. David was very like his father in some ways. I closed my eyes, thinking of Tanganyika and the hard life I'd led there, and then I felt a hand on my shoulder.

"Well?" David asked, and when I nodded almost without thinking, he passed me a rifle. "I take it you know how to use it?" He had another, which he handed to bin Suleiman, and a revolver with holster and belt, which he strapped to his own waist.

The stark reality of what I was doing came with the feel of the well-oiled breech under my hand. It took me back to days I thought I'd forgotten—to the deadly slopes of Monte Cassino, to Anzio and the Gothic Line. I rose quietly to my feet. Salim and Ali were loading cartons of explosive cartridges on to one of the camels. Hamid and his brother, a squat, hairy man with wild eyes and a low-browed head, were packing coils of fine wire and a contact plunger with its batteries into the saddle-bags of another beast.

The camels staggered to their feet, bulking suddenly large against the overcast, and we were on our way.

A lone figure standing by one of the tents watched us go. It was Colonel Whitaker. He made no move to stop us, nor did he call out. We left the camp in silence, and though they knew we were going, no man stirred from the camp-fires. It was as though they feared to have any contact with us; it was as though we had already passed beyond the shadows of death.

Clear of the camp, we turned east, working our way silently up the face of a dune in short zig-zags. At the crest we stopped to mount, and then we were riding, the dark desert all around us and the swaying shapes of our camels the only movement in the stillness of night.

The clouds thinned and gradually cleared, leaving us exposed in bright moonlight. But if the Emir had men watching Whitaker's camp, we never saw them. Dawn found us camped amongst sparse camel thorn on a flat gravel plain. Sharp-etched against the break of day stood the jagged tops of the mountains. Dates and coffee, and then sleep. "We start at dusk," David said and buried his face in his head-cloth.

The withered camel thorn gave little shelter, and as the sun climbed the burning vault of the sky, it became very hot. Flies worried us, clinging to the sweat of exposed flesh, and we suffered from thirst, for our water-bags were empty and all we had was the contents of two water-bottles. We took it in turns to keep watch, but the shimmering expanse of gravel that surrounded us remained empty of life.

As the sun sank we lit a fire and had a huge meal of rice and dried meat. A bowl of warm camel's milk passed from mouth to mouth. Our four Arabs talked excitedly amongst themselves and, the meal finished, they began to oil their guns, cleaning them with loving care. In contrast, David and I sat silent, doing nothing. The sun set and in an instant the sky had paled. The visibility was fantastic in the dry air, everything sharp and clear, as though magnified.

"You'd better tell me what you plan to do," I said, and my voice reflected the tension that had been growing in me all through that long, inactive day.

David was staring at the distant line of the mountains and for a moment I thought he hadn't heard my question. But then he said: "It isn't easy to explain to somebody who has never been to Hadd."

"I've flown over it," I said.

He looked at me then, a sudden quickening of interest. "Did you see the fort of Jebel al-Akhbar? Did you see how the town is backed right into the rock?" And when I explained how I'd passed close over it in Gorde's plane, he said: "Then you know the situation. That fort is the key to Hadd. Who holds that fort holds the people of Hadd in the hollow of his hand. It's as simple as that." He was suddenly excited, his eyes bright with the vision of what he planned to do. "When there was trouble here before, the Trucial Oman Scouts moved into the fort and that was the end of it."

"We're not the Trucial Oman Scouts." I thought it was time he faced up to the facts. "There are six of us, that's all. We're armed with rifles and nothing else. And our ammunition is limited."

"There's ammunition for us in the fort," he said. "Two boxes of it and a box of grenades." Apparently he and Khalid had found them left there by the TOS and half buried under a pile of rubble. They were out hunting as the Emir's guests and had taken refuge in the fort during a sandstorm. "It's a long time ago now," he added, "but I think we'll find the boxes still there. We buried them pretty deep. As for numbers . . ." He gave a little shrug. "One man, well armed and determined, could hold that tower for as long as his water held out." He smiled grimly. "Water. It always comes back to water in the desert, doesn't it?" And he slid to his feet and gave the order to move.

As we rode he pointed out the fort to me, small as a pinhead on top of a hill that miraculously detached itself from the line of the mountains, standing clear in the last of the daylight and much nearer than I had expected. "Dawn tomorrow," he said, "that's where we'll be." He looked very much like his father as he stared at me, his youthful features set in the grimmer mould of an older man. "God willing!" he breathed. "And when we're there you'll understand." He rode on then with his four Wahiba, talking with them urgently in their own tongue and leaving me to ride alone, prey to my own forebodings.

Dusk fell and merged imperceptibly into night. The stars lit our way, and in no time at all, it seemed, there was the Jebel al-Akhbar, a black hat of a hill bulked against the night sky. We rode slowly in a tight little bunch. The time was a little after ten. "We'll water our camels at the well on the outskirts, fill our water-bags. . . ." David's voice was taut.

"And if there's a guard?" I whispered.

"We're travellers from Buraimi on our way to the coast. Bin Suleiman will explain. He's known here."

"And after we've filled our water-bags?"

"Ssh!" The camels had stopped at a signal from Hamid. We sat still as death, listening. There were rock outcrops ahead and the dim shapes of buildings. A solitary light showed high up on the slope of the hill, which now towered above us, a dark mass against the stars. Somewhere a goat bleated. There was no other sound.

A whispered word from David and we moved forward again. The well-head appeared, a simple wooden structure topping a crumbling wall of mud and stone. We dismounted and the leathern bucket was dropped into the depths. The wooden roller creaked as it was drawn up. One by one the camels were watered; one by one, the skin bags filled. And all the time the wood creaked and we stood with our guns ready. But nobody came. The solitary light vanished from the slope of the hill, leaving the whole town dark as though it were a deserted ruin. Salim and Ali left with the camels and David went to work with cartridges of explosive and detonators. And when he'd mined the well, we went forward on foot, running the thin line of the wire out behind us.

The second well was close under the walls and there were camels couched near it. We could hear them stirring uneasily, could even see some of them, dark shapes against the lighter stone. A man coughed and sat up, dislodging a stone. The sound of it was magnified by the silence. And then I saw his figure coming towards us. Hamid and bin Suleiman moved to intercept. They talked together in whispers whilst David went on working and I helped him, glancing every now and then over my shoulder, expecting every moment to hear the man cry out and raise the alarm.

But nothing happened. The camels quietened down, the man went back to his interrupted sleep, and David was left to complete his work in peace. He worked fast and with absolute sureness, but it all took time. It was past midnight before he had finished, and a paler light above the mountains warned that the moon was rising.

As we trailed our wire towards a gap in the crumbling walls, two shots sounded far out in the desert behind us. We checked, standing there motionless and sweating. But there were no more shots. "Somebody out hunting gazelle," David whispered. "They do it at night by the lights of their Land Rovers." And we went on through the gap, which led to a narrow alley. There were no doors to the buildings on either side, only window openings high up. The alley led into the market place. More camels, some goats and figures asleep against the walls of the houses. The well was on the far side. There was a baby camel there, and a small boy lay curled up beside it. The camel, its coat fluffy as a kitten's, rose on straddling, spindly legs and gazed at us in amazed silence. The boy stirred, but didn't wake. A dog began to bark.

I caught hold of David's arm. "You've done enough, surely," I whispered.

"Scared?" He grinned in the darkness and shrugged me off. "We can't climb to the fort till the moon's up." And he squatted down in the dust and went to work. The boy suddenly sat up, staring at us, round-eyed. I thought: My God! If he kills that child . . . But David said something and the boy got slowly to his feet and came hesitantly forward, gazing in fascination. David gave him the wire to hold. A man moved in the shadows by an archway. The boy's father. As he came forward, other figures stirred. A little knot of men gathered round us. But the boy sitting there in the dust beside David, helping him, made it all seem innocent. They stood and watched for a while, talking with Hamid and bin Suleiman, and then they drifted back to their sleep.

The moon rose. The mud walls of the houses on the far side of the open place stood suddenly white, and moment by moment the dark shadow-line retreated until it touched the base of the buildings and began to creep across the ground towards us. At last David tied his mine to the well rope and lowered it. We left then, and the boy came with us, trailing the baby camel behind him. Other figures followed us, curious but not hostile. "They don't belong to Hadd," David whispered. "They're

Bedou in from the desert to sell camels. Otherwise we'd never
have got out of there alive."

"What did they think we were doing?"

"I said we were testing the wells before installing pumping-
equipment. They know all about pumps. They've seen them in
Buraimi and also in Saraifa." By the second well we picked up
the line of our wire, clipped on another coil, and trailed it to
the limit up the hill just outside the walls. There David fastened it to the terminals of the plunger, and then he handed it
to the boy and told him what to do. "He'll tell the story of this
moment till the end of his days." He patted the boy on the
shoulder, smiling almost cheerfully as he turned and left him.

We climbed quickly, came out from the shadow of the wall
on to the moonlit slope of the hill, and on a rock well above the
rooftops of the highest houses we halted. The boy was squatting there beside the detonator, his face turned towards us.
David raised his hand above his head and then let it fall. The
boy turned away and his shoulders hunched as he thrust down
on the plunger.

The silence ceased abruptly, the stillness of the night rent by
three deep, rumbling explosions that were instantly muffled and
snuffed out by the collapse of the earth walls of the wells. The
sound nevertheless went on, travelling back through the mountains, reverberating from face after face and gradually fading.

The boy still hadn't moved when all sound had ceased. The
baby camel stood beside him. It was as though the shattering
effect of the explosion had turned them both to stone. Then
suddenly he was jerked to life. For an instant his face was
turned towards us, white and startled in the moonlight, and
then he fled screaming down the hillside, the camel breaking
away in ungainly puppet strides.

VI

Fort Jebel al-Akhbar

We turned then

and followed a zig-zag track that climbed by crumbling outcrops, and below us the town came to life—the sound of voices, the glimmer of lights. A shot stabbed the night, but it wasn't directed at anything in particular and we were close under the fort before the pursuit got under way. We could see them clear on the moonlit slope below us, zig-zagging up the path by which we had come. There were about a dozen of them, climbing in single file and moving fast with the agility of mountain goats.

The fort tower hung on the lip of the cliff above us, a white stone keep crumbling to decay, and where the track doubled back through a narrow defile in the rocks David posted Hamid to guard our rear. "I hope to God we find Salim there," he panted. The path had steepened, so that we climbed with our hands as well as our feet, rocks slipping away from under us. And then we reached the walls and the track led through a narrow opening.

We were inside the outer defences then, an open space of half an acre or more that occupied all the top of the hill. The walls had originally been about twenty feet high, with a firing-step round the inside, but they were now in a bad state of repair and there were few places where they were higher than ten feet. They were horseshoe-shaped, the two ends finishing abruptly at the cliff edge, the tower between them. There was no sign of the camels.

"Damn the old fool! He should have been here by now."

David's sudden uneasiness made me wonder whether perhaps Salim had taken the opportunity to desert us. But when I suggested this, he shook his head. "Why do you think I sent Ali with him? That boy knew what those camels meant to us. No, something has happened to them."

A shot ripped the silence apart. Hamid had opened fire on our pursuers, and the sound of it echoed back from the naked rock faces that surrounded us. A scatter of shots sounded from lower down the slope and a bullet hit the wall close by us with a soft thud.

"Wait for me here. I'm going to see what's happened." David ran quickly across the open courtyard of the fort and out through the main gate on the north side, and when he was gone I climbed to the broken top of the wall and threw myself down beside bin Suleiman. From this vantage point we commanded the final approach to the fort.

Perched high on the edge of the sheer cliff face, I could see right down into the town of Hadd. The market square, where we'd mined the third well, was clearly visible, a white rectangle with people moving about or standing in little groups. It was not more than a thousand feet away, an easy rifle shot. And the wells outside the walls—I could see them, too. I began to understand then why David had been so sure those damaged wells would stay out of action.

Immediately below was the defile. I could see Hamid stretched out on top of one of the rock shoulders. His rifle gleamed as he raised it to his shoulder. A stab of flame, the crack of the shot, and then silence again. On the slope beyond there was now no sign of pursuit. The men who had started to follow us were pinned down amongst the rocks. It was an incredible position, impossible to take from that side so long as it was defended by men who knew how to shoot.

A bullet whined low over my head and I ducked automatically, poking my rifle forward and searching the steep slope beyond the defile. But there was nothing to fire at. The night was still and without movement.

We remained in that position for two solid hours whilst the stars moved sedately round the sky and all away to our right the desert stretched its white expanse. The sense of isolation, of a long wait for ultimate death, gradually took hold of me. It had a strange effect, a throw-back, I think, to the mood that had filled me as we lay pinned down like rats on the slopes of Monte Cassino . . . a mood compounded of fear and the desire to survive that expressed itself in the need to kill, so that when a figure moved on the slope below me, my whole being was concentrated in my trigger finger, and as he stumbled and fell my only feeling was one of elation, a deep, trembling satisfaction.

A little after three the first glimmer of dawn brought the mountains into sharp relief. A small wind whispered among the stones and it was quite chill. It was the time of night when the body is at the lowest ebb, and I began to worry about David, and about our rear. By now men from the village below could surely have circled Jebel al-Akhbar to climb by the camel track to the main gate. I called to bin Suleiman and made a motion with my hand to indicate what I was going to do, and then I abandoned my position and started on a tour of the walls.

The result was encouraging. They were built on sheer rock slopes. Only on the north side was there any means of reaching the fort. There the camel track climbed steeply from the desert below to enter by the only gateway. Old palm-tree timbers sagged from rusted iron hinges. This was the way attack must come if it were to succeed. Bastion towers flanked the gate on either side, and from the top of one of them I could see down the whole length of the track. It was empty. So, too, were the slopes of the hill. There was no cover, and nowhere could I see any sign of David or the camels.

I was turning away when my eye caught a movement on the white floor of the desert below: four shapes moving slowly, their shadows more sharply defined than the shapes themselves. They were camels moving towards the bottom of the track, and as they turned to start the climb, I made out the figure of a solitary rider on the leading camel.

I lay down then on the broken stone top of the bastion and pushed the safety-catch of my rifle forward. Our camels had numbered six, and with David there should have been three riders. They came on very slowly whilst the grey of dawn overlaid the moonlight and the whiteness faded out of the desert.

As the light improved and they came nearer, I saw the body of a man lying slumped over the saddle of the second camel. Skin bags bulging with water confirmed that the beasts were ours, and soon after that I was able to recognize David. I met him as he rode in through the broken gateway. He didn't say anything as he dismounted, but his face looked grey. "What happened?" I asked.

"Those shots we heard . . . They rode straight into a party of the Emir's men camped outside the town." He asked me then whether they'd tried to rush us yet.

"No," I said. "They're still pinned down less than a third of the way up the slope."

"Good. Give me a hand, will you?" He led the second camel to the foot of the tower and got it couched. The body tied with cord across its back was Ali's. "He's badly hurt." We laid him gently on the ground. He moaned softly, barely conscious. He'd a ghastly wound in the chest. I'd seen the effect of a soft-nosed Bedouin bullet on the metal of a Land Rover; now I was seeing its effect on human flesh, and the sight appalled me. He'd a knife wound in the shoulder, too, and he'd lost a lot of blood; the dark, broad-lipped, girlish face had taken on a sickly pallor.

David stood for a moment, staring down at him. "Poor kid," he murmured. "I found him lying in a pool of blood by the ashes of their camp-fire. I suppose they thought he was dead. Salim's body was close beside him. They'd slit his throat." His voice shook. "The murdering, dung-eating bastards! Why did they have to do it? There were at least twenty of them there, twenty of them against an old man and a boy." Apparently he'd found the camp deserted, our four camels wandering loose. "They must have been disturbed by the sound of the explosions," he said. "Otherwise, they wouldn't have left the camels. They only took one. It was the other that led me to their camp; it was wandering around on three legs, bellowing with pain. I had to finish it off." He gave a quick, angry shrug as though wanting to dismiss the whole thing from his mind. "Well, let's get him up into the tower. He can't lie here."

He got the camel to its feet and stood it close by the wall of the tower. Standing on its back, he was just able to reach the hole halfway up the tower's side. He scrambled in and from the dark interior produced a crude ladder made of palm-wood. We dragged the boy up and laid him on the dirt floor and David plugged and bound the wounds again, using his head-cloth, which he tore in strips. "A bloody lousy piece of luck," he said. "I'd planned to get you away before daylight. With Salim to guide you, you'd have been in Buraimi tomorrow, in Sharjah by the next day. I'd got it all planned. Now . . ." He shrugged. "We'll have to do some fresh thinking."

It was daylight now. It came filtering into the interior of the tower through the entrance hole and through four narrow slits in the thick walls. They were firing-embrasures, and they reminded me of the turret room I'd occupied in Saraifa. But the view was vastly different. Two of them looked out east and west, each covering an arm of the walls. The other two, close together, faced south; they looked straight down on to Hadd itself.

"Well, that's all I can do for him." David got to his feet. "You stay here. I must have a word with Hamid and bin Suleiman. And then we must deal with the camels."

He left me sitting by one of the embrasures and I had time to think then. The excitement of action that had sustained me so far was gone now. The future stared me in the face and I began to be afraid of it. However impregnable the fort's position, there were still only four of us, and right there below me was that Arab town teeming with life and utterly hostile. I could see men clustered thick in the open square and some of them were armed. It could only be a matter of time.

They had already started work on the well inside the walls. Men were being lowered into it and every now and then a bundle of stones and rubble was handed up. The sun was rising behind the mountains. The sky was crimson and all the desert flushed the colour of a rose. It looked very beautiful, so serene in the clear morning air, and the mountains standing like cutouts painted purple.

It was just after the sun had lipped the mountain-tops that

David climbed back into the tower. "They've started work on that well in the square, haven't they?"

I nodded. The little square was teeming like an ant-hill.

"What are they—townspeople or the Emir's bodyguard?" He had his rifle with him and he came straight over to where I was squatting on the floor beside the embrasure.

"Both," I said. The men working on the well were mostly stripped to the waist. But, standing about, watching them, were a number of armed men, their bodies strapped about with cartridges, bands of brass that glinted in the sun; their rifles, untrammelled with silver, had the dull gleam of modern weapons.

He pushed past me, kneeling in the embrasure, steadying himself with his elbows on the sill as he brought the rifle to his shoulder and fired. The sound of the shot was very loud in that dim, confined place. "That's one of them that won't go murdering old men and boys again." He was trembling slightly as he sat back on his heels.

The crowd in the square was scattering. A little knot gathered in one corner, and then that, too, melted away and the square was suddenly empty. "An occasional shot like that and they'll learn to leave it alone. In a day or two they'll begin to understand what it's like to have the sources of water cut off, the wells dry." He got up and set his gun against the wall. "Not that they'll die of thirst. They're better off than the people we saw in Saraifa." He went back down the ladder and left me staring at the empty rectangle of the sun-drenched square, littered with the balks of timber they'd brought in to shore up the inner walls of the well. Behind me the wounded boy moaned restlessly, muttering words I couldn't understand, and when I went to him, I found his dark eyes wide open and staring, his skin dry and parched. I gave him some water, and then David called to me.

He and Hamid had started unloading the camels. Bin Suleiman kept watch from the eastern wall. We worked fast, but the sun was high above the mountains before we'd humped all the stores and the last of the water-skins up into the tower. "What about the camels?" I asked as we lifted the saddles from their backs. It was already blisteringly hot, the bare rock acting as a fire-brick and throwing back the sun's heat. There was no vestige of vegetation inside the fort for them to feed on.

"I'll keep one for you. The other three will have to be slaughtered."

They were fine beasts in the prime of life and in beautiful condition. But when I started to remonstrate, he cut me short. "What did you imagine we were going to do with them? We've no other meat." He stared at me angrily. "Even the Bedou, who love camels a damn sight more than I do, don't hesitate to kill them when they're short of food. And we're going to be short of everything before we're through."

I stood and stared at him. Without camels, he'd have no means of retreat. He'd be trapped here. . . .

"Do you reckon you could get through to Buraimi on your own?"

I hesitated. But I knew now there was no alternative for me—only death here on this pitiless hilltop. "I could try."

"Good. We'll keep the one you've been riding, then, and get you away tonight as soon as it's dark."

Immediately after we'd breakfasted, bin Suleiman butchered the three camels, slitting their throats and letting the blood drain into a tin bowl. The carcasses were then disembowelled, and the meat cut into strips and hung to dry in the sun. Flies buzzed and the place smelt of blood, and yet it didn't seem unnatural. Sand and rock and the blazing sky, that boy lying in the dim interior of the tower, his breath gurgling in his throat and blood seeping on to the floor, and below us an Arab town ruled by a man consumed by a murderous greed. Death didn't seem so hateful when life itself was so cruel.

Action followed hard upon my thoughts. Hamid, from his lookout post on the very top of the tower, called down to us: men were circling the hill to the north. From the walls we watched them climb by the camel track. They were well spaced out, their guns ready in their hands. Others were coming up by the zig-zag path direct from Hadd. Lying prone on the blistering stones, we waited, holding our fire. The stillness seemed to break their nerve, for they began shooting at a range of almost three hundred yards.

The attack, when it came, was a senseless, ill-directed affair, men clawing their way up the last steep rock ascent to the walls without any supporting fire. We caught them in the open, unprotected, and the attack petered out almost before it had begun. They went back down the sides of the hill, taking their wounded with them and not leaving even a single sniper to harass us from the shelter of the rocks.

"It won't be as easy as that next time they come." David's eyes had a cold, dead look, untouched by the light of battle that I'd glimpsed for a moment on bin Suleiman's broad animal face.

We had used, I suppose, no more than two or three dozen rounds, but it was sufficient to make David anxious about his ammunition. Whilst the two Wahiba kept watch, David and I lowered the ladder through a hole in the mud floor of the tower and climbed down into the black rubble-filled pit below. It was slow work, searching in the dark, for we'd nothing but our hands to dig with and after so long David wasn't at all certain where he had buried the boxes. We must have been down there at least an hour, and all the time we were scrabbling at the rubble with our hands, Ali lay delirious on the floor above. Twice Hamid's rifle cracked as he carried out David's orders and kept the wells in Hadd clear of people. Those sounds and the darkness and the feeling that at any moment we might be overwhelmed through lack of ammunition gave a sense of desperate urgency to our work.

Finally we found the boxes and hauled them through the hole to the floor above—more than a thousand rounds of ammunition and two dozen grenades. We'd barely got the boxes open when Hamid reported a Land Rover leaving the palace. We watched it from the embrasures, blaring its horn as it snaked through Hadd's crooked alleys and out through the main gates of the town. It headed south towards Saraifa, and David let it go, not firing a shot. "The sooner Sheikh Abdullah is informed of the situation here," he said, "the sooner his raiding force will leave Saraifa in peace." His eyes were shining now, for this was what he'd intended. That little puff of dust trailing across the desert was the visual proof of the success of his plan.

"But what happens," I said, "when Sheikh Abdullah attacks us here with all his forces?"

He smiled, a flash of white teeth in the dark, lean face. "We're not short of ammunition now."

"But we're short of men. There are only four of us. How many do you think Sheikh Abdullah musters?" I thought it was time he faced up to the situation.

"It's not numbers that count," he answered tersely. "Not up here. Whoever built this fort designed it to be held by a handful of men." And he added: "We're bloody good shots, you see. Hamid and bin Suleiman, they're like all the Bedou—they've had guns in their hands since they were kids. And me, I learned to shoot out hunting with Khalid." He was almost grinning then. "I tell you, man, I can hit a gazelle running with a rifle bullet —and a gazelle's a bloody sight smaller than a man. Anyway," he added, "no call for you to worry. With any luck we'll get you away under cover of darkness tonight."

"And what about you?" I asked. "You've no camels now."

"No." He stared at me, a strange, sad look in his eyes. And then he gave a little shrug. "There comes a moment in every man's life, I suppose, when his destiny catches up with him."

Again I was conscious of his strange choice of words, the sense of fatalism. "If you don't get out . . . if you stay here until Sheikh Abdullah's men have surrounded you . . ." What could I say to make him see sense? "You'll die here," I told him bluntly.

"Probably."

We stood there, staring at each other, and I knew there was nothing I could say that would make him change his mind. He didn't care. He was filled with a burning sense of mission. It showed in his eyes, and I was reminded of the word Sue had used to describe his mood—the word "dedicated." All the misdirected energy that had involved him in gang warfare in Cardiff docks—now it had found an outlet, a purpose, something he believed in. Death meant nothing.

"What about Hamid and bin Suleiman?" I asked. "Will they fight with you to the end?"

"Yes," he said. "They've a blood feud on their hands and they want to kill."

There was nothing more to be said, then. "If I reach Buraimi and get through to the coast, I'll inform the authorities of the situation at once."

"Of course." He said it with a bitter little smile, so that I was afraid he'd read my thoughts and knew I was thinking that help would arrive too late. But then he said: "It's no good talking to the authorities, you know. They won't do anything. Much better give the story to the newspapers. I wouldn't like to die without anybody knowing what I'd tried to do." Again that bitter little smile, and then he turned away. "Better get some sleep now. You've a long journey and you'll need to be fresh for it."

But sleep wasn't easy. The only place where there was any shade was the tower, and there Ali's agony of mind and body was a thin thread of sound piercing each moment of unconsciousness, so that I dreamed I was listening to David's death throes, at times to my own. He died as the sun sank—a brief rattle in the throat and silence. And at that same moment David scrambled in by the entrance hole to announce that there were vehicles coming from the direction of Saraifa.

"I think Ali is dead," I said.

He bent over the boy and then nodded. "I should have put him out of his misery," he said. "Without a doctor, he hadn't a hope, poor kid."

From the embrasures we watched a trail of dust moving in from the desert . . . three open Land Rovers packed with men, a machine-gun mounted in the back of each vehicle. David called down to Hamid, who was cooking rice over a fire, and he grabbed his gun and climbed the outer wall to lie prone beside bin Suleiman. David motioned me to the other embrasure. "Don't fire till I do. And, remember, every man you hit is one less for us to deal with later." He had dropped to his knees, his rifle ready in the slit of the embrasure.

The three Land Rovers reached the main gates and there they halted, stopped by the crowd of people who swarmed round them, all pointing and gesticulating towards us. An Arab askari in the leading Land Rover swung his machine-gun, and a long burst ripped the sunset stillness. Bullets splattered against the base of the tower. The guns of the other two Land Rovers followed suit—a sound like ripping calico. Several rifles were let off.

It was a demonstration designed to restore morale. My hand trembled as I set the sights of my rifle to 500. And then David fired and I was conscious of nothing but my finger on the trigger and the third Land Rover fastened like a toy to the V of my sights. The smell of cordite singed my nostrils. Fire blossomed like a yellow flower against the dun of desert sand. Men scattered. Some fell. And in a moment there was nothing to shoot at.

One Land Rover in flames, the other two deserted; some bodies lying in the dust. Tracer bullets exploded like fireworks from the back of the burning vehicle, and almost immediately a second Land Rover caught fire as the petrol tank went up.

"I'm afraid they won't give us an opportunity like that again." David sat back on his haunches and cleared his gun. "It will be night attacks from now on."

Hadd was deserted now. Not a soul to be seen anywhere, the alleyways and the square empty. The Emir's green flag hung limp above the palace; nothing stirred. Hamid went back to his cooking. The sun set and the excitement of action ebbed away, leaving a sense of nervous exhaustion. "You'd better leave as soon as it's dark," David said. Dusk had fallen and we were feeding in relays. He began to brief me on the route to follow, and as I listened to his instructions, the lonely desolate miles of desert stretched out ahead. The embers of the fire were warm. The dark shapes of the surrounding walls gave a sense of security. I was loath to go, and yet I knew the security of those walls false, the embers probably the last fire for which they would have fuel.

He gave me dates and a bottle filled with water, sufficient to take me to the first well, and then began to saddle the camel. "You'll be seeing Sue?"

I nodded.

"Give her my love; tell her I'll be thinking of her and of a day we spent on the Gower. She'll know what I mean."

"She thinks you're dead," I reminded him.

"Well, tell her I'm not—not yet, anyway." And he laughed and slung the heavy blanket over the wooden saddle.

Ten minutes and I'd have been away. Just ten minutes, that was all I needed. But then the sound of a rifle cut the stillness of the night and a man screamed and went on screaming—a thin, high-pitched sound that had in it all that any one could ever know of pain. Bin Suleiman shouted a warning from the east-facing wall, and David let go the camel and raced to meet the attack. "Get out now," he called to me over his shoulder. "Get out now before it's too late!" He called something to Hamid, who was posted on the far side of the fort by the main entrance gate, and then the darkness had swallowed him. A stab of flame showed high up on the wall, and the echo of the shot cut through the man's screams as though it had severed his vocal cords. A sudden silence followed, an unnatural stillness.

The camel, startled by the noise, had fled into the night. I found him close under the wall of the tower. Bewildered and obstinate, the wretched beast refused to move, and by the time I had coaxed him to the main gate it was too late. Firing had broken out all round us. A figure appeared at my side, gripped my arm, and shouted something in Arabic. It was Hamid, and he gestured towards the tower. Rocks thundered against the wooden timbers of the gate we had barricaded that afternoon. Hamid fired, working the bolt of his rifle furiously, the noise of his shots beating against my ear-drums.

And then he was gone, running for the tower. I let the camel go and followed him, my gun clutched in my hands. Bin Suleiman was at the ladder ahead of me. David followed close behind as I flung myself through the hole and into the darkness beyond. As soon as we were all inside, we drew the ladder up. Bullets splattered the wall—the soft, dull thud of lead, the whine of ricochets. "Didn't expect them to attack so soon," David panted.

We heard the wood splinter as they broke down the gate. They were inside the walls then, vague shadows in the starlight, and we fired down on them from the embrasures. The shouts, the screams, the din of firing . . . it went on for about ten minutes, and then suddenly they were gone and the inside of the fort was empty save for half a dozen robed figures lying still or dragging themselves laboriously towards the shelter of the walls.

From the top of those walls our attackers kept up a steady fire. Bullets whistled in through the entrance hole so often that the slap of lead on the opposite wall became a commonplace. They caused us no inconvenience, for they struck one particular spot only, and the convex curve of the wall prevented them from ricocheting. We kept a watch at one of the embrasures, but did not bother to return their fire. "Let them waste their ammunition," David said. "Our turn will come when the moon rises."

Once they misinterpreted our silence and left their positions along the outer walls. We waited until they were in the open, and as they hesitated, considering how to reach the entrance hole, we caught them in a withering fire. Our eyes, accustomed to the darkness of the tower's interior, picked them out with ease in the starlight. Very few got back to the safety of the walls or out through the gateway. And when the moon rose about an hour later we climbed the ladder to the very top of the tower, and from there we were able to pick them off as they lay exposed along the tops of the walls.

Below us Hadd lay white and clearly visible. There was great activity round all the wells. David fired one shot. That was all. The people scattered, activity ceased, and in an instant the whole town appeared deserted again.

We took it in turns to sleep then, but there was no further attack, and sunrise found us in command of the whole area of the fort. With no cover from which they could command our position, the Hadd forces had retired. We took the guns and ammunition from the dead and dragged the bodies outside the walls. Nobody fired on us. The hilltop was ours, and the sun beat down and the rock walls became too hot to touch. We buried Ali and retired to the shade of the tower. The camel that was to have carried me to Buraimi had disappeared. There was nothing for me to do but resign myself to the inevitable.

"How long do you think you can hold out here?" I asked.

"Until our water's gone," David answered. "Or until we run out of ammunition."

"And Hadd?" I asked. "How desperate will they become?"

He shrugged. "There's a well in the Emir's palace, and they can always evacuate the town and camp out in the date-gardens. There's plenty of water there. It's more a question of the Emir's pride. He can't afford to sit on his arse and do nothing."

And each night we'd be a little wearier, the hours of vigilance more deadly. I closed my eyes. The heat was suffocating, the floor on which we lay as hard as iron. Sleep was impossible. The flies crawled over my face, and my eyeballs felt gritty against the closed lids. The hours dragged slowly by. We'd nothing to do but lie there and keep watch in turns.

Shortly after midday a cloud of dust moved in from the desert —men on camels riding towards Hadd from the south. It was Sheikh Abdullah's main force. They halted well beyond the range of our rifles, and the smoke of their cooking-fires plumed up into the still air. There were more than a hundred of them, and at dusk they broke up into small groups and moved off to encircle our hill. They seemed well organized and under a central command.

It was that and the fact that they were mounted on camels that decided me. I went to where David was standing by one of the embrasures. "I'm going to try and get out tonight," I told him. "Whilst it's dark, I'll get out on to the hillside and lie up and wait for a chance to take one of their camels." And I added: "Why don't you do the same? A quick sortie. It's better than dying here like a rat in a trap."

"No." The word came sharp and hard and violent. His eyes burned in their shadowed sockets, staring at me angrily as though I'd tried to tempt him. "To be caught running away— that isn't what I want. And they'd give me a cruel death. This way . . ." Again I was conscious of that sense of mission blazing in his eyes. "This way I'll write a page of desert history that old men will tell their sons, and I'll teach the people of Hadd a lesson they'll never forget." And then in a quieter, less dramatic voice: "Think you can make it on your own?"

"I don't know," I said. "But it's dark and there's bound to be a certain amount of chaos when they put in their attack."

He nodded. "Okay, it's worth trying. But they're Bedou. They've eyes like cats, and they know the desert. And, remember, the moon rises in four hours' time. If you're not away by then . . ." He left it at that and stood for a moment, watching me, as I gathered together the few things I needed—a canvas bandolier of ammunition, my rifle, the water-bottle, a twist of rag containing a few dates and some pieces of dried meat. My matches and my last packet of cigarettes I left with him and also something I'd become very attached to—a little silver medallion of St. Christopher given me by a mission boy in Tanganyika after I'd saved his life. "You're travelling a longer road than I am," I said.

Ten minutes later I was saying goodbye to him by the splintered timbers of the main gate. When I told him I'd get help to him somehow, he laughed. It was a quiet, carefree, strangely assured sound. "Don't worry about me. Think about yourself." He gripped my hand. "Good luck, sir! And thank you. You've been a very big factor in my life—a man I could always trust." For a moment I saw his eyes, pale in the starlight, and bright now with the nervous tension that comes before a battle. And then with a quick last pressure of the hand, a muttered "God be with you," he pushed me gently out on to the camel track.

Behind me the timbers creaked as he closed the gate. I heard the two palm trunks with which we'd shored it up from the inside thud into position.

I started down the track then, and in an instant the walls had vanished, merged with the dark shapes of the surrounding rocks. Black night engulfed me, and I left the track, feeling my way down the slope, my feet stumbling amongst loose scree and broken rocks.

High overhead a thin film of cirrus cloud hid the stars. It was this that saved me, for I was lying out in the open not two hundred paces from them as they climbed to take up their positions on the north side of the fort. I kept my face down and my body glued tight to the rock against which I lay. My rifle, clutched ready in my hand, was covered by my cloak so that no gleam of metal showed, and the two grenades David had given me dug into my groin as I waited, tense and expectant, for the moment of discovery.

And then they were past and the scuff of their sandalled feet faded on the slope above me.

I lifted my head then, but all I could see was the dark hillside in my immediate vicinity. No sign of the men who had passed, no shadows moving on the edge of the darkness. I slid to my feet, found the track, and went quickly down the hill. And at the bottom I walked straight into a camel. I don't know which of us was the more surprised. It had been left to graze, and it stood with a tuft of withered herb hanging from its rubbery lips, staring at me in astonishment.

There were other camels; they seemed to be all round me, humped shapes in the dark, champing and belching. I seized the head-rope of the one facing me, forced it down, and, stepping on to its neck the way the Arabs did, I found myself sprawled across its back as it started into motion with a bellow of fear and rage. There was a guttural Arab cry. A shot rang out, the bullet whining close over my head. But the only thing I cared about at that moment was whether I could hang on, for the brute had gone straight into a gallop.

If it hadn't still been saddled I should undoubtedly have come off, but the saddle gave me something to hold on to, and after a while the crazy motion slowed and I was able to get my feet astride and, by means of the head-rope, obtain some control. And when I had finally brought the animal to a halt, there was no sound of pursuit. There was no sound of any sort. That wild, swaying gallop seemed to have carried me right out into a void.

And then, behind me, the sound of shots, carrying clear and hard on the still night air. The rip and blatter of a machine-gun. Twisting round in my saddle, I saw the firefly flicker of the attackers' guns high up on the black bulk of Jebel al-Akhbar. Distant shouts and cries came to me faintly. More firing, and the sharper crack of small explosions. Three of them. Grenades, by the sound of it. The cries faded, the fire slackened. Suddenly there was no longer any sound and I was alone again, riding across an endless dark plain, haunted by the thought of David, wondering what had happened.

The silence and the sense of space were overwhelming now, particularly when the curtain of cirrus moved away and the stars were uncovered. Then I could see the desert stretching away from me in every direction and I felt as lost as any solitary mariner floating alone in an empty sea. Far behind me the Jebel al-Akhbar lifted its dark shape above the desert's rim, for all the world like an island, and all around me were small petrified waves, an undulating dunescape that seemed to disappear into infinity.

In the darkness, without any stars to guide me, I had trusted to luck and let the camel have its head. Now I saw it had carried me westward—towards the big dunes of the Empty Quarter and Whitaker's lonely camp. I kept going, not changing my direction. It was a dangerous decision. I knew that. I'd only the one bottle of water and there were no wells where I was heading, no caravan routes to guide me, nothing but empty desert. My decision was based on the fact that Whitaker's camp was much nearer than Buraimi—and, after all, he was the boy's father.

I had two chances, that was all—our own camel tracks and the tracks of Whitaker's trucks. If I missed both of these, or if they had become obliterated by wind-blown sand, then I knew I'd never get out of the desert alive. I rode through the night without a stop, guiding myself as best I could by the stars, and when the dawn came I turned so that the rising sun was behind my right shoulder. If my navigation was right, then I had placed myself to the south of the line between Jebel al-Akhbar and Whitaker's camp. Some time during the morning my new course should intersect the tracks made by our camels three nights back.

It was the first time I had ridden in the desert alone. The solitude was immense, the emptiness overpowering. The heat, too—it came at me in waves, so that time had no meaning. It seared my eyes and beat against the membranes of my brain. I drank sparingly from the water-bottle, rinsing the tepid liquid round my mouth. A wind sprang up and small grains of sand were lifted from the gravel floor and flung in my face, a fine-ground dust that clogged nose and throat and made the simple act of swallowing an agony without any saliva. To look the desert in the face, searching for our old tracks, was like pricking needles into my eyes.

By midday I'd finished the water and still no sign of our tracks. I was trembling then, but not with the heat. I had reached the sands, and the dunes were growing bigger, like an ocean's swell building up against the continental shelf. Dune followed dune, and the sense of space, the feeling that this petrified world of sand went on and on without end, appalled me.

A dirty scum formed in my mouth as I rode, and my tongue became a swollen, leathery mass. The camel's pace was slow and reluctant. We had passed no vegetation, no sign of anything growing, and as the sun slanted to the west fear took hold of me, for I knew I was headed into a desert that was four hundred miles across. Memory plagued me with the vision of a stream I knew in the Black Mountains of Wales where the water ran over rocks brown with peat and fell tinkling to a cool, translucent pool. The sun sank into a purple haze, and the sense of space, with the dark, shadowed dune crests stretched out in endless ridges ahead of me, was more terrifying than the close confinement that produces claustrophobia.

And then a chance turn of the head, a sudden glance, and there it was: a diagonal line ruled faintly across the back of a dune away to my left. I stared at it through slitted, grit-swollen eyes, afraid I was imagining it. But it was real enough—a single, scuffed-up thread scored by the feet of camels and half obliterated by sand. In the hard gravel at the foot of the dune I counted the tracks of six camels. I had actually crossed the line of our three-day-old march without knowing it. If the sun had been higher I should never have seen that faint shadow-line. I should have ridden on to certain death. I realized then why David had insisted on my making for Buraimi. I had been very fortunate indeed.

I headed into the sunset then, following the tracks, knowing they would lead me to Whitaker's camp. The camel seemed to know it, too, for its pace quickened.

The sun set and darkness came. I camped at the foot of a

dune, not daring to go on for fear of losing the faint, intermittent line of those tracks. The desert lost its warmth immediately. I ate a few dates, but my mouth was too dry and sore to chew on the meat. Tired though I was, I couldn't sleep. The moon rose just before the dawn, and I went on. The tracks became more difficult to follow; at times I lost them and had to cast about until I came upon them again. A wind was blowing and the sifting sand was covering them moment by moment. The sun rose and it was suddenly very hot.

Long before I reached Whitaker's camp, the sound of the drilling-rig was borne to me on the wind. The steady hum of machinery was utterly incongruous in that empty, desolate world. One of his Bedouin guards brought me into the camp, and as I slid exhausted from my camel, I saw Whitaker himself coming towards me from the rig.

I must have passed out then, for the next I knew I was lying in his tent and he was bending over me, holding a mug of water to my cracked lips. The water was warm, but its wetness cleaned my mouth, eased the swollen dryness of my tongue, and as I began to swallow, I suddenly wanted to go on drinking and drinking, for my body was all dried up. But he took the mug away. "Are you alone?" he asked. And when I nodded, he said: "What happened? Is he dead?"

I sat up, staring at him. Something in the way he'd said it . . . But his face was in shadow and I thought I must have imagined it. "He was alive when I left him."

"I see. So he's still up there." And he added: "He'd made his gesture. He'd carried out a successful attack on the wells. Why couldn't he leave it at that?"

I started to explain about David's determination to keep the wells from being repaired, but he cut me short. "I know all about that. I got the news from Hadd yesterday. My chap said the streets of Hadd were deserted and no man dared venture out of his house for fear of being fired at. He also said that the inhabitants had made a daylight attack on the fort and had been driven off by heavy fire."

"There were just the four of us," I said. And I told him how Salim had been killed at the outset and Ali fatally wounded.

"And he's alone up there now with just Hamid and his brother, bin Suleiman?" He was silent for a moment, and then he said: "I gather the Emir sent to Saraifa for Sheikh Abdullah. Had his forces arrived before you left?" And when I nodded, he said: "What happened? Were you there when they attacked the fort?"

"No." And I explained how I'd got out just before the attack started. "I don't know what happened. But if David did manage to beat off that attack, there'll be others, or else they'll just snipe at him from the rocks until they've worn him down or his water runs out."

"So he's got himself trapped." And then almost irritably: "What's wrong with the boy? Does he want to die?"

"He will," I said angrily, "if you don't get help to him somehow."

"I've done what I can. Yousif was just back from Sharjah and I sent him straight off with letters to Colonel George, who commands the Trucial Oman Scouts, and to Gorde. It's up to the authorities now. Fortunately, I don't think the Emir has any idea yet who it is holding that fort."

It was something at least that he'd notified the authorities, and I lay back, exhausted. He gave me some more water and then left me, saying he'd arrange for some food to be brought. When it came, it was a half-cold dish of rice and camel meat. I ate it slowly, feeling my strength beginning to return, and then I slept. I hadn't intended to sleep, but the food and the heat in the tent . . . I couldn't keep my eyes open.

I woke to the sound of voices speaking in English. It was almost three in the afternoon. The camp was strangely quiet. The drilling-rig had stopped. I peered out of the tent. An Army officer in khaki shirt and shorts and a peaked cap was standing talking to Whitaker. There was an RAF officer there, too, and resting on the gravel beside the silent rig was a helicopter.

Whitaker saw me as I came out of the tent and called me over. "This is Colonel George of the TOS."

He was a short, thick-set man, bouncing with energy, of a type that a Frenchman in Zanzibar had once described to me as a typical officer of the *bled*. Small, protruding eyes stared at me curiously from beneath the peaked cap. "I was in Buraimi when I got Whitaker's message. The RAF had loaned me a helicopter, so I thought I'd fly down and see what it was all about." His words were sharp and crisp. "Understand young Whitaker's alive and that he's playing merry hell with our aggressive little Emir. Correct?"

I didn't answer, for I was staring past him to a strange figure walking towards us from the rig—a short, fat figure in a powder-blue tropical suit that was now crumpled and dirty and sweat-stained. "Ruffini!" I called.

He came almost running. "Mister Grant!" He seized my hand. I think he would have liked to embrace me, he seemed so pathetically glad to see somebody he knew. "'Ow are you? I 'ave been so concerned for you. When you don't return with Gorde, I am asking questions, making a dam' nuisance of myself, and nobody tell me nothing."

"What are you doing here?" I asked.

"What is a newspaper man ever doing? Looking for a story. I go to Buraimi, by invitation of the sheikh and an Italian oil man who is there also. Then this gentleman is sent by the British authorities to remove me. They don't wish for Ruffini to be in Buraimi or anywhere else in the desert. So I am under arrest."

"No question of arrest," Colonel George snapped. "I've explained to you . . ."

But Ruffini wasn't listening. "I tell you once before, signore," he said to me, still holding on to my hand, "I think you are sitting on the story I want. Now I talk to some of the Bedouin 'ere and I know it is true. What is this boy doing? They say you are with 'im in that fort, that you come from Hadd this morning."

I could have wished it had been a British journalist. But that wasn't so important as the fact that chance had put me in touch with the outside world. Ruffini might be prevented from filing his copy immediately, but the knowledge that sooner or later David's story would become known might stir the authorities to action.

But when I suggested this to Colonel George, he shook his head. "I don't think you quite understand the official view." We were back in the tent then and I'd been talking and answering questions for more than an hour. The TOS, he said, had been reinforced with Regular Army units some time back and had been standing by for more than a month, ready to move at short notice. The attack on Saraifa and the battle at the Mahdah *falaj* were just the sort of trouble their Intelligence had expected, and as soon as he'd received the news he'd given the order to prepare to move. "It was two nights ago. We'd everything lined up, the convoy spread out round the perimeter of Sharjah airfield and everybody ready to go. And then the Foreign Office clamped down, the Political Resident called the whole thing off."

"But why?" I asked.

"Why? Because of Cairo, Saudi, the Americans, the United Nations, world opinion." Cairo Radio, he said, had first referred to the Hadd-Saraifa border dispute two weeks back. There were reports from Riyadh that Saudi intended to raise the matter at the next meeting of the UN.

The Political Resident came under the Foreign Office, and to the Foreign Office this wasn't just a local problem, but a small facet in the pattern of world diplomacy. Until that moment I had seen the attack upon Saraifa as it appeared to David, a personal matter; now I was being forced to stand back mentally and look at the situation as a whole, from the viewpoint of authority.

"Twenty-four hours," Colonel George said. "That's all we needed. In twenty-four hours we could have put paid to the Emir's little game and saved a hell of a lot of lives. I know we've no treaty obligation so far as Saraifa is concerned, but it lies within the British sphere of influence and we've certainly a moral obligation to protect them against this sort of thing." He shrugged. "Well, there it is. I'm just a soldier, not a politician." He glanced at his watch and then at the RAF Pilot Officer. "Time we were moving, eh?" Outside the tent, he turned to Whitaker. "That boy of yours. He's going to get himself killed if somebody doesn't do something." The protruding eyeballs stared. "You've been out here a long time, Colonel. Couldn't you see the Emir? Talk to your son? You must have considerable influence still."

"A little. But not with my son, it seems." Whitaker was clearly disconcerted. "He's acting contrary to my advice—contrary to my express orders, in fact." He hesitated. "Of course, if the Political Resident authorized me to negotiate a settlement of the Hadd-Saraifa border dispute, I have some influence with the Emir. But," he added, "a just settlement for Saraifa would almost certainly require the backing of British military forces."

"That's out of the question at the moment."

"Then . . ." Whitaker gave an awkward little shrug.

Colonel George grunted, a small, peremptory sound. "Pity! That boy's got a lot of guts and he's going to die." He started towards the helicopter, but then he stopped and faced Whitaker again. "I've heard stories about you. . . . And if half of what I've heard is true, your son's doing just the sort of thing you'd have done yourself in your younger days, eh?" He paused, and then in a harder voice: "I'll tell you something, Whitaker: if that boy holds out for a week, he'll go down in desert history, his name remembered long after yours is forgotten." He stared at him hard for a moment and then marched off across the gravel towards the helicopter. "Sorry I can't give you a lift out, Grant. No room. We've got to deliver this damned journalist to Sharjah. But I've got one of my company commanders with a wireless truck up at Buraimi. I propose to send him down to patrol Hadd's northern border and keep tabs on the situation. I'll tell him to pick you up, if you like. Name's Berry. Sound chap. Understands the Bedou. That do you?"

I nodded, and behind me Whitaker said: "You might tell him to keep an eye out for my two vehicles. My fuel tanker and the supply truck should have been in two days ago."

The rotor blade of the helicopter began to turn. Ruffini gripped my hand. "*A riverderla.* I see the story of this David Whitaker reaches London. Don't worry. We 'ave an arrangement with one of your newspapers." He was sweating already as he ducked into the oven heat of the fuselage.

Colonel George paused in the open door. "Want to give me a message for his sister? I could send it straight down to the hospital. She'd get it this evening."

I hesitated. "Just tell her he's alive. That's all she needs to know at the moment."

"I should have thought something more personal was called for." He stared at me, playfully tapping my arm. "Probably you don't realize it, but she's been raising hell on your account. As soon as she knew you were missing, she came straight down to Sharjah. She caught that oil chap, Gorde, just as he was boarding his plane, and the story is she tore him off such a strip for abandoning you that he dropped his stick and took off without it. Since then she's been badgering the life out of me. I'll be damn glad to be able to tell her you're safe. Well?" He cocked his eyebrow at me and grinned. "I'll give her your love—will that do?" And without waiting for a reply he got into the helicopter and slammed the door.

Whitaker and I watched it take off, a mechanical dragonfly whirring in the clean, bright air. I turned then, conscious of the quickened beat of my pulse, the sudden desire to be alone. It was strangely heart-warming to know that somebody had been concerned about whether I got back safely or not. I walked to the steep, shadowed edge of the dunes and lay there, longing for a cigarette. The drill, so useless now without its fuel, stood like a toy, dwarfed by the dunes, the Arab crew lying about, listless with nothing to do. Whitaker had gone to his tent. The shadows lengthened and I wondered what was happening on that hilltop forty miles to the east. Was David still alive?

The answer came next day, just after Whitaker's two trucks had pulled in and the noise of their arrival had wakened me from the first long, uninterrupted sleep I had enjoyed in well over a week. Everything was confusion, stores being unloaded, the rig started up, when a bullet-scarred Land Rover appeared, flying the Emir's green flag. Out of it stepped a big, portly man with very black features under a large turban. "The Emir's secretary," Whitaker said and went forward to greet him. A bodyguard of four askari sat silent in the back of the vehicle—wild-eyed men with greasy locks hanging to their shoulders, who fingered their weapons nervously.

Whitaker took the secretary to his tent and they remained there over an hour, talking over tinned fruit and coffee. Finally the man left, but before getting into the Land Rover, he made a long, angry speech, a harangue that was clearly intended for the whole camp.

"What did he want?" I asked as the dust of his departure finally settled and the men returned to their jobs.

"If I don't go at once to Hadd and get David out of that fort, the Emir will hold me responsible." Whitaker's face was very pale, his whole body trembling. "*Allah akhbar!*" he muttered. "Why did the idiot have to choose this moment, when I'd talked the Emir into agreement and had obtained the financial backing I needed? Why now?"

"He's still alive, then?"

He turned his eye on me, a fixed, glassy look. "Yes," he said. "He's alive. The night you left him, he beat back the attack, captured a prisoner, and sent him to the Emir next day with a message. It announced who he was and the terms on which he'd vacate the fort and leave them free to repair the wells." The terms required the Emir to declare publicly that he accepted the present borders between Hadd and Saraifa for all time, and this declaration was to be supported by a signed document to the same effect, lodged with the United Nations. David also demanded an escort of the Trucial Oman Scouts to see him and his men safely out of Hadd territory.

But it wasn't the terms that upset Whitaker. It was the fact that David had disclosed his identity. "Did he have to involve me?" he demanded angrily, staring towards the rig.

"I don't suppose he meant to involve you," I said. "You're involved by the simple fact that you're his father."

"His father!" He turned on me. "I took a servant girl," he said harshly. "A moment in time, a passing need—but that was all. It ended there, and I made provision for her."

"You can't buy immunity from your actions."

He ignored that. "Twenty years, and the moment catches up with me and I'm faced with the brat; a raw, undisciplined boy with a vicious background." He glared at me. "And you sent him out here."

"He'd have come in any case," I said, "once he knew you were his father." I was angry myself then. "I don't think you realize what a shock it was to him to learn that he was illegitimate—to discover that his mother had been deserted in childbirth."

"She'd no claim on me," he said quickly. "And even if she had, it doesn't justify his coming out here with some idea at the back of his mind that he was going to kill me. Did you know about that? I had it all out of him shortly after he arrived—that and his criminal background and how he was wanted by the police for causing the death of that man Thomas." And he added: "I should have sent him packing. I should have realized the boy was bent on destroying me, on ruining all my plans."

"You know that's not true," I said.

"Then why did he pretend he was dead when he wasn't? And now, when the truth of my theory is within my grasp, when the thing I've been searching for all my life is here, he gets me involved in this stupid, useless demonstration of his." He was sweating, and there were little flecks of white at the corners of his mouth.

"What he's doing," I said, "he's doing because he's accepted the things you believed in; he made your world his own, Saraifa his home. And the background you complain of is the reason he's doing it so successfully. He's got the Emir to withdraw his forces from Saraifa. Now is the time, surely, when your influence—"

"My influence? What influence do you think I have now? Men have been killed, and that's something only blood can wipe out." And he added, staring into the distance: "If I'd gone with the Emir's secretary, I'd have been held hostage for David's submission—his life or mine. And when next the Emir sends an emissary, he'll come in force. That was made very plain."

He put his hand up to his head, covering his eye as though to shut out the desert and concentrate on what was in his mind. "It's madness," he breathed. "Madness. He can't achieve anything. . . ."

"How do you know?" I demanded angrily. "Ruffini has the whole story now, and—"

"That Italian?" He let his hand fall, staring at me in surprise. "How can he affect the situation? The authorities aren't going to take any notice of him." He said it as though to convince himself, and then in a voice so hoarse it seemed to be torn out of him: "He'll die up there, and that'll be the end of it." The look on his face was quite frightening. He turned and walked slowly to his tent. I didn't see him again that evening, and the next day his manner was still very strange. We hardly exchanged a word, and I was glad when Captain Berry arrived.

Looking back on it, I suppose I should have tried to understand his predicament. He hadn't enough men to get David out by force and he was probably right in saying the situation had gone beyond the reach of his influence with the Emir. What I didn't realize was that I was seeing a man in the grip of events, forced to a reassessment of his whole life and the values by which he had lived—and being driven half out of his mind in the process.

It was late afternoon when Berry got in. A lean, bony-looking Scot with fair hair and a face that was almost brick-red in the slanting sun, he brought a breath of sanity into that sultry camp, for he was from outside and not emotionally involved in what was happening forty miles to the east. He had a message for me from Colonel George picked up on his radio that morning. "I'm to tell you that your Italian friend got his story out in time and that you're not to worry. Everything possible is being done. The Colonel has been ordered to Bahrain to report to the Political Resident in person. Oh, and he said a Nurse Thomas sent you her love and is glad to know you're safe. Okay?"

I nodded, not trusting myself to speak. For the moment I could think of nothing but that message from Sue. Captain Berry was speaking to Whitaker, something about his son showing what one determined and resolute man could achieve. He was one of those soldiers that believe action is the solution to everything. "You must be very proud of him, sir."

Colonel Whitaker's face was without expression, but a nerve flickered along the line of his jaw, and he turned away.

Berry watched him for a moment, a puzzled look on his face. "That's a man I've always wanted to meet," he said. "But I'm surprised he left this to his son. After what's happened in Saraifa, I should have thought he'd have been busy raising the

desert tribes. It would have solved our difficulty if he had. We
might be allowed to support a desert rising against the Emir."

"I take it," I said, "you'll be leaving at once." It wasn't only
that I wanted to know what had happened since I'd left Jebel
al-Akhbar. I wanted to get away from that camp.

But he told me it was out of the question. They'd been driving
for over twenty hours. Both the wireless truck and the Land
Rover had to be serviced, the men needed sleep. He had a wireless operator with him and five levies of the TOS under a corporal. "Leave at first light. Makes no difference, I'm afraid,"
he added, seeing my impatience. "I can't help Colonel Whitaker's son. Mine's only a watching brief. Anyway, it's no good
bashing these dunes in the dark."

He'd brought spare kit for me, so that I had the luxury of a
camp-bed that night. And in the morning I was able to discard
my Arab clothes, which by then were very filthy, and put on
clean khaki shirt and shorts. We breakfasted on bully-beef and
tinned peaches, washed down with a brew of strong tea, and
then we left.

Colonel Whitaker was there to see us go, and as he said goodbye to me he gave me instructions that were to have considerable significance later: "If anything happens to me, Grant, I
leave you to look after my affairs. I think you know enough
about me now to understand what I want done if they find oil
here." We drove off then, and I remember thinking he looked a
very lonely figure standing there with the clutter of the rig behind him. We went north, taking the shortest route across Hadd
territory and driving fast. Keeping to the flat gravel stretches
between the dunes, we were clear of Hadd's northern border by
ten thirty. We turned east then, and the going became much
slower, for we were crossing the lines of the dunes.

At set times we stopped to make radio contact with TOS HQ.
The only news of any importance was that Colonel George, before he left for Bahrain, and therefore presumably acting on his
own initiative, had ordered Berry's company south into the desert for exercises.

Shortly after midday the dunes began to get smaller, and in
an area where it had rained quite recently we came upon the

black tents of a Bedouin encampment, and there were camels browsing on untidy bushes of *abal*. Berry stopped and spoke with some of the men. "Well, your chap was alive yesterday," he said as we drove on. "I thought they were Al Bu Shamis, but they were of the Awamir and they came up past Jebel al-Akhbar yesterday. They say they heard intermittent firing. They also told me that the people of Saraifa are beginning to return to the oasis, that two *falajes* are running again and Khalid's half-brother, Mahommed, is calling men to arms."

It was the first indication I had that what David had done had not been done in vain.

Soon after that we became bogged down for several hours in an area of small dunes so confused that it looked like a petrified tidal race. As a result, we didn't sight Jebel al-Akhbar until late afternoon. We stopped at sunset. The hill looked deceptively close in the clear still air, the colour of the rock almost mauve, the sky behind quite green. "It's about six miles away," Berry said, handing me his glasses. I could see the fort quite distinctly then, the tower in silhouette against the fantastic sky. Nothing moved there. No sign of life.

I was tired after the long drive and I felt depressed. Darkness fell. We had our food, and after the meal Berry disappeared into the back of the truck. He wanted to hear the BBC news. It kept him in touch, he said; but what he meant was that it brought home nearer and made the desert seem less remote.

Nature's needs took me into the desert and when he called to me I didn't hear what it was he shouted, but only caught the excitement in his voice. Back at the truck I found him seated with the earphones pressed tight against his head. "It was in the summary," he said. And then after a while: "Your chap's made the headlines, apparently. A big story in one of the papers this morning." He removed the earphones and switched off. "They even got his name right and the name of the fort. . . . And the Foreign Secretary is to be asked a question about it in the House tonight." He rolled his long body over the tailboard and stood beside me. "Funny thing," he said, "if it had been a soldier up there on the Jebel al-Akhbar, they'd have taken it for granted, or more probably somebody would have raised hell because the fellow had disobeyed orders. But because he's a civilian . . ." He gave a quick, derisive laugh. "Not that it makes any difference. One newspaper story and a question in the House won't change my orders. We'll be left to sit here and watch him die. That is, if he isn't dead already."

We'd heard no sound since we'd gone into camp. The night was deathly still, not a breath of air. And Berry made it plain to me that he couldn't go any nearer. His orders were to stay in Trucial territory, and in front of us stretched the invisible barrier of the Hadd border. "You can be certain we're under observation. If I cross that border the political repercussions would be endless. As it is, my colonel's sticking his neck out sending me down here on his own authority."

We stayed up late to listen to the last news summary from home. The item we were waiting for came towards the end. *"Questioned in the House this evening about reports that a British civilian, David Whitaker, with two Arabs, was holding the fort of Jebel al-Akhbar in the Arabian Emirate of Hadd, the Foreign Secretary said that the newspaper report emanated from a foreign source and was almost certainly without foundation. He added that he was having enquiries made. . . . Cairo Radio this evening accused Britain of concentrating a large force on the Hadd border, including armoured cars and artillery. . . ."*

"Armoured cars and artillery!" Berry snapped the receiver off. "Why the hell do they repeat that sort of nonsense?" Like most soldiers who know what the situation is on the spot, he was contemptuous of the organs of publicity. "And you heard what the Foreign Secretary said. It's all going to be hushed up. Oil and politics—it's always the same out here in the Middle East. For the sake of peace and quiet a petty tyrant is going to be allowed to get away with murder." He jumped out of the truck and stood staring a moment towards the Jebel al-Akhbar. Finally he gave a little shrug. "Care for a drink? I've got a little Scotch left."

I shook my head. I was wondering whether any of the other papers would take the story up, and, if so, whether they'd make enough of it to stir up public opinion. Only public opinion could force the Government to accepts its responsibility for

Saraifa and take action; and without that, David's sacrifice became pointless. "I think I'll turn in now," I said. "I'm still very tired."

I slept like the dead that night, and in the morning it wasn't the sun that woke me, but Berry shaking my arm. "Somebody's still in the fort. I heard shots just after dawn—very faint, but definitely rifle fire. I've reported it to HQ."

I scrambled up, sweaty from lying in my sleeping-bag in the blazing sun, but even through the glasses there was nothing to be seen: just the Jebel al-Akhbar shimmering in a heat haze.

Berry glanced at his watch. "You might like to listen to what the newspapers are saying back home."

We went into the back of the truck and switched on the radio. It was an overseas service of the BBC with a round-up of news and opinions from the national press. I don't know what I expected—what Berry expected. A few references, perhaps a leader. Instead, every newspaper had taken up the story. For almost ten minutes the thin voice of the announcer came to me through the earphones, speaking as though from another world, and giving variations on the theme of the story I had told Ruffini. David was headline news. One I particularly remember: BORSTAL BOY HOLDS FORT FOR FOREIGN OFFICE. And another popular paper was quoted as attacking the Foreign Secretary for trying to hoodwink the public.

But the press reaction seemed to have made no impression on the official attitude. The only indication of increased interest was that radio contact with TOS HQ was every hour now on the hour. Colonel George, we learned, was back in Sharjah. Ruffini was still there. Berry's company was in a position ten miles west of Buraimi and about a hundred miles to the north of us. The day dragged on. The sun rose until the sky was a burnished bowl, a throbbing ache to the eyes, and the desert sand beneath our feet as hot as the lid of a stove. Several times we heard the distant sound of shots, but though we took it in turns to keep watch through the glasses, we saw no movement.

We dozed between watches, ate snacks out of tins, and waited. Water was rationed and we became thirsty. Boredom set in. We listened to the BBC, but David was no longer in the

news. Time was running out for him, and my presence here
seemed to serve no purpose. Those occasional, intermittent shots
didn't tell me whether he was alive or dead; they only indicated
that the fort was still held. Repeatedly I tried to persuade
Berry to move forward and recce under cover of darkness. But
he was absolutely adamant. "I cross that border with British
military vehicles and God knows where it would end."

By the end of the day we were beginning to get on each
other's nerves. The truth was that nothing would have pleased
Berry more than to be allowed to call up his company and go
in and settle the whole business. In his quiet Scots way he was
so tensed-up over the situation that the battle would have been
a welcome relief. Instead of which he was tied down within
sight of the Emir's stronghold in the company of a man who
was becoming more and more irritable at the delay.

It wasn't that I didn't understand his difficulty. If he acted
on his own initiative he might plunge the whole of Arabia into
war, involve his own country, and certainly ruin his career. It
was a diplomatic tight-rope that I couldn't possibly expect him
to walk. But understanding his difficulty didn't help me to bear
the inaction. To have to sit there, doing nothing, whilst six
miles away that boy was dying by inches . . . The heat and
frustration, they nearly drove me mad.

I suppose it was the strain of the past fortnight. Berry gave
me salt tablets, a large whisky, and sent me to bed at dusk. At
midnight he woke me to say we'd be moving at first light. "The
Colonel's finally got Bahrain to agree to my making an attempt
to get him out alive. I'm to try and arrange an audience with the
Emir in the morning."

"And suppose he refuses to see you?" I asked.

"He won't. What's more, he'll accept my offer to mediate."

"You seem very confident."

"I am. I'm offering him a way out that'll save his face. If we
do what the men of his bodyguard have failed to do and get
young Whitaker out of the fort, then the Emir at least gets credit
for being cunning. That's something to set against the laughter
of the Bedou round their desert camp-fires. I take it you'd like to
come with me?"

"Of course."

He hesitated. "I think I'd better make it clear that I could be wrong about the Emir. He hasn't a particularly savoury reputation, and if he did decide to turn nasty . . ." He gave a little shrug. "So long as you understand the position."

Six hours later we were on the move, motoring across the flat, stony plain with the Jebel al-Akhbar growing bigger every minute until it towered above us, a grey sugar-loaf mass against the rising sun. A Union Jack fluttered from the Land Rover's bonnet. There were just the two of us and Berry's driver, Ismail, a tall, dark-skinned man, very neat in his khaki uniform and coloured TOS head-cloth. No sound reached us above the noise of the engine. I could see no sign of movement on the hill above us.

We rounded the shoulder of Jebel al-Akhbar by a dusty track, and there suddenly was Hadd, yellow now in the sunshine, with the Emir's green flag hanging limp above the palace and the town silent and strangely empty, with the tower I had known so well perched above it on the lip of the limestone cliffs. We passed a camp of the Emir's men. Smoke spiralled blue from their cooking-fires in the still morning air, and they watched us curiously, wild, lank-haired men, their bodies strapped around with cartridges, their rifles slung across their shoulders. Several were wounded, the blood caked black on their bandages.

The well outside the town was as we had left it that night, the wall destroyed by the explosion and nothing done to repair it. We entered Hadd by the main gate. The streets were empty, the little square deserted. Balks of palm timber still lay where they had been thrown down in panic beside the damaged well. "Looks as though the population has moved out into the date-gardens," Berry said. "Three men, and they've stopped the life of this whole town dead. It's incredible."

But as we looked up, it wasn't quite so incredible. That tower hung right over the town. All the way to the gates of the palace we could see it perched there above us. The narrowness of the streets was no protection; it looked right down into them.

Berry's appreciation of the Emir's situation proved correct. After keeping us waiting for over an hour, he received us in a

small room off one of the palace rooftops. There were armchairs in the Western style and a table on which stood an
expensive German camera and some models of tanks and armoured cars. The walls were hung with finely silvered guns and
pictures of the Emir driving through Hadd in a glossy American car.

The man himself was small and wiry, with a face that somehow managed to combine craftiness with great dignity; it was
a long, rather cruel face, its length emphasized by the big nose
and the little pointed beard glistening black with oil. His eyes
were heavily made-up with *kohl*. Sheikh Abdullah was there,
and several other notables, including the Emir's secretary, and
though I couldn't follow what was said, I was conscious of the
atmosphere, which was distinctly hostile.

The audience lasted a long time, with the Emir insisting at
first that Berry storm the fort with his own troops, take David
prisoner, and have him shot. When he refused, the Emir
launched into a harangue that was so violent that the spittle
actually flew from his lips.

"I thought for a moment," Berry said afterwards, "that we
were for it." Threatening us, however, didn't solve the Emir's
problem, which was that he was being made to look a fool before
his own people and all the desert world. After a long argument
he finally agreed that if we were able to persuade the defenders
to evacuate the fort they would be allowed to go unmolested.

We waited whilst Sheikh Abdullah gave one of his men orders to climb the slopes of Jebel al-Akhbar under a white flag
and announce a cease-fire. Berry had guessed that there were
snipers posted among the rocks below the fort walls, and he was
taking no chances. "The extraordinary thing is," he said as we
hurried out of the palace, "that they're convinced there are at
least a dozen men up there in the fort."

We drove back through the silent town, out past the deserted
wells and the askari encampment, and took the dusty track that
led round the shoulder of the hill. We left the Land Rover at the
foot of the camel track on the north side and started up on foot.
The sun was high now and the heat throbbed back from the
bare, scorched rock, beating up through the soles of our shoes.

For a time the fort was lost behind ridges, but as we climbed higher the walls gradually came into view. There was no sign of Sheikh Abdullah's snipers, no movement on the hilltop. The air was very still, the silence and the heat appalling. It was just over five days since I had come down this very track in the dark. Five days—just over one hundred and thirty hours, to be exact, and under constant attack . . . It didn't seem possible that David or any of them could still be alive. And yet Hadd was deserted and the Emir had agreed to Berry's terms. We climbed fast, hoping for the best—fearing the worst. They must be out of water by now, wounded probably, perhaps only one of them left alive.

The timbers of the main gate sagged open, splintered by the rocks that lay at the foot of the two crumbling bastions. As we climbed the last steep rise, the tower appeared, framed in the gateway, pale yellow in the sun, with the shadowed opening halfway up yawning like a mouth agape. No sign of life. No sound. I called out: "David! It's George Grant!" The rocks echoed back his name and nothing stirred. "David!"

And then, unbelievably, he answered—a hollow, croaking sound from the interior of the tower.

"I have Captain Berry of the Trucial Oman Scouts with me." My throat was parched, my voice hoarse. "The Emir offers you a safe-conduct." Even as I said it I wondered, the stillness and the heat beating at my nerves. Concealed amongst the rocks below us were men with rifles. How did we know they wouldn't open fire on us? The hairs at the back of my neck crawled; treachery seemed to hang in the hot air, and even as David told us to come in through the open gateway I knew we shouldn't have trusted the Emir. The open expanse of the fort's interior was a shambles. There were the remains of fires, the tattered remnants of camels' carcasses—those things I remembered. But now there were bodies of Arabs, too, lying where they had fallen, unburied and rotting, buzzing with flies. I counted nine of them; the place smelt of death, was littered with the debris of attacks beaten back. And the sun—the cauterizing, sterilizing sun—blazed down.

Something moved in the black mouth of the tower and the

rickety ladder was thrust out of it. It fell the last few feet to the ground and David appeared, climbing stiffly and very slowly down it. At the bottom he paused as though to gather his strength together, and then he turned and faced us, standing very stiffly erect, a bloodstained strip of cloth round his right forearm and blood showing in a black patch below his left shoulder.

Berry took a tentative step forward. "We've just seen the Emir. If you leave with us now, he's agreed to allow you to cross the border into Trucial territory unmolested."

"And you believed him?" David started to move towards us, but then he stopped. He was swaying slightly, too weak to walk.

"He's ordered a cease-fire."

He nodded slowly. "That's true. I heard the order given. A man came up by the path from Hadd a little while back. He carried a white flag. But then he disappeared; went to earth amongst the rocks." His voice was thin and very weak. "I don't trust the bastards," he added, coming towards us very slowly.

Close to, he looked ghastly. His eyes had gone quite yellow, the skin of his face yellow, too, and all the flesh fined away so that the cheeks were sunken, the bones staring. His body seemed smaller, dried up and shrivelled. He looked about half his normal size, completely desiccated. The death's-head face, the yellow, burning eyes, the croaking voice . . . I thought he couldn't last much longer, and I pleaded with him to take this chance. But he was like a man in a trance. "Have the authorities decided to act? Will they support Saraifa?" And when we told him no, all he said was: "They will. They will. If I hold out long enough, they'll be forced to act." The eyes fastened on me. "Why didn't you go to Sharjah? Why come here? This isn't what I wanted." His voice sounded desperately tired, utterly dispirited. "Didn't you understand? I wanted the world to know. If people at home don't know what I'm trying to do . . ."

"The people at home do know," I said, and I told him about Ruffini and how the story had been taken up by the national press and a question asked in the House.

His eyes lit up, his whole bearing suddenly changed. "Wonderful!" he breathed. "Wonderful!" He was standing erect now, his head up, his voice much stronger. "Time," he said. "Time and a little luck. That's all I need now."

"Time is against you," Berry said. "This is your last chance to get out of here alive."

"Is it?" The dry, cracked lips produced a twisted smile. "Do you really believe the Emir would let us get out of here alive—particularly when they see how few we are? He'd lose too much face. Anyway, I'm not going. I'll stay here till I die unless the Emir agrees to my terms or the authorities make some move to safeguard Saraifa."

"Surely to God you've done enough," I said, and I gave him the rumour we'd heard about the two *falajes* running again at Saraifa and the people returning to the oasis.

Berry, more practical, said: "How much water have you got left?"

"Not much. But it's cooler inside the tower. We're drinking very little."

"And your two men?" Berry asked. "Are they alive?"

"Yes, they're still alive. Hamid's very weak—a bullet through the shoulder and a splinter of rock from a ricochet in the back. Bin Suleiman's leg is smashed. But they'll both last as long as the water."

"So you won't leave with us?"

"No."

Berry nodded, accepting his decision as final. He seemed to understand David's attitude and he didn't attempt to reason with him. Instead, he unstrapped his web belt, slipping his water-bottle from it. "It's not much," he said, holding it out. "But one day could make the difference. I'll report your decision by radio to HQ as soon as I get back to my wireless truck."

David took the water-bottle, and though there couldn't possibly be any moisture left in that emaciated, dried-up hull of a body, his eyes glistened for a moment. "Thanks," he whispered. "I'll remember." His thin hands were gripped tight round the bottle. "One more day," he breathed. "You'll have that—I promise." He wasn't looking at Berry or at me. He was looking upwards, to the burning vault of the sky . . . a pact with God. And on this barren, burnt-rock hilltop where the air was heavy with the stink of rotting bodies, it would be an Old Testament God. "One more day," he whispered again in that croaking voice, and at that moment a rifle cracked.

The thud of the bullet, the scream of pain, the clatter of a gun barrel on rock—it was all on the instant, and I turned to see the body of an Arab writhing on the eastern wall. It reached the edge, paused, and then fell, and as it pitched, screaming, on its face, a second shot rang out.

The screams thinned to silence. The body on the ground arched, a series of violent jerks; something sounded in the throat and after that it lay still. I glanced at Berry. He hadn't moved. Nor had David. The click of metal on stone drew my eye to the top of the tower. The glint of a rifle, a thin wisp of smoke. Everything was still again; it was difficult to believe that in that instant a man had died.

"You see! That's all the treacherous bastard's safe-conduct is worth." David gave a dry little laugh. "You'd better get out of here whilst you still can."

Berry hesitated, and then he nodded. He reached into his pocket and produced some field dressings and a small first-aid kit. "Had an idea these might be required." He handed them over and then drew himself up and gave David a formal parade-ground salute. "Good luck!" he said, and turned quickly.

David looked at the first-aid tin and the dressings, his eyes quite blank, his face suddenly fallen-in, the flesh tight on the bones of the skull. I could only guess what he was thinking. A few more days and if he hadn't been killed by a bullet, he'd be dead of thirst. He looked up. "This is goodbye, sir." He held out his hand. "Tell my father, will you, that I hope it's a bloody good well . . . but if he lets the Emir get his hands on one penny of the royalties I'll haunt him to the grave and beyond."

His skin was dry, the bones of the hand like an old man's bones. I stared at him, not knowing what to say, for I was sure I wouldn't see him again. He was so damned young to die—and like this, in cold blood with his eyes open, trading life for the sake of a gesture. And yet, like Berry, I didn't try and argue with him. "Goodbye," I said, and turned quickly before my eyes betrayed me.

At the gateway I paused and looked back. He hadn't moved. He was still standing there, quite alone and swaying slightly, all his muscles slack with weariness. We stared at each other for a second and then I went out through the gateway, and I knew if the Emir attacked again that night, it would be the end. "What a waste!" I said to Berry, stumbling almost blindly down the track.

He looked at me. "I don't agree." His voice was hard and there was a ring to it, as though I'd struck a chord deep down. "If there weren't men like David Whitaker . . ." He shrugged. "It's a big question, isn't it? Why we're born; what we do with our lives." And he added after a pause: "I'd like to think, given his circumstances, that I'd behave the same way." He had loosened his pistol holster and his eyes searched the rocks as we hurried back down the track. But we saw nobody and the only sound was the heat throbbing at our temples. The Land Rover was still there with Ismail standing beside it. Treachery had gone back to its lair, and high up over the fort the black speck of some carrion bird planed on the still air.

Berry had seen it, too, and as we drove off he said: "I give him four days. In four days I reckon he'll be dead of thirst."

"He's weak," I said. "They've only got to make a determined attack now."

But Berry shook his head. "So long as there's one man left in that tower capable of firing a rifle or tossing a grenade they'll never take it, and Sheikh Abdullah knows it now. Only artillery or mortars could blast them out. I couldn't understand, even from your description, how three men could hold a fort against a hundred tribesmen, but now that I've seen the place . . ." He was staring back at it over his shoulder. "I am only surprised that a civilian should have appreciated the military possibilities of it."

"He was a gang leader in Cardiff docks before he came out to join his father in Saraifa," I said.

He laughed. "Well, I suppose that's as good a training as any." And after that we drove in silence.

When we got back to the wireless truck, Berry found a mes-

sage ordering him to return to Sharjah immediately. "But why?"
I said. "You're not on Hadd territory."

"They've got cold feet over the situation, by the sound of it.
My company's been ordered back, too." He stood staring towards Jebel al-Akhbar and there was an obstinate look on his
face. "I've given orders that we move at dawn and I've notified
HQ that I'm held here the night with a damaged spring on the
wireless truck. Twelve hours isn't much, but you never know.
The situation could alter."

By this simple stratagem we were still there on the border
when the slanting sun showed a cloud of dust moving across
the desert from the direction of Hadd. Through the glasses we
counted thirty-two camels, and the riders were all armed. Berry
ordered his corporal to issue additional ammunition and personally sited both the Bren guns on a low ridge. But the raiding
force kept to Hadd territory, heading due west towards the
sands. "Their objective must be Whitaker's camp," Berry said.
"There's nothing else out there." But he made no move to follow
them. "Colonel Whitaker will have to look after himself."

I thought of the lone figure we'd left standing with the clutter of that drilling-rig behind him. This was what he had feared,
the emissary returning in force. Whitaker would go with them
this time. He'd have no alternative. I wondered what would happen when he met the Emir. Would he agree to go up to the fort?
And if he did, how would David react?

But that was all in the future. I watched the dust cloud until
it disappeared below the rim of the horizon, and then I fetched
my briefcase and settled down to write a report. It was finished
by the time the sun had set and darkness was closing in. I gave
it to Berry and he agreed to have his wireless operator transmit
it to Sharjah at the next contact with HQ. The report was a long
one, for it covered David's situation, our visit to the fort, and
the treacherous attempt on his life, and I addressed it to Ruffini.
We were both civilians and I thought there was just a chance
that it might be passed across to him before any one in authority
stopped it.

"If he's still there," Berry said. The thing was sent now, and
we were sitting in the truck waiting for the BBC news. More

questions in the House, and the Opposition had attacked the Government for refusing to grant newspaper correspondents visas for any Arabian territory except Bahrain. They were accused of trying to hush up an ugly situation.

And then, in the morning, when we picked up the BBC newspaper round-up, I was staggered to find that virtually the whole national press had carried a story obviously based on the report I had sent to Ruffini. Somehow he had got it through uncensored, and the result was a fantastic perversion of the facts, so colourful, so written up as to be almost unrecognizable as the sad spectacle we had witnessed; and yet it was all there, the heroic quality of David's stand magnified a thousand-fold to give jaded townspeople the best breakfast-table reading for weeks. And the story had spread from the front pages right through to the editorial columns, an angry, outraged demand for Government action.

And when the last editorial flag had been waved by the BBC announcer and the last exhortation to the Government to act immediately had been read, Berry and I looked at each other in astonishment. I think we were both of us quite dazed by the violence of the reaction at home. It was only twelve hours since Berry's wireless operator had laboriously tapped out in Morse my long report, and in that short time David's situation had been put before the highest tribunal in the land—the British Public. Moreover, something had obviously roused the press to anger—the secretive attitude of Whitehall, presumably. As one paper put it: *Up to a late hour last night, despite a barrage of phone calls, nobody in authority appeared to be in a position to confirm or positively deny the story. The only comment was: "We regard the source as highly unreliable." This is either stupendous arrogance, or stupendous ignorance. We suspect both, and we demand that the Foreign Secretary take immediate action. The country is deeply disturbed.*

On the strength of that Berry cancelled his orders to move, and within half an hour his action was confirmed. Colonel George, acting on a hunch that political decisions would now have to be reversed—and entirely on his own initiative, I gathered later—had already turned Berry's company round and or-

dered it to drive with all possible speed to the Hadd border. "I'm
to wait here until they arrive," Berry said. "By then the Colonel
hopes to be here himself to take command."

"How long before they get here?" I asked.

"If they keep going without being stopped in the dunes they'll
arrive sometime after midnight, I imagine." He started to go
back to the wireless truck, but then he stopped. "It might interest you to know that Signor Ruffini was appointed Reuter's
correspondent with the full knowledge of the Political Resident
yesterday afternoon. But for that very odd appointment, I imagine your report would have been passed to Bahrain. In which
case I've no doubt it would now be rotting in some pigeonhole
in the Residency instead of making the world's headlines."

The official attitude was obvious. By agreeing to Reuter's request—perhaps even instigating it—they could justify their re-
fusal to grant visas to correspondents by saying that the press
already had coverage from an accredited agency correspondent, and that the very man from whom the story had originated.
No doubt they took the view that, as a foreigner, Ruffini would
be more amenable to control than a British correspondent and
therefore unlikely to cause them further embarrassment. It was
a little ironical that in their hurry to appoint him they had given
me almost direct and immediate access to the whole of the
British press.

"I am to tell you," Berry added with a thin smile, "that no
further messages for Ruffini will be accepted through military
channels. A matter of bolting the door after the horse has gone."

"What about that raiding party headed for Whitaker's
camp?" I said. I hadn't mentioned it in my report to Ruffini the
previous night. "Somebody ought to be told."

"Already done," he said. "It won't be passed on to Ruffini, but
the PRPG will be notified and so will Sir Philip Gorde. He's in
Sharjah now."

So that was that, and nothing to do now but wait. The day
passed slowly. No sound from the direction of Jebel al-Akhbar.
Not a single shot all day. The hill seemed suddenly dead. The
heat was very bad. The wireless operator was on constant watch
on the headquarters wave-band. We switched only once to the

BBC news. A Foreign Office spokesman had stated that, whilst there was no official news, there was reason to believe that press reports were substantially correct and that a young Englishman had instigated some sort of guerrilla activity against the Emir of Hadd. The whole matter was under urgent review. There were rumours of reinforcements standing by in readiness to be flown to Bahrain, and two destroyers had left Aden, steaming north along the Arabian coast. Cairo Radio had stepped up its propaganda offensive.

Late in the afternoon I was wakened from a stifling sleep in the shadow of the W/T truck with the news that the Hadd raiding force was returning. "And there's been no sound from the fort at all." Berry passed me the glasses as I stood with slitted eyes gazing at a dust cloud right in the path of the sun. "Thirty-three of them now," he said. The dust made it difficult, but as they passed to the south of us and I could see them more clearly, I confirmed his count. "They must have been travelling all night and moving very fast." The figures flickered indistinctly in the heat. "The Emir will have picked up the Arab news," he added. "He'll know he hasn't much time. Had Whitaker a radio, do you know?"

"I don't think so."

"Then he probably doesn't know what's happening at home —that the Government's being forced to take action. Oh, well," he added. "If he goes up to the fort and his son's still alive, Colonel Whitaker will learn from him what we were able to tell him yesterday. It might make some difference."

I thought of that scene: father and son facing each other in the shambles of that fort. Watching the Emir's force move past us, men and camels all lifted bodily off the ground by a mirage and turned into strange, distorted shapes by the heat rising from that sea of sand, I felt once again the cruelty of this desert world. It was so hard, so empty, so casual of human life—a crucible to transmute the flesh to skin and bone, the mind to something as distorted as those shapes dancing in a mirage. I had a premonition of disaster then; but not, I think, of tragedy—certainly not a tragedy quite so grim.

I watched them until they disappeared beyond the shoulder

of Jebel al-Akhbar, and shortly afterwards the sun set. One more night. But there was still no news, no certainty of action. "Better turn in and get some sleep," Berry suggested. "I haven't even got an ETA from the Colonel yet."

"Will we move in the morning, do you think? David can't last out much longer." And in the morning he might be faced with his father's desperate situation. "For God's sake! It's got to be tomorrow."

"You'd better pray, then," he snapped back irritably. "For only God and the Foreign Office know what action will be taken and when." And he added angrily: "I don't even know whether the Colonel's order to my company has been officially confirmed."

I took his advice then and went to my camp-bed. But sleep was out of the question. The night was hot and very still, the stars bright. Time dragged and I dozed, to be jerked awake by the distant sound of engines. It was 0155 hours and Berry's company was motoring in, dark shapes moving in convoy across the desert without lights. An officer reported all present and correct, but warned that the only orders he'd received were to wait for the Colonel and not to cross the border.

Orders whispered in the night, the dark trucks spewing men out on to the sand; the area of our camp was suddenly full of movement, an ant-heap settling to sleep, and a voice at my elbow said: " 'Ullo, Mister Grant. Is Ruffini." His pudgy hand gripped my arm, patted my shoulder; words tumbled out of him. They had rushed him up to this company to get him out of the way. He'd been made fabulous offers by several newspapers. "I am lucky, eh—lucky to be a journalist and out 'ere at this minute?" But I think he was a little scared. He was certainly lonely. His knowledge of the Arabs was based on Mussolini's short-lived empire.

A bare two hours' sleep and then the dawn breaking . . . Another day, and the ant-heap stirred and came to life, little groups of men forming and re-forming, an ever-changing pattern against the blistering yellow of sand and gravel. And standing there on the rim of the desert to the southeast, the Jebel al-Akhbar—black at first against the rising sun, but soon dun-coloured and bare. No sound, no movement to be seen through the glasses. And the desert all around us—that was empty and silent, too.

And then that solitary shot. We were sitting under a canvas awning, rigged from the side of the headquarters truck, and drinking tea. We all heard it, a sharp, faint sound from the direction of Jebel al-Akhbar. But when we looked through the glasses there was nothing to see, and there was no further sound; just that one isolated shot. The time was 10:34.

We had no reason to regard it as any different from the other shots we had heard, though afterwards we realized the sound had been slighter. We settled down again and finished our tea, an island of men camped in a void, waiting whilst the sun climbed the brassy sky and the oven-lid of the day's heat clamped down on us, stifling all talk.

Only Ruffini was active, trotting sweating from one to the other of us, tirelessly questioning, endlessly scribbling, staring through creased-up eyes at the Jebel al-Akhbar, and then finally badgering Berry until he had given orders for his copy to be transmitted over the radio to Sharjah.

And then, just before midday, the dead stillness of the desert was torn apart by the buzz-saw sound of a helicopter. It came sidling in from the north, a strange aerial insect painted for desert war, and in the instant of its settling the whole camp was suddenly changed to a single organism full of purpose. With Ruffini I stood apart on the edge of this ordered turmoil and watched the man responsible for it, surrounded by his officers, standing with legs straddled, head thrown back—a man conscious of the dramatic quality of the moment.

Ruffini noticed it, too. "*Il Colonello*—'e is going to war."

But my attention had shifted from Colonel George. Coming towards me from the helicopter was the squat, battered figure of Philip Gorde. "Grant." He was leaning heavily on his stick as he faced me. "Where's Charles Whitaker? What's happened to him?" And when I told him what we feared, he said: "Christ Almighty, man, couldn't you do something?" But then he shrugged. "No, of course not. Bloody politicians!" he growled. "Always too late making up their minds. Hope we're in time, that's all." He was staring at me out of his bloodshot eyes. "I gather he'd moved his rig up to the border. He'd started to drill, had he?"

"Yes."

"I wish I'd known that earlier." He looked tired, his face liverish. "Not that I could have done anything to help him," he added heavily. "It's a hell of a situation. And that boy of his a bloody little hero. Doesn't he realize what he's doing to his father—or doesn't he care? God!" He was jabbing at the ground with his stick. "Well, we'll just have to hope we get there in time," he said again, and he stumped off to talk to Colonel George.

The cluster of officers was breaking up now; voices shouting orders, men running, the whir of starter motors, the roar of engines, a Land Rover disappearing in a cloud of dust.

"Ah, there you are, Grant." The Colonel, neat and dapper, cool almost in the torrid heat, came towards me. "The boy's still alive, I gather."

"There was a shot fired. . . ."

"So Berry tells me. We'll just have to hope for the best. I'm sending a small force up to take over the fort. The rest of the outfit will move direct on Hadd. Berry's gone ahead to make contact with the Emir. You and Ruffini can ride in the headquarters truck."

The column was lining up now, and ten minutes later we were on the move. "If 'e is still alive, it is a great story, eh?" Ruffini said. "You think 'e is still alive?"

"How the hell do I know?" But Berry had given him four days. I was pinning my hopes to that.

"Well, it don't matter—alive or dead, 'e is a hero. And this is the biggest story I am ever writing."

That was all Ruffini saw in it—a newspaper story, nothing more. And Gorde hating David because I hadn't had time to explain his motives. I felt suddenly sad, depressed by the thought that David's action would be misunderstood. How could you explain to men like Gorde what Khalid's death had meant to him, how he'd felt when he'd seen the people of Saraifa forced to leave the oasis?

Half an hour later the column halted. We were close under the Jebel al-Akhbar. Time passed and nothing happened. The wait seemed endless. And then suddenly the Colonel's Land Rover came roaring down the column. He had Gorde in the seat beside him. "Jump in," he called to me. "Ruffini, too. The Emir has agreed to meet me at the first well." He was in a mood of boyish elation, a reaction from nervous tension. The column was moving again now and several vehicles had swung away and were headed for the camel track on the north side of Jebel al-Akhbar.

We reached the head of the column just as it breasted the shoulder of the Jebel. There once more was Hadd, jammed against the limestone cliffs, with the Emir's palace flying the limp green flag and the fort stark against the sky above it. "Hell!" Colonel George signalled his driver to stop, and Berry's Land Rover drew up alongside. The column ground to a halt behind us. "I don't like it," the Colonel said. "Too quiet."

Between us and the crumbling walls of Hadd there wasn't a living soul: no sign of Sheikh Abdullah's askari, no vestige of the camp we'd seen two days before. Even up by the date-gardens nothing moved. All the Wadi Hadd al-Akhbar, as far as the eye could strain through the glare and the mirages, was empty of human life.

"The blighter's up to something. What do you think, Berry?"

"I think we'd better be prepared for trouble, sir. I told you I didn't like the speed with which he saw me, the crafty look in his eye."

The Colonel nodded. "Go ahead, then."

The orders were signalled and the column fanned out across the level gravel plain, whilst we drove straight to the first well. Behind us the Bedouin Scouts leapt from their trucks and spread out over the sand—mortars and machine-guns, ammunition. And not a shot fired at us. We sat in the Land Rover, roasting by the shattered parapet of the well, and the tension mounted with the uncanny silence. Nothing stirred anywhere.

A full hour the Emir kept us waiting there in the blazing sun. He judged it nicely. A little longer and Colonel George's patience would have been exhausted. And then at last life stirred in the mud-dun town, a scattering of figures moving towards us across the flat, shelved expanse of gravel that lay between the well and the walls: old men and children—not an armed man amongst them. "He's going to play the injured innocent," Gorde whispered in my ear.

The old men and the children had closed around us. Some had empty drinking-bowls, others goats' skins; they whined and begged for water as they had been told to do.

"My heart bleeds." Gorde snorted with contempt. "Ah, here he comes."

Through the arched entrance to the town came a figure riding a white camel, riding absolutely alone—not a single retainer. "He's clever," the Colonel muttered. "There isn't a desert ruler who wouldn't have regarded this as an occasion to parade his full power. And to ride a camel when he's got an almost brand-new Cadillac . . ." His eyes were fixed with a puzzled frown on the solitary figure, on the slow, stately gait of that lone camel. He turned abruptly to Gorde. "What's he got up his sleeve? Something. That Cadillac was a present from Saudi. He'd surely want to flaunt that in our faces."

Gorde didn't say anything, and we sat and waited. The crowd fell back, the clamouring ceased. The Emir rode his camel through them, and, sitting there in the Land Rover, I realized suddenly why he hadn't used his Cadillac. With set face and without any gesture of greeting, he rode his beast right up to us, and when he finally halted it, the supercilious head was right over us, the rubbery lips white with foam, dripping saliva on the Colonel's beret. The Emir himself towered above us, godlike against the burning sky.

It was extraordinarily effective. The man was simply dressed in spotless robes and looked much bigger, the features more impressive, the curve of the nose more marked.

He waited in silence for Colonel George to greet him. Instead the Colonel barked an order and his driver backed the Land Rover, turning it so that the bonnet faced the Emir. But it was no good. Patiently, without expression, the camel moved, resumed the same dominating position.

And then the Emir began to speak. It was an address that

lasted almost a quarter of an hour. The manner of delivery was cold and restrained, but underlying the restraint was the hate that filled the man. It was there in the thin, vibrant tone of his voice, in the black gaze of his eyes, in every gesture—a bitter fury of hatred. And that bloody camel, slavering over my head, seemed the very embodiment of his master's mood.

Gorde whispered the gist of the Emir's speech to me. It followed a familiar pattern. It ignored entirely the unprovoked attack on Saraifa, the cruel intention behind the blocking of the *falajes*, the murderous slaughter of men driven to desperate action to save life and home. Instead, it dwelt at length on Hadd's territorial claims. These the Emir based on a particular period in Hadd's history, a period that went back more than five hundred years. He conveniently brushed aside all that had happened in the area since that time. He attacked the oil companies for sucking Arabia's life-blood. The spittle flew from his mouth as he called them "*Nasrani* thieves, jackals of the West, imperialist blood-suckers." He ignored the fact that without the companies the oil would have remained beneath the sands, that the wealth of Arabia depended on them, that the very arms he'd been given had been bought with the royalties they paid. And in attacking the oil companies, he also attacked Britain and America. Imperialist murderers! he called us.

"He's coming to the point now," Gorde muttered. The camel belched, a deep, rumbling sound that blew a fleck of froth from its lips into my lap. The Emir leaned forward, the dark, cruel face bending down towards us. *Murderers!* he screamed. I thought he was going to spit in our faces.

"Start the engine," Colonel George ordered the driver. "I'm not standing for any more of this." He said something to the Emir. The man smiled. That smile—it was curiously excited. *I call you murderers because you come here armed to protect a murderer.* He gestured with his hands, pointing towards the fort. And when Colonel George tried to explain David's motives, the rough justice of his action in depriving Hadd of water, the Emir silenced him. *You do not think it is murder when an Arab man is killed. What do you say if he is the murderer of a white man—one of yourselves?*

He turned, raising his body in the saddle, shouting and signalling with his hand. A closed Land Rover emerged from Hadd. The crowd, which had drawn in a tight circle round us, scattered before it, and as it roared past us a figure in Arab clothes was thrust out of the back of it, a limp rag of a figure, battered and covered in blood.

It hit the sand beside us, rolled over once, and then lay sprawled face upwards in an undignified heap; and as the cloud of dust settled, I saw what it was that lay there: the dead body of Colonel Whitaker.

He had been shot in the face, and his head was badly battered, his arms broken. His clothes were black with blood. Flies settled in a swarm, and I felt suddenly sick.

You know this man? the Emir demanded. And when Colonel George nodded, the Emir explained that *Haj* Whitaker had that morning agreed to go up to the fort and reason with his son. What had happened up there he did not say. He merely gestured to the body. *This man's son has murdered my people. You say it is not murder. Look now at that which lies before you and tell me—is that murder?*

Colonel George sat there, his eyes hard, his face set. He had no answer. "His own father!" His voice was shocked, and he made no attempt to challenge the Emir's version of what had happened.

"You can't be sure," I said.

It was Gorde who answered. "Do you think it would have occurred to him to have the body flung at our feet like that if Charles had been killed by one of his men?" He was staring down at the bloody figure lying in the dust, his hands clenched. Then he looked up at the Emir and demanded to know where the body had been found, and when the Emir replied that his men had picked it up at the foot of the cliffs directly below the tower, he nodded his head slowly. As far as he was concerned, that settled it.

It was very hot there in the sun, yet a cold shiver ran through me. I was remembering the solitary shot we'd heard that morning, and into my mind came Mrs. Thomas's words: *It was never Dafydd that was going to die.*

Colonel George was the first to recover. Ignoring the body, he dealt with the terms on which the fort would be evacuated and his forces withdrawn. And when the Emir finally agreed, he made the prearranged signal to his troops waiting on the Jebel al-Akhbar and withdrew his force into the desert, taking Whitaker's body with him.

Back at our old encampment we found the helicopter gone and one of the trucks belonging to the Jebel al-Akhbar detachment already returned. After interviewing the driver, Colonel George announced: "David Whitaker is apparently still alive. The helicopter's gone up to bring him out." He said it flatly, and behind me I heard Gorde murmur: "God help him! He'd have been better dead."

The helicopter took off from the fort, and when it landed they carried David to the shade of the headquarters-truck awning. When I saw him, I thought for a moment it was all over. His face was relaxed, the eyes closed; the flesh, tight-drawn, was bloodless. It was a death's head, all skull and bone, and the skin like parchment. But then the eyes flicked open and he saw me. The cracked lips smiled and he tried to say something, but no words came. He was too dried up to speak. The eyes closed again and he went into a coma.

The helicopter had also brought bin Suleiman out. He was badly wounded and very weak, but he was alive. Only Hamid was dead. They brought his body down and buried it beside Colonel Whitaker's within sight of the Jebel al-Akhbar. Gorde stood with bared head and hard, frozen eyes as they laid his old friend to rest in his shallow desert grave, and Ruffini was there, sitting on the ground, his pencil moving steadily across the pages of the notebook held against his knee.

The burial over, I went to talk to him. I wanted to persuade him to soft-pedal the fatal news. I was thinking of Sue rather than David. The boy was a hero and the newspapers were avid for news. And now the world was going to be told that he'd killed his father. I was probably the only person who could justify it, who understood the provocation. The public's reaction would be one of revulsion. Sue would be torn to bits, her life made hell. I touched Ruffini on the shoulder. "About Colonel Whitaker," I said.

He paused, his face creased against the sun's glare as he glanced up at me. "We talk about 'im later," he said. And he added: "It is fantastic, the most fantastic story I ever write. There is this boy David, who by 'imself has forced the British Government to take action. And now this man they 'ave just buried—'is father, who is a great figure in the desert, a sort of . . ." He clicked his fingers, searching for a name. "It doesn't matter. What matter is that 'e is dead, killed by a stupid tyrant, a sort of Arabian *condottiere,* in a lousy little mud town in the desert."

"You mean you think the Emir . . ." I checked, staring down at him.

"And for what?" he demanded, his mind concentrated on assembling the English phrases he wanted. " 'E kill him to blacken 'is son's name, a ridiculous attempt to destroy this heroic young man. It is a tragedy, a great tragedy. And with the death of Colonel Whitaker, it is the end of an epoch in the desert, the last great Englishman in Arabia. . . ." He bent his head, his pencil flying again.

I stared at him in astonishment. He'd been there. He'd understood what the Emir had said. And he didn't believe him. His story would accuse the Emir of Colonel Whitaker's murder, and because he was the only journalist here, the press would carry his version. I could only hope that the authorities would leave it at that.

Colonel George took that story with him when he left shortly afterwards in the helicopter. He also took David, and because of that Gorde was left to travel by Land Rover. I was standing beside him as the helicopter took off. He turned to me, and I can still remember the rasp in his voice as he said: "If that little bastard of Whitaker's lives, you'll have a lot to answer for."

"How do you mean?" My mouth felt suddenly dry.

"You sent him out here, knowing he'd killed a man, knowing he was a self-dramatizing little gangster. Fellows like that don't change, and patricide is something every society abominates. He's a hero now. But when the public learns the truth . . ."

He stared at me, his eyes cold and hard. "Charles Whitaker was a man in a thousand, probably the greatest Englishman who ever made the desert his home. I've known him since I first came out to Arabia, and you can rest assured I'll see to it that the truth is known." He turned abruptly, without giving me a chance to say anything, and I watched him as he limped across to where Berry was organizing his convoy.

Colonel George had placed a Land Rover at Gorde's disposal and he left immediately, so that I had no opportunity to talk to him. And when I finally reached Sharjah, he was on his way back to England and it was already too late. David had been placed under arrest and an official statement had been issued to the press.

Part Three

The Court
Stands Adjourned

I

It was the third day
of the trial and David Whitaker had gone into the witness box
immediately after the lunchtime recess. Counsel for the Defence
had taken him through the salient points arising from my evidence, with the object of showing his relationship with his father
in the best possible light. Now, late in the afternoon, he had
arrived at the crucial point—Colonel Whitaker's visit to Fort
Jebel al-Akhbar. The packed Court was very still, every eye on
the fair-haired boy standing, neat and tidy, in the box, his arm
in a sling and the sun-burnt face looking almost black in contrast with his light tropical suit.

"I would like the Court to have a clear picture of your situation on that particular morning." Counsel glanced down at his
papers, his hands resting lightly on the desk in front of him.
"By then you had been on the Jebel al-Akhbar seven days. Is
that right?"

"Yes."

"And there were only two of you left. Salim, Ali, and Hamid
were dead; Grant had gone. There was just yourself and bin
Suleiman, and you were both wounded."

"Yes."

"Had you been attacked during the night?"

"No, it was some days since they'd made any attempt to take
the fort."

"But you were under fire?"

"They'd got men lying out in the rocks all round the fort, but
we were all right as long as we remained in the tower. They'd
fire a few shots once in a while just to remind us they were there,
and at night they'd move up to the walls. But they didn't bother
us much. We were pretty used to them by then, you see." Just

the trace of a Welsh accent to remind the Court that this was the same boy who had run wild in Cardiff docks.

The reporters were scribbling furiously. This was the big moment, and when the Court adjourned there would be a rush for the telephone to catch the daily papers before they went to press.

"On the morning in question, were there any shots fired—other than the shot that killed your father?"

"No, none."

"Did that strike you as unusual?"

"I can't remember that I thought about it. It was some time since any shots had been fired. They were lying quiet, you see, hoping we'd think there was nobody there and get careless. But we knew the bastards were there, waiting for us."

"So you remained inside the tower?"

"Of course. I hadn't been out of the tower since Mr. Grant came up to talk to me. There wasn't any point. It was cooler there and the walls were good protection."

"Was there any other reason you didn't leave it?"

"I tell you, man, they were lying out there waiting for us. I wasn't risking being shot at when there wasn't any point."

"Quite so. But what I'm getting at is this: wasn't it a fact that you were too weak by then to attempt a descent from the tower?"

"Well, yes, I suppose so. Anyway, there wasn't any reason for us to be wasting what little strength we had left to no purpose."

"Were you weak because of lack of water or lack of food—or was it because you were wounded that you hadn't the strength to leave the tower?"

"I tell you, there wasn't any point." His tone was irritable; he didn't seem to understand what his Counsel was trying to establish.

"When had you last had any food?"

"I can't remember. We'd some dried camel meat left, but it wasn't any use to us. We couldn't swallow it. We did try and chew it, but it was very painful, and in the end we didn't bother."

"You couldn't chew because of lack of water?"

"Yes. We'd no saliva and our tongues were swollen and quite black. Our mouths were absolutely dry."

"Had you any water left?"

"Captain Berry had given me a water-bottle. We'd finished our own supplies and now that bottle was half empty."

"Your situation, then, was quite desperate."

"Pretty desperate."

"I want the Court to be absolutely clear about this." Counsel paused, glancing from the Judge to the crowded press desks. "In your opinion, how much longer do you think you could have held out? In other words—" and here he spoke slowly and with great emphasis—"how long before you were dead of thirst?"

David shook his head. "I can't be certain. We'd have finished the water-bottle that day. If we'd been left alone we might have stayed alive a few days more."

"You heard the evidence of Dr. Logan, who saw you when you arrived at Sharjah. He said you were in such a weak condition that he didn't believe you could have lasted more than another twenty-four hours."

David's head went up. "That all depends on how urgently you want to stay alive, doesn't it? I'd have lasted longer than that. But not if they'd attacked us."

Counsel seized on this. "You say, not if they'd attacked you. Do you mean you were too weak by then to defend yourselves?"

"That's about it."

"Could you stand?"

"I don't know. I didn't try."

"Could you have lifted a rifle to your shoulder and fired it?"

"If they'd attacked us, I expect I'd have managed somehow."

"But you were so weak that it would have required the urgency of an attack to give you the strength to lift even a rifle to your shoulder?"

David hesitated. "I suppose so," he murmured. And then in a clearer voice: "It's difficult to explain to you people here. But everything was an effort by then. Everything," he repeated.

"Quite so. And if you couldn't lift a rifle to your shoulder except in a moment of great urgency, then you'd hardly have had the strength to descend from the tower by that ladder and then climb back up again and pull the ladder—"

"Objection!" Counsel for the Prosecution was on his feet, facing the Judge. "The Defence is putting words into the witness's mouth."

But Counsel for the Defence had made his point. "I will rephrase the question, then." And, turning to the witness box again, he asked: "Did you at any time on the morning in question, and before the Trucial Oman Scouts arrived to take over the fort, leave the tower for any purpose whatsoever?"

"No, sir."

"Did you at any time attempt to lower the ladder?"

"No."

The Court breathed an audible sigh.

"One more question before we come to the moment of the meeting with your father: Did you know that the Trucial Oman Scouts would move into the Emirate of Hadd that day? In other words, had you any reason to suppose that your ordeal was nearing its end?"

"None at all."

"We have the evidence of Mr. Grant that from their position six miles away beyond the Hadd border they could see the fort quite clearly through field glasses. Could you see them? In other words, could you see that over a dozen vehicles had materialized at that position during the night?"

"No."

"As far as you were concerned, nothing had altered that morning—your situation remained as desperate?"

"Yes."

"All you knew of what was going on in the world outside was what Mr. Grant had told you two days before."

"That's right."

Counsel paused, again consulting his papers. "Now we come to the moment of your father's arrival at the fort. You'd no reason to expect him?"

"How could I?"

"Quite so. I suppose you've no idea what time it was when he arrived?"

David shook his head. "My watch had stopped. I'd forgotten to wind it a few days back. All I know is the sun had been up some time."

"Had you any warning that you were going to receive a visitor?"

"There was some shouting—an order in Arabic not to fire. It was given by a man holding a white flag. The last time that had happened was when Mr. Grant came with Captain Berry."

"That was the occasion on which a treacherous attempt had been made on your life?" And when David nodded, Counsel added: "And on that occasion you had taken the precaution of sending bin Suleiman to the top of the tower, just in case. Did you take the same precaution this time?"

"No."

"Why not?"

"He was unconscious."

"And you hadn't the strength to climb up there yourself?"

"No."

"Would you tell the Court, please, what happened when your father arrived?"

"Well . . ." David hesitated, his eyes glancing quickly round the courtroom. Finally he turned towards the Judge. "I thought it was an Arab at first—one of the Emir's men. He came in by the main gate, and he was dressed in Arab clothes, you see. I didn't recognize him—my eyes weren't too good. But then he stopped just inside the gate and called me by name and said who he was."

"Were you surprised to see him?"

David shrugged. "He was there. That was all there was to it." And he added: "No, I don't think I was surprised. When you're in the state I was, you just don't register anything."

"What happened then?"

"Well, he came to the foot of the tower and we talked."

"What about?"

"I don't remember."

"He wanted you to abandon the fort, didn't he?"

"At first."

"He changed his mind then?"

"Yes."

"What made him change his mind?"

An obstinate look had come into David's face. "He just changed it, that's all."

"Was that after you'd told your father that your defence of the fort had made headline news back home?"

"I don't remember."

"You did tell him that, didn't you? You did pass on to him this information which you had obtained from Mr. Grant?"

"I don't know. I expect so."

"Was your father surprised?" And when David didn't answer, Counsel went on: "What I want the Court to know is whether or not Colonel Whitaker knew about the newspaper stories of your exploits and the fact that there had been questions in the House. The evidence at the moment points to the fact that he couldn't have known before you told him. Would you agree?"

"I really can't say."

"But he must have made some comment, shown some reaction?"

"I tell you, I don't remember. I wasn't in a fit state to remember details."

"You were talking to him from one of the embrasures of the tower or from the entrance hole?"

"From the embrasure. I should have been an easier target if I'd dragged myself to the entrance hole, and I was afraid of getting sniped at."

"And the whole interview was carried on with you in that same position. You didn't move at all?"

"No."

"Where was Colonel Whitaker?"

"Standing right below me."

"Could you see him?"

"Yes."

"And when the interview ended—where did he go then?"

"I think he moved nearer the tower, away to my right. I can't be sure, but I lost sight of him."

"Towards the cliff-top?"

"Yes."

"And what happened then?"

"Well, a little time passed, and then . . . then there was this shot."

"A rifle shot or a pistol shot?"

"It was a rifle shot."

"You're certain of that?"

"Yes."

"And after the shot, was there any other sound?"

"Yes, a sound of falling stones. That's when I knew he'd gone over the cliff."

"What did you do then?"

"I dragged myself to the southern embrasure, but I couldn't see directly down the cliff face, so I didn't know what had happened. I tried to call out to him, but I don't think my voice made any real sound."

Counsel leaned forward, his voice pitched low. "You've heard a ballistics expert give it as his opinion that your father was killed by a bullet from a pistol, not a rifle."

"It was a rifle."

Counsel stared at him, and the whole Court could see the quandary he was in. But the evidence that had gone before had to be disposed of. "You have also heard Dr. Logan's evidence. He has said that post-mortem examination strongly suggests that the shot that killed your father was fired at close range. He, too, thinks it was a pistol shot."

"How do they know?" David said almost belligerently. "They didn't find the bullet, did they? And they weren't there. I was, and I'm telling you it was a rifle shot."

The Judge leaned forward. "I would like to get this quite clear. You have said that your condition was such that you cannot remember what passed between you. You have, in fact, left the Court with the impression that your powers of perception at that time were at a very low ebb. Yet on this point of the shot, you are quite categorical. You say it was a rifle shot?"

"Yes, sir."

"Had you a rifle in your hand?"

"No, sir. I didn't fire the shot. It was fired by one of those treacherous—"

But the Judge stopped him. "You will kindly confine yourself to answering the questions put to you. Am I to take it that you're absolutely clear in your mind that the fatal shot was fired from a rifle and not from a pistol?"

"Yes."

The murmur of a sigh filled the courtroom. They didn't like it. The Judge sat back, nodding to Counsel to continue. I glanced at Sue. Her face was white. She, too, felt the change of mood in the room. It was obvious that David was withholding vital evidence about what had passed between his father and himself, and he'd been altogether too determined to put the blame for his father's death on the Emir's men. I heard the man next to me whisper to his companion: "He hasn't a hope if he goes on like this."

Counsel stood for a moment staring down at his papers, undecided whether to pursue the matter further. Finally he lifted his head and faced the witness box again. "Suppose we consider for a moment that you were in no fit state to be certain on this point and that it was, in fact, a pistol shot that killed your father. Had you a pistol?"

David stared at him, sullen and white-faced. "You know I had. That ballistic chap's already given evidence that he examined it."

"Quite. A six-chambered revolver with two rounds still left in the chambers. And you had some spare rounds loose in a leather bag. Exactly how many rounds had you fired with that weapon?"

"Just the four. I didn't use any of the spare rounds."

"Why?"

"A rifle was more useful. I only used the revolver once. That was on the night Mr. Grant left. They got pretty close then, and when I'd emptied the magazine of my rifle, I used the revolver."

"And you fired four rounds with it that night?"

"Yes."

"I see." Counsel paused. And then, speaking very slowly, he said: "If we accept the medical evidence, based on Dr. Logan's post-mortem following the exhumation of your father's body, and the evidence of the ballistics expert, then the possibility of your father having been killed by one of the Emir's men is ruled out entirely." He leaned forward, staring at David. "I want you to be quite clear on this point. There remain then only two possibilities. Either you killed your father or he killed himself." A long pause this time. And then the question, put bluntly: "Did Colonel Whitaker kill himself?"

"He hadn't got a rifle. He wasn't armed."

"Are you sure? He might have had a pistol concealed under his robes." And then Counsel put the question again, trying for the way out, pressing the issue in an attempt to give David the one chance that might save him. "Did Colonel Whitaker shoot himself or did he not?"

David stared at him, his eyes unnaturally big in his dark face. And then his mouth opening slowly and the courtroom hushed, some sixth sense warning us all that he was about to close the door on this one hope of acquittal. And finally the words: "I've told you before—he was killed by a rifle shot fired by one of the Emir's men." And then, turning from Counsel towards the Court, he added in a firm, clear voice: "Does any one imagine my father was the sort of man who'd kill himself?"

That, more than anything else, settled it in the minds of the Court for he was voicing what everyone there felt. And after that there was nothing Counsel could really do to help him. "The Defence rests." He sat down abruptly and the stillness in the courtroom was absolute.

The Judge spoke then, his thin, tired voice sounding remote and detached. "It is almost five thirty." He was leaning slightly forward. "And I gather there are certain gentlemen here who have deadlines to catch." The dry humour produced an easing of tension, a little whisper of relieved laughter. "I intend to adjourn now until tomorrow. But before I do so I think it is my duty to address a word to the prisoner. Your Counsel has advised you to go into the witness box, and you have elected so to do—rightly, in my view, since otherwise the Court would have no means of knowing what happened on the morning of your father's death." The voice was warmer now, almost fatherly. "Today you have been answering questions put to you by your own Counsel. When the Court resumes tomorrow, however, it

will be the Prosecution's turn to cross-examine you, and I must
warn you that he is likely to question you most closely on what
passed between you and your father. The witness George Grant
has shown in his evidence that there was a great deal of misun-
derstanding, not to say friction, between the two of you. I feel it
my duty to warn you, therefore, that it will greatly prejudice
your case if you refuse to tell the Court what passed between
you, and I would ask you to take advantage of the adjournment
to consider very carefully your attitude here. Justice is depend-
ent on the evidence of witnesses. You are now a witness. You
would be wise not to withhold, from whatever motive, vital evidence." For a moment he remained leaning forward, staring at
the prisoner. Then he picked up his gavel and rapped. "The
Court stands adjourned until ten o'clock tomorrow morning."

The Court rose, the Judge bowed, and the rush for the doors
began. Still standing in the box, David glanced slowly round
the courtroom. He was sweating and he looked tired. For a brief
moment his gaze rested on his sister and he gave her an uncertain, almost apologetic smile; then police guards closed round
him and he was lost to view beyond the milling heads of the
crowd.

"I suppose the Judge meant it kindly." Sue's hand was on my
arm and I could feel her trembling slightly. "But David won't
change his mind, and tomorrow the Prosecution will make a
strong case out of his silence, won't they?" She sounded nervously exhausted, her voice tired.

"It won't look good," I said.

"And it was a mistake, wasn't it—trying to blame it on one of
the Emir's men?"

"Yes." No point in pretending it wasn't a mistake. "The medical evidence is against it; the ballistics expert, too. . . ." We
passed out into the sunlight, and the humid heat of Bahrain engulfed us like a steam bath. The street was crowded with cars,
packed with people, a solid mass of Bahrainis.

Gorde was waiting beside his car, and he called to me. "A
word with you, Grant." He took me aside. "That boy's going to
be convicted if somebody doesn't persuade him to talk."

"I thought you were behind this witch-hunt," I said angrily.

"I made a statement; but I hadn't all the facts, had I?" He stared at me accusingly as though I were to blame for that. "Now that I've heard your evidence, seen the way he's behaving in the witness box . . ." He hesitated and then turned abruptly towards the car. "Get in, Grant. You, too, Miss Thomas. I want to talk to you." And as the driver nosed the car through the crowds, he turned to Sue and said: "I think I could arrange for you to see your brother tonight."

She gave a hopeless little shrug. "It wouldn't do any good. I think he'd rather be convicted, you see, than have the world know that Colonel Whitaker, that legendary figure of the desert, committed suicide." She was very near to tears, and she added with a hint of wildness in her voice: "Just because his father's dead, all David's feeling for him, the hero-worship my mother fed him when he was a kid, has returned, magnified a thousand times by the friction there was between them when he was alive. Nothing that I can say will make him change his mind. I know that."

"I see." Gorde didn't seem surprised. "Then we must think of something else. Nobody's happy about the situation, least of all the authorities." He put his hand out, and his gnarled fingers rested for a moment on Sue's arm. "Miss Thomas. Your father was a strange man. And he'd been a long time in the desert. A hell of a long time, and alone." He spoke with surprising gentleness. "He was a great man in his way. You should be proud of him."

She stared at him, dry-eyed, her face white. "Well, I'm not. I don't care about him. To me it doesn't matter a damn whether he killed himself or was killed by somebody else. He's dead. All I care about is David."

Gorde sighed. "Would it help you to understand him if I told you that he tried to join David in that tower—that David either couldn't or wouldn't lower the ladder to him? He actually got as far as the entrance hole, but couldn't pull himself in."

"How do you know?"

"Bin Suleiman. After he left hospital, he disappeared. I've had men scouring the desert for him ever since. They brought him in two days ago. Your brother says he was unconscious. So he was, most of the time."

"You mean he regained consciousness?" I asked. And when Gorde nodded I thought he'd found the witness who could save David. "Why didn't you notify David's Counsel, then?"

"Because it wouldn't help. Bin Suleiman heard them talking, but he didn't know who it was David was talking to and he didn't know what they were saying. They were talking in English. And the fact that Charles climbed up to the entrance hole, which is the only material fact he can add to the evidence, would only operate against David. Bin Suleiman thought it was one of the Emir's men trying to get in, and he reached for his rifle. The effort, or more probably the pain of movement, caused him to lose consciousness again, so that he knows nothing of what happened after that."

"But it's sufficient to cause you to change your mind about David's guilt," I said. "Why?"

"Oh, it's not that. That's only a fragment of the picture that's been building up in my mind. One of the first things I did was to send Entwhistle down to take over at Charles's camp on the Hadd border. He reported the rig gutted, the seismological truck burnt out, the place deserted. He had the sense to go on to Saraifa, where he had a talk with some of Charles's men. That raiding party you saw heading into the desert towards the rig attacked the camp at dawn. They came in firing their guns, and when they'd got hold of Charles, the Emir's secretary had him bound to a camel and made him sit there whilst they set fire to everything. When they started back towards Hadd there wasn't a thing left that they hadn't destroyed."

Visualizing the scene, I began to understand how desperate Whitaker's mood must have been. "He said he had some sort of hold over the Emir," I murmured. "I can even remember his words. He said: 'I know that little Emir inside out.'"

"Probably he did—certainly well enough to know that the man was in a vicious mood and prepared to go to any lengths. I sent a couple of the best Bedouins we've got on the pay-roll into Hadd a month ago. They reported that when he reached Hadd the Emir gave Charles the choice—either he brought his son down from the fort, alive or dead, or he'd be taken out into the Empty Quarter and left there to die."

"Didn't it occur to him that Whitaker might throw in his lot with his son?" I asked.

"Oh, it was more subtle than that. The Emir also thought he knew his man. That was why he ordered the destruction of the rig. He offered to finance Charles's drilling operations once his son was out of the way and the Jebel al-Akhbar in his hands. That's the story, anyway."

"But surely the Defence had a right to know—"

"Rumours," Gorde growled. "It wasn't evidence. Besides, how could I be sure what had happened till I knew the facts? I wanted your evidence and David Whitaker's evidence. . . ." He shrugged. "Even now I can't be sure."

"But you think you know what happened?" Sue was leaning forward, staring at him.

"Yes, I think I know now. I think Charles realized, after talking to his son, that what he'd regarded as a useless demonstration had, in fact, a chance of succeeding. He wanted to join David then, but probably he hadn't told his son what the alternative was and David refused to lower the ladder. Charles tried to get into the tower and failed, and then he stood on the edge of that cliff looking down on to Hadd, knowing that if he went back to the Emir he'd be going to his death. It's a slow death to die of thirst, and it would serve no purpose. Whereas to die quickly, by a bullet . . . I suppose he'd been allowed to carry a pistol with him, and I've no doubt he thought that a dramatic end like that . . ." He sighed. "He'd nothing to live for any more—the rig destroyed, his son doing what he might have done himself. But he could still do something. He could still die. And like that, tumbling down from that cliff-top, the news of his death would be spread by camel men from water-hole to water-hole. He still had a great reputation amongst the Bedou, and his death would be attributed to the Emir's treachery. I suppose he thought it might provoke a desert rising against the tyrant." He hesitated, and then he gave a little shrug. "I'm just guessing, that's all. I knew Charles very well, and that, I think, was what was in his mind." He looked at Sue then. "That's

why, Miss Thomas, I think you should be proud of your father.
And he was right in a way. His death did influence the situation. If he hadn't died like that, the Emir might not have agreed
to Colonel George's terms. There might have been fighting, and
God knows where it would have ended."

"You must tell this to the Court," Sue said.

But he shook his head. "It's no good, Miss Thomas. The Judge
trying this case has been brought out from England. He couldn't
begin to understand the sort of man Charles was—the sweep of
his vision, the almost Arab subtlety of his mind. And the only
absolute proof—the pistol with one bullet fired—I don't possess.
My men searched the ground where his body was picked up,
but they couldn't find that or anything else that has a bearing
on the case. Doubtless the Emir had it destroyed, since he
wanted to show Charles as a defenceless man murdered by his
son. No," he said quietly. "This is a matter for action now." He
turned and ordered the driver to head for my hotel. "We'll drop
Grant and then you'll come on with me, Miss Thomas. I'll arrange for you to see your brother tonight. When you do, give
him this." He pulled his wallet out of his pocket and removed
a thick wad of East African notes. "There'll be a message, too."
He handed the notes to Sue.

She stared at him, too startled for a moment to say anything.
And then she burst out: "I don't know what you're planning
to do, Sir Philip. But, whatever it is, you're not doing it for David. You're doing it because you want him back in Saraifa.
You're signing a concession, and you want to be sure you'll be
drilling—"

"How do you know we're signing a concession?" Gorde
barked in that peculiar rasping voice of his. "Alex Erkhard
knows. A few other executives, but that's all. How the devil has
it got to your ears?"

"It's true, then." She turned to me, her voice tired. "In Court,
when you were giving evidence—I sat next to that girl-friend
of David's. She told me. She'd got it from one of the oil men at
the al-Menza Club, and she said she was telling me because,
if things went badly for David, I might be able to make use of

it." She glanced at Gorde and there was suddenly a glint of that irrepressible Celtic humour in her eyes. "She thought you'd need David—alive and free."

Gorde caught the glint, and the hard, battered features relaxed in a smile. "She sounds a clever girl. What's her name?"

"Tessa," I said.

"And she's a hostess at the al-Menza?" He nodded. "I'll remember that. But please understand this, Miss Thomas: free, your brother could be very useful to us. I admit that. Arabs respect force, particularly the force of a strong and fearless personality. The Emir is afraid of him, and in Saraifa he'd be worth more to us than a hundred armed men. We don't want any more trouble on that border. But I promise you this: anything I can do will be done for one reason only—because I'm satisfied now that he's innocent."

"Of course, Sir Philip." Sue's voice, the little smile on her lips, were tinged with irony. But I noticed also that her eyes were alight with excitement.

The car slid to a stop. We had reached my hotel. "You get out here, Grant. I'm taking Miss Thomas on with me." Gorde's hand gripped my arm. "Don't try and get in touch with her tonight, and don't talk to anybody. What we've said here is between ourselves. Understand?"

I nodded and got out. The car drove off then and I went into the hotel. It was full of newspaper men; they crowded round me as soon as I entered. What did I think of David Whitaker's chances? Was he going to talk? I told them I'd no comment to make and escaped to my room. I had my dinner brought up to me, read the papers, which were full of the trial, and went to bed early.

To this day I don't know what part Gorde played in the events of that night. Sue saw David shortly after ten o'clock. She was allowed to see him alone, and she said afterwards that he looked tired at first, though he was quite cheerful. She gave him the money and also Gorde's message, and after that the tiredness seemed to drop from him. The message was simply: *Bin Suleiman is in Bahrain. He and another Bedouin will be waiting by the side entrance all night.* He asked her a lot of questions then, about Gorde's attitude to him and what he thought had happened up there in the fort. And when she had answered them all, he seemed anxious for her to go, his eyes very bright, his manner tense, almost nervous.

It was hot in my room, and I didn't sleep very well. My nerves were on edge and I kept worrying about Sue. And then just as it was beginning to get light I heard footsteps in the corridor outside and the door of the next room was flung open; muffled conversation and the movements of a man dressing in a hurry. I looked at my watch. It was just after four. I got dressed and went down. By then the hotel was in a ferment, reporters and camera men trying to telephone for cars, the word "escape" on everybody's lips. Within half an hour the hotel was deserted.

I got one of the house-boys to bring me some coffee and sat over it smoking endless cigarettes, waiting, and wondering what had happened. In less than an hour the first of the newspaper men were drifting back and it was official—David had escaped. I never got the details absolutely clear. I doubt whether any one did, for the thing was hushed up and there was no enquiry of any sort. There was a lot of talk about a force of Bedou from the desert, but that was clearly a story invented by his guards to cover themselves. The only Arab definitely implicated was bin Suleiman, and that only because a strolling reporter happened to recognize him loitering outside the walls. FAITHFUL COMPANION RESCUES AL-AKHBAR HERO ran the headlines of that particular newspaper. But it was more subtly managed than that, though whether David bribed his guards to unlock the doors or whether it was all arranged by some outside agency I don't know. The fact is that David was able to walk out of the place, and from that point it must have been very carefully organized, for when his guards raised the alarm at 0335 hours he had completely disappeared. There were rumours that he was being hidden in a rich merchant's house, that he was lying up, disguised as an Arab, in a house on Muharraq, that he had been got away in a dhow. The whole of Bahrain seethed with rumours, but nobody knew anything definite and neither Sue nor I dared go and see Tessa, who was the one person we both thought might know where he'd been taken.

The newspaper men stayed another twenty-four hours and then they were suddenly gone, like a cloud of locusts moving on, the story dead. And all Gorde would say when I went to see him was: "I don't know anything, and I wouldn't tell you if I did. But this way it's a lot easier for everybody." The heavy-lidded eyes stared at me. "Tell his sister not to worry. I expect she'll hear from him in due course."

. . .

We were married in a registry office in Cardiff four months later, and when we got back from our honeymoon there was a letter waiting for us. It came in a parcel containing a silver coffee pot, very intricately worked. The letter was headed Saraifa:

A mutual friend of ours in GODCO has sent me word that you two are getting married. Congratulations! I thought you'd both like something from Arabia as a wedding present. It should have been native work from Saraifa. But I came to the conclusion that only the best would do. The coffee pot comes from Riyadh, by courtesy of GODCO, and is as good as any Arab potentate possesses. Remember me sometimes when you use it.

The situation here has settled down. I have a small force under my command, composed mainly of men of the Wahiba and the Rashid, and the money for its upkeep is provided. All five falaj *channels are running with water and we hope within about a month to have the first of the old channels back in use. The Concession agreement has provided the funds, and we are running the channel right through the oasis to irrigate the camel thorn we'll be planting as a break against the sands of the Empty Quarter.*

As soon as you have time, I want you both to come out here for a holiday. I think I can promise you more comfort than you had last time, and there'll be plenty for you to see. Come next winter. The weather is perfect at that time of the year. We'll have struck oil by then. And if it's all that we hope, it will be called the Whitaker Oilfield.

*Not much news, except that the Emir has invited Sheikh Ma-
hommed and myself to go hawking. We shall go in force, exchange presents, and I hope live in peace thereafter. God bless
you both!*

Affectionately,
"The Brother of Sheikh Khalid"
(By which title I am now known)

A Note about the Author

HAMMOND INNES, born in England in 1913, wrote his first book at the age of nineteen. A journalist before the Second World War and an army officer during it, he has become an increasingly successful novelist since the publication in 1952 of *Air Bridge,* a novel that dealt with the Berlin Airlift. Next came *Campbell's Kingdom* with a background of the oil boom in Canada. *The Naked Land* was set in French Morocco. A return to England, France, and the seas between inspired *The Wreck of the Mary Deare,* probably Innes's most widely read book thus far.* Following this came *The Land God Gave to Cain,* the result of two trips he made to Labrador. Readers of his next book, the non-fiction narrative of his travels entitled *Harvest of Journeys,* will recall the vivid section on Arabia and the Persian Gulf. It is these experiences that provided the setting for his latest novel.

October 1960

   * Aptly enough, his latest boat, which was built for him and in which he has made extensive voyages, is christened the *Mary Deare.*